**Dr. Michael S. Horton,
Westminster Seminary in California**
*"Church history is exciting, but not always told in an exciting way. As historical fiction, **Trunk of Scrolls** transports the reader to another time and place while making it all seem less remote. Written in vivid—sometimes almost poetic—prose, this is a page-turner. I'm sure that it will reach the wide audience that it deserves."*

Dr. Joel R. Beeke, President, Puritan Reformed Theological Seminary, Grand Rapids, Michigan
"This exciting and engaging story takes us back to the sixth century in order to consider the most critical question of every age: Who is Jesus Christ? A great read!"

Jill Nelson, World Magazine correspondent
*"**Trunk of Scrolls** is an illuminating story written with the novelist's eye for the telling detail. Darlene Bocek does more than tell a story—she breathes life into church history and inspires us to reverence for the Sacred Writings. A sparkling tale that is rich with meaning."*

Dr. Darrell Bock, Dallas Theological Seminary
*"**Trunk of Scrolls** is a fascinating and entertaining story. A joy to read. If you like to be engaged as you read and see how Scripture can help you make good choices through difficult situations, this story is for you."*

Valeri Marsh, mother of four, Goodreads review
*Beginning with the excitement of its opening scene of a young man being kidnapped on horseback, through every twist and turn, heartthrob and heartbreak, all the way to its final and satisfying resolution, this book had me gripped. **Trunk of Scrolls** fell open and I fell in, and throughout the adventure, mystery, drama, action and romance, I found myself lost in the author's world and deeply attached to and caring about her characters. They became my friends; I hated her villains and loved her heroes and heroines...MY heroes and heroines. Their stories thrilled my soul and warmed my heart for many weeks after I finished the book.*

DARLENE N. BÖCEK

TRUNK OF SCROLLS

A FAMILY ADVENTURE

Entrust Source Publishers

For more information, please go to: www.entrustsource.com.

ISBN-10:1-942308-12-4
ISBN-13:978-1-942308-12-6

Cover created by Diana Buidoso
Layout and design created by Entrust Source LLC, Judy Buckert

Printed in the United States of America

Entrust Source Publishers
281 Camino la Pasida
Rio Rico, AZ 85648

www.entrustsourcepublishers.com

Dedicated to the One
Who thought to make this beautiful earth for us
and if that were not enough,
He condescended to make it possible
for us to live with Him for eternity
by His coming to this minuscule planet
and pitching His tent with us,
leaving us with salvation, a life to emulate,
and a Book like no other.

And dedicated to my husband, Fikret Böcek,
who is my best friend, my inspiration,
and God's greatest gift to me on earth.

TOME the FIRST

Episodes of My Young Life

TOME the SECOND
Episodes from Experience

He needs not fear confiscation,
who has nothing to lose;

nor banishment,
to whom heaven is his country;

nor torments,
when his body can be destroyed at one blow;

nor death,
which is the only way to set him at liberty
from sin and sorrow.

St Basil, AD 370

He was despised and rejected by men; a man of sorrows,
and acquainted with grief...upon him was the chastisement that
brought us peace, and with his wounds we are healed.

Isaiah 53:3,5 ESV

TOME THE FIRST

EPISODES OF MY YOUNG LIFE

GOTHLAND THE DREADFUL

BEARDED MEN

MARCH 15, AD 529

I opened my eyes to darkness and light—the stench of strange meat on an open fire, the pungent body odor of bearded men, and the bitterness of my own bile assaulting my senses. Ropes, like snakes twisting tightly on my hands and feet, restrained me from righting myself. Across the night, pulsating flickers of a fire shifted on phantom men, dizzying my attempts to think. Waves of nausea pummeled my sideways world and heavy eyelids opposed my desperate desire to understand. I blinked and all was black again.

I awoke. My face was buried in the side of a galloping horse. Chilly twilight mixed with musky horse sweat. I tried to make sense of senseless impressions. One thing I knew, my injured body pressed against an empty stomach. The ropes now bound me behind a rider whose form I felt more than saw.

Another rode beyond us: red beard, shaggy hair, and furry cloak flopping with the speed. Tied behind him—my heart skipped a beat—*Justin!* Then a flitter of memory came back, and I groaned.

Kidnapped.

The ruddy rider's gaze met mine, and he yelled in a burly tongue to my captor. By the time they unloaded me from the horse and tossed me at a tree next to Justin, I realized our dark fate was to die under the hand of these bandits.

My young cousin and I sat in a clearing with foggy flatlands before us, a scrub-oak and pine forest behind. Frog songs mixed with the crackling brush they had thrown on the fire. *How short my life has been, like that brush turning to ash just as it lights aflame.*

Justin rubbed his wet eyes on his shoulder. "You're alive, Marcellus! I'm so glad."

"Where are we?"

"Still in Byzantium. I thought you were dead. They tied you like that. On your stomach with your hands hanging down like a bloodless corpse."

I sighed. We had seen our share of those. "Well, I'm not dead. How did I get here?"

"The night after they took me, a strange horse walked up to their camp. To their horses. And you fell off it to the ground with blood all over you. Where'd you get the horse?"

A large pool of half-dried blood stained the side of my robe and the ache under that stain reminded me of the fight, the fast plan, the horse, the Scrolls.

"How long ago was that?"

"It's been four nights. They force wine into your mouth whenever we stop, but you hardly keep it down." His voice broke just as an owl swooped down over our campsite, grabbing its prey from the field. In an instant it flew off with it to its nest. Taken. Just like us.

"Please, Justin. Stop crying. I need to think. Have you seen any scrolls?"

He sniffed and rubbed his nose. "I was sure you were dead today. Your lips are so dry. Drink something."

He tipped his head toward the pouch hanging on the tree between us. It hung lopsided so we could drink without hands, but the acidic wine did not soothe my thirst. I spit it out. It soured my stomach and now my ears were ringing.

"Don't worry, we'll find a way to escape. At least we're to-gether. *Kyrie Eleison.*"

"*Kyrie Eleison,*" he echoed in a whisper, rubbing tears away. "I'm so glad I'm not alone anymore. And of anyone in the world, that it's you with me."

I stretched a smile onto my face for him, forcing a feeling I did not have, then tried to rally my thoughts. *What had happened?* The images came to mind. We had been escaping Antioch. Rushing cross-country to the emperor in Constantinople. Bandits attacked.

Sword-swiped my back and took Justin. I had grabbed the Scrolls, rushed to the town of Tyana, bought a horse. Followed them.

That was the last I remember. I must have bled-out. *Phew! I could have been dead. What a mercy that I was here.* What was the likelihood my horse would find their campsite? What was the likelihood I, unconscious, would stay on the horse's back? No likelihood unless....

"Do you know where the Scrolls are?" I asked.

"Byziana's Scrolls? They have them."

"Tell me where."

The bandits sat opposite the fire from us. One of them studied us as he gnawed at a hunk of meat. He scratched a half-bloodied bandage on his thigh, and his eyes narrowed.

"The big guy. With the wide square beard. He's the boss. He has your things in his saddlebag." My eyes located the man and his bag.

"How did you get my sister's Scrolls?"

His sister. Byziana. Her name burned into my heart, reviving in me the scene of our last embrace. All the things I should have told her flared my urgency to escape. I would not break that last promise I made as she gave me her Scrolls.

Before I could answer Justin, the hefty Goth leader stood to his feet. Trudging over, he grabbed my hair. I resisted, trying to gain control of my head, but he stretched my chin up and stuffed a chunk of cadaverous meat into my mouth, forcing my chin shut. *Atrocious! Rotten unknown beast.* I gagged. A flash of fury behind his eyes revived my enthusiasm to eat.

He forced Justin in the same uncivilized way and made us each drink a swill of the bitter wine. Then he returned to his co-conspirators flicking his thumb in our direction. Their echoing laughter mocked us across the fire.

Trembling, I grasped at my wrists. If we stayed they would kill us. Or worse. I eyed the bag as I loosened my knot. I would not die passively—we had to get away or die trying. But preferably live trying. *I cannot die.* What would my mother do, alone in the wearld? Or the girls, with no one to keep them safe? We had to get back.

"Where are my sisters?" Justin asked.

"They're in Tyana. Waiting for us. Hold on, my knot is almost untied."

"Almost untied! I tried my ropes, but they're too tight."

"We'll leave as soon as they fall asleep," I said.

"I'm glad you're going to free us. But stop looking at the Scrolls. You got to leave them, Marcellus."

"Not a chance!" I glared at him.

The searing pain on my back kept me from analyzing our situation beyond those Scrolls. He chewed his cheek and shrugged at me, so I drew a deep breath of night air and tried to figure out a plan. *We'll get untied, get the Scrolls and sneak out.* My thinking felt slushy, making me panic. *Or is there already another plan?*

"Give me your hands," I said when mine were loose.

I gasped for air, somehow out of breath, then reached back my tired fingers and located the knot, seeing its curves in my mind's eye.

"Can you undo it?" Justin asked.

I worked at it for a bit. "I don't know. It's pulled taut."

We should make a plan. Untie his hands. I yawned. *Or sleep. That's a good idea.*

"They're watching. Stop," Justin hissed.

Without looking up, I bobbed my head against my chest and pretended to nod off in sleep. I tried not to believe my own ruse, fighting a much desired slumber. A flick from Justin roused me to return to the knot. The work rubbed my fingers raw, but soon Justin exhaled relief when his ropes dropped off.

"Stay still," I said.

I tipped onto my side, back to the fire, knees to chest. The shot of pain almost knocked me unconscious. With my back blocking the motions I tugged at my foot bindings, hoping the Goths did not suspect what I was doing.

"Can you do your own feet?" I whispered when untied. "Roll like I did."

He turned his back to the fire and worked on his feet.

"Marcellus. Marcellus." He shook me awake from a comfortable slumber. *How long was I out?*

"I'm free now. Let's go."

Go where? Do we have a plan? I struggled to remember. *Get away. Get the Scrolls. Find the girls. Sleep.*

The guards faced the fire, arguing over a game they played with dirt and rocks. *Not yet.* I settled against the tree. "It's too dangerous. Let's wait." Let's sleep, I meant.

Abandoning the Scrolls

Time passed. As the Gothic bandits lay down to sleep, I bit my bottom lip to deny sleep its right. Still we watched. Until I counted. One. Two. Three men snoring. I rallied my heavy body. Let's go. Justin followed me, inching backwards, scooting toward the bushes behind the tree, into the darkness beyond.

I tried to stand, but my muscles did not cooperate. "Give me a hand?" I whispered, trying not to cry out from the roaring pain that followed.

My eyes strained for focus as I peered through the trees, studying the sleeping horsemen. Searching. When the leader rolled over and scratched his round belly I found it, the swirled edge of my Scroll peeking out of the saddlebag under his head.

"I'll be right back," I whispered.

He grabbed my hand. "Just leave the Scrolls. Come on."

"I need them. Look. The Goths are fast asleep and the bag is wide open."

"We got to get away!"

"It'll just take a minute. Trust me."

"Isn't it more important to live?"

No! They're worth more than anything.

Justin shook his head. "My mother would understand. Don't risk it. Please."

I looked again at the irreplaceable Scrolls. "No, she wouldn't understand."

Finally they're mine and I lose them? Not on my watch.

"Forgive me, Justin."

I crept along the darkness, each step jarring my side, until I was five paces away from the sleeping giant. Dim firelight danced across the boss's face, and I hoped those shadows would disguise any I brought. From its familiar handle, I recognized the Scroll peeping out from under his head. It was John's Gospel, emerging as if summoning me to rescue it. We could not lose John.

I tiptoed a step forward into the circle of fire near the snoring man. Pulsing firelight teased my eyes to cross and shut. I shook my head and mustered my senses. Taking another step closer, I glanced at the other two men. One of them had eyes on me. I froze and stared back, tensed, ready to dart away.

He made no move, spoke no word. Then he shifted on his mat with a deep sigh and groan. Those eyes saw nothing but their dreams. The air's chill mixed with an iron taste in my mouth. Two steps to go. We were free, now to free the Scrolls.

I bent my knees, leaned forward to take hold of the bag. The next thing I knew, Justin was leaning over me, terror on his face. He tapped my cheek frenetically to awaken me and flicked his head away from the camp. I had fainted to the ground next to the sleeping Goth. My soul sighed in anguish. I had to give in. For Justin's sake. For life's sake. My energy was barely enough to run away, I could not also steal a saddlebag from under a strong titan's head.

I hope I don't regret this, my heart groaned louder than my body as I maneuvered up. With that farewell, we slipped away from the men, away from the Scrolls, away from captivity. Leaving the precious Scrolls of Scripture to God's will. As soon as we were out of earshot, we took off running down the road. Every jolt sent raging pain through my being.

"Is this the right way?" Justin asked, slowing his pace.

"I hope so. At least it's away from those bandits."

"Marcellus!" Justin gasped, pointing at my side. "You're oozing blood."

My robe was drenched. *No wonder I'm so tired.*

"Great." Drips from the hem led down the dirt path mixing with our footsteps. "We'd better get off the road."

"Your face is white, Marcellus. We should find a place to rest."

Don't give in. Keep pressing. "We left a trail," I gasped out.

"We can't stop here. The woods." *The woods will be our safety.*

"You don't look so good."

"Forget about it." I tucked my robe up around my wound and dove into a cluster of trees. The branches reached out like witch hands, grabbing at my cloak, scratching my arms and face, snagging my cap. We had barely entered the forest when Justin cried out.

"Horses!"

We froze. *Please God. Please God. Help us stay hidden.* Crouching behind a hedge, we listened to the hoofbeats approach, slow down, stop.

They must see the blood-trail ended. *Will they come into the woods? Or will they assume we went along the road?* I held my breath and listened. My heart beat in my wound and I pressed it to keep the blood in. My leg was cramping and a ringing in my ears dizzied me.

The bandits debated in their rough language then their horses cantered down the road. *They've gambled against the forest. Thank God.*

We concentrated on the sounds around us—only frogs pierced the silence now. I blew out in relief. "Phew. We're safe."

I herded him through the trees, over the fallen logs. Ducking under branches exacerbated my side, and a headache clenched my brain. I grasped for my senses.

The earthy aroma of wet leaves lulled me to lie down. "Forgive me, Justin. I've got to stop." The ringing in my ears loomed louder and louder and rushed upon me as the taste of iron came to my mouth.

"Whoa!" he said, catching me as I began to faint.

He pressed me into the crook of a log and dragged a large leafy branch to cover us. I squinted up through the trees. The early morning sun had broken the darkness. Soon nothing would hide us.

He lay next to me and every so often I heard him sniff. "Don't cry. Trust God," I said.

"I cannot," his voice cracked. That same despair threatened my own heart, but I refused to give in. *Why pain upon pain, God? Maybe this is my lot in life. Maybe this is everyone's lot.*

A branch split in the woods. We locked eyes and held our

breath. *They're here! Will this covering keep us hidden? Oh, God. I just want to close my eyes and sleep. If only this were a bad dream.*

The silhouette of a Goth tromped through the shadowy woods. His head scanned left and right. He carried a pouch. *Is he the one with my Scrolls?* My brain told me what my heart refused to accept. Even if he had the Scrolls, we were too weak to wrestle him. I watched him move through the woods. *If we can see him, he may see us.* The Goth paused, looked our way, and cocked his head. I stopped breathing. But he turned away and stomped into the deep woods.

"I need to sleep," I said when the woods were still again. "I cannot stay awake another minute."

"I'll keep watch." His voice held no hope, and I had no energy left to help.

Each time I barely fell asleep, Justin shook me awake. After the third instance, I growled, "Enough! Let me sleep."

"I'm sorry. You keep groaning and I have to silence you."

So tired but even sleep was denied me. *Oh God. Kyrie Eleison.* Eventually his rousing ended, for he fell asleep too.

The morning crows in the treetops awakened us with their caws and fast fluttering through the woods.

Sunshine shone at my feet. The angle of the shadows showed me the direction to head. *South and west until we find a river. Then a town.*

Justin had barely pushed the covering branch away from our log when their smell accosted us. And accompanying the odor, four large hands seized us by the shoulders. The bearded Goths had been waiting, and we had not listened to the crows' warning.

They met no resistance from me. I could not even lift my arms. Or head. They bound me hand and foot and gave me a large swig of that wine. This time thirst took control, and I filled my belly with their drink. I barely remember a burly man throwing me over his shoulder.

A metallic tang stung my throat . . . that black haze descended over me . . . and again I was in darkness.

NIGHT AND LIGHT

I have several dream-like memories of night and light, drifting sleep and painful handling, hoofbeats and the taste of caustic food. When I finally came to my senses, my side was on fire. I was in large tent, high and circular. I rested on my hip, furs and blankets surrounding me.

A woman with long blonde braids was wiping a burning ointment into my wound. She smiled and chattered at me in a comforting but foreign tongue.

I tried to steady my trembling. *Where am I?*

A rough-looking man peered into the tent. It was the square-bearded leader. This time the bandage on his leg brought a memory of our sword fight however many days ago.

He glared at me. Then his sharp words struck the woman, making her flinch. She dismissed the effect with a sigh and shake of the head, still working on my left side. I jumped at the prick of her needle. The woman patted my shoulder and stroked my temple with the side of her hand, pressing me to relax and lie back.

Why is she helping me?

My stomach growled like a dog. The woman failed to restrain a chuckle, and in her light-hearted laughter she said something to me. After getting no answer she called to the taciturn man outside the door. He heard her words, glanced at me, and slogged away. The woman continued sewing my side, tied off her string and spread some more fiery salve on my wound.

I tried to catch a glimpse of the aching injury but it was out of sight. On my back. She bandaged my waist and pulled the cloak over my body.

The tent flap opened and a young woman stepped in carrying steaming food on a tray. A meaty fragrance drifted to my soul, and I scrambled to sit up. This immediately tore my stitches, ripping my flesh.

"I must be famished," I said with a pitiful laugh that pulled more at my side. "Your odious meat actually smells good." A gripping helplessness swirled over me. *How can I get away from this strange world where nothing is under my control?*

The woman pressed my shoulders down and lifted her finger to chasten me for straining the stitches. Again I was on my side while she adjusted her work. So I examined the pretty girl.

She was lovely, like the first flowers of spring, with a pale face, a rosy complexion and blonde braids twisted over her head like a halo. *She must be full of life and goodhumor. I wonder what it's like for her to live . . . in tents, wherever we are. I wonder what she does for enjoyment.* I wondered a lot about her. Her face turned even pinker when she saw me scrutinizing her.

In a soft voice the nurse told the girl to feed me. She took a sliver of meat and put it in my mouth with hesitant fingers.

I recognized this meat! *Freshly roasted, familiar, delicious deer.* I smiled up at her, grateful. My stomach responded in another canine grumble, at which the nervous girl giggled then looked up at the nurse for direction.

I was famished and having wolfed down that minuscule bite, remained unsatisfied.

The nurse pointed to the wine pouch, so the girl poured out a spoonful of wine for me. This wine was sweet. *Thank God.*

Thirsty and hungry and weak. All these needs spun a cacophony of feelings. "Please may I have some more?" I motioned to a cup. My mouth felt dry and sticky.

The girl glanced at the woman, who gave permission, so she lifted the wine cup to my mouth. Though on my hip, I maneuvered so I could drink without putting pressure on the stitching.

"Thank you," I said, trying to sit up. But I was so tired and weak. The nurse lifted and lowered her hands in front of her, showing me to stay down. I was glad to recline and my eyes were heavy.

She laughed with the girl about something—no doubt about me, for they pointed my way. When the nurse left, the tent flap sent a puff of air into the room, which picked up the aroma of roses from somewhere.

The beautiful helper brushed wisps of hair away from her face. Her cheeks reddened again.

I broke the awkwardness. "Why am I here? Where is here?" I asked, hoping against hope to get answers.

She shook her head, saying some rough words I did not know. She knew no Latin.

"What is your name?" I patted my chest. "I am Marcellus. Marcellus." I pointed to her. "Who are you?"

With a bright smile that might have smitten another man, she touched her chest. "Mari," she said.

Her eyes, sparkly gray, drew me in.

"Nice to meet you, Mari." An immature grin spread over my face, but I straightened it, sobering my thoughts, and scratched my itching face. My beard surprised me. I needed to shave.

She asked me something and bit her bottom lip.

Her red lips were smiling, enticing. My attention drew to her mouth, to the teeth peeking out ever so slightly from behind them. *Who is this beautiful girl?*

I met her eyes thinking this thought, and the silent message brightened her face. She returned my gaze for the briefest moment then looked down to study the floor. Now I could see long eyelashes on her cheerful eyes. My heart surged, betraying all I stood for. It was her—the rose scent came from Mari.

"I do not understand you." I shrugged, trying to shake off the spell.

As a reply, Mari started talking as she fed me in ever-too-small bites. It must have been a story, from the rolling pitch of her voice. I kept watching her, my heart on swells. Up and down.

By the time my food was gone, the story was over. I was still famished, which awakened me to my senses. Mari stood up and said a farewell, pointing toward the exit. I shook my head to escape the stupor.

"Goodbye," I said. She turned from me with a coy half smile and put plates and bindings on the tray.

When her back turned to me, my mind took over, yanking my wayward heart into shape. *Shame on me.* I was glad to have food and drink and nursing. But I belonged with someone else. I never knew it more than now. *I must get back to Byziana. This wild girl is danger.*

I struggled to remember. *Antioch. Mopsos. Tyana. I am supposed to be protecting the girls. I promised to be back with Justin within a week. I've failed them again. I hope it's not too late.*

My vague plan pressed at me.

As soon as this bewitching barbarian girl leaves, I will untie myself, find Justin . . .

Justin. Where is he?

I eyed the tent flap. *It would be so easy to leave, to make my way home.* But discovering Justin would prove the challenge now. I shifted in place to find my legs tied. *How can I have not noticed before?*

When the flap closed behind Mari, I grabbed at the ankle bindings. Too late. A shadow above me stopped my progress. The alert guard stood between me and escape. Again.

I could guess what he sputtered now, shaking his head and glowering. He soon secured my hands behind my back, tighter than before—giving me a message that he would not tolerate another escape attempt.

I sighed and lay against the blankets. Byziana's face came to mind, her hands to the sky. That day, before everything changed, when the world was before her as a prize. The bittersweet vision chased away the enchantment of Mari.

Nineteen years may be a long time to live. And I had seen much sorrow. But nothing I had experienced to date had prepared me for these conflicting passions. The welcome warmth of hope encompassed by the threatening cold of dread.

I am so weak, so tired. How can I ever rescue Justin, let alone myself? I closed my eyes. *Kyrie Eleison.* I hesitated. *Where is God? Does He even hear me?* My mind thought of the wolves in the mountains. The story of my life, fighting off wolves. As I struggled to remember how to trust God, the meat, the wine, and the soft furs

lulled me back into the darkness of a fitful sleep.

SIXTEEN DAYS

"Marcellus! Wake up! It's time to go. We're having a picnic on Mount Silpius. Wake up, sleepyhead." My cousins were jumping on me, tickling me, pulling the blankets off me.

"Go away," I said, grabbing for my blanket, my arm heavy. "Let me sleep." In response, there was silence and a repugnant animal odor.

My eyes opened to find a hairy goat gnawing on my blanket. No little cousins. No Mount Silpius. No home in Antioch. *I am still captive.*

I heard the clinking of swords, the yelling of men and the laughter of children outside the thick wool tents. Justin lay asleep on the opposite side of the tent. Tied as well.

"Justin!" I called in a strong whisper. "Wake up."

"Ooohh." He groaned, stretching his shoulders and legs, in spite of his bindings. "Why did you wake me? In my dream I was somewhere else."

He pointed his chin at the animal. "Who's this?"

"Some goat got in. Glad to see you again. Do you know where we are?"

"Not sure. Still Byzantium, I'm sure. We were only halfway through Anatolia when they caught me."

"But who knows where we are now? I passed out so much after they found us. How long has it been?"

"I think sixteen days."

"Sixteen?" I sat up. "How can it be sixteen? Sixteen days and no money. What will your sisters do? I told them I'd be back in a week."

"Are you strong enough?"

"Yeah. My side does not hurt as much." *How did it heal so fast?*

"They take such good care of you, but they keep us tied. Learned their lesson, I guess."

"I guess so."

"I wish I understood these people so I could get answers."

Light streamed into the tent. The stocky guard entered and seeing us awake chased out the goat, made a curt demand, and left. I did not recognize the two women entering, arms full of furs. The guard yanked Justin up, and the women exchanged his robe for a furry cloak. They combed his hair and wiped his face with a wet cloth. After doing the same to me, the women picked up our clothes and drifted out.

The guard pushed us onto our mats in a sitting position and then went to wait at the door until someone called for us.

He pulled us to a huge round tent. Red wool felt covered the sides of the tent, and black wool roofing waterproofed it. "Look at the trim!" Justin whispered. The guard yanked him forward to stop his talking.

The bow-tied trim of the tent, small golden disks and rainbow gems, glittered and sparkled in the morning sunlight. Smoke streamed from one window. *A fire in a tent?*

We passed through the entrance flap and our vision adjusted to the dim light. *Just what I was afraid of. The Gothic leader has summoned us to his presence.*

In the center of the tent next to a fire, a large man sat on a throne piled with furs. The guard shoved us to our knees and stood between us, holding us in position.

Why have they not killed us? Why have they healed us? And fed us. And treated us with this strange mixture of honor and . . . honor and something? Why are we here? Questions whirled about my mind.

"Greetings. Welcome at our village," the man said in rough Latin. "I am Olufr, King of White Goths."

He paused, sharing a gracious smile. Justin showed as much surprise as I felt. *He speaks Latin?*

"Greetings." I gave a short bow of my head. Justin followed.

"You are noblemen." He motioned to our patrician robes in the arms of a servant.

I nodded.

"You have no money," he added, holding up empty hands.

I nodded again.

"Botheric says you good fight sword." He pointed to our guard. Botheric. Finally a name.

"You of interest to me."

Interest to him? *He's studying us? I am not a specimen!*

"Please let us go," I said. My voice rasped out a weak whisper, not matching the firm voice I had intended. "We need to go home. Please."

His kindly smile did not match his words. "No. This is now your home. You our prisoners. You do our command."

How could I reply? I scanned the room—the people watched with curiosity, not with hostility.

Then I noticed for the first time that Mari stood next to the king. When my attention stopped on her, her cheeks turned pink again. The king looked at her and back.

"This is my daughter Mari." He reached out for her and she nestled into the crook of his shoulder. "She good nurse." He flashed his toothy smile again.

His daughter? My mind drifted back to her calming, sing-song story. *A princess?* I felt an imbecile smile spreading over me and sternly chased it off.

Then a realization took my breath away.

His village?

"Sir, may I ask a question?" I managed to say.

"Yes, please."

"Are you subjects of the Emperor Justinian? How is your village within Byzantium?"

He laughed then said something to the others in the tent. They also laughed.

"We not in Byzans. We in Gothland. We in Gothland!" He spread his arms above him. Then he fisted his chest. "My Gothland."

What? How can we be in the land of Goths? I thought again of our ride from Tyana, of my unconscious journey.

"How many days have we been your prisoner, King Olufr? Sir."

"One moon you our prisoner."

One month! Impossible.

"No," Justin said. "It can't be. I counted. It was sixteen sleeps."

"Yes. Sixteen sleeps. Perhaps. We have good wine. Good for long journeys."

The king laughed again, and a word to the others brought more good humor. Their laughter at our misery made me wonder again if I was dreaming.

A month? No wonder I am so hungry. No wonder I am so weak. No wonder my wound healed so fast. I fought against the hazy ringing in my ears. *A month ago I left the girls alone! Where did they go? How did they pay for food? How long did they wait? God have mercy on them.*

My heart felt helpless, hopeless. Dismay threatened my faith. As if we had not lived through enough heartbreak these past months and years. As if that were not enough. Now we were captive to Goths.

Where are you, God? I begged. Wishing this was a dream, I knew we were in the midst of our worst nightmare.

The king said something to our guard, who yanked us up to our feet by our shoulders.

"Botheric will take you to servant yurt. You are our prisoners. You our servants. No fight, you will live. Run away, you will die."

He paused and smiled a fatherly smile, opening his arms wide. "Please stay." He translated what had transpired to his people.

A slight movement from Mari drew my attention. She bounced on the tips of her toes.

Can it be?

She strained to keep back a smile.

Is it possible? She wants me to stay?

Her desire bore into my heart. I gulped and tore away from her. *She's going to be trouble.*

If only she were not so . . . so . . . . I entered her smiling eyes again.

King Olufr followed my gaze to his daughter. A frown flittered across his face and for a moment his lips pressed together.

He shook off the thought, then commanded something to Botheric, who turned us toward the exit.

The king spoke to another man, and as we left over my shoulder, I glimpsed four scrolls being taken to the king. Our Scrolls. It stabbed my heart. When we escaped, I left them behind to save our lives. That was a fair trade. This was not.

And now, being so close yet severed from them took me to the cliff of desolation. The power of those Scrolls—their mysterious neglected power—was now lost to me. And our survival—our next breath—depended on a strength we no longer had.

"God, please help us. Please help us," I whispered hopelessly.

Justin sniffed to stop his weeping. His tear-stained face twisted as he tried to appear brave.

We have lost our Scrolls, our freedom, our lives. "God have mercy. *Kyrie Eleison*," I said, fighting back my own desperate tears.

For once, he did not echo. His wide eyes stared at the hundreds of soldiers in the roped-off training ground we passed—hundreds of soldiers moving together as a unit at sword drills. *We will die here!* Justin's panicked eyes screamed. Life was in my bones, but hope had truly fled.

Botheric took us into a larger tent, a round black wool yurt, and passed us off with brusque Gothic words to our new slave boss, Groufe. He in turn led us to the cots we would sleep in for—what would be—the next three years.

I tried not to think of all the if-only's.
If only we had stayed home.

If only we had left Antioch on horseback.
And brought more money.
And not lost the Scrolls.

If only I had kept a closer eye on Justin that night.
If only.
If only.
If only I knew how to trust God.
These things happened for one purpose.
If only I had known.

ANTIOCH
THE GLORIOUS

THE ASCENSION EVE BANQUET

MAY 19, AD 526
Three years earlier

She entered the room like a misty spring breeze on a dry summer day, yet none of us watching her glide between the guests that fateful evening could know this would be her last banquet.

Looking back those many years ago, I see her as if it were yesterday. I remember the swish of her robe on black and white marble tiles—sliding to the rhythm of a graceful step. I see a silver bowl glittering in her young hands, on its sides a golden gilded grapevine.

I hear her sweet questioning voice offering guests fruit from the piles of honey-dried apricots, grapes, peaches and plums. I can almost touch every curl and twist and wisp on her braid-pinned hair that night, but mostly I recall her joy as she passed in front of me. My cousin. My Byziana.

Vases of spring blossoms adorned the room. Nine-year-old Justin, chasing a smaller boy through the crowded tables, tipped a vase off its pedestal. In a swift move, Byziana caught it and lifted both the flower vase and the silver bowl over their heads as they ran past. "There is more room to run on the terrace," she directed in a singsong eldest sister voice.

Justin acknowledged his sister then called to his four-year-old friend, "Come, Simeon! Let's hide and seek between the tree-pots!" The younger boy hooted and raced from the room.

She set the vase on its stand. Its pink blossoms matched

her own bloom. My cousin Byziana loved being the hostess. Though the family owned servants to spare, she would still take the silver fruit bowl herself, catering the crowd as she wove her ribbon of courtesy between guests—their smiles bringing a sparkle to her hazel eyes. A sparkle which was never the same after her father stood.

I remember the frown of Gaius Justus, repugnant yet again at his high-born daughter playing servant. Why he did not restrain her tonight of all nights I soon discovered. Any other night, his censure would be felt by all. But tonight he searched the faces of the military guests next to him, their lack of criticism—their almost gawking approval—brought contentment to his look and restrained his usual rebuke.

This was Ascension Eve. The celebration of our Christ's ascension into heaven forty days after his resurrection. So strange of all days it was this day.

Before me the house of Gaius Justus poured forth Roman strength and aristocratic luxury, all wrapped in a Christian veneer. Unaware of what awaited them, the guests filled their bellies from the overloaded dessert platters. Happy eating and comfortable dialogue hummed throughout the Great Room and hints of fresh rain outside merged with faint lamp-oil smoke.

Katerina and Natalia, Byziana's younger sisters, sat on the floor near a mosaic juggling an armful of small kittens. Their giggles added to the joyful peace in the room that dark night. I rose to join them, walking as I should, with my chin straight and shoulders back. The conversation of some guests at the mosaic's edge distracted me from my target.

"Some of us are still paying the artist," one man said. It was Gaius Epiphrates. "But we would want no less for Justus. He gave to Antioch more than any man would or could last year."

I did not recognize the man he spoke with who studied the intricate scenes on the mosaic. "So you say all Antioch got together to commission this for the man?"

"It would seem all of Antioch. These mosaics do not come cheap, and I assure you there is no other in the empire. I would doubt even Emperor Justin has one as grand or significant as this."

"Certainly you must be mistaken."

"No. I know our mosaics are coveted throughout the empire. And I know they are not duplicated. Perhaps it is because our people are as varied as the colors of a mosaic, from origins as vast as those multi-hued marbles of pink and blue and green down there. Perhaps it is because our mosaics represent our living history—a slowly grown art form now planted onto the floors of every nobleman's home."

"They must be quite a talented group of artists. You wax poetic, Epiphrates."

"Perhaps it is that we love life, and our art reflects our love of pattern and color and story. Perhaps it is the Persians at the gate, a desire to stay in our homeland to spite all foes. For whatever reason, my friend, our mosaic artists decline to leave Antioch. Though the commissions come from the empire's four corners."

"I cannot imagine an artist denying the emperor."

"Be that as it may, our artists stay at home. They have business enough here. And we pay for it. Oh yes, we do."

"But what would spur such an act as this mosaic gift? Who is this Gaius Justus?"

"A man of great virtue. Do you see the border? The potter, the blacksmith, the baker, the fishmonger?"

"Such intricate workmanship!"

"After the great fire last year he spared no expense to repair and rebuild artisan shops."

"I see the stadium. And is that the agora?"

"Even the stadium and the agora."

"He must be a man of great wealth."

"And great generosity. And who is the woman in the middle medallion? Can you guess?"

"A Roman goddess?"

"Nay. Not a goddess. An ideal. Megalopsychos."

"Aristotle's pure virtue!"

"Yes, the crowning ornament of the virtues. Epitomized by our beloved Gaius Justus, a true Roman." His eye caught me. "And this is his nephew, Marcellus. Son of the late Gaius Dorotheus."

"Nice to meet you, son."

"Do you agree with your uncle's assessment?"

"Yes, sir. He is a great man. I am proud to know him."

The other man pointed to the space between the medallion and the border. Leopards, lions, wolves all faced a man with a sword and a torch.

"And this hunter fighting those beasts? It must also have meaning."

"The great of heart man, taming his passions. Also Justus. Generous, brave, virtuous."

"He can do no wrong, it seems. I look forward to meeting him, if he will take the time."

"He will. He will. Generous with his time as well as his gifts, I dare say. Look, he is about to rise."

The men hurried to their seats, and I to mine. The kittens stumbled over one mosaic image the men had not noticed. My favorite. A man helping a child over a bridge, symbolic of my uncle's role as *patrikios*, or city-father of Antioch.

Such was my uncle's repute. Well did they look at that mosaic, they would never again see its beauty. For he would stand and change everything.

Significant Antiochene families, men and women whose family lines heralded back even to the first Christians named in Scripture, sat at the numerous tables. We were the foundation, the cornerstone of Antiochene history. Soldiers and laborers whose daily bread depended on that foundation stood along the Great Room's edge.

The years before he arose remain in my memory as the zephyred sunrise of childhood, the years after—a storm-clouded tempest.

Gaius Justus smiled, strong shoulders back, forehead lifted. A brief word commanded the silent heed of all in the room. "Ladies and gentlemen," he said, after a simple welcome, "You are all familiar with our dear promising Captain Belisarius." Murmurs of accolades echoed around the Great Room.

"I declare to everyone present my pleasure with him. Over the years he has ingratiated himself to me in service as my *doryphoros*." He invited his head-guard to stand.

I had heard of Belisarius, the commander of Gaius Justus's personal army. My uncle's unending commendation of the man in family gatherings could not be missed. But till tonight, I had not met him. His business for my uncle kept him out of our small family circle.

"Before the sun rises tomorrow," Gaius Justus continued, "our troops will depart for Constantinople at Emperor Justin's call. As my last act before retirement from military duties, I shall accompany them. And within a month I shall introduce my dear and faithful Belisarius at court for a new service, please God."

There was an approving thrum and soft applause from those present. I bit another dried apricot my cousin had given me and listened with half interest. My eyes found Byziana again. She reclined against a pillar, the fruit bowl on her hip, tilting her head to the side as she listened to her pater. Years of comradeship as relations and neighbors had forged my care for her. I loved her strong, kind, sometimes bossy embracing of life. Oh how I loved her. Even then.

I looked back to the soldier. Belisarius was a warrior in carriage, a virile man in bearing, a young version of my uncle Gaius Justus. He seemed pleasant enough, but the overripe grin of Indulf, his Gothic hired-sword sitting by him, soured my stomach. I leaned against my seat and finished the apricot. *I like him. My uncle likes him and I can see why. What's not to like?* He was young, clean-shaven, broad-shouldered—just as a soldier should be. *You'd be a fool to not want to please him. And obey him. In spite of that fearsome companion.*

I had thought Gaius Justus's pleasure could be no more bright, no more vibrant. But I was mistaken. He called Byziana to his side. She set the silver bowl on a guest table and slid next to her pater. Not a man to express sentiments, he surprised us by putting his arm about his daughter's waist.

"And now I would like to announce to you, my dear friends," he said with added pride, added excitement and tears in his eyes, "the betrothal of my firstborn Byziana,"—at this he took her left hand and put it into the soldier's right hand—"to Captain Belisarius."

Spontaneous applause met his announcement. But Byziana's incredulity and shock warped her usual carefree expression. Looking from her father to her mother, the Lady Sophia, the girl asked through raised eyebrows if this great fact could be true. Lady Sophia tapped her fingertips together in congratulations, adding a slight signaling nod to her daughter. The confirmation caused Byziana to pull on a nervous smile and peek into Belisarius's face.

A scream drew everyone's attention to the doorway. Justin's voice echoed from the terrace and he ran toward his mother. Katerina and Natalia jumped up at the commotion, then gathered and comforted their scattered kittens.

"Mater! Simeon bit me!" He lifted his hand to Lady Sophia.

The room watched as she quieted her son. She put her hand around his shoulder and whispered in his ear, words which widened his eyes and snapped his mouth shut.

The boy studied Belisarius and Byziana while his mother took some water onto her handkerchief and wiped the wound. I see now the irony of that small accident. But who could have known?

Gaius Justus drew the crowd back to himself. "Well then," he said, clearing his throat and motioning to the soldier. "The joining of our families links our faithful Captain to the Old Order, and our family to the New. Most profitable and honorable." He lifted his cup to Belisarius.

The captain, at this signal, lifted my cousin's hand and slipped a ring onto her finger. He lifted their joined hands in his right hand, and his newly filled goblet in his left, drank a toast to himself and sat down. Applause filled the hall, turning to a drone of discussion as the guests considered the union.

Byziana's eyes flitted to the ring, which shimmered in the lamplight . . . to her father, who stood talking with congratulatory guests . . . to Belisarius, who occupied himself with Indulf. Her eyes caught mine. Not knowing any better, I lifted my cup in her direction. Her teeth showed between curved lips, but a change had come over her. She glanced at her friends, Basina and Iulia, to my right. They also lifted their cups to her.

I kept my gaze fixed on Byziana and ate another dried fruit. She sat by her betrothed, reclining against the dining couch. His arm engulfed her shoulders, his hand immediately a bit too friendly, his focus still on his Gothic friend. Indulf glanced around his captain at my cousin, looking much as a wolf who would eat her. *I'd better move closer.* Who were these mercenary Goths? They ought to stay to themselves, instead of selling their services to the highest bidder.

I admired Belisarius for his soldiering skills, for his leadership skills, for his social skills. In my young body, I felt too small for these long legs which would never do what I wanted. My sword work was strong, but my limbs were clumsy. Someday I hoped to be a soldier. *Maybe I will be as great a soldier as Belisarius. Maybe someday I will be promoted and meet the emperor, too.*

Byziana seemed pleased by the notice though she fought

his hand to stay in decent places. Her curious eyes studied the captain, who regarded her every so often with an enigmatic smile. After a few minutes she stood to leave, but this time he pulled her onto his lap. That should have told us everything. But we were blind and asleep.

Byziana looked to her father for help. But Gaius Justus heeded not his young daughter. The soldier spoke, and what he first said pleased her. The next made her blush, made her try to stand. But being restrained, she succumbed to his strong arms, paling by the moment. Soon his rough attention and bold hands shot her to her feet, and me to mine.

Her face was still pinched up in a smile, but I knew my cousin. *That is not her happy smile. That is her somewhat-annoyed, somewhat-scared smile.* He lifted her hand and brushed his lips across it. Then he stroked his finger along her jawline and down her neck. Her cheeks turned pink again. In a smooth move she pulled away, slipped over to the silver bowl, and ran with it into the kitchen.

Belisarius rolled his eyes at this, making Indulf laugh. His next words, added to an accompanying rude gesture, made his friend fall off the chair in obscene drunken hilarity.

I scanned the room. *Isn't anyone else troubled by his crudeness?* No one seemed to have noticed.

The captain leaned over to Indulf and, whispering something, flicked his thumb behind him. The ugly Goth stood to his feet and stretched, then slugged into the recesses of the house. I was soon on his trail.

POUCH OF HERBS

I made my way around the tables. The dark hall down which Indulf had disappeared was still, all its lamps now being used in the Great Room. I listened to the sounds echoing. Byziana's merry laughter came from behind the light-framed kitchen door. I followed her voice. *If she is safe, there is nothing to fear from the Goth.*

I opened the door to the kitchen and peeked in. The house servants surrounded Byziana, congratulating her. A movement at the end of the hall caught my eye and stopped me from entering the bright room. *What?* Indulf's cape swished into the library. *What business does he have in there?*

I slipped to the library door, about to enter, about to confront the Goth with trespassing, when low words in the room stopped my confidence. *He's not alone.* I pressed against the wall and listened to the sounds coming through the partially opened door. A chuckle and the words "well done" came to my ear. Then the conversation lulled to a whisper. Try as I might, I could hear no more distinct words, just murmurs. *Two men are in there.*

Never had I seen Indulf in this house, and now he moved about freely. As if he owned the place. What was he doing here? I glanced toward the Great Room. *Should I summon my uncle?*

As I looked back the way I had come, a stuffed-cheek mouse ran out from under the kitchen door. Where was the cat? It scurried into the darkness with its treasure. *If there is one rodent there are many.*

Rustling in the library drew my attention, so I pivoted my face toward the gap between the door and the wall and peeked into the room. Indulf's back was to me, blocking the other man. He wiped his hands on his robe. I saw the other man's hands rummaging through a pack on a chair.

I pulled against the wall. *Marcellus, you are making something out of nothing.* But I would not believe myself. Was this nothing? I wanted to believe so, but an alarm gripped my heart. *No, this has to be something.* I heard a crash in the room, and some swearwords. I peeked into the room again. Indulf shifted away from the now empty side-table. An Egyptian vase lay shattered on the floor, yet neither moved to pick up the pieces. Indulf wiped his sweaty hands again. His new position opened me to the shock of recognizing the other man.

Gallus? What is this Goth doing with my uncle's steward?

Steward Gallus smiled as he put a small pouch into the soldier's hand, and I distinctly heard him say, "If you put it in chicken broth, the flavor best meets your needs."

Chicken broth? What needs? I pulled against the wall, my mind spinning. The jingle of a money-pouch flooded a million questions to mind. *Who is giving money to whom? Is Indulf—or Belisarius— paying Gallus? Or is Gallus paying Belisarius? What is in the pouch? What business does Belisarius have with Gallus? And most importantly, why are they hiding here in the library?*

Gallus spoke short, directive words. I looked in the crack again to try to understand what was happening. But my timing was horrible. The moment I looked in, the steward's eyes turned toward the door and met mine. You know when you are seen. The shock goes deep into your heart. I caught my breath and pulled back. Our eyes had spoken to each other. And his message was not good. *I need to leave.*

His voice, louder than before, said, "Make sure Master Belisarius knows we are all happy for his engagement. This is from all of us—." His voice cut off into another whisper.

My nerves trembled. *I have to get out of here.* Even if this private parley between the two was unexpected, I had no business eavesdropping. The steward had responsibilities I know nothing of. *And if it is private business—private enough to hide in a library, private enough to take place during an engagement feast—I must not be here.* Mostly, I did not want to be caught spying. Or to face reprimand by Gaius Justus.

I hurried toward the kitchen and slipped through the door,

darting behind a group of servants and avoiding the Goth. Indulf's loud steps passed the door as he walked toward the banquet hall. The happy voices in this room clashed with the fleeting fox-caught-in-a-henhouse message I had read in Gallus's eyes. *What was in the pouch? Something for chicken soup? A recipe? Impossible. What was the jingle of coins? This makes no sense.*

These questions had no time to be pondered for my heart leapt to my throat. Steward Gallus had entered the kitchen! He scanned the room. *Smile!* I pulled a smile onto my face to disguise my trepidation. *Don't look at him!* I kept my attention on Byziana. Perhaps I tried too hard.

"Master Marcellus," he said, slipping next to me.

I glanced at him with a snuff, "Yes?"

He blinked once or twice squinting at me. I rolled my eyes and—in as condescending of a manner I could muster—flicked my head to dismiss him, and focused on my cousin. I was hardly an expert at being rude. *But does he know this?*

Byziana rescued me just in time. She came over with her ringed hand outstretched. "And what about my ring, Marcellus? You haven't said a word."

"Congratulations, Cousin," I said with a bow and kiss of her hand. "May God grant many years of happiness." I felt the steward leave my side.

Why would he get mad that I saw him give a recipe to someone else? Or a financial gift? The reaction, the location, Indulf's hastiness. It could not be a recipe.

I tried to dismiss what I had seen—to placate myself with unsatisfying explanations. *What do I know of the world of adult men?*

Byziana's attention was drawn again to the banquet. She filled up the fruit basket and handed it to the servant Maria, but made no move to return to the banquet herself.

I followed the servant. "Maria, wait," I said, stopping her before we came to the Great Room.

She turned toward me with a tip of her head and a curtsy. "Yes sir?"

I took a dried peach. "Does Steward Gallus often come to the kitchen?"

"Yes, master." She nodded. "He comes in and watches and

advises us on all sorts of cooking matters. I think his father was a cook."

"I see," I said, relieved. *If his father was a cook, it must have been a recipe.* I warded off the assailing questions with this new information and was about to turn away when Maria added, "Steward has a herb patch he grows himself, too. He says they keep him young. Don't know it works, but he thinks it does."

"What kinds of herbs?"

"Not sure, Master Marcellus. Never seen the likes of them. Did taste one once. So bitter it hurt my stomach."

"Thank you. Sorry for keeping you from your work." *Bitter herbs?*

"No problem, sir." She went toward the Great Room, and I followed her, eating the peach. My mind's eye recalled the captain sending Indulf away in the first place. *All for a recipe? For herbs? Of course. Why not? But bitter herbs?*

Chicken broth. I reminded myself. *All for soup. It had to be. What did I know about herbs?* In any event, Byziana was not accosted by the brute. And that was all I really cared about.

IMAGE OF THE INVISIBLE GOD

As I entered the Great Room again, I was glad Lady Gaia Sophia shook her handkerchief in my direction. I hastened to her side.

"Yes, Aunt. What service may I be to you?"

"Marcellus, I am quite hot and uncomfortable here. Would you mind helping me to my bedchamber?"

I stood next to her and assisted her off the couch. She leaned her full body weight onto my arm as we left the banquet room.

"You are such a dear," she said. "Oh, for some peace and quiet."

We got to her chamber, she sat on the bed and I took the sandalettes off her feet.

The noticeable sigh when she reposed on her pillows surprised me. Then her hand went to her stomach. I knelt on the step by her bed. "May I do anything else for you, Aunt? Shall I fetch the doctor?"

"No need. I will be fine."

The room seemed to shine. How could so much light come from one small lamp on the window ledge? Position. It was high and prominant. It could make a difference because of where it stood.

Lady Sophia mentioned not my cousin's betrothal, though she must have seen the man's strange behavior. Something was amiss. *Maybe she feels it, too. I should ask her about it. And I should tell her about Gallus's herbs.*

She spoke before I could. "Do be a darling and open the Trunk," she said, pointing toward a trunk under the window.

A smile stretched across my face. *The Trunk! Our Trunk.* Detailed ivory reliefs of Abraham and Jonah, John the Baptist, Daniel and Peter stood out from the front and sides of the sturdy trunk. My fingers traced the shapes before I opened the well-oiled latch. *What precious friends from my childhood, compatriots in faith.*

Opening the lid, I closed my eyes and inhaled. Into the room wafted the smell of papyrus and old parchment, somewhat earthy with a hint of antramentum ink. My mother and I had our own library, which had been my pater's prized possession. But the few rolled and folded and bound parchments hidden in this trunk were worth far more than our thousands.

"Marcellus, find the Parchment tied with a red leather string. You know the one. Saint Paul's letter to the Colossians."

Peaceful Lady Sophia bore the guardianship of our family's secret Scripture scrolls which had been collected and copied through the centuries. Our relatives more than a hundred years ago had been scholars in Cappadocia, men of faith. Those great uncles had been entrusted with Scriptures, and their precious treasure now lay in Lady Sophia's room.

I reached through the Scrolls and found the red-tied Epistle. My heart beat faster within me. Sitting on the stool by her bedside, I pulled the Scroll open, hoping she did not see my fingers trembling. It did not matter how often I touched these Scrolls, my soul quivered at the act. This was not a mere scroll, a piece of paper, a small book. This holy Scroll contained the very Word of God.

"Hurry, now. Take and read. Start a few digits from the top. Where the parchment is torn."

I knew the place. My eyes scanned the text up and down as I gathered self-command. I read the lovely language, sweet to my lips, poetry to my soul.

> *"The Son is the image of the invisible God,*
> *the firstborn over all creation.*
> *For in Him all things were created:*
> *things in heaven and on earth,*
> *visible and invisible,*
> *whether thrones or powers or rulers or authorities;*

all things have been created through Him and for Him.
He is before all things,
and in Him all things hold together.
And He is the head of the body, the church;
He is the beginning and the firstborn
from among the dead,
so that in everything He might have the supremacy.
For God was pleased to have all His fullness
dwell in Him, and through Him
to reconcile to himself all things,
whether things on earth or things in heaven,
by making peace through His blood,
shed on the cross—"

"Knock knock?"

I turned my head at the voice. Byziana came in and kissed her mother on the cheek, so I stood, perhaps to leave. My aunt held me in place. Byziana sat on the opposite side of the bed and wasted no time in asking, "Mater, did you know I would be betrothed tonight?"

The lady set her hand over her daughter's. "Yes, I did." She gave a soft smile to Byziana then squeezed both our hands.

"Did you agree with Pater to not tell me until we were in that crowd? Did you agree it would be a surprise for me too?"

"Your father had already decided, darling. We thought you would respond better when you saw the honor it brought the family." Lady Sophia's cheek twitched.

Byziana held the ring to the light and watched it sparkle. "Is it Pater's express will for me to marry Captain Belisarius?"

"It is."

"Then I suppose I have no choice."

"This is the system, Byzia. We submit to our fathers. It is the foundation of the patriate. The Pater makes the decisions, and we trust the Pater."

Byziana sighed. Not a sad or sorry sigh.

"Do you like him, Mater?"

My aunt shifted in her bed and glanced at me. Clearing her throat she met her daughter's gaze, "I do not know him. But your father knows him. And your father finds him worthy. You can trust Pater."

Byziana lifted her ring again. The new gold flickered reflections of the windowpane's lamp. She turned to me. "Do you like him, Marcellus?"

I shrugged my shoulders. *I don't like how he touched you. And I wish I knew what's underway with him and Gallus.*

"You like him because he is a soldier!" she laughed. "But Mater, he is old. How can I marry an old man?"

Lady Sophia's laugh sounded like the light tinkle of rain on a roof.

"You are twelve, he is but twenty-one—only nine years difference. He is certainly not old. Your father is twelve years my senior, and you see how well we understand each other."

Byziana nodded, trying to make sense of her mother's words.

"You will find as you get older that age does not matter as much as friendship. He is young for a captain, with potential. I think he may become a good friend."

"He promised me a large house in Constantinople. With mosaics and tapestries." An ever-so-slight flush came to her face. She shook the thought away and continued. "He has great plans for his life. It's a dream come true—what I've always wanted."

"Through your father's introduction he will go far . . . . It seems a good match for you. It is just . . ."

When her cheek twitched again, Lady Sophia changed the subject. "Would you like to listen to the Scriptures, dear? Marcellus is reading from the Colossians Epistle."

"Oh. I have already heard that one. I think I shall go see what Iulia is doing, and what she says of my ring!" She jumped off the bed and was about to leave the room when her mother reached out again to her.

"Byziana, please sit here a bit." My cousin glanced at her mother, at me, at the door. Her shoulders dropped, and she returned to the bedside.

Lady Sophia took my cousin's hand to her cheek. "You are getting so big and grown." Byziana blushed and looked at me, expecting a tease, but I acted interested in my fingernails. This was not a moment to tease her.

"Listen to Marcellus for a while, dear."

Byziana huffed as she sat on the bed again. I hoped Lady

Sophia did not notice Byziana's clenched teeth.

I read again,
"God was pleased to have all His fullness
dwell in him, and through Him
to reconcile to himself all things,
whether things on earth or things in heaven,
by making peace through his blood,
shed on the cross—"
Lady Sophia stopped me.

"Byziana, I hope you will one day know what it means when we say God's fullness dwelt in Christ whose blood was shed. It's all right here. God and man."

"Not again!" Byziana's eyes rolled to the ceiling. "You know this debate will go nowhere. Why bring it up?"

"Can you not listen, Daughter?"

"I hardly understand it, but I have heard enough. Let's not speak of it."

"But it is my bequest to you. It is what I can give you."

"It does not matter. Let me believe and let me be."

"Oh, no. It matters more than anything. It determines heresy or orthodoxy. Worship or blasphemy. It matters more than this home and the fine robe you are wearing. More than your daily bread. Your belief on Chalcedon identifies the very God you worship."

"Mater, please understand. I submit to Pater in this. Should I not submit to Pater?"

Lady Sophia sagged under an invisible burden. "You should submit to Pater," she acceded.

"We live in this world, Mater. We have to submit to the leaders and live according to the rules and laws they give us. Our position demands it. These days most people—well, people that matter—do not agree with Chalcedon. Philosophers say God cannot be man. He only appeared to be so."

Her mother shook her head slowly.

"Mater, do not worry. It changes nothing. He's still our Savior."

"But Byzia—"

"It's the way it is. Try to understand. Pater does. You give me this home," she lifted the skirt of her robe, "and this robe you mention. But without the regard . . . without the esteem . . . of honorable men, Pater's position means nothing. And this robe is meaningless. I wear the robe as a symbol of my responsibility to our class. We must bow to the future. Not to the past."

"You speak your father's words well." She closed her mouth, trying to keep herself from speaking. She closed her eyes, squeezing her lips together. But the words burst out. "You're right. It behooves you to believe what they tell you. Heaven knows what would happen if people actually reasoned through things."

She breathed out a frustrated sigh then let go of Byziana's hand. With a brushing flick of her fingers she added, "You should go to your friends."

Byziana hurried to the door. She could not have seen the weary look on my aunt's face. After her daughter left, Lady Sophia sighed again and combed her hair back with her fingers.

Other women would be discussing tapestry and fashion. My aunt sought Truth. The debate they referred to consumed theological circles. And yet it mattered to the Lady of the House of Gaius Justus.

At the Great Debate's heart, Monophysites claimed Christ was only God, and Chalcedonians believed Christ was both God and man.

After a while she asked me to read her favorite portion again. Her head reclined against the pillow, eyes closed, heart throbbing like mine, no doubt. It portrayed our beloved Savior— our beautiful Christ, the fullness of divinity, in whom all things hold together. There was something mystical yet approachable about the words on this Scroll.

Faith was in our blood. Though my father had taught me logic, ethics and history, Lady Sophia, my mother's second-cousin, had told me stories from the ancient Hebrew Scriptures, the Gospels and the Epistles here in her trunk.

She grabbed my hand again. *The Son is the image of the invisible God.* Her eyes sparkled with unearthly comprehension.

The idea was too abstract. "How is that possible? How can something invisible have an image?"

"It could if—"

Firm footsteps striding toward my aunt's bedchamber drew our attention.

CIVIL WAR

Gaius Justus came into the room bringing a glow to Sophia's face. His red cape, his firm stance, his raised chin—they awed me, making me want to disappear. My aunt reached out for his sun-brown hand.

"Are you well, Wife?" He sat by her on the bed and stroked her cheek.

"I am well. Marcellus is reading to me."

He gave a smiling nod in my direction, then returned his attention to his wife. I was relieved his eyes were off me. My uncle reminded me of Julius Caesar. But better. Of Caesar Augustus. But better because of Christ. Honor and faith—the best of both kingdoms—what Christ had wanted for mankind—cloaked the soldiers of Byzantium.

"Does your stomach ail you again?"

"It does."

His lips pressed together, and he began to rise. "We must summon the doctor."

She kept him near her. "Tomorrow. I'll meet with him tomorrow. Today is a day of celebration."

Gaius Justus as a soldier was fit and determined. I delighted in watching him challenge his men sword on sword. Hale and hearty, he commanded his sword like his men. No compromise. But here with his wife he was a different man. His chin jut out with a glad smile. "Yes. A good celebration. Byziana was surprised. Is she happy? She seemed out of temper when she left your chamber."

"We had a tiff over . . . over something else. Not about the captain. She is pleased with the match."

His face beamed. "Then I am glad. We could not hope for a

better match were she to marry a *patrikios* himself. I have great hopes in that man. He will go far. I assure you."

She agreed, then breathed heavily and patted my hand again. He glanced at her hand on mine, then at me, before asking her. "What was it that caused our girl distress?"

The lady shifted in bed. "Would you like to hear the reading with us, Husband?"

"Oh." He noticed the Scroll in my lap then looked back to Lady Sophia. "Oh. Uh. I had better not. The public reading of Scripture by the laity is forbidden. Two people is hardly public, but three borders on subversion."

Her laugh might have been despair.

He stroked her cheek again. "I promise we'll read together when I come back from Constantinople." His eyebrows furrowed. "Did the words of this Scroll trouble Byziana?"

"I am afraid so."

"Sophia, I have warned you not to undermine the family with this Chalcedon nonsense."

Lady Sophia picked at the lace bedspread.

"It hurts me to pain you. Let us have peace on this topic, shall we? I beg you, bend your knee to our leaders in this." He took her hand in his then added, "Or bend your knee to me in this."

"May I speak freely, Justus?" Lady Sophia answered.

He considered me then nodded. "Of course."

"I stand before God, first and foremost. If I fail to think . . . if I let others think for me . . . I risk all I hold most dear. It would be as if you, a fish, asked me, a bird, to trust you and live under the water. It would kill me. It is not prudent to go against conscience."

"I am not asking you to do wrong. Perhaps you should listen to their reasoning. It might make it clear to you."

"It is clear to me. The teachers of Alexandria philosophize in darkness."

"No! You are the one who is mistaken. They are great scholars. Their philosophical proofs are sound. Christ was God appearing as man. They are not the ones in darkness."

The lady's mouth twitched at his insinuation. "Husband, I shall submit to you in all things. Except this. Forgive me if I appear ungrateful. I cannot bend."

His demeanor clouded over like a storm. The soldier stepped to the battle. "I do not accept this. You must listen to me. I lead this home. This controversy can only end in civil war."

Civil war! This was the first I had heard that portent.

"Chalcedon must fail, or the army will lose its unity. Without unity we will have war within, and that's all Persia is waiting for. All the Ostrogoths in Rome are waiting for. Signs of weakness. It's political, yes. But our whole way of life depends on it."

"I agree. Our way of life depends on it."

His shoulders relaxed. "Good. So you will agree to drop this nonsense?"

"This nonsense. . . ?"

"Trust me. I know about these things."

"I trust you, dear. It's just—"

"That should be enough for you."

"Forgive me, Husband."

Gaius Justus smiled. His brown hands cupped his wife's white cheeks. "There is nothing to forgive. I am proud you are not a silly woman. I ask you again, please, do not worry our daughter over this."

Lady Sophia's soft smile reflected a pained heart.

He groaned. "Sophia, do not be sad. Tell me. Why can you not let go?" He shook his head and looked to the ceiling. "The Council of Chalcedon was hundreds of years ago. Just let go."

"One simple reason, dear Justus. Legacy. We carry the weight of the martyrs on us. They died for the creeds, including Chalcedon. If they were wrong who died in peril, how can we who live in sanctuary know better?"

"Reason. Reason shows Chalcedon cannot be true."

She shook her head helplessly, glancing at me with apology. "I am sorry you had to hear this, Marcellus."

"Marcellus would be on the side of Reason. Aren't you, Marcellus?"

"Of course, sir."

"Do you hold to Chalcedon?"

I felt pinned between two opinions, and not free to think. "I am not exactly sure yet, I guess."

"Well then, let me tell you. Side with Reason over anything else. Monophysite thought is the most reasonable. Christ was God. No less. Don't forget that. And I charge you to keep the family on track while I'm gone."

He stared at me steadily until I replied.

"Yes, sir." I scratched the back of my neck. *On track?*

"And now, Sophia. Do not make it difficult for Marcellus. Make the decision to not speak of Chalcedon. Believe what you want, but do not speak of it."

Her pale face twitched again, but she was silent. A draft flickered at the lamp on the windowsill making shadows dance around the walls.

"Can you not be on the side of Reason, Wife?"

"Oh yes, dear," she eagerly answered. "I promise with my whole heart. I will submit to you and be on the side of Reason."

"Finally good sense." He pulled his wife to his chest with eager affection and soft tenderness. Witnessing the beautiful display of arms entwined and cheeks pressed together bewildered me. I blushed and stood to leave.

"Marcellus, stay," Gaius Justus said, as if what I saw had been commonplace. "I'll leave. You should keep your aunt company."

"Justus," Lady Sophia said, clearing her throat, "our greatest worry is not civil war. A greater worry is this. If Christ was not man, how could He die for our sins?"

My uncle stroked her hand and got to his feet. "God has His ways."

"So you appeal to faith, not Reason."

"I do not know these things, I admit. I let reasonable others think for me. They have nothing better to do."

Her eyebrows pinched into a frown. "Really, dear."

A moving shadow at the doorway drew our attention.

"Gallus!" Gaius Justus opened his arms to welcome his steward into the room. Everything in me tensed. *How long has he been at the door? What did he hear?*

Lady Sophia sat up with a pained grimace and pulled her bedspread up to her chest.

"I trust you will take good care of my family while I am gone."

"Of course, master."

The steward glanced my way. *Do not make eye contact with him. Turn away.* I walked over to the window and looked outside. Watching the lights of Antioch flickering about the city, my attention remained on the conversation. *How long has he been listening to us? When did he arrive? What had he heard?*

"You will look after my wife's health, and if need be summon the doctor."

From the corner of my eye I saw Gallus tip his dark head in assent. "Wife, you have nothing to fear while Gallus runs my estate."

"I agree." She smiled and took the hand of Gallus. "You are a faithful servant, Gallus. I rest easy knowing you are here." My nerves twitched. *He must know I saw him. He must know.*

"It is my pleasure, madame, to serve your family." *Would they still trust him if they heard what I saw? But she sounds so confident in him. Perhaps it truly was for soup.*

"I shall be with you in a moment, Gallus," Gaius Justus said. The steward bowed and departed to the darkness of the hall. Gaius Justus stroked his wife's cheek. "Meanwhile, I must away to the Capital in the morning. And now I return to my steward and then my guests. Marcellus can keep you company."

She took his hand and kissed the palm. I do not know if they ever saw each other again. We watched him leave, his robe swaying back and forth in confident momentum, back to his guests, forward to his fate.

I helped her recline again, doing what I could to ease her obvious pain. *Now's my chance. Gallus. Tell her about Gallus.* But she spoke first.

"If only I were more articulate. If only he knew. It does matter. More than anything." She closed her eyes and shook her head in regret. "Everyone is against me. Everyone is against Reason."

"I am not, my Lady."

She studied me and put her hand to my face. "So put me on track, son. Can it be you are Monophysite?"

I bit my lip and pulled the Scroll open. "Shall I read to you?"

Her eyes sparkled, and she winked at me. "Yes. Then we will speak of this in the morning."

"Sure," I sighed. *In the morning.* I could wait to talk about Gallus then, too. It was a lot to think about. *Civil war rested on this?*

I unrolled the Scroll and continued the reading. Latin was becoming more common in Byzantium. Indeed, it was Antioch's street language. But the mother tongue of our family, and of many still in Antioch, was this same smooth Greek. I got to *'the image of the invisible God'* and again unanswered questions swirled about my head. *Tomorrow. Ask her tomorrow.* I read and read through all of Saint Paul's sacred words to the Colossians. In these moments when I would read to my aunt, my compact world would stop and I would glimpse a vast world of invisible things, of powers and truths that mattered. But I would leave the Scrolls and leave the Trunk and enter my minuscule life again, and those truths and feelings would dissipate into the invisible place above me like breath steam on a cold day.

Why I had gone sixteen years without asking to see these Scrolls more often I know not. At that moment, when truth was unclouded, I made a pact with myself to come to the Trunk and read in all my free moments. If only I could have kept my pact. Events were in play that changed forever those days of leisure and luxury. When I came to the Scroll's end and my thoughts were on this world again, my aunt's deep breathing showed me she had found rest and peace. I tied up the Epistle and placed it back into its old home, fighting the temptation to trespass and read another Scroll in that box.

Pulling the blanket up over her shoulders, I left her to sleep, returning myself to the feast in the Great Room. The peace of the room I left was heavenly, compared to the hell and distress and heartbreak that met me later that night.

THE SECRET OF
THE COLONNADES

The party over, the crowds dispersed, I sat in the dark on the terrace looking out over my city of Antioch. The scent of our rain-kissed mountain satisfied my heart with its freshness and promise. Flowers would be happy to bloom tomorrow.

Torchlights from people returning home from other Ascension Eve celebrations coasted like shooting stars on the streets of my city below. House lights dimmed one by one as people slept off the revelry. My mother and aunt and cousins had long since retired.

The deep farewell of Gaius Justus to Belisarius across the walkway joining our two homes called my attention. The door shut and the soldier banter began as Belisarius and his men donned cloaks.

"Delight of delights awaits, dear Captain," said Indulf, walking toward the road. Someone threw in a chortle about "proving manhood," which piqued my attention. I slipped to the corner and peeked around it to watch them.

In huddled groups, with crude and drunken laughter, they followed the damp, stone-paved road down the hill into Antioch. Then I, in the shadows, followed the group of soldiers until they turned onto the sewage-stenched Street of Colonnades.

Proving manhood. How does one prove oneself a man? Looking back I can see the naiveté of youth impelling me to shadow them. If you have lived long in this world, you know the answer. But I had not yet learned it. My uncle's esteem of Belisarius powered my curiosity into his life and the life of grown men of which I would soon be a part. My orphaned world was limited to a simple life on Mount Silpius. And as my father could no longer guide me into the realm of adulthood, I thought perhaps my new cousin-in-law would walk that path with me.

I followed my instinct and followed those soldiers down into the dark dank streets of Antioch to learn from them a lesson I wish I never had learned. They soon found me watching them.

Perhaps if I had taken my patrician's cloak they would have known to not accost me—but in my haste it had been left behind. Perhaps if I had taken my sword, they would have heard the voice of my blade—but who could have known I would need a sword against my uncle's own men?

I saw Belisarius with his men as he truly was. And no one heard my cries, and no one came to my aid. Yet I survived, and made it home pained in body and soul, swearing to myself I would die before speaking of it to anyone.

And she was to marry such a man.

WHAT REASON DEMANDS

To look back on the morning after the banquet brings a painful longing to my heart. Little did we know as we slept that night. Little did we know as we reunited to plan a lunch on the hills. Oh, how soon our sweet life would be poisoned—how soon our city would fall to the worst enemy known to man!

"Wake up, Marcellus. Wake up!" My cousins Justin and five-year-old Natalia were jumping on top of me.

"Later. Let me sleep," I said, turning over in my bed, knowing the futility of going against their stubborn wills.

"We are going to the hills. All of us."

"You must come, too." They bounced more.

"It's Ascension Day! We must have a picnic. It's tradition."

"Get up," with which words they tore the covers off me, leaving the cool May air to awaken my unclothed and bruised body.

"Hey!" I pulled my blanket back until they left the room in a torrent of giggles. As they left, memories overwhelmed me. My stomach surged and ousted into the chamberpot. *You should have known. You saw all the clues at the banquet. You shouldn't have followed them. What a fool you are, Marcellus.*

The sun shone its long rays across the housetops. A few peddler calls echoed in the streets below. Few people were out. Most were home sleeping off a festal evening. The inns burst with pilgrims come from over the empire to celebrate mass at the Great Church. And the Great Church itself hosted tired monks who had spent the night in prayer vigil.

Today was Ascension Day. As a Christian city, we were grateful Christ had died, resurrected, and ascended. Of this we were unified. Yet men afterward second-guessed whether the burgeoning Grand Debate in our city had caused the divine displeasure and terrible tragedy of Ascension Day.

When an army comes against you, you hear invasion rumors, you hear angry politicians debating, you see soldiers rushed to muster. When a plague comes against you, you see the weak fall first, you feel death all around. Of these I am now familiar and speak of what my eyes have seen.

But what we saw that morning came unannounced. We lived on the skirt of Mount Silpius. From our terraces we looked down upon the Antioch rooftops, and saw even the Hippodrome and the Emperor's Palace way over on the Imperial Island.

The houses of Gaius Justus and Gaius Dorotheus stood side by side, as the men had been in life before Pater died last year. Both Antiochene *patrikioi*, they were once a force to fear. A force to venerate. Now Gaius Justus stood alone and my capable mother, Lady Aemelia, managed our estate.

While the children packed food baskets I occupied myself, the distractions and a hollow stomach mollifying my broken soul. Lady Sophia called to me first thing and I knocked on her door. "Come in!" her soft voice said. She was still in bed.

"You are going for a hike?" she asked.

I nodded an answer. *Was it last night I was in here listening to her debate my cousin and my uncle? Was that last night? It seems a lifetime ago. I was a different person back then.*

"Marcellus. Come here," my aunt said.

I approached her and scratched my cheek.

"Did you get hurt?" She touched the side of my face where it itched. Had a sword sliced me? I couldn't remember.

"It's nothing," I lied. *How can it be nothing! It is everything. Everything happened. Everything changed.*

"If you ask Maria she can give you a salve for that. She knows where I keep it." She patted the side of her bed.

"Thank you." I doubted her salve could touch the real pain. I sat at the edge of the bed, my whole body ached.

"Did you get enough sleep?"

"Yes, ma'am."

"Ma'am?" she took a deep breath. "Something is wrong, and I want you to tell me now. Let me help you."

"My cousins are waiting for me. Did you want to talk about my uncle's words?" I deflected. *No one can ever find out. How could I ever voice the words?*

She nodded. "I understand, son. But I'm here for you when you're ready to talk. It's not easy growing up, I understand. But I'm a safe person."

"I know." Even I could hear the heartless cadence of my reply.

She took my hand in hers again. "So you have been tasked to keep us on track."

"I guess so."

"Like a shepherd. What do you plan to do for us?"

I was at a loss for words. How could I simply move from the heart realm, where I was a broken mess, to the thought realm? I was saved by Justin's noisy entry.

"Mater!" He ran in and jumped on the bed. She cringed at the painful collision, but pulled her son to her chest and kissed his cheek. "Good morning, darling!"

"Good morning. We're going on a hike. It's tradition."

"You sound like you did not get enough sleep, either. When did you go to bed?"

"After Simeon and Kasiais left."

"Well, Martha would leave at a reasonable hour, so Simeon was in bed early. But what about Kasiais?"

"He left, too. Then Maria took me to bed."

"Oh good. I trust Maria." She pulled Justin into the crook of her arm and turned to me. "So you're our shepherd." She took a deep breath and smiled. "You know, the most beautiful thing I've ever seen is a shepherd in the rain. There he was, his flock eating grass and drinking from the stream, but he was covered in his wool cape standing with the heavy rain falling over him. Have you ever seen one?"

"No. I'd think shepherds would keep their flocks locked up safe if it were raining."

"But the best grass and water are available in the rain. I'm glad you're our shepherd. So, last night I asked you a question. Is your answer ready?"

"I guess."

I had only promised to keep them on track. Now I was the

shepherd. A beaten up shepherd, more like.

"Marcellus, you act as if someone died." She felt my forehead. "You don't feel feverish."

Her hand went to my cheek. "I guess we should expect this from late nights and excessive food. So let's try to start up your brain. Monophysite or Chalcedonian? Or are you open for discussion?"

How can anyone talk about this when there are such evil men in the world? Who cares? Who cares if Christ was God or man or both or neither?

"Look at that frown!" She put her arm around my shoulder and held me against her. "No matter what is going on in your heart, Marcellus, I love you. And God is on your side. And at your side."

All I could do was sigh. *Then where was He last night?* I sat up and faced her, blocking any more prying with, "I am not sure which side to take. Truth seems more a political decision than a spiritual one—they both said as much last night. And I don't wish to be known as a traitor to Byzantium. Or the cause of civil war."

She propped herself on an elbow and said, "And yet you risk all. Regularly. To read Scripture aloud to me. No, dear. Though they be God's agents, neither emperors nor generals decide Truth. Truth is."

Justin turned his mother's chin toward himself. "Can you come too, Mater?"

"I won't be able to hike today." She took a breath and smiled at her son. "Justin, Mater and Marcellus are talking. If you'd like to listen to us, you may. But silently. He'll come in a minute."

"Okay. What are we talking about?"

"Shh. Listen." She put her finger to her mouth and reclined him against her. "Truth is. We must know it and conform to it. Even if everyone is against us."

"Pater said as much."

"Your father was a wise man. Now another question. To help you choose. Which—"

"I liked Gaius Dorotheus," Justin piped.

"We did, too. Hush now and listen," she whispered. To me she asked, "Which is superior? Philosophy or Scripture?"

I hesitated, my mind warming up. *Philosophers say the Son of the Trinity has only one nature, which is divine. Philosophers say Christ was not human like us. Do I believe them? But Chalcedon philosophers said otherwise.*

"I think philosophy is important. And Alexandrian philosophers teach Christ could not be God and man at the same time—how it must be impossible."

"So then, you believe those philosophers have the final word?"

"Mater?" Justin asked. She put her finger on his lips.

Truth. How could we know it? Scripture taught of a God of love. The world showed a preference for hate. I pushed away the hurt again and tried to answer based on my father's schooling. Scholars never hurt anyone.

"No. Scripture is given by God to direct us how we may know Truth." I chewed my fingernail. "So the question is, must Scripture submit to philosophy or philosophy to Scripture."

"Exactly."

Justin spoke again. "Mater, what's a 'fellasufy'?"

Lady Sophia embraced her son. "Philosophy. I'll tell you later, Justin. Let me hear your cousin's answer, okay?"

"Okay."

Which one was superior?

The flickering light on the windowpane reflected in my aunt's smiling eyes. "I will not allow you to sit on the fence," she said.

"What fence?"

"Hush, Justin."

"Scripture is from God Himself. Philosophy is filtered through the mind of man." I took a deep breath, gathering my thoughts. "It stands to reason we must believe Scripture over philosophy."

She smiled and lifted my hand to her cheek, "My question was not fair, dear. It is a false choice. Philosophy is also from God. A tool given to mankind to reason through unseen truths."

"So neither is superior?" My mind pulled and stretched this idea.

"They work together. Nothing is wrong with philosophy, with thinking, with questioning things. True philosophy always leads to Truth. And true reasoning always leads to God. It is just . . . as I said to your uncle, philosophizing in darkness can lead one astray."

"So Scripture complements philosophy, and philosophy Scripture. Hmm."

"Yes." She set my hand on the bed again and patted it. "Your deep, true reasoning proves you are a Son of Chalcedon."

Son of Chalcedon. I like the sound of that.

She stared out the window at the empty sky for a while. "I don't suppose Belisarius knows the creed."

"Mater?"

"Are you sure Belisarius is Monophysite?" I asked.

She nodded.

Of course. Politics wins again. The mention of Belisarius returned me to last night, and my shoulders dropped.

"Who is Kal-sidin?" Justin asked. His mother stroked his cheek instead of answering him, returning her attention to me.

"God's Word is plain enough, and Reason demands it. Christ was human. And, Marcellus, this knowledge affects everything we do . . . we say . . . we know. You won't have trouble keeping us on track with Reason if you remember this. The Incarnation is the answer to everything."

That drew my attention back. *Reason demands it?* My eyes squinted with the implications. *How does Reason demand such a thing?*

"Mater?"

She continued, "To balance ourselves against error, we must bind ourselves to the light, which is Scripture. And to the creeds. Do you still remember the Confession?"

The Confession of Chalcedon. I nodded, "I learned it as one of my last lessons with Pater. Before . . . you know . . . ."

"He left you with an invaluable tool, my dear. A measuring line to the truth. Keep it in your heart."

If Reason demands it, how did the Alexandrians arrive at a different conclusion than the Antiochene scholars? I took a breath and was about to ask all my questions, when Justin spoke again.

"Mater?"

"Yes, Son."

"Who is Kal-sidin?"

"Excuse me?"

"I thought Gaius Dorotheus was Marcellus's pater."

Her smile and chuckle puzzled my cousin.

I answered for her. "Yes, Dorotheus was my pater. And Chalcedon is a place."

"Oh." He still looked confused. Then he jumped up and pulled me onto my feet with a frown on his face. "That's enough talking. We've got business. Sorry, Mater."

I shall speak with her later. Of the demands of Reason. And of Gallus. Lady Sophia leaned back on her pillow and I kissed her cheek. After a deep sigh, a contented smile still on her face, she waved goodbye to us and closed her eyes. I wish I had known to never put things off till tomorrow.

Our Hike on the Hills

"You have to see the kittens before we leave." Natalia grabbed my hand as soon as I arrived on the terrace.

"Their eyes opened yesterday, and they walk faster now." She pulled me to where Katerina, Justin, and Byziana knelt over nursing kittens.

"See the white one with spots? He's mine. I named him Speckles," Natalia said.

I stroked the kitten's paw with my finger, so happily kneading for milk, newly-opened eyes closed in contentment as it nursed.

"Mine is named Honey," eight-year-old Katerina said, pointing to the yellow striped kitten next to Speckles.

"What a pretty color. Is it a boy or a girl?" I asked.

"It's a boy."

"He's bigger than the others. Got a big tomcat in the making here, Kata."

She touched its tiny legs with an eager smile. "A big tomcat!"

They nursed as if their life depended on it, not knowing it did. This was their world. Their mother. Milk. And some strange humans who handled them.

The tortoiseshell mother cat we called Belle. She licked the head of each kitten we had touched.

"Justin, is one of them yours?"

"Of course. The black one is mine, the white one is Byziana's, and yours is the white one with the yellow ears and tail."

"Mine?"

"Yes," said Byziana. "You have to name him. It's a boy."

Mine? He was a swirl of yellow on white. His large yellow paws promised he would outgrow even Kata's kitten. With his eyes closed he drunk life into himself, earnestly taking to his job of growing up. *What a creature!* "He needs a good name. What are yours called?"

"Blackie," said Justin.

"That's original," I laughed. "What about yours, Byziana?"

"I've named mine Misty," said Byziana. She looked at me with eyebrows raised.

"A perfect name," I said, nodding affirmation.

She smiled back thanks.

I stroked Belle. "Good job, Mama Cat. You've got a beautiful family here. Honey, Misty, Speckles, Blackie and this guy here. I will give him a worthy name." Her back stretched into my caress. The soft fur on my hand comforted my own tortured heart, the fresh pain still there under the surface.

Why had they done it? Why me? Why would men do that? What had I done against those soldiers?

I kept my hand on Belle—watching the kittens eagerly pressing their mother for her milk, receiving it with trust—seeing her patiently give of herself for her offspring. What lucky kittens to have such a life. I closed my eyes and drew in a deep breath. Belle startled me with her rough tongue on my hand, intimate, strong and lulling. Over and over. How is it that a mere beast can console a man? Were they created for this purpose? Her touch calmed me, brought me to the present, pushing the misery of last night deep into the back of my mind as if a bad dream.

"Are we all ready to go?" I rallied my cousins.

They jumped up with eager smiles and ran to our family's terrace, picking up baskets and parcels.

"Will you not come with us?" We gathered around my mother with last-minute pleading.

"No, I shall sit in the garden and follow you in spirit," she said, her eyes still on her stitchery.

My mother resembled Lady Sophia in grace and in breeding, for the same woman raised them. When Sophia's parents had died, my grandmother Helena raised her cousin's babe as her own. Sophia and Aemelia had grown up together, married Antioch's *patrikioi* together, lived on Mount Silpius together. This was why and how our families lived an intertwined life. We called each other 'cousin' and 'aunt' because of that intimacy.

Both women looked after the needy and the widowed. They

ran their homes in generosity and frugality. They embodied perfect matrons of the timeless Roman patriarchy. Yet they differed in a significant way—Gaia Sophia owned the Trunk of Scrolls.

Byziana ran up the winding bridle path before any of us, basket of cheese and bread and pastries swinging on her elbow.

Just as I was about to follow my cousins out the back gate, Mater took my arm and pulled me close to her. Her fingertips brushed the side of my face. "What happened to your cheek?" she asked. Her touch was painful.

I put my hand to cover the bruising. "It is of no import."

"Were you in a fight, Marcellus?"

"Not exactly."

"It would behoove you to not live like the rabble. You must remember your position in Antioch. And bear the duties of our class, even at your young age."

If only she knew. "Forgive me, Mater," I said. "It will not happen again."

"I am surprised at you. I would not take you as a man of war."

"My apologies, madame." I bowed my head to her.

"Never mind, then." She set her embroidery down and reached out to embrace me. "How can I stay angry with you when you gaze into my soul with those deep blue eyes of yours? Goodbye, Light-of-My-Heart. I shall see you in the evening."

Justin, Natalia and Katerina ran back to drag me away from Mater and up toward Byziana. The dirt was dry. The late morning sun burned off any sign of last night's rain. The heat was spring-hot, not summer-hot. Perfect for a picnic. Perfect for forgetting. Maybe.

"Enjoy yourselves," Mater called behind us. "Bring me a white snowfall of daisies."

"We will!" the children's words echoed down the path.

We ascended for about an hour. Katerina, the slowest, gathered a plethora of purple and pink and blue May flowers to fill her basket. I had been running with the younger children. Out of breath, I stopped them.

Byziana, above us on the hill crest, held her hands to the sky, soaking in the sun like a flower herself. This moment transformed her in my eyes.

I do not know why men are drawn to the forbidden. Yesterday she was my twelve-year-old relative, a neighbor, almost a sister. Today she was betrothed and suddenly, in my eye, that-which-becomes-married. A woman. I saw her slender form—her body, to my surprise, had taken on a woman's shape.

The girl I had known from birth—whose laughter and tears and friendship knit into mine, whose tenacious strength upheld her family for better or for worse—that girl had somehow become a young woman without my notice. A surge of something warm and achy struck my heart.

The sunlight reflected for a moment on the ring on her finger. The ring and the man who gave it. Sorrow and grief and shame from last night flooded over me. *Nothing short of cruelty would have spurred men to such actions. Men in the red cape should not have sullied the honor of Christian Rome.*

Her wheat-colored hair long and blowing in the breeze, her lips apple-red, her cheeks rosy, like a part of nature, her arms open to the sun—she had the world before her, and was promised to the man who led such people. I tried to chase away the despondency. She should enjoy her youth. Enjoy this innocence that so soon can be whipped away from you.

As if on signal, she also gazed at her ring and her face brightened at whatever thoughts came to her heart. Darkness hovered over my own heart.

My kinswoman should not marry such a man. I wanted my cousin to be safe. I wanted my cousin to be happy. *I should tell her.* My heart clenched. *Yet if I tell her, they'll all know. They'll never look at me the same. And how can I say the words?*

My courage betrayed me, and suppressing a deep feeling of defeat, I turned my eyes off the betrothed girl and onto the glorious city. My city. The city of our family. The Christian capital, where the Church of Christ had begun. It lay before us: noble powerful Antioch. No other came close to ours in eminence. Not Rome, not Constantinople, not Alexandria, not Jerusalem.

No metropolis had the magnificence of architecture or the deep tapestry of cultures as had Antioch. Jews, Romans, Barbarians, Egyptians, Indians, Armenians, Ethiopians, even some Persians, the Old Order, the New Order, to mention a few. It was said, if one wished to travel the world to see the colorful medley of people and life and thought, one need not travel beyond Antioch.

My eyes followed the Great Wall surrounding our city. Behind us, on Mount Silpius, towers and citadels kept watch to the east. Four secure gates opened us for trade, closed us to the Persians. And dividing Antioch down the center, a grand two-mile-long thoroughfare connected our northern Gate of Orientalis to our southern Gate of Daphne.

The filthy Street of Colonnades.

Though I did not wish to remember, my mind showed me the spot. I clenched my hands in frustrated desperation. But unexpectedly, Scripture from last night arrived with a warm, tender breeze that rustled my hair: '*In Him all things hold together.*'

The zephyr lifted my attention away from last night and landed it on, of all things, the kitten my cousins had given me. My kitten. His yellow tail and ears, his eager peaceful nursing, his big white paws. *Trusty. That will be his name. If he can trust in his first weeks of life, I can trust. God will hold me together. Keep me from unraveling. I hope. Trusty.* I took a deep, brave breath of the wind, and my eyes continued their caress of my city. *Life can move on.*

The Street of Colonnades, as backbone to our city, networked into the master-planned grid of streets and bridges housing life and breath in Antioch.

Ten percent of our citizens were rich, ten percent poor, the rest well-fed and happy—for meandering through Antioch and around the Royal Island, the river Orontes served as our potent lifeline to the world of affluent commerce. Out beyond the city toward the sea were our fields. The fields of Gaius Justus and Gaius Dorotheus grew the largest sections of wheat and cotton in the region.

None was like Antioch in its envious situation, its pleasant climate, its gentle breezes, its fertile lands. Most of the serfs worked our fields, many mouths depended on those fields, many pocketbooks filled our accounts. For this reason, our houses were secure, our servants many, our troubles small.

Until that moment.

A roaring thunder shook our feet, as though a giant beast beneath the mountain had awakened. Katerina shrieked and lost her balance. Beyond us, a huge boulder bounced down the hill as would a child's ball. Another boulder, then another.

The roaring continued. Our mountain shook as if to arise, throwing the others to the ground. Natalia tumbled down the hill, Katerina screamed in terror, Justin tried over and over to stand, then their eyes all plastered on the city. I retrieved Natalia before she had time to cry for help and brought her up toward her sister. Byziana's eyes, wide with terror, faced Antioch. I had kept my balance. But when I turned back toward the city the sight I saw brought me to my knees.

The buildings moved back and forth, left and right, like a feast table shaken by its corner with vicious anger. The table shook until every single building . . . every stone in the Imperial palace . . . every marketplace column . . . separated from its neighbor and crashed to the ground. The expansive baths, the high colonnades, the protective walls, the grand aqueducts. The residences of the rich, the tenements of the poor . . . collapsed to the ground, flattened like a loaf of bread with startled yeast. The earthquake, no respecter of persons—rich or poor, male or female, young or old—showed no mercy.

Earth had even the audacity to tear the magnificent Great Church asunder. The minute or more of earth-work destroyed centuries of man-work. Famed projects of Hadrian, Trajan, Caligula, Theodosius, Antiochus Epiphanes, Caesar Augustus . . . all returned to the ground whence they had arisen.

And when the sound of falling stones subsided, our imaginations took over. Our loved ones might now be under those fallen stones. Breath failed and we found ourselves running in one accord, back down the path to our homes, around the crest of the hill, past the sun-scorched flowers, our only thought our mothers.

Running home our legs felt heavy and slow. Limited and ineffective, as in a dream. What normally would have taken twenty minutes felt like days.

Natalia insisted on being carried, crying the whole way, and the other children, afraid of the ground, afraid of another quake, gripped our hands and slipped and slid down the gravelly path.

When we finally came around the last curve of the path, what we saw froze us in incredulity. Aqueducts below our homes had foundered and fallen, leaving precarious stones balanced on thin pillars.

Yet by some strange twist of fate none of the residences on Mount Silpius had collapsed. The relief we felt was a cruel joke—life as we knew it had ceased.

STONE VERSUS MAN

We ran through the mountainside gate into our courtyard. My mother was nowhere. Her stitchery and needle lay discarded on the ground.

"Mater!" I called, searching our house.

Byziana and her siblings ran through the courtyard and across to their front door. "Mater!" they cried. A rushing servant directed me, "The lady is next door, young sir."

I hastened in to find several men hoisting a pillar off Lady Sophia. My mother wept at her side. Though the heavy stone had fallen on her already weak body, my aunt insisted, "The others. Look after the others. So many hands should not idle by me."

We sent the servants to help our household but we stayed with Lady Sophia. My mother's tears pooled on the ground, "Dear Sister, stay brave. Stay brave."

I carried my aunt to her couch, and she rested while we surveyed our home. A girl's scream echoed from the terrace. "Marcellus! Marcellus." I hastened to Natalia's side. Face streaked with dirt and tears, she pointed to where Belle's bed had been. Hints of stilled tiny paws and tails stuck out from under a collapsed wall. I stared at them.

"Do you see Belle anywhere?" Justin asked. Our search was over in a moment.

"Oh, no!" Katerina called from the walkway between our houses. We found the mother cat lifeless under a roofing slab.

In her mouth was a kitten.

"She was trying to help him."

"Poor kitty," Natalia murmured.

I fell to my knees and could hardly breathe. *Trusty.* She failed to save him. He would never trust again. *The irony. It's not fair!* I touched his little limp paw and uncontrollable weeping took over.

My cousins stood behind me, silent and confused. There must have been rushing all around, the servants and neighbors helping each other. But I could not see. My face was in my hands. *Why the kitten?*

"We better tell Mater," someone said.

"Just let him cry it out."

Natalia sat next to me and rested on my shoulder. "It will be all right. Don't be sad."

They don't understand. Kittens should not die. Not like this. Not when the world is filled with such evil men.

"I didn't know he loved kittens so much," another said.

"Me neither."

Sobs drew my mother. She leaned close to my ear. "Son, pull yourself together! People are at death's door. Why do you weep for beasts?" Her cross, hushed words shamed me further.

I tried to stop the tears, but the assault was fresh a-mind. *No one understands. Trusty was my hope. Hope that things would hold together. Things won't hold together. Nothing could be worse.* The trembling began from deep in my soul.

"Marcellus, we can get you another kitty," Natalia said, wiping away her own tears.

"It will not help," I groaned. Emotion surged again, and I held my robe's edge to my eyes.

My mother put her arm around me again and hissed in my ear, "Marcellus, the servants are speaking of this. Think of your position. Leave this place at once or you have lost your honor in front of the servants. Their future master weeping for kittens? Now really!"

I steadied my nerves and muscles and tightened my gut. Cold flushed down my spine. *The servants must not see me weep. She is right.*

"Marcellus, my mother is calling you," Byziana said, coming up beside me.

I hurried to her bedside. Lady Sophia held my hand. "It is a dark day, Marcellus. It is not shameful to have deep feelings. But when life knocks you down, you've only got two choices."

If you are down? Two choices? I squinted my eyes, trying to understand, and ran my hand through my hair, grabbing the sides. What choices?

You're down. I looked into her face and the meaning dawned on me. Two choices. She was right. All in a nutshell.

I sighed. *I have to stand.*

"We must be strong, for one another. Can you be strong, dear?"

"I can try," I said, steeling myself. I clenched my hand, nails piercing my palm. At least it was a goal to aim toward, as impossible as it seemed.

"What is the status of our households? Do you know?"

"I do not," I said.

A frown flittered across her countenance. *She is right, I should have known.*

Byziana updated her mother as my mother entered the room, "Several servants are injured. Nothing serious." *Except for you*, her eyes said what her voice could not.

"Thank God" Lady Sophia said. "Is the city suffering?"

We looked out my aunt's window at the destruction below, then nodded. Words would not suffice. The damage was great, every structure unfaithful.

"Antioch. Oh Antioch," she moaned. One lone tear dripped from the corner of her eye—what I wouldn't have done to undo that teardrop.

Byziana suggested a plan of action. "Mater, we ought to help. Down in the city. They must need a hand." Her callowness did not strike me until much later.

My mother called Dynamius asking for his service. Gallus appeared next to him and my rage welled. *Too many things made no sense.*

"I have me a hoist. I can take that. Joseph and Petrus the Foreman, and some gardeners can come," Dynamius said. "Gallus, the moment you arrange for Gaius Justus's servants to join us we will start."

I left the room before I said something I'd regret. Mater took charge of Lady Sophia's business, at her request. Soon a crew of twelve people followed me to the city, arms filled with ropes and pulleys and makeshift hoists.

The sight besieging us added to the scalding pain already in my heart. I do not know why there are earthquakes. The ancients claimed them as a method of divine execution. I cannot claim that the only reason. But the caliber of disaster in Antioch pointed to an act of God. Antioch was an unthinkable horror, a post-war battlefield of fragile man versus hefty architecture. Lives extinguished by stones lay flattened between their earthen enemies.

How easily I write that which horrified our souls. Men can pull up the strength to face such atrocities. God created us with that ability. But it comes at a cost. We lose a part of ourselves any time we face epic catastrophe.

At each building we came to we called out, "Hello!" and responded to the need. The futility of our quest was clear from the start. We found Thomas, an old playmate of mine, half under a pile of marble slabs. The grand edifice had collapsed over him as he had dashed through its doorway. He called out to us, his arms furrowing the road, his fingers clawing the dirt, body and soul attempting to extradite his lower body from beneath his home.

He called out in terror, "Help me, Marcellus. Get my legs out. That's all." His eyes bulged pain and fear. "I just want to live."

Byziana ran to him and put water to his lips. Her eyes begged us to free him. The men ascertained the labor needed. Fifty-odd precarious stones pinned him to the ground. Hoisting the stones would destabilize the heap even more, endangering everyone, the men said.

We decided to dig out the soil under him, hoping to free him this way. The men steadied the stones as we began. After twenty minutes of our digging and shifting and hoisting, Byziana stood up and patted my arm. Tears glistened in her eyes. "He's gone."

We stopped our work, stepping back to take a weary breath. His body had succumbed, the stones above him had won. Youth—and all its potential and vitality—extinguished in a moment. Indeed the kitten was nothing to the sight of my lifeless friend whose voice I had just heard, who had clung to the earth and begged to live.

Six of us and twenty minutes were insufficient to save him. I looked at the wreckage that was once our city. The magnitude of the need petrified me. Antioch was filled with four hundred thousand people, plus holiday pilgrims. *How many now lay under rubble? How many will yet perish as we try to help?*

We cloaked the body of Thomas and continued in search of life amidst death. Our daunting task not lessening by its futility. We called out again, "Anybody there? Hello?"

Two voices echoed up from earth's living hell. We set up our hoist and lifted stones and pillars and lifeless bodies until we reached the living ones. Heavy, vicious stones would be put to the right, weak pitiful corpses lined up to the left. Nobody mentioned burying these broken bodies, our only concern help for the living.

This time, we delivered a family from death: a woman, a young girl, a baby. The baby nursed, the young girl whimpered, the grateful woman clung to us. Success pushed us onward for we might save some.

Byziana guided the family to our home. She returned with several other women. "People are flocking to our homes. Our mothers have set up sick rooms, and other survivors are nursing the injured."

"How is Lady Sophia?" I asked.

Byziana bit her lip. She shrugged her shoulders and said, "She is on her feet. Helping too. But she is in a lot of pain. She'd never say it though."

"She wouldn't," I agreed, turning back to the group of men and our hoist. She directed the new women how to help. Thus went our system. We would spend an hour or so extraditing a person, and the women would lead or carry that person all the way to the refuge on Mount Silpius. Truth be told, we lined up more bodies than we saved. We raced against time, hardly resting, hardly drinking, hardly taking time to wipe our flowing tears.

Intolerable life and death choices grind at our humanity. Too much pain can cause the softest of hearts to harden to human suffering.

Blood-curdling screams and a trample of feet closed in on us. The unavoidable fire had arrived, its appearance paralyzing us with fear. Starting somewhere, catching on everything not stone, the blaze turned the city to a cauldron of flame. We stared at the racing flames. Last year we had watched a fire sweep over our city. But last year from our terrace vantage point we had been mere spectators, above the fray. Now we were its prey.

Flames crossed the street before us. It cut us off, as if a bodiless hand directed it. We could not get home.

Fingers reached out at us from below the wreckage. "Do not leave us to the fire!" we heard buried voices call.

Time stopped. Eye to eye, hand to hand, life to life—the call came. I saw, under the crevasse, several people alive but trapped. Hands reaching out. Eyes catching mine. Fumes scalding my face.

We have the brace and hoist. We have the manpower. Only we above can rescue them. My eyes lifted to meet Byziana's, and in her eyes was the same fear of those below the rubble.

But we do not have time. I can still remember that horrid feeling of raw betrayal—betrayal of my humanity—for not staying, for choosing my life over theirs. Leaving my fellow citizens to their own fate, I left my conscience to burn.

Eye to eye, hand to hand, I fled. *Who am I to decide their fate? Am I a coward for leaving? Could I have saved them?* Eternal questions with no answer.

"Run!" the rushing citizens shouted, clambering toward and past us. Our men stumbled with the brace and hoist.

"Leave it. Save yourselves!" I commanded them. I took Byziana's hand and pulled her down the street, parallel to our mountain.

"We'll never get out, Marcellus!" Byziana cried. "Look at the fire!"

The fire chased us onward. The heat tempting to scald our treacherous backs. Suffocating heat soon shut the cries of those under the rubble. The ground rumbled beneath our feet, an aftershock that tempted the precarious stones all around. Perhaps it was the groan of God.

All about was bedlam, pandemonium and hell. The world was collapsing in on us, bent on wiping us off its surface.

A man running by me screamed as he ran. It was Gaius Epiphrates's friend who had been at the mosaic, so changed. He spewed delirium, bawling over and over, "The Lord sent it, the Lord!"

"The Lord sent it? Marcellus!" Byziana panicked and tried to pull her hand out of mine.

I held tighter to hers. "Where will you go? Flee like a madman into the hills? Stay with me."

The indecisive wind blew the manic fire northward and then southward, chasing us with that fire. It stalked us across the river . . . to the Imperial Island . . . down toward the Big Church.

"Stop! Stop! This island has no exit!" Byziana pulled me back.

Catching our bearings, we peered behind us. The winds shifted and the fire on our heels slowed its pursuit.

A man beat his head against a large marble structure, "Not again! This fire must be put out! Not again!" People stared at him and kept running on, as did we. Last year's deadly fire was on everyone's mind.

"There's a footbridge up ahead," I said, pulling her down a side street. Turning the corner, we collided with a crowd. Disheveled men and women blocked the road.

In spite of the mass hysteria, everyone had slowed to a congested walk. Our men, running behind us, ran into us now. Shocked eyes froze every God-fearer's feet at the patriarch's home. Bishop Euphrasius lay in this road's line of the dead. We passed and paused in silent shock. In horror. His peaceful expression showed a man merely asleep, his melted body showed a man gruesomely killed.

Pointing whispers circulated, "He fell out his window there into that vat of tanning pitch."

The prayer, "*Kyrie Eleison*," reverberated.

"The Lord sent it, the Lord!" the man's voice echoed above the people in the alley, as if a prophetic utterance.

Byziana's eyes widened. "Did God do this to us, Marcellus?"

"Stop saying that. I don't know."

"Then we're cursed. Cursed."

Others parroted her declaration. "This is the curse of God."

"The judgment of God. The bishop was Chalcedonian!"

Women and children nearby lamented in reply.

"The Lord sent it, the L—" the force of my fist in his face cut off his words and he collapsed to the ground.

"What did you do!"

"He's filling everyone with hysteria. How do we know this is God's judgment?"

"You shouldn't have hit him."

"All I know is I want to live. Don't blame me. Don't blame God. Don't blame anyone."

"But what if it's true?"

I huffed and bent down to check on the man. Stunned but conscious, he took my hand. I pulled him to his feet and told him to follow us.

A burning roof shifted toward us. "Watch out!" I cried, shoving Byziana down an alley. The surrounding flames flared up as the roof met the ground.

The sun had gone down long ago, the only light now the fire's steady glowing heartbeat. We maneuvered to stay alive, running down channel after channel of terror. I pulled her onward until I found the small footbridge on the island's north side. Trekking the outskirts, we discovered a road where the fire had come . . . taken its plunder . . . and ceded. We crossed the southern part of our city and found ourselves free of the stalking fire.

"It's got to be the curse of God, Marcellus. If we're his prey, we're doomed." Her ominous words threatened my own sanity. *Don't panic. Just do the right thing.*

We hurried toward the mountain, noticing men hard at extradition. I sent the servants behind us to help them. But with no hoist they struggled with bare hands.

"They all need help," Byziana whispered, letting go of my hand.

My hand had melded into the shape of hers, and I rubbed it to bring blood back into it. *Are we under the curse of God?* I looked behind me at this darkened, broken, charred city. *In His power over earth and sky, in His sovereignty He could send earthquake and disaster as a punishment. But had He?*

"What if it just happened? Where do earthquakes come from? I don't know."

"It's got to be punishment." She gasped and lifted a finger in realization. "Marcellus, it's the Debate!"

"What?"

"God took our patriarch. A Chalcedonian. Euphrasius is proof enough. We need to unify and believe the Monophysite teachers of Alexandria. This is a warning."

My eyes widened at her claim. "Byziana, look around you.

This is not the time for blame. We've got to help the city."

"Hey girl!" a frustrated worker cried. "For the love of God! Take this family to safety!" Out of the shadows, a man carrying his son and a woman carrying her daughter approached.

"I want to go home, Mater," pleaded the little girl, "I want to go home."

"We haven't any home, darling," the woman said in the most comforting of voices. "Lie down in Mater's arms and let Mater take care of you. I shall bring you somewhere safe." My eyes met Byziana's tear-filled ones. She took a deep breath and responded as I hoped she would.

Her war-torn compassion found life again. "Let me take you to Mount Silpius. They'll take care of you there."

We parted ways without another word, and I watched her until she was no longer visible in the shadows.

"Why? Why, God? Why?" A man walked in groaning stupor, his small daughter dead in his arms. "What did I do that you took my baby?" His eyes met mine, expecting an answer. He waited, but I could say nothing. Yet I did not break our gaze. I wanted to send him silent hope, even if my voice could not speak it. But from his eyes my heart heard the opposite loud message, then I fought back intense despair. The father disappeared into the darkness, and my gut pounded his questions into my soul.

We are human. We will ask questions of tragedy. We seek meaning in meaninglessness. By nature we appeal, as Job did, to God. For some reason tragedy makes us demand something of God. We men always have reasons for our actions. So we hold God accountable for His actions—acts of God, like earthquakes and floods and plagues. *He must have a reason for disaster. But how are we to know them? Why would he do this?*

Questions burned in me as hot as the fire in the upper city. *Is the patriarch's death proof that God is against us?* Euphrasius was a gentle, kind man, learned in Scriptures. But my friend Thomas also died—as had, it seemed, most people in the city. Surely people on both sides of the debate were lined up. Surely people who held no view on the debate were lined up. Was this disaster a message from God? About the Controversy? *If so, either side can blame the other.* My thoughts returned to the forlorn man embracing his dead child. *How can we know what God's saying? Who can ever know?*

"Hey boy, we need your help moving stones! Hurry up. Think later, act now!"

I turned, and taking a deep breath to regain my courage, ran to help the men extricate the frantic worker's mother. In this darkness, with the distant fire casting its warring shadows, only a scattered few workers continued the dark task. All others had fled the city like madmen.

The ground rumbled again, spawning terrified screams, threatening to topple the remaining upright structures. The weary workers recoiled into the open street's false safety. When the tremor stopped, we returned to the pile of columns.

I had not recognized this street.The red fluted Corinthian pillars lying scattered all around . . . this was the Street of Colonnades! What a strange revelation. My tragedy of last night paled next to this assault of nature. I could not even resurrect my sorrow. *My city. My majestic glorious city, gone in a moment. And God did this.*

Straining with all my strength, I held a rope as another man shifted a pillar off the wreckage. Antioch's people, under the city they loved, fighting for life . . . and so few to help them.

Imagine ten thousand intricate mosaics uplifted and flicked-away by nature. Imagine countless gold-painted frescoes split down the middle by toppled walls. If you can imagine such terrific destruction, imagine now that each of those works is a family—knit together as a beautiful piece of art—and you can perhaps comprehend the kind of horror consuming us as we awoke the next morning and the morning after and the morning after. Lives and families shattered. Torn apart. Ruined. Hopeless. *But why? Why?*

GOD OF THE EARTHQUAKE

The sky had been dark when we went to bed and remained dark as we awakened. The men rallied us to return to the rubble, some having worked through the night.

Gaius Epiphrates, the only *patrikios* in our provisional hospital, summoned me. When I arrived and saw his broken leg I cringed. His expression acknowledged the severity of this wound. If things went well and it healed, he would be crippled for life. If not, our city would lose one of its last *patrikioi*. My mother had brought him a rubbed-out parchment from our library, and on this he had written a letter.

He held it out to me. "Marcellus, please send this by the fastest horse to Emperor Justin in Constantinople."

"Yes, sir," I answered, taking the scroll across the path between our houses.

Lady Sophia sat on the terrace speaking with Byziana and Steward Gallus. They saw me, and Sophia motioned for me to sit on the bench a moment.

"Madame, as long as we have money we will be safe. But if you do not protect your provisions, we will starve alongside the poor," Gallus said. His attention on me turned into a frown.

"My good man, with all respect, it is mine to use as I wish. I will not have my fellow citizens starve as long as I have food in my larders. I wish to walk in the way of faith and generosity, and trust God to provide and keep our larders full."

"May I then, Madame, arrange a guard to keep these . . . these guests . . . from helping themselves to our food? I fear they plan to steal it all. If this happens, we have nothing."

"If you wish to station one of our men at the larders, you may do so. But they must not hinder Cook and his helpers. He is responsible to feed all I have housed."

Gallus bowed and left. His self-satisfied look dropped off his face the moment his gaze met my eyes. I watched him leave and had to force myself to release my tight fist. I needed to warn her about him. But this was not the time.

"Now Byzia, how can I help you?" Lady Sophia pulled her daughter to her side.

"Mater, I cannot see all those dead people again. Do you know what it feels like to touch a clammy-skinned man? A death-claimed child? It smells of death and hurts my heart, and my best robe got torn and bloody."

My aunt stroked her daughter's back and her smile and outstretched arm welcomed me.

"Yes, Marcellus, what is in your hand?"

"A letter from Gaius Epiphrates. He requests the fastest courier, and I thought your horse Willow is ideal."

"Is the letter sealed?"

"No."

"Read it to me, dear."

I lifted it and read the short message.

"From Gaius Epiphrates, Antioch, to our Beloved Honorable Emperor Justin,

Our Glorious City Antioch has been entirely demolished by earthquake on Ascension Day. Most people have been killed. We are abandoned by God. Oh great August, would you not please help us"

The man's poetic bent was gone, today's words blunt and to the point.

Lady Sophia's hand was on her lips. "While I disagree with being abandoned by God, I will not begrudge him the message." She waved her hand toward an attendant standing at the doorway to their Great Hall and arranged for the courier.

"Marcellus, Byzia does not want to go down today."

I pinched my lower lip, looking from one to the other. "I understand. Yesterday was difficult. You can only do what you can do, Byziana. It's your decision. Meanwhile, I've got to go." I flicked my thumb to the men in the walkway behind me.

Lady Sophia looked down on Antioch. The fire burned yet

in the upper city. "Byziana, your carrying water was such a help. Then you brought them to the safety of our hospice. Can you not find the strength? This may be our last chance to help people. With no water few can survive."

"But if God wants them dead, we shouldn't fight Him!" Byziana blurted.

"You cannot mean that!"

"I do mean it. It's useless trying to please an angry God who can throw an earthquake down on you."

"It is not useless. It is not difficult to please God. Look to your heritage of faith."

"I don't want to be here."

None of us want to be here. I felt the tension along my arms and shoulders.

"This is where we are," her mother answered. "Sometimes we need to think of others instead of ourselves. Christ said we need to be ready to give even our cloaks to those in need. We must please God in all we say and do."

"My cloak? My robe is my status!" She fingered the flowered embroidery neckline of her robe. "Who knows what would happen if I didn't have this . . . proof. I cannot give this away." I knew what could happen.

"You misunderstand me. Helping others has everything to do with trusting God. Your God determines who you are and what you do on days like this."

"But God rejected Antioch. How can we know a God who hates us? Gaius Epiphrates agrees. Everyone agrees. Who are we to fight God?"

My aunt began coughing, which turned into a struggle to breathe. She gripped her throat. I ran for a cup of water. Byziana knelt and held it to her mother's mouth.

The attack passed. Her mother's voice trembled. "Our country is torn because they do not know God. Show them who your God is by your actions."

"Yes, Mater. I will go. I am sorry. Please don't worry yourself. I will go."

Lady Sophia took my hand and Byziana's hand in hers. "God has not forsaken us. Not as we have life in our bones."

"Mater, I'm sorry. Just you be well. You be well." Byziana walked her mother to her room. I shook away the dread and followed the other men down the road with our makeshift hoists and low spirits. I'd keep my eye on Gallus and tell my aunt about him in the morning. What could he do in one day?

Byziana came down behind us, and did as she had promised, and we worked through the day's heat and the fading light, until we could no longer see, and yet we worked on.

They lit torches, and we called, and some answered, and we rescued some of those. They got their water, and some resurrected from the throes of death. And most did not. The earth won its fight, the rocks covered those who would never answer. Huge cornerstones, square boulders quarried for the roads, painstakingly fluted pillars and intricately chiseled capitals, now lay strewn in broken shattered piles like abandoned toy blocks. Spiraled rocks and floral shards now ugly, useless and dead.

The spirits of those who lived and worked got heavier and heavier as the spirits of our buried compatriots relinquished their earthly temples. The smell of death seeped into our deepest parts, and our limbs would work no more, and we went home for sleep.

DEATH OF A SAINT

That third day, when the sky filled with vultures and the air with the smell of sun-heated death, a glimmer of hope came as our family shouldered great pain. We lost my aunt to the earthquake. Her body, already weak, could not long bear the internal injuries she had suffered.

We stood around her grave. In spite of endless demands of strangers living in our home, the servants had dug this tomb. It lay beside the path we took that last beautiful day, Ascension Day. The red and white marble reinforcement along the grave's edges would be her final resting place. Natalia grasped her wet face to my hand, hiding her eyes from the sight of her lifeless mother.

The priest said a prayer, and we sang a hymn. Byziana knelt down and put a bouquet of carnations into her mother's hand, tidying a curl of her hair. Lady Sophia smiled. Perhaps this was the hardest for everyone. On this dark day she wore a smile. Not taunting us, for we knew her. But it mocked us in its own way. She was at peace, and we bore her burden now.

The girls sprinkled basketfuls of wildflowers over her body. Then Katerina handed Byziana the linen, and they covered their mother, shrouding her from the sky, from the world, from the family she had loved.

We could not read, for fear of the priest, so I quoted verses from the Epistle to the Colossians. Yet without her to hear it, it felt empty and meaningless.

Then we lowered the lady and covered the tomb. Byziana took a handful of soil, and dropped it onto her mother, then collapsed in tears. "I am sorry, Mater. I am sorry." She took another handful of soil and squeezed it over herself.

The soil clodded over her hair, over her robe. She fell forward, face in the mound that would soon cover the lady's remains. "Mater, I cannot," she said. "But you didn't have to die."

She can't do what? I looked at my mother, she shrugged her shoulders, so I sat next to my cousin and waited, my arm over her back. Her body trembled and shook silent grief.

My mother tossed dirt from the mound onto her friend, then directed the other children to each add soil. After a long while, when their tears had subsided, Mater turned the children away from the grave.

I helped Byziana stand and brushed her off, picking up a handful of moist soil. *Ashes to ashes dust to dust.* A rush of dread filled my heart and my ears pulsed with heat. *How can it be? What is man that we turn into dirt?* I could not throw the earth onto the shroud. Opening my hand, I let it crumble through my fingers onto the ground.

With heavy hearts and spinning questions, we joined the others in a quiet place in the house, away from the crowds of sympathetic compatriots who also lost loved ones. Maria was ready with sweetened hibiscus juice.

"It looks like blood," said Katerina, leaving her cup on the table. "I've had enough blood."

"Drink it dear," my mother encouraged. "The sweetness will remind you of your mother's sweet life."

Katerina gasped a cry, "Sweet Mater!" and sipped the juice, reverent eyes shut.

"Where is Mater?" Justin asked. "Her body is dead. But where is Mater's thinking part?" Two days ago he had volleyed his guileless questions at her. Now she was gone. Could life be so swift?

Natalia lifted her head from her hiding place and waited for my mother's answer. My mother took Justin and Natalia in her arms, "She rests in the Lord, dear ones. Wherever God is, there she is, with Him in Heaven."

"Can she see me?" Natalia's eyes lifted to the sky.

"I do not know, sweet Nati. But our Christ promised the thief on the cross who just met Him, 'Today you will be with me in paradise.' How much more is that promise for Mater who lived so many years for Christ. We may not see her again. She may not see us now. But someday we will be together, on that Great Day."

The death of Thomas, the death of Euphrasius, the clammy bodies lined up, the unreachable bodies buried alive under our city. These were distant from my heart. But the death of my godly, loving, intelligent, life-giving aunt, the mother of my cousins, the mother of my soul, this put an emptiness in me I could not shake.

"Take . . . my family . . . to Chalcedon," my aunt had charged me this morning, moments before her passing.

With red, swollen eyes, Mater had roused me and my cousins from bed and ushered us into my aunt's room just as the sun rose.

Lady Sophia spoke to us, one by one. Each of her children turned from her with broken hearts, not willing to let go of her hand, not willing to return to the doorway. Then she had called me.

"Marcellus . . ." she fought to speak, she fought against death's call. "Emmilia's faith," she said at last.

The mention of our *atavia* brought to mind all she represented. I looked in my aunt's face, unsure. She tried to speak, but struggled to breathe.

"How may I help you?" I asked.

I tried to prop her pillows behind her but she grabbed my hand, staring into my eyes. She turned her other hand over and over in a circle, landing it on my heart. And then she told me to take her family to Chalcedon. She meant something more than the town across the waters from Constantinople.

I knelt on the stool and stared into her eyes, trying to read her meaning. Finally, I guessed, "Do you mean the faith of Chalcedon, my lady?"

She nodded and squeezed my hand, her strength stronger than her weak body should boast. *Byziana's will is too strong for me. And I've sworn the opposite promise to my uncle.* I could not keep my eyes on hers. They darted from the torn curtains, to the tapestries on the floor, to the buckled mosaics below our feet. *I can't hold the charge she's giving me. How can I lead a sad, broken family of which I am barely a part?*

"I will try," I said. *I know I cannot succeed.*

She did not accept my answer. Nodding her head, she touched my heart again. "Take them."

Her intense eyes gave me the courage to make an impossible promise. "I will," I said, taking her hand into my hand. Inside I cringed as I gave my word. *I am sixteen years of age, the son of a widow, living in a destroyed city, now responsible by a vow to persuade four children and their father of truths they are against?* "With the help of God, I will," I promised.

She leaned back, a radiant rest glowing about her. *You shouldn't make empty promises. Not to a dying woman.* But I had. And then a strange thing happened. A light supernatural shone upon her.

The others at the door saw the light and ran toward her. Natalia raced to the window. "Look! In the sky!"

Hastening to the window, I gasped in amazement. I threw my gaze to Lady Sophia in fright and awe. "You must see this. It is a sign from heaven, dear Aunt." She reached out toward me, as a child learning to walk reaches out toward its mother, eager to experience the miracle.

"Hurry, before it is gone," I said. When I yanked the precarious curtain, it fell off its brace, its heavy rod hitting my head then the marble floor, the clang echoing throughout the room. *Ouch!* I rubbed my head then carried my aunt to the window.

The open window framed the miracle of the Ascension Day earthquake: in the sky over the mountains, through the clouds shone a giant glowing cross. "*Kyrie Eleison.*" Lady Sophia whispered our prayer of mercy and hope and faith.

My mother kissed her hand. "*Kyrie Eleison*, my friend."

With her eyes on the miracle in the sky, with her thoughts on her Savior, Lady Sophia took a deep contented breath, closed her eyes and was with us no more. She died in my arms.

The glowing cross remained for hours, the clouds never changing shape, the wind powerless to take away the hope it stirred in the hearts of the living victims of this great disaster.

And so we buried the wife of Gaius Justus. We had written a letter to my uncle that first day. He must have otherwise heard of the earthquake—such news traveled fast on the Pilgrim's Way. How far away could he have been? We wrote that Gaia Sophia was injured. But we received no word in reply. We waited, she worsened, he did not come.

And so we buried the wife of Gaius Justus between red marble slabs on the skirts of our mountain. And her beloved husband knew not the sorrow that awaited him on Mount Silpius.

THE DIM TORCH

Lady Sophia's soul was with her Maker and we existed in a broken-down house in a broken-down city amidst broken people. The children were orphaned. Gaius Justus did not come. So we sat. And waited and waited and sat. They were content to be locked in the Fireside room. I stared out the window.

"I want to do something," I said. "Why can't I go out and build up the city? I'm wasting my life."

"We are not the class that works, son. You know this."

My hands tightened into fists. Thirst and hunger, our daily companions, demanded the city be fixed.

"When will the aqueduct be completed?" Katerina asked. "I'm thirsty."

"The servants are exhausted and grumpy having to walk so far to fill buckets at the spring," Byziana said. "Who's working on it? Is anyone in charge?"

"I believe Gaius Epiphrates is managing things."

"With his broken leg?"

"What are we waiting for? All we do is sit."

Mater sighed and leaned back in her chair, lowering her embroidery.

We lived in the Fireside room, where Mater stacked our personal possessions, wrapped parcels of precious vases, and our clothing atop the Trunk. These were the only stacked and ordered things in our life. Everything else was like the aqueduct—useless and thrown to the ground.

"Where is Pater?" Katerina asked one of those days in the Fireside room. "It's been weeks and weeks. If he's not here, it means he doesn't care."

"Well, God is supposed to be here, and he clearly doesn't care."

My mother's mouth dropped. "How dare you say such a thing, Byziana?"

Tears welled, filling up little pools in the corners of Byziana's eyes. "Then why does He hurt us?"

Mater opened her arms to my cousin who sat at her foot, head in her lap. "Aunt, he put the cross sign in the sky to barb us, to tell us He did it. He slaps our face and then laughs. And we can do nothing. If even God is against us, who can stand?"

A shaking startled us, earth's rumbly gurgle. Terrifying memories raced to mind. We watched the walls—*will they fall this time?* Eyes darted one to another. *Is it another big quake? Is this our last moment?* We held our breath . . . and the earth held her peace.

Just another tremor.

Katerina's eyes widened, and she spoke in a frightened whisper, "It's almost as if God answered you, Byzia."

Byziana ducked into my mother's robe, hiding from the world.

"We forget where we come from. Let me tell you our story. Our song. About your great-great-grandmother Saint Emmilia." Byziana's pinched eyebrows relaxed and her eyelids closed.

Mater took a slow breath, eyes on me as she sang the soft, familiar, mournful song,

> *The sun rose slow on Pontus road*
> *While Saint Emmilia wept.*
> *Her heart was broken, her son had left*
> *Down Pontus road in the fall.*
> *"Oh why, Naucratius, do you insist*
> *To leave me to serve the lost?*
> *Where are your sons I dreamed*
> *To rock to sleep upon my knee?*
> *Where is your laughter and glad smile*
> *To comfort me all my days?"*

She felt a presence at her side,
She saw her faithful child.
Her daughter Macrina shared the tears
But rallied her mother's will.
"Dear Mater, do you
Who trained us so
Now undo what you have said? Your son,
My dear Naucratius,
Was shaped by your word and deed.
Did you think by your meeting
The cry of the poor
Or feeding the hungry man,
That he though cradled on your knee
Would see not the model you gave?
My father, Saint Basil, my grandparents too
Walked steadily down Christ's path.
Did you think your son would not also take
That torch and follow in stead?
Come threat of emperor, come famine or plague
You said we will faithful be.
Should we not, like Christ, leave family, friends,
To spread that warm light of God?"

The mother embraced her oldest child,
And gratefully thanked her Lord.
"The Lord has given. Blessed be
The marvelous Name of God."

Naucratius lived among the poor
He fished and chopped their wood.
And sharing his life and breath with them
He showed the great name of Christ.

The sun set slow on Pontus road
While Saint Emmilia watched.
Her heart rejoiced, her son would come
Down Pontus road in the spring.
She saw three strangers walking forth
Her summons within their hands.

Emmilia knew ere words were shed
The portent of sorrow they bore.

"We now know Christ because of him
Who came to live our life.
We ate with him and heard from him
And extend out the fire he lit.
But dear Naucratius has left this world
The boat dropped him from the side.
We grieve with you and ache your pain
For he left you, to meet our need."

Emmilia swooned onto the ground
Her heart yearned to stop its beat.
No more his glad smile to meet her soul
The world lost one such as he.

She felt a presence at her side,
She saw her faithful child.
Her daughter Macrina shared the tears
But rallied her mother's will.
"Dear Mater, do you
Who trained us so
Now undo what you have said?
Your son, my dear Naucratius,
Was shaped by your word and deed.
Let us not mourn, as those who have
No hope of eternity.
We shall see
Our gentle man again
And shall always together be."

The mother embraced her oldest child,
And gratefully thanked her Lord.
"The Lord has taken. Blessed be
The trustworthy Name of God."

The room was silent for a long while.
She stroked my cousin's long hair. "You mourn, dear Byzia,

but you must not lose hope. *The Lord gives and takes away.* It's his right. We must hold on. Never forget, you have her blood in your veins. The blood of a saint and mother of saints."

She traced the blue line along Byziana's arm. "It was her sons Basil and Gregory who started the Cappadocian cave-schools. Five of her ten children were sainted. Her son, your Grandfather Marcus, bequeathed that faith to his children. And your mother and I are proof of this. As are you." Her firm eyes met each of ours.

"I hate that story," I mumbled, watching Antioch again from the window.

"What!"

I glanced back to ensure their shock then turned back to my city. "It makes no sense."

"To trust God, no matter what?" Mater said.

"Exactly. Is life a sad song and we merely its stanzas?" No one responded to my heart's cry. "It's insane. Life's got to be worth more than that."

The Incarnation is the answer to everything? It sure isn't the answer to this crumpled city I can't go out and fix. Or secret talks in libraries. Or unstoppable wicked men. Or invincible death. Or sad songs of dead people.

"That's how I feel," said Byziana. "What kind of God just lets people die in an earthquake?"

Weeks after the destruction, Justin burst through the doorway with the news.

"Emperor Justin's help has arrived!" he exclaimed. We rushed outside to watch large carts pulling supplies to the outskirts of town. Gaius Epiphrates found me on the hill scrutinizing the army set-up. He walked with a cane, but his leg had healed otherwise.

"Good thing they're not on the food fields," I said. "Antioch desperately needs those future crops. A camp atop would ruin two seasons."

"True. This work force will help restore our city though. The emperor has put a man named Count Ephraim in charge of repairs."

"If they had been here at the earthquake, they might have saved many people."

"We did our best. No use second-guessing God, or fate. Do

you ever reflect on those people, Marcellus? Under the rubble but alive?"

"Yes, sir. I do." *Hands reaching out. Oh, I often did.*

"My friend left the city. He could not recover his sanity, poor fellow."

I wish him luck. Where could he go? Into the hills?

"Son, a captain below told me news I'm sure will interest you. As soon as Justin received my letter, he tore his robe in two and dressed in sackcloth and ashes to pray at the Hagia Sophia."

"He did?"

"His act speaks tomes. If such a great city can be destroyed in a day... and if the emperor must humble himself and bow to God and intercede for his people. . . we all need to repent and remain in prayer."

"Hmm." The thought overwhelmed me. *Byzantium's great emperor on his knees before God?* "In a way, it lights a small fire in my heart. About the world. About our country."

"I know what you mean. Mine, too," the *patrikios* answered.

When I told Byziana the news, she put her head in her hands and shook it back and forth, raising our great question. "But where is Pater? If the emperor so far away has heard, what about my father?"

"Pater never comes when we want him." Katerina looked to my mother for an answer.

But Mater offered no reason. She stitched and stitched at her handiwork as if the threads would generate our new future.

Natalia took Byziana's hand. "Where is Pater?" she lisped. "Are we worried?"

The smile Byziana forced was comforting, deceiving enough for a six-year-old, but not for the rest of us. "Never mind, little one. He loves us. He is surely providing for us as we speak. We must trust him, even when he is not seen."

Justin laughed. "You speak of him as you should speak of God. Except you don't trust Him."

"Hold your tongue!"

"When you know God better, you will understand His ways." Mater said.

"That'd be good."

"He must have His reasons. Doesn't He have the right to rule this world His way?"

Even if it means killing off half a city? It doesn't make sense. What kind of God would do that? Again my aunt's words haunted me. *The Incarnation is the answer to everything.* I pushed away the thought. *It's not the answer to this.*

"It's love and hate. Light and darkness. We must carry the torch into this dark world," Mater added.

"Torch? What torch?" asked Natalia.

"The torch of truth. Of Emmilia's faith. It's the light we shine to the dark world around us."

Justin scratched his head, wondering with me no doubt, *How can a torch fight back darkness?*

"And do not believe lies the world tells you. Least not words of God abandoning us. If this is of God, we will learn from it and be better for it. Just hold to the torch, no matter the darkness or the noise in the darkness."

My mind spun with questions stemming from my mother's words. *Carry the torch? These days? No one will notice, they are too busy fighting over a new patriarch. Will he be Chalcedonian or Monophysite?* I sighed. The ugly topic still divided our inflicted city. Civil war brewing. Unless the winds of change brought back a reform of faith, Truth and Falsehood would keep battling for the minds and hearts of our weary cityfolk. *And Persia watches at the gates.*

Mater tucked the children into bed, prayed God's blessing on us, then left to speak with Gallus. The firelight twinkled in the hearth and soon Byziana's deep breathing enabled me to relax as well and lean back into the couch, watching the flames flick and flutter. The others slept on their mats. In the angry silence I thought of Mater's words. *What does God want from us? Sainthood? Life is hard enough without aspiring to sainthood. I just want to live.*

My mind drifted to our larders as I fell asleep. *Food is scarce, need is everywhere. Our foremen fight off continual raiders, yet still a month before the wheat is ripe . . . .*

THE RETURN OF
THE PATRIKIOS

L ife found root again under Ephraim's leadership. Men are impacted by earthquakes. As are animals. Occasionally mountains and trees and rivers are moved by geological shift. But life goes on. As if obeying a divine mandate.

The wheat stood its ground and blessed many. The cotton harvest came. Our laborers harvested, twilled, yarned, and wove blankets and clothing to meet the great demand. In Lady Sophia's absence, Steward Gallus helped Mater set the prices. While demand provided opportunity to increase prices, compassion required selling low. Everyone was poor. Everyone was hungry. We did our best to fill the bellies of our workers' children.

Then one late summer night Gaius Justus arrived, stumbling into the Fireside Room as we were preparing for bed. He held his hand out to my mother, a scratchy voice saying, "Lady Aemilia. You are here."

My uncle looked ready to collapse. We leapt to our feet. My mother hastened to the door and with a gentle smile led him toward us. The younger children feared to approach their father but not Byziana. She embraced him, "Pater. Come, sit by the fire." She directed him toward the warmest softest seat. "Your hands are like ice," she exclaimed. A small bit of ember glowed in the fireplace. Justin put wood on the embers and fanned it to flame.

In truth, I have never seen a ghost, but if I had, I believe it would appear as the honorable Gaius Justus appeared that day. One look at his ashen face, scraggled beard, and hunched, gaunt body, removed any doubt of his concern for us. Something—or someone—had kept him against his will.

Pulling the blankets off her bed she wrapped them around her father. A sign from Byziana directed the children to bring their coverings. They stood around him, waiting for him to speak.

Mater ensured her neighbor was comfortable then summoned a servant and whispered a word. Within minutes Maria set a table and a tray of warm stew before Gaius Justus. His grateful gaze blinked on the servant then my mother. Mater was busy with embroidery again. Byziana lifted the spoon to her father's mouth, and he ate each bite, his own hands securing the blankets to his neck. He did not speak, but shivered in the summer heat.

When his bowl was almost empty, he looked from Mater to Byziana. "Strangers fill Lady Sophia's bedchamber . . . . I surprised them."

My mother sighed and set her work into her lap. She shut her eyes for a moment, and a gentle smile formed on her lips. She answered, her hand on his, "Dear Justus, our friend and sister sleeps in Christ now."

The man did not speak or eat for a long while. He stared at the fire, shaking his head from side to side, fists clenched to the blanket, face straining for placidity. The last time they were together he had been cross with her. And then had caressed her. *Is he thinking of that, too?*

Finally, with tearful eyes and a trembling voice, my uncle said, "She was a good woman, full of Christian virtue, wisdom, courage, temperance, justice. Truly a good mother, a loyal wife."

His children drew near to him and he surprised me by opening his arms and embracing them, kissing them. This was a different man.

His eyes met mine, and he saw me as if for the first time. "Marcellus!"

"Yes, sir," I stood up and approached him, giving him my hand. He held it with an appreciative smile.

The sweet scent of the fire's crackling oak sap could not hide the smell of urine diffusing from his clothes. *What happened to him?*

"So you have been the man of the family for us?"

I shrugged my shoulders, to which my mother answered, "He has, Justus."

He tried to take the spoon from his daughter, but her gentle heart refused to give it to him. "Pater, let me cover you. I will feed you. You stay warm." She tucked the blanket back up to his chest and helped him finish the soup.

While he ate, Mater told of the earthquake and the rescues, of Sophia's death and the cross sign in the sky. "The family in Gaia Sophia's chamber will leave before this Lord's Day," she said. "Count Ephraim repaired a residence for them."

My uncle nodded his reply, but spoke not his thoughts. Hopefulness and relief reflected in Byziana's eyes, as if life could now return to normal.

The next day as soon as the family sat for breakfast he explained his disappearance.

"I so wish I could have been here many months ago. Return was impossible. Let me tell you my misadventures. We left early in the morning by barge down the Orontes and made it to Seleucia Pieria by the second hour—yes, yes, I see by your faces you thought we traveled by land. They encouraged a last minute change.

"The ship departed upon our arrival. We were halfway to Cyprus when a series of big waves hit us, but only in hindsight do I know the waves were from the earthquake. If only I had known! I would have come home post haste."

He scratched his newly shaven chin. "We sailed to the northern point of Cyprus before mooring. Still no one discussed the earthquake. We traveled ahead of the news.

"Continuing the next day around the Cyprus coast, we set across to Attalia. On that journey, I got so ill I feared I would die. I suspected my soup was poisoned. That was the last thing I remember. I woke up weeks later in the care of a priest in Attalia."

My memory flickered to the pouch of herbs, and my hand flew to my mouth. I tried to dismiss the thought, but to no avail. *Chicken broth most meets your needs*, the man had said.

The sudden darkening of the Fireside room drew my attention to the window. Wind outside whipped the trees to block the sun. I glanced at the door. *Of course Gallus is there, listening.* Shadows danced inside and outside of the room.

"When I regained consciousness then strength, the priest told me of Antioch's destruction. Waiting in my bed, unable to return was tortuous. Only several days ago I had the strength to take the journey home. I returned through the priest's generosity. Francio. I must remember to recompense him."

"Did they leave you no servant? No one?" Byziana asked.

"I do not know. I had no money-pouch when I awoke."

"How did you find the priest?" Katerina asked.

"He found me. Walking around moaning. I do not remember it, or anything except the departure from Cyprus and stomach cramps on the ship."

"Did someone poison you?" I asked.

"I do not know."

The memory was vivid. The pouch. The culpable look on his face. *Had he planned to murder my uncle?* The steward was studying me. A quick smile appeared when our eyes met. What was he thinking? Yet again Reason attempted to rescue him. *It makes no sense. Why would the steward bite the hand that feeds him?* But his ready grin condemned him. It was up to me to resolve this, to confront him.

"I'm surprised Belisarius left you," Byziana said.

Gaius Justus shrugged his shoulders. "I doubt he left me on purpose. I must have left the ship in my delirium. He may not have known."

Byziana's voice got stronger, "And when he discovered you missing—they do not send word to us? His future father-in-law, a *patrikios* of Antioch, a defender of the emperor's frontier, leaves his possessions, disappears off the ship and he doesn't search for you?"

"I cannot say. You ask important questions which have also worried me. But at least I am well now."

"Dear Pater," said Natalia, "if this is your wellness, how sick your sickness must have been!"

Gaius Justus patted her hand. "Sweet Natalia. Now where is my breakfast? I must get my strength back for they await me in Constantinople."

How does he know this? No messenger arrived. My attention returned to Steward Gallus at the doorway, same snaky grin plastered across his face.

As Ephraim rebuilt the city, hope vitalized our lives. Rebirth came with the steady rhythm of new life. The earthquake, my assault and the pouch of herbs were so intertwined that to conquer the malaise I applied myself to sword-training, a sport which chased away the pain, invigorated my body and dulled my senses. And the Trunk remained in place now in my uncle's room, under the other parcels of storage, getting dustier and dustier. It called to me. *Take and read.* But I would have to request my uncle's permission, and I knew how he felt about the Scrolls stirring up ghosts and civil wars.

Since my mother supervised the cooking, in a month's time Gaius Justus recovered, if one can recover from such loss and tragedy. Gaius Justus and Steward Gallus sat late into the nights drinking mulled wine as they spoke of business matters. My uncle's mind was sharp as ever but I sensed an inexplicable change. A weariness growing within him. His shoulders seemed narrower—was that even possible? A bridled urgency pressed me whenever I passed the library.

Gaius Justus had immutable trust in the steward. I refused to trust the man, in spite of my uncle's undying reliance. I feared something dark was brewing. If I kept alert, I would find the crack in the cup, and his duplicity would show itself. Hopefully, before it was too late.

I prodded a few of the servants, seeking any distrust of the man. But I only found quickly closing mouths. Is lack of evidence evidence in itself? Is silence proof? If it was, my case was strong. But no one else would give it a second thought.

My eyes always gravitated to that wine. Its spices whispered of a bitter herb garden. If I was right, and his motives were sinister, it was poisoned. Of one thing I was sure. He had conspired to kill my uncle on the ship. I had to do something. But what could I do?

In early fall my mother came with a commission. "Marcellus, from this day on, please accompany Gaius Justus on the rounds. Learn from him. And require of our workers what he requires of his."

I was more than willing to do so.

"Here is a new robe for you, for your business." She handed

me a robe trimmed with the embroidery she had been stitching all along. "One more thing. If you are to fill the role of a Roman proprietor, you must appear as you are, the son of a *patrikios*, not as a wild barbarian. Jarva here will shave your whiskers. He will expect you every morning."

My hand went to my face. *I need to shave?* I felt pieces of beard hair here and there. Jarva had a basin of water and a straight razor, and he seated me on our terrace. And so I had my first shave, overlooking our renewing city. Only Natalia commented on my new look. She rubbed her hands and then her cheek on my cheeks, "So soft, Cousin." Byziana watched her sister with a smirky smile.

I had taken rounds with Pater when I was young. Those had been enjoyable, especially watching how Pater's quiet speech elicited straight-backed respect from the servants. At some point my immature priorities spurned those tours, so he stopped inviting me. Then he died. So now, renewing my place over our properties, I found a bittersweet connection to Pater and a sense of life purpose.

And so began my responsibilities as proprietor. I observed the way my uncle acted toward his men and studied his decisions and mannerisms. Based on his model, I directed our own men. When Gaius Justus accompanied me, the men held to my instruction. Hope returned in full force. Life had meaning in this work. It was a wonderful season, except for the haunting suspicion of Gallus hanging over my head.

One day, in late summer, as we rode our horses across the fields, my uncle said, "Marcellus, I see much of your father in you." I looked out at my father's bountiful fields. A faint whiff of bread whisked across the sun-kissed wheat sheaves. Reapers sang their harvest song as they swung their sickles. Crickets chirped happily as if they owned the world, and starlings fluttered in thick black flocks making patterns across the azure sky. My life was Antioch.

"There is nothing I want more than to be like my father," I said.

"If that is true, you will be a great man."

These simple words shot strength and pride into my heart, fueling in me a desire to prove myself to Gaius Justus. It gave me the courage to speak of Gallus, to expose the darkness, to chase away darkness with light. I struggled to frame my words of suspicion. It all pivoted on trust.

"Do you trust me, Uncle?"

"I do." He scanned the busy fields. "Why do you ask?"

"I need to tell you something I saw," I said. Then I detailed the Ascension Eve liaison between Gallus and Indulf, connecting it with his sickness on the ship.

He frowned and rubbed his lips, thinking.

After a long while, he answered me. "I have no reason to doubt my steward's faithfulness. I cannot confront him based on what you saw. I'm sorry, son."

"But he might have poisoned you. He might still be poisoning you."

"He's not poisoning me. You've just got an active imagination."

I clenched my fist. The steward's glare when he saw me watching him that night spoke guilt to me as loud as any words. But what kind of evidence was this? I needed something physical.

The wine itself. If I could take a sample of the wine to the druggist, or the herbist, they could find the evidence I needed to rid our family of the steward and his secrets. I lay in bed that night and planned what to do. Tomorrow night I would wait outside their house, on the terrace. When everyone was asleep, I would sneak into the library and get the wine bottle. That would prove I was right.

But the next day my uncle was gone. Like that. He departed. When I came in from my rounds that evening, I found Byziana. "He left this morning for Constantinople," she explained, "leaving us in the care of your mother again."

"Did a courier come? Did you see him send or receive a message?"

"I did not. But a letter must have arrived. He would not go without assurance. I can ask Gallus."

"No, no. Don't ask Gallus," I said, understanding more than I could say.

His departure angered me. Antioch needed every able-bodied man. We needed our *patrikios*, and he left. I needed our *patrikios*. And on top of all this, my plans for tonight were foiled. There would be no more wine bottles on the table. Why would he abandon his children again? He had been stranded in Attalia by those men. Why would he continue to the Capital to be with them?

Yet as my cousin said, he would have waited for assurance. Things were not as they seemed.

Byziana must have seen my frown. She explained, a slight blush coming to her cheeks, "He goes to Belisarius, to enable him to join the soldier school and to introduce him at court."

I heard a ringing in my ears. *Belisarius?* At that moment, she—who was my friend, my co-sufferer—became the otherly, she-who-marries. Mixing with the anger, something sliced down my neck to my gut—a misery, sharp and longing, a kind of protectiveness.

Why does she have to marry Belisarius? During the citywide fire, my hand had melded to hers, and had cramped when I let go. My heart was cramping now at the mere thought of her leaving. I knew what he was. *Would she truly go from us to that vile man? Would he be a part of our family?* Excusing myself, I went in a stupor to my bedchamber. My heart felt warm and strong, and achy and weak. *Belisarius, Indulf, Gallus. All of them brought disaster.* What do you do when life pins you down?

The moment my head touched my pillow again an idea came to mind. *Maria!* She knew where the man's garden was. I leapt up and hurried over to our neighbor's kitchen.

"Excuse me," I asked the cook. "I'm looking for Maria."

His eyes widened. "You are? What for?"

Propriety was on his side. I had no good business asking for the neighbor's servant. "Never mind," I said. "I have a question about . . . something."

"She went to the well." His eyes narrowed. "Don't keep her busy, Master Marcellus. I need her help for dinner."

"Of course," I said and hastened to the well. She was sitting by its side, gossiping with some other maids. They jumped up when I approached, and curtsied.

"Maria, may I ask you a question? Privately?"

"Certainly." The other girls winked at her as she walked to the side of the terrace with me.

"You once mentioned an herb garden. Belonging to Gallus. Would you tell me where it is?"

"Why do you need that?"

"My own reasons. Just tell me where it is. Please."

She walked out toward the well and pointed up the side of Mount Silpius. "Almost straight up from here. You can't miss it, though the path is not well worn. Straight up," she repeated.

I walked past the servants to the faint path she had shown and pressed forward through the brush and brambles. A few minutes later I was at a rough patch of garden. By the side of the path a dead rabbit lay collecting flies. I took out my handkerchief and gathered leaves from the different plants. I could take these to the herbist. This might be what we needed.

A man cleared his throat behind me. I jumped up, the leaves spilling onto the ground at my feet.

"Master Marcellus." It was Gallus, and he did not seem surprised to see me there.

"What is your fascination with all things Gallus?" he smiled.

I could think of nothing to say. Behind his smile, in his eyes I saw a spark of cunning. He would attempt to slip out of this like a fox, so I had to be on my guard. Before me was all the evidence I needed. The herbist would identify these poisons, and the steward would be gone. Our precarious life would be safe again. No longer would danger hang over us like an executioner's axe. No one could force pain on us anymore.

"My master told me of your accusation, boy." *Boy?*

"Just leave well enough alone. Come, shall we talk?"

I gulped. He sat down on a rock near the garden and motioned for me to sit on one across from him. My eyes darted to the path.

"No. Don't leave. Where can you go? I know where you live. Let's have a talk. Man to . . . boy."

Boy again? He could not talk to me in this manner.

"You are curious about my herbs, I understand." He chuckled and winked at me. "I see you are surprised I know your thoughts. It's my job to know everything that happens on our estate."

He pulled off a leaf from one of the plants and rolled it in his fingers. "You think I'm poisoning your uncle. Now why would I do that?" He put the leaf in his mouth, chewed it, and swallowed. Then he stood up and picked a leaf from each of the plants in the little garden and sat down again. I wondered how fast these poisons worked. Would even touching a leaf kill you? I looked at my fingers.

"I assure you, you are mistaken about me. Indulf wanted to know about the herbs on the chicken. They are unique, brought from the far east," he said. "Yet because you are accustomed to the flavor, they are no longer delightful to you. But to Indulf they were worth discovery. He's a Goth. Who knows what they eat up there?"

I scanned the garden again. It looked like a little old woman's vegetable patch.

"But son, I need you to stop. Stop challenging my honor in the household. For some of us, who were not born to wealth, all we have is our honor." He ate one after another of the leaves, raising his eyebrows as he swallowed the last one. If they were poison why would he so fearlessly eat them?

"Please believe me and let this go. You're on the cusp of manhood. Just starting to shave. Taking on responsibilities of a proprieter. Stop being a boy about this, and embrace life. As a man."

He stood up and gave me his hand. I reluctantly took it, and he pulled me to my feet.

"Do we understand each other?"

Gallus had eaten the herbs without hesitation. His father had been a cook. I shut my eyes, taking it all in. My uncle had said it was my imagination. Gallus claimed it was my immaturity. He ate them, and showed no sign of sickness. I took a deep breath.

I was wrong about this. I had to be wrong. Chicken soup. Nothing was wrong asking for that. Why was I begrudging Indulf the right to new tastes? My fingers went to my temples, and I rubbed them. It was a lot to make sense of. Gallus put his arm around my back and led me to the path. In truth, I was relieved. Knowing the herbs were not poison removed my heavy burden.

Over the next months, gifts of silk and perfumes arrived with steady funds from Gaius Justus, assuring us of things going well for him and for their family. My uncle retained a courier whose sole chore was to deliver these parcels. Gallus was jovial and helpful. My cousins' situation scarcely suffered by their father's absence. Or so we thought.

OFF TO ATHENS!

Tremors continued. Families fled the city. Season followed season. Farmers harvested their summer fruit and their winter vegetables. Animals were slaughtered, sheep shorn, blankets woven. Business centered on immediate needs. But mosaics and frescoes and families stayed shattered and scattered.

At final count, more than half the people in our city, two hundred fifty thousand souls, had died in the destruction. The service of the emperor's troops and Ephraim's city planning soon made our city a landscape of hoists and pulleys. The Great Church, our beautiful Domus Aurea, still split down the middle, could not yet be repaired. But Ephraim was now our patriarch, and he assured us Justin's nephew, the new Emperor Justinian, had guaranteed its rebuilding. Anticipation of hope and renewal displaced thoughts of debate and reason.

Domus Aurea, unrestored, still housed Sunday services and weekly prayer. We and our households attended every Sunday, so God's teaching smoldered yet in our family in spite of the Trunk's location.

One Lord's Day, the old priest Paulus taught on the spirit world. I suppose he was trying to take our eyes off of the immediate adversity in Antioch. But he stirred up a hornet's nest in our lives.

"Demons are all about us," he said. "They seek to do us ill, so we must do all we can to oppose these forces. Our primary weapon is the greatest enemy of demons. The Spirit. And the Spirit dwells in saints, and in items touched by holy people. Peter's shadow, Elijah's bones, the hem of Christ's garment. These relics carried miracle power. Peter's shadow and the hem of Christ's garment brought healing. Elijah's bones brought the dead back to life."

Up to this point, I had no trouble with his words. Scripture spoke of such things. But his next words stunned me.

"You see, John the Gold-Tongue, of Antioch, our illustrious teacher, knew of these secret things. He said: 'For as the waters of a spring that pour forth, and are not held back by its bank, but overflow and overcome, thus it is with the grace of the Spirit that resides and inhabits the bones of the saints who hearkened unto Him, and proceeds from their bodies to their clothes, and from their clothes to their shoes, and from their shoes to their shadow.'"

I started to shift in my seat. Byziana and Justin sat wide-eyed, absorbing the words.

"'As a result, not only did the bodies of the holy apostles work wonders, but even their napkins and aprons, and not only the napkins and aprons, but even the shadows of Peter worked wonders stronger than life. For beholding these sun-like rays, the demons cannot suffer it, for they cannot bear the light emanating from them, and they are blinded and struck down, and flee from the area.'"

He paused for emphasis. "For this reason, friends, you must spend time in prayer here in Domus Aurea. Our relics will bless you, and the demons will not suffer your presence."

After mass, I sat in the Great Room of Gaius Justus, mulling over those words. *How can anyone know about those invisible rays? How could John the Gold-Tongue know the goings-on in the invisible world?*

A foundation crack ran through the center of the *megalopsychia* medallion, its once beautiful face upturned. I took a stone and looked at it. *Just a rock. A pinkish rock. By itself, worth nothing. But in that mosaic it had meant something. Tiny but significant.* I tossed the little square back into the pile of misplaced tiles. *Nothing makes sense outside of a system.*

Everything I heard at church fostered doubt. But who was I to question them?

Just then my mother came in, "Oh, there you are. I've been looking for you." She sat down and must have noticed my frown. "Are you all right?"

"I don't understand, Mater. How do the priests know what angels and demons think? There's nothing like that in the Scriptures we have."

"Peter's shadow?"

"Yes, but it doesn't make sense. How do priests know these things? There are so many questions. . . "

"I wish your father were here. You would have had a good time talking together about your questions. He loved these kinds of debates. You get that from him." She smiled and bobbed her head in recollection. "He's missing an important part of your life."

"If only he were still alive."

She took a deep breath, and then her voice changed. "So it's a good thing I found you right now. You'll like what I have to say. "

Good news is always welcome. She stroked my cheek. "Darling, these are trying times for us all. You've been an invaluable help in this work of ours. But watching you with Gaius Justus reminded me of your father's desires for your life."

Her eyes sparkled with the news she would share. "Gaius Dorotheus wanted you to study, and from your education to manage his property upon his death. What you don't know is he arranged many years ago for a place to be held for you in Athens."

I caught my breath, gasping, "Athens?" *I can't believe my ears.* It was like a sunbeam peaking out, promising the end of a storm at sea.

"You may find what you seek in Athens, I think." She patted my leg. I threw my arms around her.

"Oh. Yes. I shall. I know I shall." My father had taught me much. Law and history, the creed, eloquence and rhetoric. But there was still so much to know. Imagining myself surrounded by teachers and learning and books and discussions boiled within me my passion for knowledge. I would have chosen this over anything else. Debating with priests was not my right. They spoke the words of God and the words of wisdom. But my questions were too big. Athens would have the answers.

"Can you manage by yourself?" I asked, restraining my eagerness for a moment.

"I am not alone, Son. I have our steward Dynamius. He is a faithful servant. Your grandfather trusted him, and I trust him. With my life. I have Byziana and the children to help me and I them.

Their property is secure again as is ours. This is the perfect time for you to move on in your studies. If you would like."

"I would. Most definitely."

"In a few years you will return, Light-of-My-Eyes, and by then I shall need your help."

My heart soared as a bird. *I am going to Athens!*

"So you will be a scholar?" Byziana asked later that day. "Great Uncle Basil went to University in Athens. Will you follow in his footsteps?"

"I suppose I am following—"

"Will you move to a cave in Cappadocia? Will you be a monk, too?" Katerina asked. "I can't imagine you a monk."

Pushing her away I said, "I'm not going to be a monk."

"Then why are you going to Athens? What about us?" Natalia asked.

"What do you mean, 'What about you'?"

"Who will watch after us?"

"My mother, your servants, your father."

"Aunt Aemelia is here, but Pater is not. I want you to stay!" Natalia said, taking my hand to her face.

"Marcellus needs to make his way in the world, dear," said my mother. "He'll be back soon enough."

"Before the harvest?"

"Oh, no. Several years."

I measured her against my chest, her head came to my waist. "When I get back you'll be up to my shoulder, right here." I showed her.

"That's too long!" said Justin.

I shrugged my shoulders. *I'm going to Athens!* My eyes dwelt on Byziana. *And so our paths will part, Byzia.* She just watched herself twist the ring.

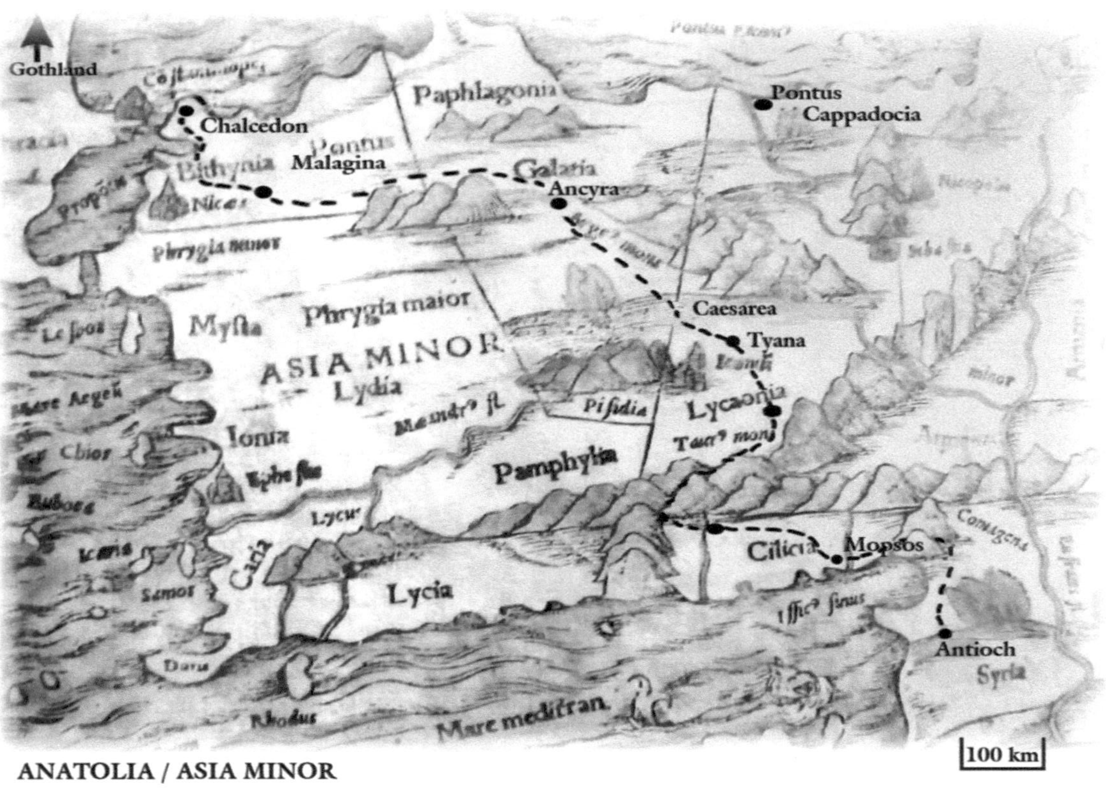

ANATOLIA / ASIA MINOR

97

'NATOLIA THE TREACHEROUS

FIERY FEARS

NOVEMBER 28, AD 528

Timing always surprises me—even still, after all I have lived through. My mother had never mentioned Athens before. Now, leaving was forefront in my mind, in my heart. Studying from the masters. Learning philosophy and logic, mathematics and physics, rhetoric. Where I would go from there, I did not know. But I would be a man. I would be educated.

Proving manhood. The phrase crept in from my haunted past and I grabbed it in a chokehold. *Maybe Belisarius knows how to wield a sword, but I will wield a pen. I will wield words. He may be brawn, but I will be brains. And brains ruled the world.*

The Pater makes the decisions, and we trust the Pater, I tried to remind myself. She was promised to Belisarius; I was promised to Athens. My desire to go to university was as strong as the guilt I felt for leaving her to that fate. I hoped for confirmation from a family friend in Athens before my final departure.

Gray November clouds covered the sky, our second cotton harvest since the Ascension Day quake lay bundled in bales and our lives and future seemed secure. I sat on our terrace, looking out over our slowly re-forming city, ruminating over my future as an educated landholder when suddenly it happened again. It was not a tremor.

The heavens roared thunder. I watched, eyes wide, expecting an apocalyptic beast to come soaring through the air. Instead, earth replied to sky with a furious grinding tearing screeching bull's roar.

I started to black out, but the buckling marble terrace under me awakened my wits.

I grabbed at a stone planter around a stoa pillar, the most secure thing about me.

"Help!" Girls next door shrieked. "Earthquake!"

My mother's voice resounded from somewhere, "Marcellus! Marcellus! Earthquake!"

This earthquake did not stop. Much worse than last time, it shook and shook, as if it were not satisfied leaving a single stone on another.

"Where are you?" Mater's voice came again.

Rattle! Squeak! Crash!

Byziana's house next door collapsed. A dust cloud from the crash billowed into our courtyard.

Our own house shook and groaned and began folding in on itself. The ground convulsed. I needed to make sure the women were safe, but did not trust the way between me and them.

"I'm outside!" I shouted to Mater. "Come to the terrace!" Could she hear me?

Where I stood seemed the safest of all places, until the re-taining wall holding our terrace gave way and I barely escaped sliding down the incline.

I clambered up the marble and stood beneath the terrace crossbeams. Mater appeared next to me, grasping me, trembling in disbelief, weeping in terror. The doorway she had just passed through was no longer a doorway but a collection of brick and stone and torn curtain tapestry.

Below us the noise of the bull, the earth's deep moan, tore our attention to the city at the very moment Ephraim's rebuilt city collapsed again.

Imagine how a servant shakes the blanket as she makes a bed, whipping the wrinkles off.

The movement whipped across the city-as if these struc-tures were mere blanket-folds and not living beings and lifeless stones residing on earth's blanket.

The rumble and shifting lasted and lasted. Later I heard it had continued an hour—but to us it lasted a lifetime! The world's end.

We held on to each other, in the safest place we could find, whispering tearful farewells.

There were no sounds anymore from Justin or the girls. Then, like an innocent cart halting on a street, it stopped with a rumble and creek.

A death-curdling scream from next door threw us to our feet. *Natalia!* "We're coming!" I called, grabbing Mater's hand and rushing through our home. Over pillars and collapsed roofs. Out the front door, which was askew on its hinges. Toward the gate and garden. And to Gaius Justus's front door.

An interior wall had collapsed on the huddled girls. I threw bricks and furniture off the girls, left and right, until they were safe. Thanks be to God, besides bruises and terror, they were intact. Justin climbed out from under a table. Natalia clung to my hand, the girls to Mater's chest.

Surveying our homes, we rescued anyone we could. Miracle of miracles, each beloved, faithful servant of our household had escaped alive. Again.

The house of Gaius Justus had not fared as well. Their servants' quarters had collapsed, and dozens were dead. My cousins had survived, alive but battered. Steward Gallus, and only a few others, had made it. Their home had not—the grand palace of two years ago now a skeleton framing misty memories.

Faint cries echoed from the city. Reminders of our former trauma flooded our souls. The children huddled together. Trembling with memories, they refused to look at the city. I am glad they did not. It was not a pleasant sight. Well did I relate to their trembling. Yet again would we take out the hoists?

If you have ever faced this magnitude of disaster, you recall the moments of motionlessness. Petrification. Not wanting to move. Wishing for life to be other than it is. Hoping to wake up. Urging yourself to leave the nightmare. But then reality alights on you, like the dew. This is your new life. This is what now is.

"Get ready, children," my mother said, her voice weary and duty-bound. "You know what to do. Katerina and Natalia, you will help nurse the wounded here again. Byziana and Marcellus—and Justin too, this time—will help rescue our fellow citizens. We begin in our homes. Then on to the city. Without delay now, children."

I took a deep breath and moved toward the door. The others' inaction stopped me. Byziana with shoulders squared, chin out, and lips clenched, gripped a wrinkled letter in her hand.

"I have had enough of this God-forsaken city," she burst out. Her eyes shot stubborn fire.

"God has not forsaken us, Byziana," I said, but she did not hear me.

"Me too!" said Katerina. "We must get away from here. Or the ground is going to eat us alive!"

Mater disagreed. "Patriarch Ephraim says we must turn our hearts back to God."

"Why would a good God destroy our city twice? You mean this is how He asks for faith? Does that make sense?"

"Absolutely." Mater's response startled me. How could that make sense?

Byziana pushed ahead, not allowing my mother to explain her answer.

Looking back, I think we could have avoided many future problems had we asked Mater what she meant. But as it was, Byziana took the conversation a different direction.

"No. It means He does not wish us to live here. Think about it. The Great Church, Domus Aurea, was split. Split, like the city over the Debate. And is still not repaired. God spoke, and the people ignored Him. We did not make peace so God's patience is exhausted."

"Byzia, what are you talking about?" my mother said, looking at me. "What debate? Why are we talking about this?"

"The Chalcedon debate," I explained. But Byziana kept talking.

"I have tried to trust Him, as you said to, Marcellus. I have tried, but I am done."

"I want my mater," Katerina cried.

Byziana nodded. "Every single minute since Mater died my heart aches for her. Regret fills my soul. Every day I determine I will do what she commanded me to."

Byziana's voice rose to a crescendo. "Every single day I have tried to live in honor of her wishes. But I can no longer carry that burden. No more!"

A few servants had gathered at the doorway, waiting for Mater's direction in the rescue efforts. My mother held up her finger, asking Byziana to pause a moment, then answered their questions. I took that moment to excuse myself. Duty called.

"Don't you leave, Marcellus. Katerina, Natalia and Justin, stay right where you are."

Time was against us, people were dying, and Byziana wanted to talk. Mater turned her tight-lipped attention back onto my cousin, nodding for her to continue.

"I have no compassion left. I have tried to have the faith Mater demanded of me. But it is useless. She wanted me to read her Scrolls. Did you know that? She begged me before she died. And I have not. 'Become a Chalcedonian,' she said. I will not. What a curse! She wanted the impossible. I am sick of this house and these memories. I am sick of a falling-apart world. I cannot carry her deathbed wishes anymore. I will not do it. We need my pater."

Justin, standing next to his sister, asked, "But where is Pater? How can you find him?"

Natalia wrapped her arms tighter around my waist.

Byziana held up the letter. "Serendipitously, I received this from him this morning. Thanks to Gallus it did not get lost. It solves all our problems. We shall go to Constantinople, Children."

Mater drew toward Byziana and tried to calm her with an embrace. "Enough said, Byziana. Before you make such a decision, you know we must help our wounded. We'll talk about this in a couple days."

Byziana pulled out of my mother's arms, "Let me read it to you,"

"No. Your servants are dead and need burial. That is your responsibility. And we must help those down in the city. You must cease this complaining and assist the people. We've wasted enough time here."

Byziana went forward with the reading.

"Gaius Justus of Antioch, to Byziana his daughter.

Greetings, Daughter. I write to inform you of the great success we have had in Constantinople. Your betrothed, Belisarius, has become not only known by court, but honored and esteemed by our new emperor, Justinian. He has been on several expeditions.

The emperor has put his faith in your betrothed's exceptional abilities. I believe he will soon be ready to marry, so prepare yourself for nuptials, my daughter. Greetings to all et cetera."

I clenched my fist at the mention of that man's name. She should keep herself as far from him as possible.

"You may not go, Byzia. He does not summon you, he merely informs you." Mater's voice was unusually firm. "You are needed here. To care for the wounded again."

Byziana rolled her eyes and groaned. "I cannot. Not again. Please, Lady Aemilia. Please, Aunt, understand. I cannot. I have nothing left in my heart."

A servant was at the door, "My lady, neighbors are here. Shall I open the Great Room for them?"

Mater looked at Byziana, and at me. She shook her head in frustration. Then, turning to the servant she said, "Yes, show them in. Please pack up the valuables. We will live in this Fireside Room again."

She turned to Steward Gallus. "Please gather what you can of your master's valuables and bring them here."

The servants left, but Byziana touched Mater's arm.

"We will not be moving into your chamber, Aunt. We have no home left here. It collapsed. We go to my pater in Constantinople. To my new home there."

Mater tried to brush off the comment, "Crossing Anatolia, Niece? Do you know what you are saying? You face wild beasts, wild men, months and months of weariness on that road you speak of. Certainly you will come to your senses. You're frightened. Come, sit down."

Justin eyed the roof and walls of this uncollapsed room as if doubting their stability.

Katerina sat on the couch and started crying, "We'll die if we stay here. What did I do, God? I just want to live."

"Stop it, Kata. I've decided. We'll leave first thing in the morning. We need to prepare ourselves, Children."

Mater's voice rose. "You're frightening your sisters and brother. Now stop pitying yourselves. Think of these people we must tend to. Your own servants need your help. People under your care are dead. They need proper burial. That's your duty. Your broken home needs to be managed. Rebuild it, if you choose to ignore Antioch."

I saw fire in my cousin's eyes. Anger and hatred of nature. Fear. Or was it dread?

"Cousin, it is not safe for you to travel alone," I offered, to which I received the most startling directive I had heard in my life.

"Which is why you must come with us, Marcellus. You can use a sword."

"I will not go," I said. She looked at me with surprise, then up at Gallus.

"You won't?"

"Absolutely not. And neither should you."

I swept out with those words and ran to help the servants nearby. Yet wherever I was, Gallus appeared.

A couple hours later I was resting with a cup of water, brushing sweat off my brow, when Gallus slid up to my side. "About the young lady. I agree with you, Master Marcellus. You should not go with them. Your mother needs you here."

I frowned. Who was he to speak his opinion so boldly? *He's a servant. Of a neighbor's house. Has he no consideration of etiquette?*

"I will send Trolius the eunuch with them. He is excellent with a sword. Have no fear for them, young sir. Antioch needs you." His eyebrows were pinched with concern as he nodded his encouragement.

My thoughts returned to that day by his herb garden. My worries had been asleep since then, but now his urgency for me to stay awakened them. *Have no fear for them?* I tried to control my expression. Who was he to direct me? It made no sense for him to be concerned. Why should he care what I did?

Unless he wanted her to be alone.

I blinked slowly, lifting my eyes to his. *Trolius alone with the children? Is that what he wanted?* As I looked into his face, the dead rabbit next to his garden appeared in my memory. Things quickly fell into place. It all made sense, and I condemned myself for missing it. Yet he must not know my suspicions.

I forced a yawn. "Thank you for your thoughts, Steward. Still, I prefer to make up my own mind."

He nodded and backed away, disappearing into the broken-down house. Later that night my mother came into my chamber. I shifted pieces of roofing off the bed, making room to pack my baggage.

"Oh! Are you going with them?"

"Yes. Something happened to change my mind."

"I don't want to ask." She covered her face with her hands, steadying her nerves.

Who was Gallus to manipulate me? He had tricked me in the garden. The dead rabbit showed it all—he was immune to his own poisons. Of course. How else could he drink the wine with my uncle and not be affected? He had maneuvered me from suspecting the garden, and I fell for it, for months. *Now he had plans against the family that need me to stay here. I will not fall for his cunning this time.* I refused to stay. I would be with them. My sword against Trolius's.

"Yes. I agree. Darling, you should go—it's only right. You are family and Trolius is not."

I lifted two cloaks. "What am I supposed to take on such a journey?"

She shrugged her shoulders. "I cannot say. Flint for fire. You have your money-pouch. Warm clothes. Oh . . . if only you were packing for Athens," she said, her eyes pitying my dilemma.

"Marcellus, I am saddened our plans for Athens are postponed. I so wanted to educate you." She pulled me into her arms.

"It can't be helped." Loss kicked at my life again, beating me in the darkness of the Colonnades.

I pulled away and walked over to my shelves. Lifting and tossing my clothing, blindly choosing what to pack. My mother watched me. "As I walk over the shattered remains of our broken vases, fine pottery, and imported glass, I have no feeling of regret, no sighs nor even tears. Everything seems so insignificant, Marcellus. And that world so far away. What we valued yesterday is valueless today. The only thing worth consideration is human life."

"I remember those feelings. From last time."

"The number of our hospice guests increases by the hour. Given our position in Antioch, you should be out there, helping save lives, as you did last time."

"I want to stay here. I want to help Antioch. That's how we can make this right." I had no desire to leave on an unknown road into an unknown wilderness facing unknown dangers. I raised my eyebrows to my mother. "But—"

"But your path leads to the Capital, protecting the lives of your cousins. I do understand. It is a different calling on this dark day. Byzia will not be swayed."

I sat heavily on my bed.

"She will not openly defy me, but will do what she will do. Yet . . ." She paused, and sighed. "Byziana, with many others, flees toward that which she can never acquire. I hope she will soon learn this and come home."

"What is it, Mater? What can she never acquire?" I searched my mother's face for the meaning of her cryptic remark.

But she did not answer my question. Instead, she said,

"Never forget the importance of humanity, Son. You did much to help our people today. But now you must rest for your big journey." She kissed my cheek and returned to our hospice guests.

I considered her words again as I began to sleep—a sleep startled by heart-stabbing thoughts of people trapped again under rubble. People anxiously watching for someone, anyone to approach the gaps in their earthbound prisons. And here was I, warm in bed.

How does God lead us? In a still small voice? Yes. With a raging fire and heartless earthquake? Yes. Through the blazing fears of a girl? Yes. In, through and around our sinful desires, our weakness, our inability to do the right thing at the right time—He guides us.

In the end, this was the best thing that could ever have happened. It all happened because of the Scrolls and their power in our lives. But we had no idea. I only knew I was abandoning our people, and I prayed God would forgive me.

TOOTH OF A SAINT

So we sneaked away. We departed for the midlands of 'Natolia. Antiochia, Pontus, Cappadocia, Galatia, Asia, the heart of the Byzantine Empire lay before us.

We left at first light the next morning, not the only ones to flee, nor the only ones to abandon survivors to their own means. Preparations were quick. None of us packed wisely. I brought my sword and my money-pouch. Tied on two donkeys were bundles of food and clothes—and Lady Sophia's Trunk of Scrolls, which Byziana insisted accompany us. "I shall not start life as mistress of a manor without Mater's treasure next to me. And I refuse to leave her Trunk to any more earthquakes."

Mater could not overcome my cousin's plans. Byziana, as Lady of Gaius Justus's estate, had decided the fate of her family. I could say nothing. My cousin's sensible heart was frozen with ice-cold determination. If I crossed her, she may exclude me from the trip altogether. And then who would protect them? She did accept one recommendation from Mater, to take our dog, Captain. This saved our lives.

Thus we stood at the crumpled walkway between our refugee-filled homes and said goodbye to life as we knew it. Mater gave us half-hearted attention, torn by her responsibilities to our guests and now two properties to manage. This last view of my mother troubled me for years. Distracted, disapproving, taciturn, frustrated . . . abandoned and alone in a broken-down house. So we bade a bitter farewell to overburdened Mater and much-abandoned Antioch. And we stole away from the call for help.

We left up through the mountains, along the bridle path, as

the straightaway would lead through our fields, and I did not want silent criticism from the foremen protecting our fields. In truth we were slinking away.

"Let's stop at the monastery," Byziana said.

"Why?" I asked.

"To get a blessing on our journey. And it's on our way."

"Do you not find it hypocritical?"

"Why are you so antagonistic? You don't have to come, you know?"

"You claim God is making you leave, as a judgment. But you still want a monk to bless your journey. Isn't that hypocritical?" I said.

"Is it so bad to want a blessing?"

"How long is this trip going to take?" Justin asked his sister. "A week or so?"

"Four weeks."

"What do you mean, four weeks?" I asked Byziana.

"I heard it takes four weeks to get to Constantinople."

"Oh, that's true for those on horseback. Walking will take us more than three months!" I cocked my head. "I remember my mother specifically mentioning it."

Byziana smiled a nervous, worried smile.

Justin stopped in his tracks as did Katerina and Natalia. "Three months? Just to get to Constantinople?"

Justin asked again, "Do you mean we have to walk every day, all day, for three months to get there?"

"Yes."

"Are you ready to go back?" I nodded to encourage Byziana. "It's not too late."

She bit the inside of her mouth, thinking. Then she shook her head, "No. We've already left. If we go back, we earn nothing but ridicule."

"Your siblings are too small for a three-month journey," I tried again.

"If we return, we will face all that death again. Those dead bodies. Our home's destroyed. I'm not going back."

"What if God tells the monk not to bless us?" Katerina said. "If we do not get a blessing, we should go home."

Byziana looked behind us at Trolius prodding the donkeys

along. "Of course he will bless our journey if we leave a coin," Byziana said.

Money for blessings? Another contradiction.

"Whew! What a long trip we're on," Justin wiped his forehead with the back of his hand. "I'm tired."

"We won't go too fast. We'll get there by February," she promised. Then she added in her most big-sister-acting-like-mother voice, "I don't want to hear another word about it."

"My feet hurt," Katerina said as we approached the Monastery of the Admirable Mountains on the side of Mount Silpius.

"We have come for a blessing, Brother John," Byziana smiled up at a man on a pillar inside the monastery gate.

"Welcome, Pilgrims!" he said.

"Hey! Justin!" a voice called. We were shocked to see Simeon, the young playmate of Justin, on a pillar across from John.

"Hey-a, Simeon!" Justin called. "Where have you been and why are you on that pillar?" I had not seen the boy since the Ascension Day feast.

"I'm now a Stylite," he boasted matter-of-factly, feet dangling over the tall pillar's edge, one finger in his mouth. Below his column, Martha, Simeon's mother, bowed in prayer. John the Stylite, across the courtyard on a much taller pillar, beamed at Simeon.

"Is he not too young for this business?" Byziana asked.

I scanned the columns. Had they fallen during the earthquake? Roofs and their supporting pillars around the courtyard had shifted or collapsed. A nearby hoist and pulley still held righted stonework.

"He has proven himself to be worthy of this task," the man answered. "I witnessed his miracle. God be praised!" He raised hands to heaven.

"God be praised," repeated the mother.

"What miracle?" Justin looked to his friend for an answer. But Simeon just kept his finger in his mouth.

Martha stood up and swaggered her shoulders, "He met with a leopard, my dear son. And not knowing what it was, put a rope on its neck and brought it to this monastery, saying he found a cat. A miracle!"

"I knew this boy had a special gift," John the Stylite continued, "since he tamed a ferocious beast. I told him to hoist himself a pillar here across from me to fulfill his calling."

"When God gave this special blessing to my son, his father and I were honored. He has been here a year already." She sniffed and raised her eyebrows, waiting for our acknowledgment of her son's superior holiness.

"Uh . . . ," I fumbled. "I am surprised he's been on the pillar for so long."

"Hey!" shouted Simeon. His hand came out of his mouth holding a tooth.

"*Kyrie Eleison*," Martha said. "He has lost his first tooth! And on a pillar. Praise God and the Lord Christ!" She fell again on her knees in prayer.

Our eyes questioned each other.

"Children, take this special tooth with you on your journey," said John, motioning to Simeon. "It may bring you its blessing. As you have the first tooth of an infant saint."

"Infant saint?" whispered Justin.

Simeon handed the tooth to Natalia, smiling ear to ear. Her hands together, her eyes gazing in awe at the tooth in the center of her palm, Natalia carried the relic to her sister.

Byziana took the tooth and wrapping it in a kerchief put it in the fold of her garment. The holy reverend John the Stylite blessed our journey with a sign of the cross, and after dropping a coin in a box by the gate, we left, stunned.

"Why is Simeon on that pillar? How long will he stand on it?" Natalia asked.

Byziana pulled her to her side as we walked along, "He will be there for life, Nati. It's his calling."

"On a pillar for life? How can he play?" Justin said.

Katerina answered, "He's a holy man now."

"Man? But he's only six years old."

Justin's mind moved on. "Will we be going through mountains?"

"Yes, big mountains and rolling hills and flatlands." I answered. He whistled surprise and picked up a stick off the road, now hitting tall grass as he walked along.

Natalia's simple question rang in my head. *How can a child consecrate himself by living on a pillar? How could God want that?* "Byziana, what do you think God expects from us?" I asked.

"To leave Antioch, that's all I know."

"I mean, does He want us to stand on pillars our whole life? How do we please Him?"

"I have no idea. I never could figure it out, which is why I am going to Constantinople. My mother called it easy, but I never found out."

"Your mother used to say Emmilia had taught it to her children."

"It would be nice to know. Then we can all be saints, too. Meanwhile we have this tooth to keep us holy, I suppose." She held the tooth up for me to see.

It dumbfounded me. *It makes no sense. A tooth can make us holy, a pillar can make a saint, and a God we can't understand drives us from home.*

I took a deep breath and exhaled heavily. *Will I ever understand?*

Byziana echoed my sigh, twisting her ring as she walked. I wished she would stop playing with that ring.

Pilgrim Road

On our fifth night I poked at the fire, alert to any sound. Staying out of doors was neither safe nor wise. However, the donkeys would go no further. And carrying our burdens they determined our pace.

Here I was, on the Pilgrim Way with children—children more interested in the wildlife, the trees, the view, delay, delay, delay. We had hardly progressed. After all, how far can children walk in a day? A grown man, a healthy man, can walk to our Imperial Capital in ninety days on foot, they say. A three-month journey for a strong man. How long for us? Four months? Why had we decided to walk? *At this rate, we'll face winter in the mountains above Tarsus. What a lack of foresight.*

Trolius was neither help nor threat. He carried his pack, prodded the donkeys, and never spoke. Yet his connection with Gallus made him suspect.

Today I had pushed everyone, and still we had not made it to Alexandretta. Instead, we spent the night in a field, away from village or town. Unsafe. Unwise. Yet practical. I wondered how well Trolius could use a sword.

Byziana had arranged all the beds around the fire, and now the younger children slept. Trolius, with his disapproving gaze, watched me. Justin's snores and the girls' deep breathing reminded me even more to stay alert.

The weather was cool. Autumn winds beginning in earnest and a ring around the moon promised bleak weather tomorrow. *Four months of this?*

I walked over to the edge of camp and rested my shoulder against an oak tree. Captain came to my side and looked out into the flatlands beyond us, growling at the darkness.

I tried not to think about Athens, about what I had given up. But it weighed deeply on my heart. *With the cost of new guests, Mater won't be able to send me for another year or so, I guess. I'll be home in eight months at the very least. Why did life always change so suddenly?* I turned to see Byziana's eyes on me.

"You should sleep," I said, coming back to her. "Captain and I will keep the bandits away."

"Mmm," she nodded. "Can we talk, Marcellus?"

I pulled my sleeping mat toward her and sat cross-legged on it. The light flickered through her hair, a halo of brightness shining over her, reflecting on her face.

"What do you honestly think? About the earthquakes? Do you think we weren't supposed to save those first people? What if they were supposed to die? Maybe that's why there was a second earthquake."

"It's not right, Byziana. If God wanted them dead, they'd have died. We were duty-bound to help them. We did the moral thing. Maybe the earthquakes were a warning. Or a wake-up call."

I shifted on my mat and watched the fire shadows flickering over my sleeping cousins. "You know, I remember hearing a story from one of the Gospels where a tower fell on a dozen or so people. The disciples asked Christ, 'Who sinned, that such a disaster came?' Christ answered something like, 'It's not for you to know why it happened to them. Rather, make sure you yourselves are not judged.' In other words, God will do the right thing. And we must do the right thing ourselves. We had to rescue those people. It's right to save lives."

"If God wanted them dead, they'd be dead."

"Yes."

"Like your friend Thomas?" She raised her eyebrows to emphasize her question.

I shrugged. "It is hard to understand. Why would God want Thomas dead?"

"Or my mother. Why would God want either of them dead?"

"There has to be a reason. Honestly, I've been thinking a lot about this."

My words surprised her. Five days of thinking time had awakened those questions which had plagued us after the first quake. I was glad to put words to my thoughts.

"It comes down to one question. Who is God, really? We say He is all-powerful, over nature. So He can decide about an earthquake happening or not. We say He is love, so He wouldn't want people to die. But they die. So how can an all-powerful God exist when people die?"

"That's right." The question shifted in her mind.

"You could stop there and say, therefore there's no God. But that's not the answer. You've got to keep asking, so who is God?"

"Well?"

"We can only know the Why of God's acts by knowing the Who of God. If we know His character, we can know His reason for letting bad things happen. It's not only about His power versus His love. But there's something else."

She pulled her knees up and wrapped her arms around them. "So what's the other thing?"

"Well, that God is good. Holy. Infinitely moral. There's no room—no logical possibility—for evil in Him. God did this, or let it happen, so it can only be for a good and just reason. Something that agrees with His power and love but also His goodness and justice."

"Makes sense." She looked hopeful, like a child who expects you to fix their broken toy. "So is it punishment? Does that agree with goodness?"

"It could be. A happy, good life feels right. But why should it, if we are sinners? I believe two things. First, I want a good life, and a good life is what I should have. But then I know I shouldn't have a good life, because—"

"There is no but to that. You're speaking nonsense! Of course we should have a good life."

"I'm not speaking nonsense! Hear me out."

"If God is good, He would want us to have a good life. Look at the beauty of the world and tell me he doesn't want us to have things good." She lifted her hand and pointed to the sky and to the land. "Look at the trees. Or the birds. Or the moon up there. Or that fire. That's beautiful. That says it should be good. No but about it."

"But Byziana, the second thing I believe is my sin deserves punishment and I should not have that good life because of it. My conscience condemns me. Even for little things. Doesn't your conscience ever prick you?"

"Of course it does."

"For murder? For adultery? For stealing?"

"No! I don't do those things."

"Then for what?"

"The little things. Like you said. Being mean, saying something unkind."

"That's my point. Why did God give everyone a conscience to prick us, unless to tell us of the law, to warn us of punishment for breaking the law?"

"I get it."

"But for some reason God waits. Have you ever wondered why we don't get the punishment our conscience tells us we deserve?"

"Of course because God will forgive us."

"No. He can't forgive us just by His sheer will. That would make him party to the crime. Think about it. A good judge can't forgive a murderer. If he dismisses the murder, he disregards the law as law. And he compromises justice. If there is no consequence for breaking the law, it means breaking the law is not wrong in the first place. It means the judge does not consider the murder to be worthy of punishment."

Her face paled as my words found meaning. "You're right. He can't just forgive. Since God is a good judge, there must be a penalty."

"And Jesus said that hatred was equal to murder. So we're all guilty."

"Are you saying God punishes us for our sin by throwing suffering down?"

"Yes and no. I just know that God waits. Evil keeps getting worse, yet He waits. Warning and waiting."

Above us the dark clouds shifted, opening the orange moon to peek down on us. A flutter of wings flew across the moon and into the night. It was silent for a while.

"Then why is there such beauty in the world?" Byziana said. "Doesn't that give false hope?"

I nodded. "You're right. Hope never leaves our hearts does it? But we mustn't misread that hope. He's not indifferent to sin, yet He's waiting for something."

"What would God be waiting for?"

"I don't know. Your mother told me the answer to everything is in the Incarnation."

She looked up at the sky and shook her head. "But how are we to know? I have the same problem with saying Christ had two natures. We don't know. It doesn't make sense. Marcellus, I can't believe with my heart the things I don't understand with my mind. I wish I could, but it's impossible."

"It's related to Who He is. There must be a bigger purpose. Because of His love."

"I still think it has to do with the split church," she said. "Besides, if even the priests don't know what God is saying through this, how should we be expected to understand?"

"Pater always said some things demand a lot of mental work to comprehend." I shrugged my shoulders. "We just have to figure it out."

When you know someone from childhood, you can almost predict how they will act in any situation. But this second earthquake had begun a change in both of us, opening new avenues of thought.

Speaking with Byziana from my heart on these deep truths of God powered something in me. It bound my soul to hers in a way I had never known before, like a rope and hoist pulling our hearts together. And I liked the feeling.

"There are so many things I don't understand. But I want to know what is True. My father always told me Truth will prove itself. Maybe that's what he meant."

My eyes caught on the Trunk. "Do you want me to read a Scroll? Maybe the Gospel of John could help us."

She eyed the Trunk. "Not right now. It is too hard to get untied."

We gazed at the fire, each in our own thoughts, listening to everyone's deep breathing. After a while Byziana looked at me again. "I wanted to ask you something else."

I watched her touch the ring, rubbing its band.

"I was thinking of Belisarius. Of being married to him."

I bit my lip and tried to calm my breathing. *Not him!* She could not know the pangs stabbing my heart. The memories surfacing. That ring and that man and the unfairness of life. *Captain*

Belisarius. Strong, handsome, skilled, and oh-so-honorable. But he's a louche, and she to be his wife.

Looking across the fire I could only grunt, "Oh." The word did not match the raging in my heart. *How can I trust You, God? With pain and death and things I can do nothing about. Who are you?* That hoist and pulley that had moments before been drawing us together had been let loose, and my heart fell to the ground with a thud.

"It occurred to me you saw him elsewhere. Maybe at the baths. Maybe on the streets. So you might know. What kind of man is he?"

My eyes met hers. *What kind of man?* There comes a point in a man's life when everything he hopes for pivots on a word. My heart raced within me. *If only she knew*, I had been saying to myself for years. *If she only knew what he was, she could not agree to the match.*

This was my moment. I would tell her the truth about that man! A strange vengeful passion stirred in me. *So how to phrase it?* My pulse raced. She'd be free of the man, we'd be free of him and the memory of him.

But then in my mind's eye I saw Gaius Justus at that same banquet with his goblet raised. The joy, the hopes with which he had written us. Gaius Justus had shaken hands in pledge. And I remembered the banquet guests in Antioch.

My hopes lost their wind. *If she were to speak against her betrothal, if she were to break the will of her pater, they would to-a-one despise her, shame her, shun her. She'd become a tainted woman. An undesirable.*

In the end, my thoughts of the man—my memories even— were of no import. She had no choice but to accept him. Certainly there was no other choice. Even Grandmother Emmilia married against her will, and things worked out. If she had gone into a convent as she wanted, she would never have birthed saints.

"Yes, I did see him. Briefly," I said, pulling my disappointment in check. "Just during the night of the feast before everything changed." *Everything changed. The night his troops saw me, and all that.* Captain put his head on my lap and closed his eyes. I looked over at Trolius. He seemed to be asleep. *Can he hear us?*

My cousin's eyebrows rose in anticipation. I could see in

her face the hunger for a tasty morsel of gossip to mull over, to treasure in her heart. "So what is my husband like?" she asked again, her voice teasing. "How does he behave when he's not the guest of honor?"

Her husband. I have the chance to speak daggers into the situation. I can change the direction of her life. But to what end? Her pater has determined her marriage. And we trust the pater. I shrugged my shoulders, hoping to shake off the question. *Can't she remember how he touched her in public . . . even when he was the guest of honor?*

"Please, Marcellus. Just tell me what comes into your mind. Any memory. Something he did or said. I have such a limited memory of him." She would dwell on him as she fell asleep.

I sighed, avoiding the answer.

The recollection coming to mind was so vivid. After the banquet. Belisarius, the captain Belisarius, newly betrothed Belisarius, standing face to face with a prostitute, his arm against the wall behind her. Did I remember any other act? At this moment that was the one. Yet she would marry the fiend.

"What a leader he is," I said, a stabbing pain of hypocrisy in my heart. *I am too weak to tell her. Too ashamed.* "His soldiers follow his example in word and deed. This is a reliable fact."

Why I allowed the chance to slip from my hands, I cannot say. At that moment, I saw her precious future like a fragile perfume bottle tipping . . . off a pedestal. Yet instead of protecting it, reaching for it, hindering its fall, I had stepped away, letting it smash to the floor into tiny pieces.

I remembered her words just days ago of God's abandonment. If I told her what he truly was, she would have no hope left. Yet I had said nothing, so she could not flee.

"A good leader," she smiled. "He will lead the family well. Be a good Pater. And will give me a large home, with mosaics and tapestries. A home that will not fall down." Her words bore the hopeful dreaminess of youth.

Oh, how I wish she could have the house she dreams of. But it will not be his. Such a man will not provide that kind of happy home. I knew the fire lit up each shadow on my face, so I turned away. My facial muscles twitched as I hid my revulsion. I stood, stepping into the darkness outside the firelight.

He will not be. He is weak, full of vice. Yet he is strength in the eyes of the power-hungry. Irresistible in the eyes of the blind. Why has God put Belisarius in my life when every mention of the man drives a wedge between me and Byziana?

I heard her turn in her bed, and soon she fell asleep with a sickeningly blissful expression on her face. There was my mat, still next to hers. I pulled it over to the tree. *So, Marcellus, you sleep instead of speak.* Like the hissing and wuthering of the fire, thoughts flickering in my head would not rest. Self-condemnation raged inside of me at the missed opportunity, my sick cowardice bringing me anything but bliss.

What Is Mankind?

Little by little the children abandoned their sightseeing until all they did was plod on, plod on.

During our meal stops, Justin had whittled a little box, a reliquary, for Simeon's tooth, and had tied it around his neck to keep the tooth close. But most of the time, he rolled the tooth between his fingers.

"Why do you do that?" I asked him.

"It is for good luck," he answered. "It's the tooth of an infant saint, you know. I think it keeps away bandits. And maybe it can make the road shorter."

How can anyone know a six-year-old will become a saint?

"After all, he tamed a wild beast. A confirmed miracle."

Just because he stands on a pillar? He gives up any other sort of service in this world to stand on a pillar, and he is presumed to be an 'infant saint'?

"Or mere good luck," I said. "Or the sovereign hand of God keeping a child safe. In any event, Simeon can't make the road shorter. You can, though, by moving in a straight line."

I kept my eyes on the weather, my pace as fast as their little feet could follow. Then the rains began.

"Byziana, I fear we have to winter in Mopsuestia." I lifted my hand to show the drops of water accumulating. "It must be snowing on the Taurus Pass."

"The Taurus Pass?" asked Justin.

My prediction did not please Byziana. "No, we keep going. We can walk in snow, can we not, children? We've got to get there. I've got to get there."

Katerina's eyes teared up. "Ohhh. I am so cold and wet. I can hardly feel my toes. If it gets any colder I'll freeze to death."

"It will be much worse on the mountain pass with freezing winds. We may not even make it. Why'd we leave in November?" I said.

"We can make it. Stop cursing the journey!"

"The Cilician Gate, Byzia. The Horns of the Bull." Justin said. "That is what we must pass through. Everyone knows their danger."

"We must not stop. We must keep moving. Through the mountains. There won't be much snow."

"The gates are notorious. They mean death. When I say we can't make it, I mean one or even all of us may die. Die. Do you want to risk our lives? Will you choose to put your sisters' and brother's lives to that test? We can't survive. Winter has come. We were too slow and must winter before the Horns of the Bull."

"I don't agree," she answered. "No one wants to extend this trip any longer than necessary. We'll keep moving. If we make it through the pass, we have only flatlands left."

"If we make it."

She ignored my wry comment, so I added, "I suppose you have to see for yourself." Her willfulness would get us killed.

We had been traveling a long two weeks by the time we reached beautiful Mopsuestia. The Pyramos River coming toward us from the mountains made this a verdant, tree-rich locale. Myriad myriads of streams trickled past as we approached the Great Gate into the city. Yet our shivering feet and icy backs kept us from appreciating anything in nature.

As we searched for an inn in this town they called Mopsos, it started to snow. People and animals were already locked indoors. We hired a large room for our party at the first inn we could—not a clean place, but it would do for a short while.

Justin and Natalia huddled before the fire, "My bones are cold," Justin said. "This fire is not hot enough. Put more wood on it!"

I asked Trolius to find more firewood, which I added to the fire. But the damp wood smoked, refusing to flare up.

"My bones aren't thawing," Justin complained. Natalia was trembling, teeth clattering. I lifted her into my lap and rubbed her arms to warm her up.

"I can still see my breath," Katerina said, pulling her head under the thin blankets.

No one spoke of tomorrow, though I guess most of us had the snowy mountains in mind. We slept be it ever so uncomfortable in the damp and dirty room.

The next morning we met disaster.

"Marcellus!" Justin was shaking me awake. "Marcellus! We've been betrayed!"

"What? What happened?" I grabbed my sword and jumped to my feet.

"Trolius is gone. So is Byziana's purse. Where's your money-pouch?"

I reached below my pillow and found it missing too. Our hands flew to our mouths in shock.

"How can we pay for this room?" Katerina asked.

"Be quiet! Not so loud!" Byziana whispered.

"What are we going to do? We don't even have money for breakfast." We had no money to keep going, no money to return home, no money to stay. We sat in despair.

Byziana twisted her ring. Justin rolled Simeon's tooth. Katerina mourned our dire strait, "How can we live? What'll we do? They don't know us in Mopsos. What if they throw us onto the streets?"

"They won't throw us out. I won't allow it, Kata."

"We must write a letter," said Byziana, "and ask Gallus to send money."

"Writing would be a fine idea. But where will we get money to pay for the courier?"

"We can return home," Justin suggested.

"Impossible. How can we buy food? It took us two weeks to arrive here. Two weeks back, in the rain, with no food?"

I found my thumbnail between my teeth and lowered my hand. "Let's step back. Take a breath," I said.

"What do people do who have no money?" Katerina asked.

The answer was simple. "They work. And earn money." We looked at one another, willing for it to not be so. Our fallen-apart world was falling apart more.

Silence followed my answer. No one knew how to work. Work was the job of servants. "You have worked before. Think of how much you helped the people who were in our homes. You have worked."

"We are not allowed to work. Pater would not like it," Justin said. "He said we are not the class that works. We are the class people work for. He wouldn't allow it."

Byziana's answer was just as sure. "It's one thing to help earthquake victims, when you can lift a stone or give water or tend to a wound. But to work in a field. As a common laborer? It's shameful. Impossible. We've got to think of something else."

"There is another option. We can sell what we have. But I don't know how long it'll last."

We pulled our possessions together. Bedrolls, clothes, donkeys, dog, trunk. Everyone's eyes were on the Trunk of Scrolls.

"We must work," I said to Byziana.

"Sell the Scrolls. We can get money for those," Katerina suggested.

"We can't sell Mater's Scrolls," Byziana said. "Those are more precious than anything."

"Then we must work for our living." No one consented until I offered, "Or only I will work."

This being less abhorrent to the group, they agreed. "But just temporarily, Marcellus. Till the courier arrives."

After breakfast I went out to look for work. I found a farmer in his field alone and called out to him. "Do you need help?"

He scanned my clothing, up and down, then shook his head, "No, I do not need your help."

"Please, sir. I need a job."

He approached the fence. "You are a landholder yourself. Your dress betrays you."

I looked at my robe, the one Mater had made for me bearing the markings of my class.

"It is forbidden for me to hire you."

"It is not against the law, sir. True, it is not acceptable. But please know my desperation." I scratched the back of my neck as I explained. "We are on a journey, my four young cousins and myself. Last night our servant stole all our money. And now we are in a strange city. We have nothing to live on. And—," I hesitated mentioning the shameful fact, "—and no funds to either continue or to return home."

He put his hand to his chin and sighed, swaying his head with indecision. *Please, God.*

"Sir, you are correct. My name is Marcellus, son of Dorotheus, Patrician of Antioch. I do know the shamefulness of a young man of my position to labor, or to be without funds. But, sir, I will do any kind of labor if only my cousins have bread and shelter."

His eyes softened in pity. "I do need help in my cattle barns," he said, "if you'll do dirty work . . ."

"Yes sir, I will!" I shook his hand. "Yes sir."

He laughed, "In all my life . . ."

The farmer took me to his barns and showed me how to clean stalls. I took off my robe, pulled up my sleeves and went to work.

After three days we had funds for a parchment and courier. Byziana wrote, asking Steward Gallus to send funds. With great expectations we watched the courier ride off.

I worked in the man's cattle barns, but when the inn's matron heard of our situation, she threatened to throw us out.

"If youse all do not work for your keep, I gots no option but to kick you out!"

Natalia trembled against me. I looked at Byziana. She would have to decide. "Yes, madame, we will work. But our funds will be here. We are good to our word."

"Ah yes, I have known many such people 'good to their word,' who come to Mopsos and end up robbing me of weeks of income. So pardon me for not believing youse all."

She took the girls to the kitchen and put them to work peeling vegetables and washing dishes. Justin joined me at the barn. Thus we continued for more than a week.

One night, as we were warming our tired hands by the fire, eating a meager meal, Katerina's ever-present tears overflowed into speech. "My hands hurt from washing in that icy water. My back hurts. My feet hurt. God has forgotten us. Sister, you were right. He has abandoned us. He must have wanted us to die in the earthquake, so He squashes us here."

"You're wrong, Katerina," I said. My eyes rested on the Trunk. "Why have we neglected this, in our most desperate moment? Let's listen to the Words of God." I hurried to open it, knowing these Scrolls would pay comfort into our empty heart-chests.

Opening the first Scroll my hand met, I found Saint Paul's Epistle to the Hebrews. Everyone sat close to the fire, food bowl in hand. I scanned the lines then started reading at the beginning,

In the past God spoke to our ancestors
through the prophets
at many times and in various ways,
but in these last days He has spoken to us by His Son,
whom He appointed heir of all things,
and through whom also He made the universe.
The Son is the radiance of God's glory
and the exact representation of His being,
sustaining all things by His powerful word . . . .

The fire was not nearly warm enough, so everyone huddled together for extra heat, our breath showing itself in puffs of steam. No one else spoke, so I continued and read on and on into the night. As I read, my heart surged within me.

These beautiful truths had been next to us all these weeks, yet we had continued on in our own pitiful strength and feeble wisdom. And here Truth was, answering those questions we had asked, assuring us that Christ sustains all things—even us, in the midst of the tribulation we were living through.

What is mankind that you are mindful of them,
a son of man that you care for him?
You made them a little lower than the angels;
you crowned them with glory and honor
and put everything under their feet.

Everyone watched the fire and listened. No one slept. No one spoke. And I read on and on. Unbeknownst to us, those nuggets of Truth were making a slow and sure place in our hearts, hiding where no thief could ever steal them.

Now may the God of peace,
Who through the blood of the eternal covenant
brought back from the dead our Lord Jesus,
that great Shepherd of the sheep,
equip you with everything good for doing His will,
and may He work in us what is pleasing to Him,
through Jesus Christ, to whom be glory
for ever and ever.
Amen . . . . Grace be with you all.

When I read those last words, I rolled the Scroll closed, and all was still. No one dared break the holy silence.

At that moment, a knock at the door brought the matron and—*praise be to God!*—the courier we had sent.

At that moment!

We looked from one to another as if a miracle had happened. The package for which we had waited. At that moment. Hope filled my heart. Perhaps He found in us *'that which was pleasing to Him'* as the Epistle had just said.

I stood and took the rolled parchment, and a parcel from the courier, then handed him our last coin as a tip. I gave the note to Byziana with a relieved smile. She opened it.

Her face turned white making my own stomach clench with fear. Stepping close I whispered, "What happened?"

"It is for you. From Lady Aemilia," she replied, then bit her bottom lip as she waited.

"For me?" I took the note, scanned it, and my hands began trembling. They stood around me, wide and fearful eyes looking at my face for my response, for an explanation. I looked from one to the other. They expected something from me. If I failed them, all would be lost. I closed my eyes and paced my breathing.

Natalia took my hand. Hers was ice cold. "What happened? What's it say?" Justin took the message, but had not yet learned his letters so handed it back to me.

"Sit down, everyone. I have unpleasant news." I collapsed into a chair, fighting back tears of frustration. From such a high to such a low. Why this? Why now?

Byziana pressed her hands together at her mouth, waiting for me to begin. I opened the roll and read Mater's careful and small print to myself with my thumbnail between my teeth. Then forcing my face to remain calm, to not reflect my trepidation, I read it aloud.

"Gaia Aemilia of Antioch, to my dear son Marcellus, son of Gaius Dorotheus of Antioch, and to Byziana, daughter of Gaius Justus of Antioch,

"Greetings. Our assistance to the people and the repairs to the city are continuing on, though not as earnestly as before. We have rebuilt the Great Room of Gaius Justus and have buried our dead. Many people have abandoned the city in despair. Your presence

would have comforted my heart in these trying days. Since your departure, we have had two deliveries from Gaius Justus in your name, which I delivered to Steward Gallus.

"*I am grieved to hear you were robbed by Eunuch Trolius. His association with Steward Gallus makes me understand events here as well, for another event worse than this has happened to your family.*

"*After the second delivery, a terrible tragedy occurred to the house of Gaius Justus. Your steward has not been a true steward. Gallus has taken the holdings of Gaius Justus, the proceeds from the harvests, the gifts sent from Constantinople, your gold and some silver dishes recovered from the quake, and has fled to an unknown location.*"

"Oh no!" Katerina wailed.

I stopped, looking up at the children whose faces were white from weariness, from hunger, and now from horror. Guilt washed over me. *The shrewd man needed me to leave, so he told me to stay.*

"All our money?"

"Our dishes?"

Byziana's pale face was stoic, lips pressed together.

My eyes found the Hebrews Scroll, now on the table next to me. *That Scroll has words of hope. If only we could be reading that letter instead.* I started to close the parchment, but Byziana stopped me.

"Hush. Let him continue."

I rubbed the corner of my eyes, as if they itched, but to wipe out any sign of tears. *It's my fault.*

"Go on, Marcellus."

Inhaling deeply, I continued reading,

"*Dear Byziana, your father has been robbed completely and thoroughly. I have since learned that over the past year Gallus, in the name of your father, loaned money at exorbitant usury, and prior to his departure robbed the people of Antioch as well, in lieu of the debt. There is great distress here at your steward's departure.*"

My cousins gasped again and I condemned myself for believing his ploy. The silent room hung with gloom. Byziana, chewing her bottom lip, the children looking at me for hope. They motioned for me to continue.

"*I am sending you money to speed your journey. I pray you*

will journey home, as my heart breaks for you. After the snows melt, if you still desire, you may continue on from Antioch to Constantinople.

"Marcellus, do all in your power to impress upon your cousin the necessity of returning home. Gaius Justus expects his servant to return to Constantinople with harvest funds in the spring. I shall set aside some money to send with him, and the children can accompany the servant. But consolidation is necessary, and I think the children living with me in Antioch is the best solution to this tragedy until the next harvest in May.

"My dear children, do not despair. Come home to me and all will be well.

"Grace and peace to you. Kyrie Eleison on your journey home."

There are moments in life you wish you could rub out, like one would rub out words on an unnecessary parchment. This is one of those memories of my life. Guilt assaulted me. *I shouldn't have let my uncle dismiss my accusation. I shouldn't have let myself be tricked by the steward's words.*

"There is all the proof you need. We are under the curse of God." Byziana's words were matter-of-fact. Not even sad. My hand shielded my face, covering my eyes.

"We are cursed," Katerina whined.

What had we read a moment ago? '*What is mankind that you are mindful of them?' Why, God?* I prayed. *Why, after we read those comforting words, do you send this tragedy?* I felt like a hundred marble slabs were piled atop my back, that my fingers were clawing the soil, that I just wanted to live.

"Don't even tempt me, Marcellus. Don't say a word of how we don't deserve a good life. Everyone knows life should be good. Ask anyone." No emotion was in her voice, as if discussing the weather.

Our soul cries out for it. The soul of everyone calls out for it. Peace on earth. My heart begged God for help. *Oh 'Great Shepherd of the sheep.' Where's that peace?*

Though Mater had urged me to persuade Byziana to return, she knew Byziana. Reasoning could win nothing against Byziana's tenacity. She was a boulder rolling down a hill—impossible to stop without a great crash.

"You know I am determined to press on to the Capital. Constantinople is where our hope lies, where our family will be secure, where our new home is. Pater is there. We must be there, too. Since God is not with us—"

"You can't say that—"

"—I will pull us out from under His heavy hand."

She gritted her teeth and turned away.

'Jesus Christ, to whom be the glory for ever,' We need you.

"If we can't trust God to help us, we will have to help ourselves. We must finish this journey or die trying. We got our money, so we'll keep going when morning comes."

"Won't you listen? It's even colder outside than before! We can't make it through that mountain!" Justin's words fell on deaf ears.

Katerina moaned. "I don't want to go to Constantinople. Oooh, but I don't want to go to Antioch, either—our reputation is ruined there. And God hates Antioch. Oooh! I just wanna die!"

If Byziana did not change her mind, the death Kata called for was exactly what would happen. Natalia curled up on her sleeping mat and began to sleep, turning and shivering and groaning. I watched for Justin's response, but he shrugged his shoulders. He knew his sister must make this decision for the family.

I was speechless, could only pray. *Why God, when men are so wicked to each other, do you also serve us one evil upon another? Who are you that you do this?*

Looking at Natalia, then back to me and to the others, Byziana pulled her lips into an unconvincing smile. "Let's get our sleep. We start our journey in the morning." She sat in front of the dying fire again, pulled her cloak around her and refused to speak anymore.

Sometimes wisdom comes through listening to others. Other times wisdom comes through great tragedy. But sometimes foolishness speaks louder and more persuasively. Byziana was determined to draw a straight line and walk on it toward her goal, regardless of naysayers.

I breathed in the strength air alone could give. I would keep her safe until the last moment on the mountain, which was where our journey would end. *What are we, God? Are you mindful of us? Kyrie Eleison. Lord have mercy.*

HORNS OF THE BULL

A t first light the weather froze us to the toes. Natalia had to be dressed, helped along, carried.

"I'm cold. Sleepy," she whimpered.

"Hush. The cold air will awaken you. Let's get outside," Byziana answered.

It had rained in the night, of course, and icy mud and slush filled our path. We started off, Byziana in front with one donkey, followed by Justin, Katerina, and Natalia. I was at the end, leading the second donkey. Natalia sat at every chance she got, on stones, fallen logs, fence-beams.

"She's tired, like I am!" Katerina whined as we rallied her sister from the ground yet again.

"Come, little one. Let me put you on Byziana's donkey," I said lifting Natalia atop the luggage. As soon as we started, the donkey's clumpity movement knocked her off balance.

"Whoa there!" I caught her before she slipped off. She had not seemed to notice, but remained asleep.

"Tie her on," Justin suggested, handing me a rope. We secured her so she could sleep as we moved. I covered her with a blanket, and we advanced again toward the dreaded mountains.

Around nightfall, we met the snow-capped mountains in all their threatening glory. The moment we came around the curve of a hill and caught sight of the mountains, Justin, Katerina and I stopped in our tracks.

In front of us, the snow-covered Taurus Mountains stood like the menacing, angry, ominous bull they were named after. Our path lay between its horns, through the valley. My feet would move no closer. A roaring river pummeled out next to the road, swearing it would pull us in. The white mountaintops taunted us from the clouds, forbidding passage.

We would die on this mountain.

Byziana kept walking, pulling the hesitant donkey with Natalia shivering atop. Justin stood frozen in place, hearing the cliff's threat. Katerina came back toward me, tears running down her face, her arms around herself to stay warm.

Byziana called out. "We can make it," she insisted, pulling her robe and furs around her and pressing on. "We will only be safe in Constantinople! Justin, give me the tooth. I will lead us on with the holy rays."

Justin removed the reliquary from his neck, shaking his head in fearful unbelief. At fourteen years of age, Byziana found nothing impossible. That outlook threatened our lives, for she would not stop pushing us.

"Come on. We can find a warm cave there somewhere ...." She gazed at the mountain, her eyes following the ridge line. "There must be a village up there ... where we can stay."

"It's the Cilicia Gate, Sister," said Justin.

He had heard of the wars over this pass. She must not have. He had heard of its sharp rocky paths and raging rivers. She must not have. The moments continued. We, standing stock still. Byziana, tramping on.

And then, in a stroke of slow-coming surrender, Byziana turned the donkey around, coming back to us snow crunching underfoot, staring into a void. As soon as we met she took the reliquary from Justin.

"I should have told you from the beginning. Gallus gave me the letter after the earthquake, not before. As I looked at that mountain just now I remembered his eagerness. He meant for this all along. "

She stopped by us, shaking her head in recollection. "We left in November, at his suggestion. Walking, at his suggestion. Taking Trolius, at his suggestion. Who knows how he manipulated Pater? Maybe he even forged that letter."

My heart found bitter relief. I was not alone. We had all been deceived by the man. But how long would we pay for it?

"We have no money. Our family is ruined. Gallus would have our whole family dead."

Though I could not change the past, I could mend the future. "All is not lost, Byziana." I opened my arms. "Anything I have is yours. You'll never be destitute as long as I'm alive."

She did not acknowledge me, shrugging around my open arms with saddened shoulders.

"Don't worry, everyone," I turned as she passed me and tried to rally the others' spirits. "Home awaits us." No one answered, everyone followed Byziana back the way we had come. She pointed out lights to the west, and those lights drew us to a small village on the top of a crest. At the first house we came to, an old widow opened her door to us. We took Natalia down from the donkey and found her frozen.

FACING DEATH ALL DAY LONG

Natalia was unconscious as we lay her on the widow's bed, in the corner of the one-room cottage.

"This girl is on the brink of death. Cold as an icicle. Why are you children on a journey in winter?" the Widow Arité chastened. "Who is looking after you? Where are your parents?"

She asked good questions. When no one else answered, I said, "I am looking after them."

Byziana frowned at me and Widow Arité noticed her look, humphing, "I see! You will stay with me until she gets better."

After introductions, she hurried us next to the fire and hung a pot of stew over the flames. "God be praised you found me. You must stay here till it's warm. Natalia may still live, though it's in the Lord's hands. Let's not lose anyone else. Welcome."

Hearing this news, exhausted Katerina collapsed into her arms. "I never knew my Grandmater. But I wish she'd been you!" Byziana shared my surprise at her sister's rare affection.

"I shall be your Grandmater then, dear Katerina. Having raised seven young ones, I know how to care for children. I have many questions, but those can wait. Let's put a heap of wood on this fire. With big boys to cut firewood for us, I can keep this house nice and toasty for you all."

Justin and I brought in a large load of firewood, and warm soup soon filled our stomachs. Arité opened a wardrobe and took out a dozen thick blankets. "My mother and grandmother and I made these," she said. "I never could part with them. This is why.

They were waiting for your family to show up." Soon cots lay along the edge of the room. Her home was seven paces from door to far wall, yet somehow the cots made the room look larger. As we got settled, Arité sat by Natalia, holding her upright in her arms.

"How is my sister?" asked Katerina. "Is she going to wake up?"

"Only the Good Lord knows."

Natalia groaned, and Arité's eyebrows lifted. "Oh! Groaning is a good sign. She is somewhat aware."

The widow motioned for the girls to bring more blankets, and she lay Natalia on her side and covered her.

"She should awaken when she warms up," she said.

And yet she did not awaken. The white child on the corner mat contrasted with the cozy, colorful home. Everything had a place. On the small windowsill sat crocks of herbs tied with dried blue flowers and pink bows. The fireplace blazed away with a welcoming crackle.

Outside, the winter winds blew the reed chimes hanging by the door, the clunkity clunk sound bringing a peaceful rhythm into the home. Yet Natalia was blind and deaf to this warm and orderly cottage.

The third day Arité gathered us together.

"We need to prepare ourselves. She is so little. If she does not eat and drink . . . you know what happens."

Byziana kneeled next to the bed. "What can we do? Can we give her water, at least?" Natalia groaned and shifted in the bed, but her eyes did not open.

"Oh, Nati, this is my fault!"

Arité sat on the bed and took Byziana's hand.

"How is it your fault?"

"God hounds me, he stalks me, he chases me. Where can I go that he doesn't hunt me down? For what? Just to hurt me more. No death for me, just pain."

"Child! Do you blaspheme God? In my peaceful home?"

"I'm not trying to blaspheme. It's like I'm a dried up apple core. All that's left for me is to bury me already." Byziana hid her face in her hands. "I give up. If she dies, I promise I'll go back to Antioch. If she dies, I know God wants to kill us there."

"That still sounds like blasphemy. It's not always about you. God has all things in mind."

"Forgive me, Widow Arité," Byziana's soft voice answered.

"I understand your turmoil. But you mustn't blame yourself. The darling may live. I have noticed, every so often she swallows."

"If she swallows she might eat," I said, my mind spinning with ideas. "Can we make her swallow?"

"But how?"

"If you close a dog's mouth and rub his throat he swallows."

Justin looked at me surprised, "It does?" Byziana sat up.

"If that doesn't work, we can watch for when she swallows."

"That'd take a lot of time. To watch."

"What if we take turns?" said Byziana. "We can take small bits of bread, soak them in a thick broth, and put them in her mouth when we see her swallow."

The widow agreed. "That might work. But if she inhales anything she can die. Poor thing."

Byziana's hopeful smile faded.

Death?

Kyrie Eleison.

"Salt," Justin suggested. "People swallow when their mouth is salty."

"That is a good point," Arité said. She went over to her windowsill and lowered a jar of salt, putting it on the table next to the cot. "Dear Lord, help us," she said, looking up to heaven as she touched the salt with her finger.

She gently opened Natalia's mouth and touched her tongue. Natalia groaned and swallowed.

"It might work," the widow said with a gentle smile.

An hour later the broth was ready, and we stood in a circle around Natalia waiting for a miracle.

"Turn the child to her side. We must keep the food from slipping into her lungs."

Arité took a piece of bread the size of a fingernail, dipped it in the broth and placed it on Natalia's tongue with a touch of salt.

"Natalia, we need you to swallow dear," she said.

We watched. Her mouth remained closed, the food on her tongue.

"I knew it wouldn't work. We've killed one person. Now we're all going to die." Katerina collapsed next to her sister and wept.

"We'll find a way," Byziana said. "She must be hungry. Maybe we can rouse her."

"She's in one of those deep sleeps," I said.

"Marcellus, she always listens to you. You tell her."

I knelt by the bed and leaned my head next to my cousin's ear. "Nati. You hungry?"

There was silence. I shrugged my shoulders, but tried again. "Eat, little one. So you can get better. You've got a bit of food on your tongue and we need you to swallow it." *God, help us.*

I pressed bread on her lips, and she surprised us by swallowing the food in her mouth. I tried it again. Dipping the bread in broth I touched her mouth and pressed it through her lips. She swallowed again, so I repeated the procedure several times in a row.

"I don't know how long this will help her," Arité said.

"How much does she need to eat?"

She tore off a chunk of bread. "I think if she eats a piece of bread this big, and a bowlful of vegetable broth daily, she may get through this. But who knows when she'll awaken?"

"I will help," Katerina said, wiping her eyes.

"I'll set aside her daily rations. If we're all willing to do our part, we perhaps can keep her alive."

Perhaps? The flash of hopelessness crossing the widow's face told me all I needed to know. Nati would not survive.

I scanned the others. I think Byziana shared the realization. *Will she really return to Antioch if Natalia dies? Is that what it will take?*

The big snows were coming. Until then, we needed to gather more winter stores to keep the rest of us alive. Again we worked. Again with heavy hearts. Katerina helped the widow tie herbs in pouches and peddle them door to door. Justin chopped wood for villagers. Byziana washed dishes at two different inns. I helped farmers plant their wheat, a dreary chore in the rainy weather, but at least it brought us income. Somehow physical labor revives the soul like nothing else can.

Day by day we saw Natalia eat what Arité had set aside. Night by night we rejoiced when she finished the last bite. Often Natalia would groan, thank God she swallowed at the taste of food, but she never opened her eyes.

One evening we sat around the fire, wearied in body but eager for talk. Sautéeing garlic wafted through the room as Katerina and I finished chopping vegetables for our stew. Widow Arité hemmed our threadbare stockings and the others just watched the fire.

"I miss Mater," Katerina said, lowering her knife. "It hurts me, like I'm hungry and thirsty but in my heart."

My mind went back to when I would read to my aunt. "I miss those days as well."

Byziana agreed, pausing to feed Natalia, "I think about her almost every moment. I wish she had not died."

"*'Precious in the sight of the Lord is the death of his saints,'*" Arité said, eyes on her mending. "That is from the Psalter."

We turned toward the widow. "Have you read the Psalter?" Justin asked.

"My grandmother knew many of the Psalms. And spoke them to me as she rocked me on her knee. She was the servant of a saint, you know."

"She was?" we echoed. "She was?"

"Yes, of Saint Macrina." Our jaws dropped at the name.

"Saint Macrina believed everyone equal before God. Her mother, Saint Emmilia, was a noblewoman. But Macrina persuaded her to share her wealth with the household, young, old, family and servant alike. My grandmother was a child when she lived with them. And served them until the death of Macrina—if you could call it serving, since servants and masters shared equally in the chores. Macrina would read from the Psalter morning and night. They had a copy, don't you know. My grandmother never forgot the Psalms she had learned by heart."

She lifted her attention from her work. "Why do you have mouths of a sea-bream?"

No one could speak. *How can we explain? What should we say?*

Byziana stood up and walked over to our piled luggage. She lifted the bundles off the Trunk and opened it, taking out a bound caudex and handing it to me.

The widow's eyebrows lifted in surprise.

I began, "*Blessed is the man who walks not in the counsel of the ungodly, nor stands in the way of sinners, nor sits in the seat of scoffers, but his delight is in the law of the Lord and on His law he meditates day and night—"*

But my words were overtaken by the wide-eyed widow, who hobbled over, quoting, *"He is like a tree planted by streams of water that yields its fruit in its season, and its leaf does not wither. In all that he does, he prospers."*

"Where did you get this Writ?" the widow asked, tears welling.

"It has been in our family for generations," Byziana said.

"I thought the monasteries had gathered to a one each Blessed Writ. How came you by this? And why have you kept it?"

"My mother was the keeper of our family trust. We believe it's safer in our possession than in a monastery."

"Why your family? Who is your family?"

Katerina and Justin grinned, but waited for their sister to answer. Byziana's proud smile reshaped into a concerned frown. "Widow Arité, we have told you too much. If anyone were to find this Trunk, they'd take away our family's most prized legacy."

The widow frowned. She hobbled tight-lipped and dropped into her chair. "Don't you trust me? After all this time?"

"Madame," I said, handing the Psalter to Justin, kneeling next to her and taking her hand in mine. "We trust you to keep our secret. Byziana, do not fear this fine lady. Tell her about the wonderful Trunk."

Byziana approached the widow. "Saint Emmilia, whom you spoke of, is our great-grandmother. Her son, Gregory of Nyssa, gave a trunkful of Scripture scrolls to his brother Isodorus. Then he gave it to his son Marcus."

She waited until Widow Arité nodded. "Marcus had twin daughters. Mary and Elizabeth. Mary was Marcellus's great-grandmother. Elizabeth, our great-grandmother got the Trunk and gave it to her son Ioseph, our grandfather. And now we have it."

Byziana's surveyed the bundles she had taken off the Trunk and her face paled. *Oh, how we'd failed that trust.*

"You are indeed blessed, my children." Widow Arité reclined in her chair and watched the fire sparkle and crackle.

"Yet I ask one thing of you . . ." We waited for her to continue.

"To date I have not spoken of the lodging, for I opened my

home to you not as guests but as family. I ask not for lodging fees. Of course not. Your practical aid these cold days has been invaluable."

She looked at us with a pained, hopeful expression. "But one thing I now do ask. While we wait for dear darling Natalia to heal and awaken, Lord willing, will you read to me from these Scrolls? Is it too much to ask? My grandmother learned from these very same Scrolls. Oh, how I long to hear those Words."

"Of course, dear Grandmater." Byziana said.

"I think we dropped the torch." Justin gave the Psalter to Byziana who returned to the Trunk.

"What torch?" Katerina asked.

"The torch Aunt Aemilia said we must carry," he answered.

"Yes, we must hold the torch up high," I said.

Byziana brought me another Scroll to read, the Gospel of John.

"Take and read to us, Marcellus." As I took the Scroll from her and my hand brushed hers, a feeling rushed over me like a fiery wind. I saw my life, as a vision. A small cottage, a loving family together in a warm home, and Byziana there with me. Not a large house with mosaics and tapestries. Not fields with servants at my beck and call. I wanted her handing me a Scroll by the fireside, saying, 'Take and read to us, Marcellus.' I knew what I wanted as I wanted my next breath. I wanted her and a family with her. I wanted this moment forever.

I looked into her face. *I know this is what I want. I am sure this is what I want.* Her cheeks turned pink.

My hand brushed against her hand as I took the Scroll, and the smooth metal of her ring skimmed over my finger, scalding my soul back to reality. This would end. I would never have that home because she belonged to him.

Taking a deep breath, I buried my raging disappointment and stared at the words. A peace flowed through my fingers to my heart. At least I had a Scroll in hand. So I read,

"In the beginning was the Word,
and the Word was with God and the Word was God.
He was with God in the beginning.
All things were made through Him,
and without Him nothing was made that has been made.
In Him was life, and that life was the light of men.
The light shines in the darkness,

and the darkness does not understand it.
There was a man who came from God,
and his name was John . . . ."

No wind passed through the windows, no icy air under the door. Homey and snug, we passed our winter by the fire of Arité, warmed from within by both the fires of Scripture and the togetherness of family. We hoped against hope Natalia would awaken. She remained in a still sleep, as though dead. Breathing and swallowing, spoonful by spoonful, she withered away, yet lived. Pale but warm.

THE GREAT DEBATE

nd so it went. To keep our promise we fed our souls. We read from the Psalter in the mornings, and the other Scrolls in the evening. Hebrews. Corinthians. The Gospel of John. Ephesians. Philippians. The Gospel of Matthew. The Beginnings. Exodus. We read through all twenty-one Scrolls that winter. Our souls would be lifted to God as we heard His Word. The lively discussions afterwards encouraged our faith. And yet we avoided topics.

The earthquake, unspeakable.
Lady Sophia's name, unspeakable.
Goodness of God, unspeakable.
We feared Byziana's censure so our conversations revolved around non-debates . . . until one evening the unspoken exposed itself in a *maskil* of David.
"You have rejected us, God, and burst upon us;
you have been angry—now restore us!
You have shaken the land and torn it open;
mend its fractures, for it is quaking.
You have shown your people desperate times;
you have given us wine that makes us stagger.
But for those who fear you, you have raised a banner
to be unfurled against the bow."
Byziana had been fidgeting, but at this point she cried, "Stop! stop! Read no further!"
Jumping up from her seat she threw herself face-down on her sleeping pallet.

Katerina left the dinner preparations and sat by her sister. "What's wrong, Byzia?" She did not answer but pushed herself deeper into her pillow. Katerina stroked her sister's back and flipped her wrist to question me.

I knew girls went through mountains and valleys in emotions. But this was Byziana. Steady Byziana. I looked over the verses. "The passage was about an earthquake."

"I heard about your Antioch earthquakes. I never asked you," the widow said.

"They were horrible! We had all these bloody people coming to our house. And lots of people dying. We left after the second one, in November. We didn't want to be swallowed up too," Katerina explained.

I kept watching Byziana. I had never seen her like this. *I've got to help her.*

"Did God reject us, Marcellus?" Justin said. "The Psalter says He rejects us using earthquakes."

I looked at the verses again. "Then it says, '*But for those who fear you, you have raised a banner.*' It means the faithful shouldn't worry."

Byziana groaned and pulled the blanket over her head. *Oh Byzia.*

"Come now, child," Widow Arité said. "Tell us your sorrows. Don't press it within you."

"I don't wish to discuss my sorrows!"

"You should trust us, darling. Let us help you."

"You can't help me. God is against me. He has rejected me. He took my mater from me. And my house. He has '*shaken the land*' as it said. Given us '*desperate times.*' For what? Because of the Debate."

The widow looked at me, perplexed.

Byziana came out from under the blanket. "Listen. The earthquake said we should not be divided. But Mater said I'm supposed to be Chalcedon. And Pater says to be Monophysite. Even in our family we are divided. And this whole argument has made us poor!"

"Poor? How did it make you poor?" Widow Arité asked.

"God took it all from us. '*Given us wine to make us stagger.*' If my life does not make me stagger, I don't know what will."

"Byziana, dear, why do you only accept good from God? Can He not send pain?"

"Why would He send pain? I thought He was a God of love."

"In my long life, I have seen good men suffer while evil men prosper. In fact, King Solomon said the same thing."

Byziana's eyebrows twisted in confusion.

I wished, with all my heart, to relieve her of the pain. But suffering kept coming upon us. Beyond our ability to bear. There was Nati in the corner, fighting for her life as she slept. We were snowed in. Our homes lay in ruins. Our families broken up. *How can I help her when I'm equally lost? How can I fix this for her?*

The window drew me to gaze at the night, where the Milky Way lit up the darkness in a great swash of light. It insisted I trust God. *But why was there so much darkness to fill in the first place?*

The old woman continued. "Many weeks ago you said God was stalking you. He's not after you. Suffering comes to all men. It's just the way life is. Oh, the stories I could tell."

At her age, she must have seen much suffering. Byziana nodded in understanding.

"So, you feel it's personal. Then what are you doing about it? Are you listening to God?"

"Who knows what God says? I'm faithful to Pater. Trust the Pater. The Pater makes the decisions."

"Which is important, too. What is this Monofite thing? I've not heard of it."

"Monophysite," Byziana corrected. She peeked at me, but I shrugged my shoulders and welcomed her to explain. *I wish I could wipe away your tears forever, Byzia.* She sat up on her bed and dried her eyes.

"Dear Widow Arité," she said, gaining composure with a sniff, "A great debate has shaken the Church today. It is about Christ's nature, setting Christianity in two camps. We carry two different torches." Her lip twitched as she formed those words. "We believe in the Lord Christ Jesus. We believe He came to earth as our Savior. He died and was buried and rose again."

"That sounds right," said Katerina.

"Yes, it is right," said the widow. "And the problem?"

"Well, our torch does not match the Chalcedon Confession, which Emperor Marcian twisted in his favor," said Byziana, shooting me a look. *Why does she have to turn this into a fight? I only want to help her.*

"Oh brother," sighed Katerina returning to chopping leeks into the vegetable pot.

"In the Chalcedon creed they claimed Christ was *'of very nature God and of very nature man.'* It's about a thing called hypostatic union, which Pater says is illogical and absurd."

She turned to me. "I'm sorry, I know you disagree."

I forced a smile and stood up to return the Scroll to the Trunk, then changed my mind. Having it in my hand kept me calm. I was not wrong about Chalcedon. I was on the side of Reason.

"My point is, whatever we say about Christ has to be logically consistent."

Justin turned to his sister in a confused grimace. "What did you mean? Hippo-what?"

"Hypostasis," I said bluntly, sitting down. "It means essential substance. Monophysites say Christ has one hypostasis meaning one nature. The Chalcedon Council declared Christ has one hypostasis but two natures. Two natures but one person."

"It sounds complicated," said Justin. "How are we supposed to know which one is true?"

"You use Reason," Byziana said. "We say Christ was God. The Chalcedonians say Christ was two opposite things: man and God."

That's not so.

She touched her upper lip. "Justin, can two opposite things be the same thing at the same time? Can something black be also white?"

"No, it would be gray. Or it would be like Captain, a black dog with a white stomach." He patted the dog next to him.

We're not talking gray.

Widow Arité continued knitting away, listening. I watched the flickering fire-dance on the logs under the cooking pot. How could I ever have a hearth-fire with her when she hated something so important to me? It would never be. *Just let go, Marcellus.*

"Right. So if you take God and make Him man, He is either God in a man robe, or He is no longer God and is just man," Byziana continued.

"Okay . . . ." He seemed confused still. "But why is it important?"

Justin's question echoed over and over in my head, my heart awakened the never-answered question. *Why does it matter more than anything, Marcellus?*

Byziana thought for a moment. "For one, He cannot be all God and all man at the same time. That would make Him gray and contradictory. Second, this fight caused the earthquake. God is cross with Antioch for saying Christ was dual nature. He has *'shaken the land and torn it open'*!"

"Other cities have this debate," I said. "Why was there only an earthquake in Antioch? And not in Constantinople or Alexandria?" Alexandria was where it started.

She looked over at me, "I don't know. But you said once it had to do with God's character. This must be it."

"So people made the earthquake happen?" asked Katerina.

"God wanted to show his anger."

There had to be another explanation. I read the words again and said, "But what about the next part? *'Now restore—'*"

"Our dear cousin thinks it's possible for opposites to be simultaneously true."

"I do not," I mumbled. *I've got to get rid of my concern for her. I need to sever it from myself.*

"Does Pater know which one is true?" Justin asked.

I leaned back in my chair with a huff. *The ultimate authority on all things. The Pater. Give her a ring. Bind her to that man. Tell her what to believe.*

"Pater agrees with me. He is the one who explained it to me."

Katerina rolled her eyes, "Can't we all say Jesus Christ is God and be done with it?"

I cleared my throat and everyone got silent. "It matters more than anything. The problem with that, Kata, is both opinions cannot be true. One is a lie. Two opposites can't be true at the same time and in the same relationship."

"My point exactly, Marcellus," laughed Byziana, lifting her eyebrows at me.

My frown did not lift. "To keep the facts straight, Emperor Marcian only made the Council of Chalcedon possible. Pope Leo's input—the Tome he sent—swayed the decision."

"Well, that's debatable."

"I don't think so. And you are wrong, Byziana, in two ways. First, by saying this debate caused the earthquakes."

"How do you explain the earthquake, then?"

"Bad things happen because the world is broken. It's |a message to us—to find out why. Conscience proclaims the same message."

"Well, I would have to agree with you on that, son," said the widow.

"Your second error is saying God and man are opposites.

"Of course they're opposites."

"It may seem to break the rules, but what if it doesn't? What if there is something about God we don't understand yet? Besides, the opposite of God would be something equally powerful but all negative and darkness."

"Well, what if God is Bad?"

What! "Believing in a 'Bad God,' is not only blasphemous, it's unreasonable—as if any goodness could come from a Bad God—you have the same problem in reverse."

"Could the opposite of God be an all-weak, powerless, evil creature, like man?" Byziana suggested.

Widow Arité took a deep breath and shook her head. "All I know is Jesus Christ died on the cross. And how could He die if He was not man? Only a man could pay for man's sin. That's enough sense for me."

"You're right. It wouldn't make sense." Byziana sighed and shrugged her shoulders.

"Exactly," I said. "In the end, Pope Leo used Scripture to prove Christ to be both fully God and fully man. That became the orthodox position and clear in the Confession they wrote up. Our belief on this affects everything about our relationship with God."

Stop talking before they ask how. How does Reason demand Christ be both God and man? How does the Incarnation answer everything? They'll find out you don't know what you're talking about. I pressed my lips together, hoping to have ended the assault.

Byziana's soft eyes crinkled at the corners. "Oh, go ahead, dear Cousin. Enough from me. Your turn. Why don't you tell us that Confession? It might help us."

My heart was in a knot. *First she cries, and all I want to do is comfort her. To wipe away all her tears. Then she accuses me, blames me, insults me, and mocks me. And now she asks for the Confession? I'm going to tear my heart out.*

But then, deep in her eyes I saw a spark of something that awakened me. Something I hungered for more of.

I kept staring. *What was it I saw?* My heart flipped. *Friendship. Care for me.*

My heart returned her peace-keeping smile. *She's not angry. She just doesn't understand the earthquake.* I kept looking in her eyes, tasting that spark, when Truth spoke. *And she likes to argue philosophy. Like her mother.* I was smitten. Eye to eye I watched her light sparkle, until Widow Arité cleared her throat to capture my attention.

"What? Oh. The Confession." I gulped. "Gladly."

I tilted my head to accept the request and ran my fingers through my hair. *What was that?* My insides thundered like a waterfall splash, bubbling and powerful.

The Confession. I forced my eyes to avoid her, and concentrated on the words. Taking a deep breath, the old words and memories of Pater's drills flooded to mind. I poised my hand and tucked away my distracted heart, collecting my thoughts and beginning:

"We, then, following the holy Fathers,
all with one consent,
teach people to confess one and the same Son,
our Lord Jesus Christ,
the same perfect in Godhead
and also perfect in manhood;
. . . truly God and truly man,
of a reasonable soul and body;
. . . consubstantial with the Father
according to the Godhead,
and consubstantial with us
according to the Manhood;
. . . in all things like unto us, without sin;
. . . begotten before all ages of the Father
according to the Godhead,
and in these latter days, for us and for our salvation,
born of the Virgin Mary, the Mother of God,
according to the Manhood;
. . . one and the same Christ, Son, Lord, only begotten,

to be acknowledged in two natures,
inconfusedly, unchangeably, indivisibly, inseparably;
. . . the distinction of natures being by no means
taken away by the union,
but rather the property of each nature being preserv—,"

I stumbled and caught my breath. Goosebumps appeared on my arms. *Something's here. I'm close to a Truth, but I can't see it.* I scratched my neck, wanting to pause and contemplate this.

"Did you forget the words?" Katerina asked. I shook my head. "Excuse me."

What's here? Think. But the urgent whisper had disappeared. I focused again and continued:

"—The property of each nature being preserved
and concurring in one Person and one Subsistence,
not parted or divided into two persons,
but one and the same Son, and only begotten God,
the Word, the Lord Jesus Christ;
. . . as the prophets from the beginning have declared
concerning Him,
and the Lord Jesus Christ Himself has taught us,
and the Creed of the holy Fathers
has handed down to us."

"It sounds important," Justin sighed. "I wish I understood it."

A motion from Byziana brought applause for my soliloquy. I met her eyes again, but she looked away. So I pulled Justin to myself and hugged him. He squeezed me back. "Some day, my little man, you'll understand why it matters more than anything else. This Truth is our torch. He was like us. It matters."

Widow Arité added, "Such poise and eloquence, Marcellus. You have a way with words."

"What is 'consubstantial'?" asked Katerina. "It said that a lot."

"Sharing the same substance," I said. "He is made of what we're made of, and He is made of what God's made of."

"That's strange." Katerina rubbed her eyebrow.

I agreed. The widow called us, "Children, let's get food into your growing stomachs. Katerina has made us a nice stew. Thank you, Kata. I am sure this debate won't be solved tonight as important as it truly is."

In the back of my mind, a nervous whirring worried me

about the Confession. *Something's in there I'm not seeing.* But before I could consider it, we were seated and my attention turned to Byziana across the table. I determined two things as I stood to pray. *First, I will persuade her of Chalcedon. Second, I will figure out how to make her eyes sparkle again.*

Listening to God. The widow had asked us to pay attention to what God was saying. But how to do that— when life and its problems were always in front of us—was the bigger challenge. So we kept doing what we could to survive and to keep our spirits up. And left knowing God to another time.

Days turned into nights and into days again. Hoping for Natalia to awaken. Working. Eating. Talking. Besides reading Scripture aloud, I took evenings to teach Justin his letters using the Scrolls as text. The widow also learned some letters during that time, and she showed her pleasure—at accomplishing such a feat at such an age—by feeding us with flourish.

We remained in her cottage at the Horns of the Bull, at God's mercy—God who made the wheat hibernate, the snows come, the land turn fully white, the river rise, the days lengthen, the snows melt, the skies open, and the flowers blossom. In our favor, the house was small, the stove heavy, the room warm. This was what saved Natalia's life.

On the day Katerina came in with the first spring crocuses, she looked at her sister and screamed, "Nati, you're awake!" Dropping the fragile bouquet to the floor, she ran to her sister's cot in the corner. They say Natalia stretched her arms in the air and grinned, like a sleeping bear waking after winter.

The widow summoned us from work, and soon we all huddled around our dear Natalia, giving endless embraces and laughing kisses. We had witnessed God's miracle through the widow's broth. Widow Arité's broken-toothed smile warmed our hearts. We did not forget to kiss her hand in thanks and to praise God that evening for bringing Natalia back from death's door.

VALLEY OF DEATH

Spring arrived with vigor. The lingering snow on the mountains melted into the rising river, and eager flowers burst from the cold ground toward the warm sun.

"Travelers are traversing the Cilician Gate!" Justin charged through the door with the announcement, then leaned forward on his legs to catch his breath. We watched several caravans passing below the window, along the main road, and noted travelers from nearby inns getting their pack animals ready.

My eyes caught Byziana's. "It's time to decide. The melts are here and we can leave. I'm sure the progress in Antioch is phenomenal. Wouldn't it be good to see?" My hopes surged with the thought. "Shall we go home?"

She turned away from me and observed the procession, biting the inside of her cheek.

Natalia was well now. Her voracious appetite had fitted her for travel. Since we had worked for our keep we still had the money Mater sent. Money-pouch full, spirits revived, we were all ready for home.

"We will leave on the morrow," Byziana said.

Widow Arité moaned, "Oh. Will my new family leave so soon?"

"Please say we're going home." Katerina approached her sister, wide-eyed.

Byziana shook her head. "Sorry, Kata."

"You're still going to Constantinople?" A knot forming in my gut.

"It is my destiny. My father has called us."

She meant, *I am to marry Belisarius.* I was sure.

"Besides, my sister didn't die. I said I'd go back if she died."

"That's horrible!" I said. "You can't use your sister's life to test God. Her living is not God's stamp of approval for this trip. You've got to use your head. Make the right decision."

"I am using my head," she answered simply. "We're going to Pater."

The words soured my stomach. I stared at her. *How can you still want him, and his house, after living in this cottage so warm and happy? Has this meant nothing to you?*

Natalia put her hand in mine. "Cousin, why is your face all bunched up like you ate a lemon?"

Why do you insist on going to Belisarius? What does he offer that I don't? I rubbed my mouth to wipe away my vexation. Katerina watched me as if she were trying to read a book in a difficult language. If I was a book, she put me down, for she was soon helping Widow Arité in lunch preparations.

We had the afternoon to buy provisions, so I tended the donkeys, purchased new strappings, a wool tent, and warm travel clothes and took our shoes to the cobbler for repairs and strengthening.

When I came back, the girls, sitting by Widow Arité, jumped up. My face must have registered surprise and concern. "What are you ladies hiding?"

"We were talking marriage, Marcellus," Katerina's face turned pink and she looked to the others to take over the conversation.

Widow Arité stood. "Let's not bother Marcellus with female matters, girls. He will learn of women when his time comes."

I am eighteen years of age! What secrets am I not old enough for? What about women do I not yet know? I said nothing, but again Katerina read my face. This time she understood. "Marcellus is not happy. He's offended."

The old lady limped over, leaning on her cane. She put her arm around me and whispered in my ear, loud enough for everyone to hear, "So, you cry for kittens."

Ringing in my ears told me my face had turned red. The taunt touched such a deep pain, I strained to keep tears from my eyes. *Pull yourself together. How could they know?* I could almost taste the dirt in my mouth again.

Widow Arité pulled my face to her level and stroked my

face with her thumbs, "You'll be a fine husband, dear. Don't you worry. You have a strong, compassionate heart. Keep doing what you're doing."

Her words soothed like salve, the kindness giving hope to my sorrow. I shoved the bitter thoughts away and embraced her. *Life goes on. We've got to keep moving forward.* Byziana covered her face to hide a snicker.

"Do not laugh at me, Byziana. You would not want to lose your guide through the mountains."

"Oh no, dear Marcellus. I am not laughing at you. I am laughing at how serious your face got." *She has no idea what she's laughing at.*

"Stop teasing him, Byzia. Widow Arité is right. He'll be a wonderful husband." Natalia pulled me to her level to kiss my cheek. "Some lucky girl will get to look deep in his pretty blue eyes day by day. I wish it were me."

"What?" I asked with a chuckle, enveloping her in my arms. *I'm so glad you didn't succumb to death!*

She pulled away to look in my face. "Will you?"

"Will I what, Nati?"

"Marcellus, will you marry me when I grow up? Will you marry me?"

"Natalia!" Byziana scolded.

But Nati kept her eyes on me, waiting for an answer. I smiled a half-grin and tried to laugh it off again.

"Honey, you can't marry your cousin," Arité exclaimed.

Katerina must have wanted to prolong my torture. She answered the confused woman by piping, "Oh no. He's fair game for Nati. Our grandparents were cousins, remember? No problem there." Then she added with false solemnity, "You owe my sister an answer, Marcellus."

Poor Natalia. She's serious! I sat down and took her in my lap, looking into my dear cousin's eyes with the love I had for her.

"Your offer is delightful, sweet Natalia. But I'm not ready to make that kind of commitment to you."

"Oh, I'll wait," she assured me, adding a quick nod.

I gulped and looked up. Byziana followed our conversation, a strange curiosity on her face.

I tried again. "Nati, we'll find you a great guy to marry when it's your time. Don't rush into these kinds of things. You have lots of time."

She sighed, "I know. I just wanted to get you before someone else did."

I squeezed her. "You're very sweet to say so. I love you so much, Nati. I'll always love you. But let's forget this marriage thing, okay? We've already got something really special don't we?"

She kissed my cheek. "Yes. We already and will always love each other. I'm okay with that." Hopping down, she ran off to join Justin outside.

A heavy silence hung in the air and the women kept their strange grins on me. I gulped again. *I'd better get out of here!* I slipped out of the house to join Justin. We were packed and ready to leave in an hour.

Our farewells to the widow were as difficult to me as our final farewell to Lady Sophia. Because of her, we had been a close-knit family. Because of her, we were all alive.

I placed a letter and coins for a courier in her hands. "Please make sure this gets to my mother. She must be fearful, not having heard from us since we left Mopsos."

"I shall send it tomorrow. But, Marcellus, remember to visit me on your return."

"I will, Madame, I will. Look for me in the fall." I would be glad to see her again.

As we departed, I reflected at how strange a circumstance had thrown our paths together. She, a village woman. We, high-born of Antioch. So different yet joined by faith, our hearts one in a close eternal bond.

And so we were on the road again, on the road to Constantinople. "Carry the torch!" the widow's voice echoed behind us as we walked to the main road. We waved our answer back.

The Cilicia Pass was indeed treacherous. Not so much from cliffs below you, but from the sharp ridges rising on either side of the raging river ravine. The snows had loosened the boulders, and with the melt, often man-sized stones and tree-sized avalanches slid onto the path before you. The road led alongside the water. Melting snows turned the pathway into slippery mud, which threatened at every step to launch you into the river.

It would be impossible to traverse using a cart. I had considered purchasing one. The children could ride when they tired and the donkeys could carry more of our burden. But not wanting to awaken the donkeys' pertinacious natures, I determined to continue on with bundles and feet. Now in this muck, I affirmed my decision.

We hopped over rock and stone, through avalanche snow, and still our damp feet were caked in mud by the time the sun began to go down. Along the ridge I saw a party of three bearded horsemen following a high trail. Some merchants from Susa whom we had paced all day began setting up camp. I chose a place near them.

It is always a difficult task to judge the motives and hearts of another. One in our own party, a man whom we had known for years, had robbed us. What might happen while we slept tonight was forefront on everyone's mind. Justin did not trust the foreign merchants.

"Why do we have to set up right next to them?" he argued. "If we get robbed here, they'll throw us in the river. And it'll be the end of us."

Katerina studied the men while I continued unpacking the bundles. Our safety was my responsibility, and I had made this decision. "They could kill us in our sleep," she whispered.

"Hush now. There is strength in numbers. We either have to stay near them to avoid the bandits in the hills, or we set ourselves as easy prey."

"They are looking at us!" Katerina whispered. "They'll attack us no doubt!"

"The likelihood of being robbed by these men is slim. What do we have they'd want?"

"Nothing. There is only one way we can bring relief to this tension . . . ." Byziana took us over to meet the foreigners, two younger men and a silver-bearded one.

"Hello!" Byziana threw them a sparkly-eye smile that sought to turn strangers into friends.

The younger men surveyed Byziana and Katerina, up and down. I slipped my hand into my sword hilt, but the bearded man waved his hand and the two men went back to their setting up.

The silver-bearded fellow assessed our party before cracking a smile in his beard and saying in broken Latin, "I am Kartir. Merchant. Scholar. These are my son, Amr and Bekr." The two men did not acknowledge us, but continued their work.

"Look at Captain!" Natalia whispered.

The dog's hair bristled, his teeth bared. Two large white dogs approached the merchant. They had brown muzzles and ears and were as big as lions. Captain came between us and them, hair on his back raised high, snarling and tensed to leap.

"Do not be afraid. These are precious Sarabi dog. This is Nero. This is Diocletian." The dogs stood at attention, their half-cut ears alert, listening for their master's word.

They were majestic, but deadly. I was glad when his son whistled and tossed two large bones toward the dogs, which took the canine attention away from us. The beasts wrapped their huge paws around the bones and tore away the meat.

Captain sat by me, whining and salivating at the sight.

"Roman names for your dogs?" I stared across at him. That these emperors had attacked Christians clenched dread into my heart. *Who are these men?*

"Strong names, not insult to your nation. No. No. Lion killer. Lion killer. Alexander's dog."

The names did not offend my cousin. Tilting her head and raising her eyebrows, she said, "May we pitch camp next to your camp?"

He laughed and his beard flopped on his chest. "Of course, of course. No a problem."

The men behind him grunted something in their language and snapped and clapped at ropes as they unbound their animals. Their train included seven camels and two sad-looking donkeys of their own, all overburdened.

I felt sorry for the animals, but asked leave to return to our camp. We were losing light and still had the tent to hoist and our belongings and ourselves to pack inside it. Justin and I tied and bolstered the tent while the girls worked on the meal.

The sky was pitch black when we got around the fire to eat a meager meal of toasted bread. We had packed plenty of bread.

Without warning Captain growled, hair bristling again. I stood up hand on hilt, gazing where the dog directed. Old Kartir appeared out of the darkness, in his hands a plate full of roasted meat. His generous offering and eager gestures helped us trust him. Byziana took the plate. "Thank you. You are a true friend."

Was she planting the idea or convinced of this, I was not sure. But the bearded merchant merely laughed again, hands on belly, and returned to his campsite.

"I think he is a sweet old man," said Natalia. Her trust went a long way for us. But Justin was still uncomfortable.

"Why are his sons so angry and suspicious?" he asked. "I think they're planning to rob us tonight."

"Silly goose," Byziana said. "Bandits worry them as well. They may think you a dwarf robber come to take their fine spices and eastern treasures. Have you ever thought of that?"

Justin was not moved, promising, "I'll stay up all night to fight them off." He leaned against a tree by the fire and took the tooth from the reliquary.

"Why do you keep playing with the tooth?" I asked.

"Just in case it's a relic. In case it will help."

"Are you praying to it?"

He studied it, and then said, "I don't know. I think it connects me to God. They said it's the first tooth of an infant saint."

"But Simeon is not sainted, yet. He is still alive. He cannot hear your prayers to intercede for you."

"Well, maybe it will bring us luck."

I asked to see the tiny tooth. Small dark blood bits were still visible at the root. "I'm not sure God approves of a talisman. I do not think it's taught in Scripture."

"But you are not sure?"

"No. I don't know all of Scripture. Which is why I need to study."

"Then I'll still use it. Just in case."

Byziana joined us. "Of course relics matter. The Antioch Teacher said '*the Spirit resides and inhabits the bones of saints who hearkened unto him.*' If Simeon is a saint, if the Spirit abides in him, then demons will flee from this tooth."

It was wrong, but I could not explain.

"I know it's true. The '*sun-like rays of holiness*' in that tooth blind the demons. They can't approach us, so we're safe. Just don't lose the tooth, okay?"

"Okay."

"At least promise me you will pray to God, not to the tooth."

"All right," he promised me. "You should sleep. I will stand guard."

"I think I'll stay up, too," I said.

He lasted a short hour before he fell asleep. I roused him to take him to the tent, and he did not resist.

As I took him to bed, I debated within myself.

Look at that tent, so warm with huddled bodies. Look outside. Spring mist making everything freezing cold and wet. Stay here.

No, Marcellus. Go out, stay alert. They're depending on you.

Your belly is full, the tent is perfect for sleep. There's a bite in the air out there. You've walked all day. It's time to sleep. Nice and warm . . .

My will could not resist the lure of the heated tent. So I chose to stay and sleep. *The dog will protect us . . .* my final thoughts as I trusted our deceptive strength in numbers.

The Merchant's Gift

You would think by this point I would accept we were going to Constantinople, I would accept Byziana's fate, or else I would try with all my might to stop her journey.

The fact is, each day as I awakened my only thought was that day alone. I did what I had to do that day and hoped for the best. I was with the children to bring them to their father.

I hoped against hope the two would not marry, but I knew Gaius Justus. He was not to be crossed, and he was a man of power. Belisarius would fight for it, too. Belisarius was chosen, Belisarius it would be. The Pater's doomed decision.

The roaring river, chirping morning birds and donkey haws awakened me. Soft murmurs in the distance came from the merchant family. I stretched my long arms and legs and got out of bed. Everyone else was still asleep, so I crept out of our close quarters. I would start the fire, begin our morning meal preparations, then awaken them. We had a long journey ahead of us, and rest was essential to make it through these mountains by sundown.

I opened the tent flap to a sorry scene. One of our donkeys had died in the night and Captain the dog was nowhere in sight. Merchant Kartir and his sons had doused their fire and were moving toward the trail, camels and donkeys packed. The merchant waved at me when I looked down the road.

What'll I do with this donkey? Worse, what about our luggage? We're down to one pack-animal.

I set the thoughts aside and put wood on the smoldering fire. The wood we cut the night before was still damp from its snow-logged winter, so it made much smoke and little heat. I filled our water crock and put it on the fire to heat.

Justin came out of the tent, stretching. When he found the dead beast, his proceeding yell awoke the girls. "What happened to our donkey!"

He ran toward the animal and touched it.

"It must've frozen to death," Byziana said with a gasp, looking at me horrified. Her hand covered her mouth. *Does she realize it could have been us frozen on the mountains?*

"How great a punishment we bear, Marcellus," she said.

"Things like this happen in life."

"More so in our lives. God's wrath seems unfairly against us."

I did not want a repeat of her breakdown over the Psalms. "Byziana, this is not God's ill favor. Have you ever considered how big He is? His wrath could not be borne by any man." A pounding in my heart and a gripping in my gut overwhelmed me. I grabbed my chest and scanned the road in terror. I surveyed the surrounding cliffs. *Are we about to be attacked?*

"What's wrong?" she asked. "What's happening?" She followed my gaze.

"I feel uneasy. Like we are in serious danger." I calmed my anxiety with deep breaths.

"Of course we are. It is our continual state." When she was sure no one was on the cliffs, she joined Katerina stoking the fire.

My clenched gut stayed as we packed up camp. The girls prepared our meals, boiling a chunk of meat for breakfast and a broth for our noontime meal. But the fire was low and smoky. It would take a while.

"We'll have to carry things on our backs. Things we cannot carry we leave behind," I said.

"My pack's too heavy." Katerina's eyes scanned the sharp jagged cliffs rising above this narrow river canyon. "Will we ever make it out of these dreadful mountains?"

"I can see why this place is called a Gate," said Justin. "If bandits wanted to keep people from passing, they'd blockade them right here." He watched his sisters and his eyes twinkled as he added, "I'll bet they're up there right now."

"What?"

"Oh no!"

I scanned the cliffs but saw no sign of the riders I had seen yesterday. "Justin, don't scare your sisters," I said. "It does no good."

"But it's fun to see them squirm."

"It is not right for a man to frighten women." I frowned at him until he acquiesced, then I pulled Byziana aside. "This won't be easy. We need to divide up our baggage."

"I'll take care of it," she said.

"Katerina, you and I shall empty the tent. Hurry now. Natalia, you clean up and pack up the food. Justin, you and Marcellus care for the animals and then roll up the tent when we're done inside." She looked around. "Where's the dog?"

I shrugged my shoulders. I had no idea.

"Captain!" she called. Katerina and Natalia joined her in the search.

"When did the merchants leave?" asked Justin.

"They'd just started off when I got up this morning. I wonder why they got such an early start. They may know something about these mountains we don't." I scanned the cliffs. "We'd better hurry. We should've been gone before now, too."

Justin and I fed the donkey. Captain could not be found so the girls came back. The tent was rolled, all our possessions sorted, many things left behind, with the hope new ones could be picked up at the next village. Losing the donkey also cost in the loss of those supplies, which annoyed me to no end.

Just before we left, Natalia called out. "Marcellus, come here." She was petting the dead donkey's nose. I went to her side. She held up a sliced rope. "I don't think this is our donkey. Over there that's Luka. I named him for my silly friend in Antioch. This is supposed to be Giluki, but it's not. I know that Giluki had a big brown spot under his chin right here that I used to scratch for him and he loved it. But this donkey doesn't have that spot."

She showed me the rope. The cut end did not match the dead animal's halter rope. Byziana and I exchanged a worried look, and our eyes went to the path the merchants had taken. *Could it be true?*

"Would they've done this to us? Why? Why'd they cripple us like this?" Byziana asked.

"It will be okay. Step back. Take a breath."

"Better them than us, I suppose they figured," said Justin.

They knew they could not have divvied up their possessions onto their already-burdened beasts. They assumed our possessions were not as important. Nor our lives.

"I told you not to trust them."

The enormity of our neighbor's crime hit me fist in gut. I had never felt so betrayed, even when Trolius left us. This duplicity was worse. Here we were crippled in the middle of nowhere.

Yet I did not want the others to be discouraged, so I cleared my throat. "Let us not blame anyone, but let us trust ourselves to God who will judge the thieves, and who will, by His mercy, give us strength for our journey."

Byziana did not accept my proposal. "You are wrong. God is punishing us. Even the Psalter tells us this." Her eyes darted up the trail and along the mountain tops. "I said it before, I say it again. He is angry with us because of you-know-what. I wonder what He will throw at us next."

I did not have the energy to disagree. Why did no one blame me? *Falling asleep made it my fault.* "Justin, give her the tooth."

She took the tooth and tied the reliquary around her neck, making a sign of the cross and kissing it. At least the tooth stopped the debate.

After we packed camp, we huddled in the late morning mist and ate the boiled meat and tack-hard bread from Widow Arité.

Then we tied our bundles to our backs and to the lone donkey and, burdened in spirit and body, traversed again down the muddy, mucky road.

Our Circle of Fire

As far as I could recall from maps I had seen, this road continued northeast up and over the mountains. We should spot villages as we came out of the Gates, then the road led up to the northwest between Nyssa and the Salt Sea, past a town called Tyana, and on to Ancyra. If we so desired, we could detour to Caesarea, but this added two days to a journey which had already taken months too long.

We plodded along and had made little progress by the time the sun was straight above us.

"Can we eat while we walk?" I asked. "We need to keep moving."

Groans and whines echoed over the party.

"We must stop."

"I am so exhausted."

"Let's rest. Please. Just a bit."

"Will this valley never end?" Katerina moaned, collapsing onto a log in rebellion. She lifted her foot and rubbed it. "These shoes don't fit. My feet are blistered." Byziana stopped the donkey.

She took out ointment, courtesy of Widow Arité, and rubbed it on the blister.

"I am starving," Justin dropped next to his sister. "Give me food. Now!"

I scanned the forested mountains ahead of us and the elongating shadows, my anxiety increasing. The bearded riders observed us from the top of the cliffs to our right. I bit my lip, peeking at the others. Justin noticed the men and his eyes met mine. I smiled to reassure him but my gut buckled. *We've got to master these mountains before dark.*

The drudgery of seeing the same scenery over and over made even me lose hope of ever getting through. But we needed to put distance between us and those men. "We can stop for a short time. We'll sleep tonight, but now we need to walk more than we ever have walked or we'll lose the sun." I scanned the crest, but they were gone.

"I am too tired already," cried Katerina. "Our tent was so warm last night. Why can't we put the tent up here and sleep? It looks safe."

Justin yawned and lay prostrate on the ground. "Sounds good."

"This will be a very, very brief stop." Byziana lowered the broth-filled bladders. "Everyone, drink some of this, and put bread in your pocket to eat as we walk. You can drink from the stream as you need. But we've got to walk. I'm not staying another night in this valley."

The others complained and begged until she snapped, "What if we lose another donkey to the cold wind?" This encouraged them to keep moving for another hour or two. I had thought the canyon dreary and difficult. But that was before we saw the long steep road going up the mountain.

"We'll never make it up the mountain!"

"Hush, Kata. We will and we must."

"What happened to the valley?"

"Can we not go between the mountains?"

"No," I said. "This is the well-worn trail. We stick to it, for better or for worse."

"I'm sure it will be for worse."

"Hush, Katerina."

We tramped toward a snowy crest while the sun threatened to descend behind the cliffs. Once the sun left us, the mountain heights would be freezing.

"Stop, everyone. Put on your warmest layers," I said.

"No!"

"Oh, please. Noooo . . ." Katerina's whine reached my bones. Natalia's face mirrored the sentiments of her sister and brother.

"Do as Marcellus says." Byziana ignored their protests. "It

will be less weight on your backs, and it will keep you alive i
n the snow."

"Let's leave heavy things here. Take things off the donkey."
Katerina walked over to the pack animal. "Like. . . why do we need
this box of Scrolls? It weighs a ton."

"It's true, we don't really need the Trunk," said Justin. Each
cousin shifted uncomfortably but I know my eyes narrowed and
my teeth ground together.

"If you want to take it off the donkey, be my guest," I
snapped. "But if you decide the donkey cannot carry the Trunk, I
will strap it to my back with everything else I'm carrying."

"Cousin Marcellus, we won't do that to you," Natalia came
to my side and stroked my forearm. "Don't make your face red. I
don't like it." She patted me again and begged of Katerina. "Please
stop fighting. We are okay with these burdens, aren't we, Sister?"

Katerina shrugged and looked ahead of us. "Are there bears
in the hills?" she asked. No one answered. Her shoulders hunched,
and she wailed. "Oooh. Not bears, too! God is against us!"

"If He were," I tried to reason, "we'd have died in Antioch."

She was silent as an answer. Thus we began our uphill
march. Twinkling stars appeared, small lights in the sky blinking
in guileless, deceitful peace.

"Just remember the list in Hebrews we read about—the
saints of old who lived through difficulties, and whose names are
listed among the faithful. Wouldn't you wish to be listed
among them?"

"They had to die to be on that list," said Justin. "No thanks."

"They all died, of course. But they didn't all die because of
their faith. They died in faith. Abraham's on the list, he died an
old man."

We had left too late in the morning, and we needed to continue walking, though night had come. We trudged slower than
usual, now moving uphill. But I would not let them stop, come blister or twisted ankle.

Then Byziana pulled me to a halt. "I understand your hurry,
but if you push us like this today, tomorrow we'll be in too much
pain to move at all. The higher we go, the more snow."

"Can we try to make it to the crest, Byziana? Please?" If only

I could find a niche, a cave, anything safe to protect us from the beasts which could come into our camp, to hide from those bandits. With Captain gone I feared for the sole donkey we had left, more than that, I feared for our own lives. No use explaining all these direful reasons. "I think it will be a better start tomorrow if we mostly have to move downhill."

She noted my urgency and agreed without complaint.

The full moon in the sky shone between tree shadows upon the path. Plodding on, plodding on. We seem to make no headway, the top of the mountain always just as far away.

"Aaaaagh! Wolf" Natalia's scream froze us in our tracks. "Something ran next to me! Wolf! Wolf! Marcellus, help!" She threw herself into my waist.

Katerina hid behind Byziana and we pressed into a tight huddle. The torch I held above our heads shone barely enough to light up our own little circle. We stood back to back, donkey at my side.

All around us was silent.

We waited.

And nothing happened.

I relaxed and patted Natalia on her cheek. "You must been mistaken."

She looked at me in horror. "But I saw . . ."

"Katerina, did you see anything?" I asked.

"Maybe. I'm not sure."

"It's nothing. Hush now, Nati," Byziana said. "You imagined it."

"I thought I saw something."

"It's late. Your mind can play tricks in the dark sometimes. Especially with that flickering torch in front of us. Let's go, Marcellus."

Breathing out relief, I pulled the donkey's harness and took a step. The donkey braced its legs, refusing to follow.

"Oh no, donkey. You'll do what I say." I pulled again at its lead. "We will not be controlled by you."

But it would not budge.

Byziana patted my arm frenetically.

I looked at her, about to speak, but her wide eyes silenced me. I flicked my attention to the road and my heart about stopped. The largest wolf I had ever seen blocked our way. Brown with streaks of gray. Yellow eyes stayed on me.

I stepped between my cousins and the wolf, handing the donkey's lead to Byziana. She wrapped it around her arm. The wolf lowered its head and sniffed the air between us. In a slow movement, I pulled my sword from its sheath. The sound of metal sliding against metal echoed into the trees.

A movement to our left drew my attention. Another wolf stepped out from between the trees, lowered its head and sniffed the air, eyes turning to the wolf before us. Katerina let out a soft squeak and pushed tighter toward me and Byziana.

"Oh no! There's two more on this side," Byziana's almost-silent whisper informed me.

"And behind us," peeped Justin.

I kept my eyes on the lead wolf, put my shoulders back and stood as tall as I could.

"Go away, now!" I shouted, swinging the torch toward the wolves.

The fur on the large wolf's back bristled. Its snout curled and a deep growl echoed across the mountain path.

His eyes lingered on Natalia at my side.

"Tighter, everyone," I said. They squeezed between me and the donkey. The other wolves whined and paced around an invisible circle surrounding us, waiting for the lead wolf.

"Go away," I stomped toward the wolf with the torch.

"Don't leave us in darkness!" Katerina shrieked, grabbing my sword arm.

"Let go of him, Kata. What are you thinking?"

How could I protect everyone? I could only be in one place. And we had only one torch. The wolf shifted its stance, its shoulder to me. Eyeing me.

If I could kill this wolf, the others might run off in fear. Or they might not. Should I leave my cousins in darkness—to fight the wolves with the torch? Should I leave my cousins with light—to fight the wolves in darkness with my sword? Either way, they would attack.

I should draw the wolves out of sight. *Six wolves. Could I take on six?* Would they all follow me? Or would the wolf pack target the children when I left them?

I imagined blood-drenched snow awaiting me when I returned, and more hungry beasts turning their yellow eyes and blood-dripped teeth on me. Breathing in courage, I lifted my chin.

My heart raced and I felt made of steel. *You will die, wolf.*

"Use this to fight them off if they come for you," I said, handing the torch to Byziana, who now held the torch and the donkey.

"We need you."

"Don't leave us!"

An animal darted across the road, followed by an even larger one. Sounds of snarling and scuffling. The attack had begun.

The donkey hawed and yawled and tugged and would have bolted had I not grabbed its halter with my free hand.

"God, help us," I called to heaven.

I tried to fight off thoughts of the sharp teeth and yellow eyes of the attacking wolves. "Hold to the torch, everyone!" I whispered.

What was that Psalm? Something about a shepherd and the valley of death. But I could not remember. I could only place myself between my cousins and the beasts.

"Oh!" Without an explanation, Justin pulled away and ran out into the trees toward the wild animals. The head wolf ran after him, and the other wolves disappeared.

"Nooo!"

"What are you doing?"

"Justin, come back!"

Katerina collapsed to the ground, and Natalia stood frozen in her spot staring out into the darkness. Byziana held my arm in a death-grip. Then came Justin's screams.

Blood, teeth, glowing eyes. Thoughts assailed me. *Oh, Justin! Oh, God. Kyrie Eleison.* Terrible gnashing growls came from the woods. Justin screamed at the top of his lungs. We heard the sound of heavy weight pummeling to the ground. And Justin's screams were silenced.

"They are eating my brother!" Katerina wailed.

"Marcellus, do something! Save him!"

A muffled beastly growl came from the forest, and another whimpery-sound from poor Justin. "He must still be alive! Let me go!"

I tried to pull away from the girls, reaching for the torch. Byziana groaned as she handed me the fire. "I have his reliquary! Oh poor boy! My poor baby brother."

I was pulling out of her grasp, when Justin ran across the road, laughing and spinning, as if the middle of spring!

I watched in bewilderment.

"That was fantastic! Amazing!" he yelled.

Behind him, leaping and barking, came our Captain leading a lion-like beast.

Justin ran toward us. "It's Captain! He found us! Captain and the merchant's dog!"

The merchant's dog?

"You should have seen them tear into that big wolf. I think three are dead, the others ran off."

The wolves dead?

Wave after wave of gratefulness, of relief flooded over me. I fell to my knees. *Thank you, Christ! You saved us!*

Everyone else collapsed to the ground. Byziana did not release her hold on me, but slipped her arm through mine and leaned against my shoulder there.

She closed her eyes and breathed out a relieved sound, carrying in it the tension and sorrows and pains of the past two days, of the past four months. She pressed herself into the crook of my shoulder.

I saw her so close at my side, and the world stopped. The motions of people and beasts around me froze in silence and darkness. There was no mountain, no snow, no moon in the sky. There was only the torchlight circle on me and Byzia with her cheek on my shoulder.

The warmth of our cottage days, her handing me a Scroll, the laughter of our winter nights together. The brush of her robe on the mosaics those many years ago, her weaving among the guests, the smile on her face. Her arms up above her head on Silpius, looking out at Antioch. Her cradling the head of Thomas to give him water. These thoughts swirled in my heart as she held my arm and rested on my shoulder.

They say love comes naturally. It was simple. I reached my arm around to embrace her, putting my face to her hooded head. She did not resist, but leaned into my chest, so I nuzzled closer, breathing in her perfume, the mix of sweat and ointment. My cheek rested on her hair, her heat radiating on my face. I lifted my warm hand to her cold cheek for one brief moment, and she welcomed it.

And that moment froze in time, a circle of fire running through me and her and me and her. I felt it. An indomitable igneous bolt of lightning. *What won't I do for her? I will fight any army, kill any beast, endure any pain to keep her safe.*

She leans against me.

She trusts me.

I will live up to her trust.

I will prove my faithfulness. I will prove it all.

But the moment vaporized, a flood of movement dissolved it like salt in the sea. Katerina ran from the dogs back toward us, "I need the tor—" Then she stopped stock-still looking from Byziana to me and back to Byziana.

Byziana gasped and let go of me, leaping up, rushing away. I became a blur of mind and sight and heart. Something had happened in me. That undeniable fire circle burned and possessed me. *I don't know what this means for me, for her, for her future. But I know what I want.*

Justin called out. "You've got to see this dog. She is perfect." Standing up was difficult, for my muscles reminded me how much we had walked today. I sought Byziana, but she was helping Katerina unpack the tent.

The other dog was indeed one of the merchant's lion-killers. Was it Nero or Diocletian, I know not. But I would not use the name.

The demonesque beast faced Justin bending its front paws, waving its branch-like tail. Then it barked. The sound sent fear into my deepest part. Deep, heavy, strong, powerful. And this in play!

"Maybe you shouldn'y sport with this dog. It seems…" My words fell on deaf ears.

Next thing I saw, the white dog was wrestling Justin to the ground. Captain wagged his tail, also barking at the ruckus.

"Marcellus! He's getting attacked! Help him," Katerina begged, running over.

"No! No! It knows I'm a friend. Plus, it's not using its teeth," laughed Justin. "It's joining our pack."

The interchange amazed me, the dog's presence a true miracle. While Captain was a good protector against people—meaning he could bark a warning to us and against thieves who might hesitate—Captain still was a medium-sized dog. Compared with this beast, Captain was small.

This dog, on the other hand, was a shepherd, a protector, a wolf-killer. I took no qualms setting up camp here if I could keep the dog around camp. I tied Captain to a tree, hoping his presence would keep the other from wandering, thankful the two dogs had formed an attraction.

Natalia called the sweet-natured animal Sarabi, and the dog noted her tenderness. It never left her side. I can still see the small girl, her hand stretched over the gentle giant's back, a dog thrice her size, as it escorted her to and fro until she went to bed.

"Do you think they stole Captain?" Justin asked.

"I doubt it. Captain'd never let himself be taken. He probably ran off with that she-dog late in the night."

I wonder if the merchants made it through the mountains. What if they are close by? They could even be at the hill's crest. "I am glad the dogs arrived when they did. Looks like they'll be staying around."

We finished setting up camp, then stoked the fire large, and I scraped snow away from the base of a tree so I could sleep outside.

Byziana came over and sat by me, the warmth of her leg touching mine. *Put your arm around her, Marcellus. Smell her hair again.* Oh, did I want it! It ate me inside.

In the silence the pulsating hiss and crack of the dancing fire relaxed us. I rotated my shoulders to release the tension I had been carrying. A sound echoed from the darkness to my ear. A cough. A laugh. Nearby. *Is it the merchants? Other travelers? Those bandits? God have mercy. Kyrie Eleison.*

Byziana reached into her robe, and took out the necklace, and the tooth from its reliquary, looking at it for a while, saying nothing.

Justin asked for the necklace back. "Marcellus says not to pray to it," he said.

"I was not praying to it. Just thinking about it. Do you think it protected us, Marcellus?"

"How could it protect us, Byziana?" I asked, picking up a rock. "This rock can only protect me if I throw it, but I have to be the one to send it to flight. How can a tooth protect us? Is it conscious that it sends a message to God? Is it a receptacle of God's power that scares away demons?"

"All I meant was, do you think it helps?"

"How can it help? Do you mean does it have magical powers?"

"Spiritual powers. *'Rays of light.'*"

"Because it's the 'tooth of an infant saint'?"

"Exactly."

How could it have any power? How could God look any different on that tooth than He did on my tooth or my hand? Simeon was a boy, committed to stand for life on a pillar. I was a young man, committed to stand for God for life.

What was the difference? Did it have power? Was Simeon unique and special in God's sight, more than I was? After all, I used my life to carry burdens up mountains, not to stand on pillars.

"I do not know," I said. *How can I explain all these thoughts? Maybe God wants us to stand on pillars.*

"God protects us. If He uses a tooth or a dog, I do not know. But it's God we have to pray to. It is God who will protect us."

Byziana glanced at the dogs lying by me, then our eyes met, and that moment—our moment—flooded to my mind. I caught my breath. *Here she is right by me. That fire burns my heart. Is she thinking it as well?* I felt my eyes narrow onto her and my breathing quicken. I lifted my arm, to embrace her again. But she leapt up and slipped into her tent.

Captain slept with his head on my lap, and large warm Sarabi leaned against my leg. My hand went to Captain's back, and I slept, thinking of Byzia's head on my shoulder.

Fickle Hearts

"Give that back!" The words woke me from a deep sleep. I was outside, bundled and cozy. Someone had layered blankets over me as I slept, the heat of the dogs no longer warming my side. The noise came from Justin playing a tugging game with Sarabi.

My early-morning eyes blinked to take in the camp. Up and moving.

"Why didn't you wake me earlier?" I asked no one in particular.

"You have no worried-eyebrows when you're sleeping, that's why." Byziana's voice floated into my heart like a choir of heavenly angels. We looked at each other and the fire-circle pounded in my heart. I wanted her near me.

"Good morning, Byzia," I smiled.

"Good morning, Cousin," she said, stressing the word.

Cousin?

A rush of sensations flooded over me as if she had fist-struck me.

My hand went to my forehead. What was this? I shook my head. No.

I searched her face. "Cousin?" I opened my palms to her, welcoming an explanation. What was last night? She returned my question empty-eyed, then walked away, avoiding me, twisting her ring.

Cousin? Was I not a man, Marcellus? Could I not be a lover? Was I merely a distant cousin? A brother? Then why had she embraced me? Who had covered me with blankets?

Natalia came over to give me a hug. "Good morning, dear Cousin." My little cousin using the word comforted my heart, her words were as dear to me as if she had called me brother.

Until last night, Byziana could call me cousin. But after that . . . that . . . inexplicable communication on this mountain top, cousin was unacceptable. It was distance.

Then I felt it—a free-falling in my heart as if a giant tree reaching the heavens had been chopped and fell and fell and fell to the ground.

I understood.

She wore his ring. She was betrothed. She had embraced me as a brother.

I was mistaken.

About everything. About the fire-circle.

She was betrothed. And wore his ring. I should accept my role as her guardian, her dog, taking her safely to her father. She would be wife to that man.

I pulled my thoughts and heartbreak into check. Channeling those feelings into action, I pushed the others to a quick start. My tongue was sharper than usual, I regret to say.

The mist covered our way, but the trail, having been used for centuries, was wide enough to not completely lose. From my estimates when we got to mountain crest we would look down on the Cappadocian plains beneath us.

I had heard of Cappadocia. Not only because our ancestors, the illustrious Gregory of Nyssa and Basil the Great, had lived there, but also because of the amazing natural architecture, the soft stone mountains and small stone hillocks people had made into cave homes.

Within an hour we reached the crest. As we came around the path before us which would show the end of this mountain trek, we froze in place, for below was not a lush plain. A narrow valley of small hills lay before us with hints of another giant, cloud-covered mountain along the valley's far edge.

"This is not it?" Katerina gasped.

"Another mountain? Must we climb yet another mountain?" Justin slapped his hand to his leg.

We lost the will to continue. If not for the biting weather, we would have stopped longer. Yet walking kept our clothes warm, stopping made the layered wet cloth cold again. Heavy clouds above the mountain threatened to rain on us, sending shivers to our bones. And yet we went on.

We trudged downhill, leaving the snow-line and cloud-line behind us. About midday we lunched at the valley center. The winter of the mountain merged with spring in this green place. The clouds dissipated, and the hazy sky above outlined the dreaded mountain at the far edge of the pass. But at least the beauty of spring met us, surrounding us with the hope of cheer.

Spring bulbs bloomed in rich purples and deep pinks. "I wish my robe was this color." Natalia tucked two flowers behind her ears. "Wouldn't it be lovely if we could make a garment with these petals?"

"You are already so beautiful, my dear," I said. "Your rosy face would outshine any petal you wore."

"Not to mention your clothes would fall apart right away. *'Like the lilies of the field,'* doesn't it say in Scripture?" Justin added.

Tying his bundle onto his back, he ran ahead with the dogs. Next to us a stream rushed snow water. Swirling eddies splashed countless bulb sprouts along the shore.

Happy bird chirps sounded from the valley's trees and vultures swirled in the center of the meadow. We followed the streamside trail when we stopped at Justin hurtling back toward us.

"Hurry, hurry! You won't believe it." We found that which the vultures circled.

"Giluki! Darling Giluki," Natalia cried. For on the ground lay our lost donkey.

We all recognized the creature now. Fear gleamed as the whites of its eyes looking back at us larger than ever. Sarabi barked at it, but Captain sniffed it then led the larger dog away. Natalia's touch made Giluki lay its head on the ground. I felt the leg. It would not soon mend.

"Is it broken?" Byziana asked, kneeling close to me.

"I do not think so. It's swollen. Twisted in a rut in the road. Must've been pushed too hard with too much baggage."

"How sad."

I tried to concentrate on the donkey, but Byzia's closeness fogged my thoughts and pumped my heart. I jumped up and looked around. "There is no baggage left behind. Those poor other beasts, even more overburdened."

"Sweet Giluki." Natalia stroked its mane and kissed its cheek, then scratched the spot under its chin. "How can we make him well? If we can heal him, he will carry our bags again. And you'd like that, wouldn't you dear Giluki?"

Byziana searched the baggage for binding cloth. I stopped her, hand on hers. "We cannot take the animal. You know it."

She stopped rummaging and peeked back at the donkey. My heart caressed her face. *It had been so soft.* Her cheeks and nose so delicate, so cold on my hand. Her scent intoxicating. I still felt the same purpose in me, to protect her, to love her. *Why does she call me cousin?*

She blushed, pulling her hand from under mine. "But my sister has her heart set on it."

She lifted her eyes to mine, and I saw it. The spark. She said as if she were out of breath, "I know. The lame animal will hinder us. It will never bear a burden."

She fuddled with the baggage again. I stood facing her.

"Byzia . . .?" Could she not feel it? I waited. She must acknowledge it. Our moment.

But she would not turn. She twisted and twisted that ring instead. What else could I say? I gave up and left.

As the vultures continued circling overhead, I explained what we had to do. "I'm sorry to have to say this, friends, but there's only one way to help Giluki."

Natalia cried when she knew we had to kill her pet. Everyone understood the impending terror of predators and scavengers. She gave her farewells, whispering her love into its ear, then stood up, face full of tears. She would not watch. I wished the task had not fallen to me.

"I hate death." No one responded to Natalia. They hoisted their bundles and continued down the road.

The deed over, I caught up with them, not pointing out the vultures diving a few minutes later. We walked for another hour in this meadow valley before a delightful surprise met us—a fork in the road. Yes, a path led up into the mountains before us. But a separate path led west through the curving mountain pass to the plains of Central Anatolia. And this way was our way out! We did not have to climb another mountain. We only need follow this valley. The contagious relief renewed our energy.

We entered the flatlands while the sun was still high in the sky. And we flew to the closest village, finding a good inn and opening the door with sighs and gasps of relief.

The jocund innkeeper opened his arms to us. "Welcome, welcome!"

After a while, "I am surprised to see such young travelers so soon in the season," he said as he served our well-earned hot feast of stewed lamb and beets, fresh greens, melt-in-your-mouth hot bread, and crunchy red apples.

We took to the food like a fish takes to water, diving in with joy, not speaking a word until our bowls were empty and stomachs full. "Well, we made it." I smiled at Byziana, leaning back. My hands behind my head. Satisfied by life. Satisfied by our great accomplishment. We had not died in the Cilician Gate. "We are not abandoned by God."

Her eyes turned dark, and her glee sobered. "Why is it you always have to bring up that old quarrel?"

"What old quarrel? I only meant we survived!"

"You're not always right."

I looked at the tablecloth and my finger traced the pattern. *We survived! Our Shepherd protected us! What is going in her mind?* With our stomachs full and our lives intact, we had our whole life before us. Why was she accusing me of starting an argument?

Justin, Katerina, Natalia. No one took my eye. No one was on my side. Not even Natalia.

How is it you do your best to think of others, to help them, and then they throw your kindness back in your face like mud?

I closed my eyes, hoping the temperature of her accusation would go down.

"You cannot ignore this, Marcellus. You are pushing the Chalcedon point of view on me at every point you can."

My eyes shot open. *Chalcedon? Of course I want to persuade her. But what did I say? Only that we were safe.*

"Why are you so afraid of it?" I said. "It's like you think this whole debate is one of those African snakes that wrap around and around, tightening the life out of its prey. All you want to do is kill it."

"If it's killing me. . . "

I gritted my teeth. *God, how can I ever keep my word to Lady Sophia?*

If you have ever loved someone, really loved someone, you must have also been hurt by that person. When we open our hearts to love, the edges of the openness are raw and easily pained, because love is tender. Just last night she had spoken by her silent embrace. And now this one I swore I would die for was stoning me herself. *Why is she pushing me away?*

Natalia had stood up by her chair, glancing from me to her sister, trying to decide whom to comfort.

"Hey," Justin interjected, drawing the inn owner's attention away from our argument. "Are we not near to Cappadocia?"

"Yes, young sir." The landlord was eager to interrupt the tension. "You are nearer than you used to be. You follow the road out of town toward the northwest, west through the river valley, and then at the crossroads, straight north. You should be there by nightfall."

"I'm tired of walking." Natalia was never one to whine, but this was a bona fide whine.

Katerina lifted her foot in her hands. "My feet hurt."

Glad for the redirected conflict, I stood. "I'd love to visit Cappadocia, to see the old caves of Gregory and Basil, to see the famous cave churches, to touch a chimney stone. But another time. It's out of our way."

I left the room. Though the servants at the inn had cared for our donkey and dogs, we still needed to unpack our luggage and get arranged in our accommodations.

Byziana followed me out, hands on her hips. "Do you plan on forcing us on tomorrow?" Being near her like this hurt me and I turned my back, still not speaking.

"Answer me. We must talk about this."

I scratched my eyebrow and shook my head, wishing to rid my head of her voice. *I know we can't travel tomorrow. We pushed ourselves too far. I understand. But why are you talking like I won't be sympathetic. This is not fair.* I did not wish for a confrontation. I attempted to turn away again, but she gripped my arm.

"Marcellus, you are being unreasonable." I looked down at her hand on my forearm, her nails piercing my skin.

"You are right. We should rest for a day or two," I said. The words came from somewhere, perhaps from a wisdom that had been growing in me over the years, perhaps from my desire for her to be happy. They worked like tonic for her ailment. Or so I thought.

Our Separate Ways

We all went to bed early that night. I awoke with a song in my heart. We would not be walking.

Rest day!

My own cramped legs needed relief, so I stayed in bed even after Justin got up. We would have a day to rest, which was all my weary body and soul wanted in life.

Byziana knocked, then came from the girls' room into my room and saw me propped up in bed, reading a Scroll aloud. I assessed her, afraid of attack. Would she still be in her foul mood of yesterday?

"We need to talk." She closed the door behind her, looking at me with raised eyebrows. Fear grew in me. What happened to her? She was a ball of nerves.

"Yes?" I said, holding my finger on my place in the Scroll.

She waited, clearing her throat. Then she played with that ring of hers. "I must remind you I am a betrothed young woman."

So, she wanted to discuss this.

"I know that, Byziana."

"Then treat me as such."

"I see." I sat up taller, then motioned to the edge of the bed. "Would you like to have a seat?"

She straightened her robe around herself, then sat down and folded her hands in her lap.

"You are talking about what happened on the mountain."

She nodded.

We will talk. I felt a tug of our pulley drawing us together. *We will talk. Perhaps she will yet be persuaded.*

"I know you are engaged. I know your father wants you to

wed Belisarius. This is why we've gone through all of this." I flicked my thumb toward the road we had come. "And are you sure you want to?"

"What kind of question is that? It is my pater's will. What will all of Antioch say of me if I breathe one word against this?"

My eyes narrowed on her. "You are right. What am I asking?"

She kept her attention on her hands. "You are asking if I'll go against my pater."

"What is it you want?"

A quiet settled over the room. I felt a rush from my rebellious challenge. *Will she stand against her father? Can our relationship take the place of the one with Belisarius? Does she care enough?*

She looked down at her hands, studying them, chewing the inside of her lip.

"I want Belisarius," she said at length.

My thoughts returned to our last night on the mountain, her embrace, her head on my shoulder. "You want Belisarius?" I repeated, surprised at her answer. Breathless. *She wants Belisarius, and she had put her arm through mine, she had covered me with blankets.*

"Yes."

She wants him, not me? That man. Has he ever treated her with respect? Has he done anything but dishonor her in public? Had she not squirmed away from his rude grasp at their first introduction?

"Fine then." I crossed my arms over my chest.

She wants that man. She prefers that man.

She can have that man, and all he is.

She can do what her father commands. My eyes burned with the injustice of it.

"Fine then," she repeated, chewing the inside of her cheek. "So then Marcellus, the thing that happened on the mountain. Don't let it happen again."

"Don't let it happen again? You want me to not let it happen again!"

She nodded her head up and down.

"Yes. Just don't do that again."

I would not accept the responsibility alone.

"Okay. And you. Don't do that again, either!"

She looked up at me. "Okay." Her chest started to heave and

her bottom lip quivered. *Oh, Byzia.*

I moved toward her and took her to my heart once more. "It will be okay, Byzia. It will be okay."

"I have to marry him." She sniffed and wiped her tears.

"I understand."

My arms were around her, my face on her forehead, her cheek on my chest.

"I must marry him. If I do not do what my pater asks, the whole system will collapse. The Pater makes the decisions, and we trust the Pater."

"Shh. I will take care of you. I will take you to your father. Everything will be fine. Don't you worry."

I stroked her cheek with my thumb, wiping away her tears.

"It all fell down. Our whole life. Everything gone. And then we had no money, and all I have is this ring. Our family depends on the ring."

"I understand."

I stroked her cheek, and my face was against her sweet smelling hair. Our fire-circle burned from me to her and me to her. *Doesn't she feel it?*

"Marcellus . . ." she said when her tears stopped.

I held her warm body against mine, enjoying the boiling over of my heart.

"You . . . are . . . letting it happen again."

I let go of her, my hands up and away from her. "I apologize."

She wiped her face with her hands and took a deep breath.

"So you are going to marry Belisarius."

She nodded.

I squeezed my lips together. *That man. And all he is. It does not equate.* I gathered my rejected heart in a ball and pressed it down. Deep down. Either that or I would explode.

The Pater, I reminded myself. *No rebellion against the Pater. It will be the way Gaius Justus planned.* I tried not to hate my uncle. Yet the pressure would not stay down. My rejected heart demanded recompense. *I was a man tied hand and foot, thrown over a waterfall. If she will do as Gaius Justus willed, then I will do as Gaia Sophia wished. Chalcedon, Emmilia and the Trunk.*

"Then I need to ask you a question. Promise not to get angry."

Oh, she will get angry.

"Okay, I'll not get angry."

"Do you think the Scrolls will be safe at Belisarius's house?"

"What?"

"Will they be safe?" What I meant was more than that.

"Of course they will. Why would they not be?"

"It would be a shame, that is all. If they were lost, or given to the monasteries."

"I will be reading them. How could I give them away?"

I doubted she could predict what her future held. He would not value the Scrolls.

My heart beat irregularly, achy. *She wants Belisarius. After all we've been through.*

"I do believe in them, you know," she added.

"I know."

"They are our Scriptures, too. Not merely those of Chalcedonians."

It was "them" and "us" again.

"I suppose so." My nose crinkled and fists tightened.

"They are indeed, Marcellus. Ours is the same faith. We merely define God differently."

Warning bells came.

Be quiet. Do not say another word. Hold her again. When she was in my arms, all of these conflicts disappeared into that flame we shared.

But wisdom fled and shame burned in me, for she preferred Belisarius. So I fueled another fire, to hurt her. Vengeance is never a good reason to use Scripture.

"Defining God differently makes it a different God," I declared, lifting my chin high. When I got into the realm of the mind, I could douse the realm of the heart.

"I am sorry, but your God cannot relate to weakness, not really. If He cannot relate with us, how could Christ have taken our place? The Epistle to the Hebrews says—"

"That is not true. He can understand for He knows all things."

"He would not know what temptation is like."

"Why must He know?"

"To be our high priest."

Perhaps it would make sense to her if I showed her from the Scrolls. "There is a verse a little further down in this letter to the Corinthians . . ." I pulled the Scroll to my lap and opened it to find those words. But my hope was premature.

She stopped me with her hand on the Scroll. "I am a Monophysite. Why does this offend you?"

It offends me because Belisarius is Monophysite. And then the horrible image came to my mind. *She will be in Belisarius's arms, he will be touching her face.* A jealous rage pulsed in my gut.

And so I hurt her, the one I loved. I chose to hurt her by speaking blunt thoughtless words. And after I hurt her, my life was never the same.

"I believe it is false. No, not that I believe it so. It is false. It contradicts Scripture."

Mine was an honest answer . . . I should not have said it. Nothing done in envy is good. The other Byziana was back now, furious.

"You taunt me. You know my strong beliefs about this, but you mock my beliefs."

"Truth is not something you can pick and choose and call it true. Either you are right or I am right, not both of us. Scripture is the guide, not philosophers."

"You are against logic and reason?"

"If it negates what Scripture is clear about, the reasoning is wrong."

"Well in my opinion, Scripture supports my beliefs."

"It is not your beliefs I am against as much as your god. He is not the true God."

"I believe in the true God!" she asserted.

"You hate the god you believe in. You don't trust him and that's how you live. Your god determines your behavior. And always will."

"How can you say I hate God? How can you say I do not worship the true God? I believe what many godly men believe."

"For example?"

"My father. Many others in Antioch. Bishop Timothy of Alexandria. The Empress Augusta Theodora. People who want things to make sense."

"Chalcedon's God is one of mystery, sure. But what do the Scriptures say? That's our God. And your God determines who you become. Your mother said that."

"Do not mention my mother!"

She jumped up, hands clenched. "There's no pleasing that woman. Do not mention her."

I gawked at her unexpected words.

"Why must she haunt me like a ghost, following me, prodding me?"

"What are you talking about?"

"Nothing!"

"Byziana, please. Calm down."

I jumped out from under the covers and tied my robe around myself. Going over to her, I tried to pull her into our embrace.

"Do not touch me, Marcellus. How many times do I need to tell you?"

I lifted my hands again in surrender.

"I am this way. As the Church develops, we grow in our understanding of Scripture. We change with this progress."

Her words sounded rutty, words well worn and rarely considered.

"No. You're wrong. We must stay faithful. If we keep changing, we will end up not being the Church. This is my point. We need to hold to the faith of our fathers. We can't change our beliefs just to match what everyone else believes, just for monetary benefit."

"What do you mean? I am not—"

"You are. Think about it." I saw the ring twisting on her finger. *Stop twisting that ring!*

"Ours is a great heritage of faith. But you disdain that heritage. You only want what would be beneficial as wife of illustrious, promising Belisarius—what would please the Empress Theodora—and you conform to those faulty beliefs instead of thinking for yourself."

"My father taught me this. Pater wills this marriage."

"He is mistaken. He does not know Belisarius." I clamped my lips shut to restrain myself from exposing more.

In my mind's eye I saw his hateful character. Laughing. Mocking me.

She looked at me, astonished.

"You are sacrificing everything. Have you learned nothing from the Scrolls?"

"Pater is not mistaken. Maybe you and I look at the world differently. Maybe my people consider the future. It certainly is necessary when your house lies crushed in ruins. We have to start over, to start our family fortune in Constantinople. And why should I not regard Theodora? It is advantageous for our views to match the empress's."

"Then you are selling your beliefs to the highest bidder." I regretted my hasty words the moment they left my mouth.

"I am not selling my beliefs! As if I were a prostitute!" She raised her hand and slapped my face.

The burning sensation on my cheek was nothing to the raging volcano her disloyalty brought my heart.

The door slammed open and in flew Justin and Katerina. "What's going on? Stop shouting at each other."

"I am not shouting," I said in a furious whisper, hand to my face. The volcano drew its lava into my narrowed eyes.

"And you blame me again," my cousin answered, her chin upraised.

"Peace. Truce." Justin drew near to his sister with his hands raised. "Whatever it is about, you're both tired and need to get away from each other."

"What happened to your face?" Natalia came up to me, but I shrugged her off.

"Why do you always fight?" Katerina asked. "We need to be together, not against each other."

Byziana grabbed the Scroll from where I had set it down on the bed. "And keep your hands off my Scrolls," she snapped.

Her words sobered me in a moment. All my focus, all my attention was on her hand, on the Scroll in her hand. "But they're our—"

"My Scrolls. Mine. They were my mother's, and they are mine now. Leave them alone. Since they are mine, and we worship different gods, it is my God these are about, and I choose to keep them from you. I will keep them safe. And Belisarius will keep them safe."

Her words knocked the air out of me. *How can she say such a thing? I love those Scrolls.* I heard ringing in my ears and could hardly breathe.

"Really, Byzia . . .," Justin tried to intervene.

"Not another word from you, either, Justin. Just leave me alone. Everyone!" We fled the room. Our day of rest was doomed to be such a day. I leaned back against the door, and tried to regain composure, regain equilibrium, regain my honor.

When my breathing steadied, I crept to the dining hall and sat at the fireplace watching the coals pulsing on the fire.

Byziana would not approach me. She called her siblings to the room and whatever they discussed distressed them as well, because Katerina soon burst out the door and ran to her room. Dinner was silent and gloomy until I left the room. Then I could hear them speaking more in argued whispers.

What's happening to our family?

The next morning, I saw Justin leading two donkeys to a pile of our bundles and the Trunk. "Hey! Where did this guy come from?" I laughed, looking the new donkey over with approval. "I thought we would rest another day . . ."

Justin did not answer though in his eyes there was an inexplicable apology. He packed up the donkey with a man I had never seen before. Under his rough leather coat, the man's large shoulders hunched over, obviously from carrying burdens. His shaved round head was tied with a scarf in the manner of this region. He regarded me askance. "I can do that. Here, let me help," I said to Justin, ignoring the man and taking the strappings, securing them.

Justin allowed me to help with the strappings, but his arms fidgeted over the bundles when he saw his sister come out of the inn. The bald man crossed his arms and glared at me. Byziana tidied the folds of her robe, and brushed off unseen dust on the front, then came up to me shoulders back, chin out, blinking faster than usual. "Please leave Justin and Alcaeus to this job. We no longer require your services." That rage simmered in me again. I clenched my teeth and bolstered my chest with air.

Services? What choice of words!

Services? Is that what I was? A servant?

I kept my stance, my eyes met hers, but she turned away to say something to make Alcaeus leave us for the moment.

Eyes focusing on something over my shoulder, she added, "You should go on to Cappadocia like you wanted, or back to Mopsos from here. We have hired a guide and will continue on without you." Her sallow words declared she did not care where I went. "I was wrong about you."

Wrong about me? I had no answer for her. My mind was blank, a knot gripped my stomach, and tears threatened to show themselves.

"I will continue with you." *Services? Am I a mere slave? No, I'm a kinsman. She can't treat me this way!*

"We do not want you," she answered, still avoiding my eyes. "Right, Justin?"

"Leave me out of this!" He ran into the inn, slamming the door.

"You cannot go alone. It would be suicide."

She stared beyond me with her chin still out and lips still pursed. "You cannot leave me behind. I promised I would take you to Constantinople, and your fickle feelings mean nothing to my resolve."

Honor boiled within me with furious indignation. "I will take you there, or die in the process." I stepped toward her, my own chin out. "I am not a servant that you can dismiss me. I am a kinsman."

Her cheeks flushed, then blushed, but I continued, "You cannot treat me with such contempt. I will not leave you. I will not!" Her look toward me was enigmatic. I could not read if she was angry or stymied or happy. She looked at me with an unreadable emotion. Then, she shook her head and snuffed, and went inside again. My life tumbled downhill at a frenetic pace, and I scrambled to right myself.

APPROACHING THE FIRE

I hoped she would change her mind about separation and would repent. But a few minutes later Katerina came out, crying. "She is so unreasonable. You cannot go with us, she says. I don't know what you fought over, but can't you apologize? Can't you make it right?"

"There is nothing to apologize for, Kata. We merely disagreed on a theological point. She need not risk the life of your family over it."

"You will not?"

I thought of what it meant to apologize. At the time I believed apologizing meant denying Chalcedon. Since then I have learned that asking forgiveness is much more than who is right or wrong. It is un-offending another.

But in my weak youthful passion I said, "I am not wrong, and I will not apologize."

Katerina leaned against the fence near the paddock, face in hands, shoulders heaving in sorrow. I suppose my heart also wept, but my face refused to submit to those feelings. I still hoped Byziana would change her mind. Her finding me with the tears of an infant on my face would do nothing to strengthen my cause.

She must have heard our words, for she was soon outside, hustling her siblings toward departure, ignoring me. The guide came out with them, explaining to them his plan for the day, speed and difficulties. I listened from a distance, no one acknowledging my presence.

The others put on their packs and started off behind the burdened guide, faces northward: Byziana, Natalia, Katerina then Justin at the end. As they left down the street, only Justin glanced back at me. He flipped his head in their direction, signaling me to follow. I ran into the inn and bundled my belongings. Spurred on by Justin's encouragement, I shifted those onto my back, and hastened behind them. I kept pace not too far on their heels, loneliness overwhelming me. Only the dogs greeted me. They ran to the front of our party, circled around and trotted by me for a while, and then continued the circuit. Why are dogs faithful when humans are not? They neither heard nor heeded any word against me.

Had Byziana ever looked back? I myself had told her I would not leave them. Yet she acted as if I were not there. Who was this guide? How or why should she trust herself and two young sisters to an unknown man, with only young Justin to defend her honor were things to turn wrong? I could trust no one but myself for their safety, so I kept close behind. *They're leaving me, walking away. But it changes nothing. Family is family. A promise is a promise.*

They drifted. Too slow in my estimation. Pacing us at a distance, along the rolling hills to the west, I glimpsed the same group of horsemen. *Are they tracking us?*

When Byziana's group set up camp the first night, I looked back down the road. I thought I could still see the inn we had left. And along the skirt of the ridge I saw small shadows of the horsemen sitting around another campfire. I set up my own meager camp, then motioned for Justin to come over.

"You're poking along! You must travel faster and further than this on the morrow. We can't delay this journey through these hinterlands. It is not safe."

"I will try, Marcellus," he promised, looking toward that other camp.

"And tell Alcaeus to stay alert."

Behind us, the Taurus Mountains stood hoary-headed, reminding us of all we had been through. To the east, low hills led to short jagged hillocks blocking us from what was Cappadocia beyond. Ahead of us to the northwest, the Salt Sea flatlands continued on and on.

Traveling alone those long days, I mulled over our argument. *How can she claim I'm against Reason? I am all about Reason. Reason leads us to knowledge of God.*

In my bed I considered Abraham. He had reasoned. The Epistle to the Hebrews said Abraham reasoned God could raise the dead. His thinking faith reasoned to know Who God was. And knowing God's character, he could know What He would do. *It had to work backwards, too. By knowing What He did, we should be able to understand more about Who God is.*

I recounted . . . He had allowed, or caused, an earthquake. Had taken Lady Sophia and countless others from life. He had watched Ephraim rebuild the city, and then allowed, or caused, another earthquake which destroyed Byziana's house.

The robbery by their servant, the destitution caused by their steward, the mysterious and extended absences of Gaius Justus, the near-death of Natalia, losing our donkey to the merchant. *What do these say about God?*

And before all this, He had allowed, or willed, for Belisarius and Byziana to become betrothed. That consideration alone shot a suspicion into my soul.

Why would He decree such a thing? How can I know a God like that? I massaged my temples. The very betrothal went against what the Scrolls spoke of. *And yet she must obey her pater. Her ring is all they have to live on, she said.*

Didn't I read somewhere that all things are orchestrated by God, in His wisdom? It must have been in the Book of Daniel. Is even this argument under His control? I shook my head. *I wonder if I'll ever understand.*

Though we were in early spring, the chill was great. On the hills at a distance I glimpsed the pinprick fire and heard faint laughter of the men echoing across the lonely fields. My own fire was small, and I slept alone with no friend to heat my back. *How can we know what God is like when events in our lives spoke to a random and precarious plan?* Rolling over in my bed, I pulled the blanket up to my chin and closed my eyes.

I shot up from my mat. *The wrath of God.*

What was it I said in the valley? The wrath of God could be borne by no man.

No mere man. Preserving both natures.

My gut cramped again. My head ached, and I lay back down to rub my temples.

Christ must be man, to forgive our sins.

But no mere man.

To bear God's ultimate wrath and survive . . . .

No mere man . . . .

I massaged my temples again.

He would have to be equal to that ultimate weight.

The hair on my arms stood on end. That was it. *Only divine love could bear that divine wrath. Properties of both natures, divine and human, would be necessary. As the Confession said all along.*

Breathless, I drew deep drafts of air into my lungs. They knew what they were talking about there at Chalcedon. Reason demanded a God-man.

I need to tell Byziana.

She tossed and turned in her tent which opened to the fire. She needed to know this. It would bring her peace. She would finally understand. I lay back and took a deep, satisfied breath. *If she weren't so angry with me, I could tell her now.*

The next thing I knew the morning sun was shining on my face. Thinking of this part of our journey from my vantage point today, I can say our whole life would have been different had we gone to Cappadocia at that juncture, perhaps if I had apologized. But wisdom is learned through mistakes, and here we were in the midst of the greatest one.

Our progress that day was just as slow. I walked closer to their party, apart from them twenty paces or so. When they stopped at night, and I was debating where to throw my sleeping mat, Alcaeus came up.

"The lady hired me to show the way to Constantinople and to keep strangers away from them. You is a stranger, so you has best move along."

He tried to glare a threat, but I would not be swayed. I looked right back to let him know his place. "I am with the party. I'm not a stranger." As a conclusion to my answer, I threw my mat down next to the fire they had started. I needed to speak with her, but she refused to look on me.

Collecting an armful of wood, I took it back to their fire. The man watched me for a while. Byziana paid no heed to the exchange, so he shrugged his shoulders, and sat down to his whittling. In spite of their sister's behavior, Natalia and Justin were attentive, and soon Katerina also whispered with me. They brought me broth and bread as we ate, and when Natalia fell asleep against me, I took her to her tent.

I watched Byziana across the blazing fire. The campfire had the makings for a pleasant family time. Yet her anger closed off joy from everyone. Like a mother's death at a child's birth. *How can things have turned so sour? It feels so natural for her to be in my arms.* She stared into the fire, lost in her thoughts. *Tomorrow I will tell her what I discovered. Why it mattered more than anything. How it all makes sense. That will restore her heart. She'll be happy and we'll be at peace again.*

If I could only explain how both His natures related to the earthquakes. I stood up and walked to the edge of the circle of firelight. *How does the Incarnation explain the earthquake?*

Through the waning moonlight I could see the town of Tyana in the darkness ahead of us, less than half a day's walk. It would have been nice to stay in a real bed again. But I had no say anymore. This guide was content to stroll the road to Constantinople. I leaned my mat up against the tree, and the dogs lay next to me, sharing their heat.

Kyrie Eleison!

The vividness of the memory has never left me. Much as a dream, as one of those nightmares where you are powerless and frozen. Even the dogs did not bark until the stealthy men were already upon us.

Bandits.

We woke to the caterwaul of a donkey—being taken away into the darkness by a mounted robber!

I had fallen asleep against the tree. "Who is there?" I shouted, grabbing the sword from my lap. I saw Alcaeus on the ground, face to the fire, eyes staring into nowhere, a trickle of blood dripping from his mouth—my eyes must have bulged at the terror.

Our worst fears had come true.

"Marcellus! Marcellus!" Byziana screamed.

Her sisters' extended cries of "Help!" echoed throughout the abandoned plain.

"Stay in the tent." I shouted.

I jumped up and darted to the receding sound of the frightened donkeys. Two of the bandits galloped circles around the camp, laughing mockery at the fear their chaos caused. A man lay dead, children were terrified, and they lightheartedly rob us helpless.

Whatever kind of wicked this is I will make it stop.

Captain barked rat-a-tat, running next to me. Sarabi roared ahead toward the bandits.

A movement to my left showed a bandit hoisting our unpacked bundles onto his horse. I tried to stop him. Our struggle brought yet another bearded man to the fray.

I will not allow this. My body worked in unexpected synchrony. I fought both men at the same time. My father's fighting lessons resurrected in my memory.

Strike-step-guard-strike-backhand.

The patterns that had once tired and frustrated my young body now proved their worth. My blade and hilt and fist a trio of energy, I struck one man down with a pierce in his thigh. The other's fist met my face and the first man's knife my side.

I fell to the ground, rolled under the horse, and cut the ropes binding our bundles. The Trunk slid to the ground, barely hitting my head. As I twisted to avoid the Trunk, my legs knocked my opponent to the ground. I followed up whipping a furious strike of my sword along his shins.

Natalia's scream took my attention. Justin swung his short sword at several mocking men. Tall Katerina behind him gripped Natalia whose arms reached out toward the riders.

"Sister!" she cried out. Byziana was now the prey.

I leapt up and ran into the commotion. With a roaring dash, I sliced the arm of one and the side of another. They ran from the children and returned to the bundles. I flew after Byziana. She was over the shoulder of a mounted barbarian.

Captain barked, Sarabi bellowed and nipped at the heels of the horse, Katerina's cries filled the dark night sky.

How I leapt high enough to knock the rider off his horse, I do not know. I only remember being on top of both malodorous man and Byziana. My sword had fallen out of reach, so I fought fist to face, fist to face as she crawled away toward the others, toward the firelight.

My attention, diverting for a moment to assure myself of the girls' safety, cost me my opponent. A foreign shout came from the bandits, and the man under my assault hastened away, mounting his steed to flee, leaving his rotten onion odor behind. Sarabi howled after them. Captain, amidst our rescued bundles and the Trunk, bared his teeth and lunged at any who approached.

I ran to the others. "Are you well? Did they hurt you?" Katerina's emotions mottled frenetic words. Her hand reached out, finger pointing.

"Byziana." I took her by the shoulders. "Are you hurt?"

She shook her head, but her eyes spoke of terror.

"What is it?" I followed her pointed finger to the distant fleeing horsemen and saw to my horror that which they had seen—that of which no one could speak.

They've got Justin!

"We've got to leave. Follow them. Find my brother." Byziana surveyed the disarray, the sleeping bundles, her fearful sisters. I saw in her face my own belief. We had no way to catch them. No way to fix this problem.

The sound of hoofbeats faded out into the darkness. Frog croaks reminded us it was night and the world was asleep to us and our sorrow. We were alone facing blackness.

But then like a soft caressing breeze, my aunt's words from long ago floated to mind. *When life knocks you down. Only two choices.* I would not stay down. With that, I knew what to do. Holding her shoulders I peered into her eyes, "I'll go after them. Alone. Right now." I put my hand on her cheek and gave my word, eye to eye. "I'll get him back."

Katerina still wept. "They'll kill him. He'll be eaten by the barbarians."

"Oh God," Byziana moaned, falling into my chest. "God, where are you? How have we offended you?"

Natalia whimpered and hid on my hand. "Will they eat Justin? Oh poor Justin!"

"Yes. Or torture him," Katerina sobbed.

"I doubt it. They'd have killed him if they'd wanted to." The body of Alcaeus next to the fire emphasized my point.

Byziana sniffed, wiped her eyes, and pulled away. "Then why'd they take him? And how can you catch them? They got everything."

She looked around at what our camp. Our bundles. Our fire. The dogs. The Trunk.

Her decision sliced to my wick. Opening the Trunk she took out several Scrolls. "Take these. Sell them in the next village." In the darkness I could not see which Scriptures she had given.

"No." I tried to return them. "I have coins still in my money-pouch. Enough to buy a horse." I reached down to my waist, but alas the barbarians had been thorough.

"These are all we have left of value, Marcellus."

As much as I wished it was otherwise, Justin was worth more. She was right.

"I'll run to the next town." I pointed to the hill ahead of us where a faint light glowed from the watchtower. "That's Tyana, I think. Find an inn and wait for me there. I doubt they went far. And they can't expect us to follow, so surprise is in my favor."

The girls huddled against me.

"Look, I'll rescue him. And I'll be back. Expect me in a few days, a week at the most."

I touched the Trunk, my heart breaking.

"You make ends meet till I return. Try not to sell the Scrolls. Work with your hands."

Natalia put her arms around Byziana. "Don't worry, Sister. We'll wait for Marcellus. If anyone can bring Justin back, it's him. He promised."

Her faith frightened me because with every moment of delay the barbarians raced further ahead, in a direction I knew not. *God, please help us!*

Byziana voiced my prayer, "God, please help us! *Kyrie Eleison!*" Her words struck my heart with awe, wonder and irony. Eyes closed, face earnest, with all her heart she had called out to God. *Did it have to take such a tragedy?*

The miracle of those six words promised that hope remained. I touched her cheek that last time, pulling her into my arms. *As long as I have life in my bones I won't let her hope die.*

Her gentle, forgiving, warm, trusting embrace burned a fire into my memory, and this was what warmed me over my next life journey. For I was not back in a week.

TOME
THE SECOND

EPISODES FROM EXPERIENCE

CHALCEDON
THE BETRAYED

BYZIANA AND HER HUSBAND

OCTOBER 10, AD 531
Three years later

What happened to me over the next years could fill its own scroll. Yet my story in itself is not worth the writing, for this is Byziana's story. From my father I learned a love of books, from my mother the cost of parchment.

Happenstance is a strange thing.

What if those in Tyana had not traded a horse for the Galatians scroll?

What if that horse had not sought other horses?

What if I had bled out or fallen off before reaching the brigands?

If we look on the other side of each What If coin we can find minted the words What a Marvel.

What a marvel I lived, what a marvel I met Justin, what a marvel I was taken to Gothland, what a marvel those Scrolls arrived into the hand of King Olufr.

What a marvel. *Kyrie Eleison.*

I look back at that event, and over the next three years as the slave of barbarians, and I see the Hand of God in happenings beyond my expectation. By taking my horse and the Scrolls to the Gothic bandits, the God of the Earthquake had begun a great miracle in their tribe.

After three years they released us. The release was so sudden, so unexpected, so almost undesired at that point, we did not know which direction to go. *Does Athens still await me for learning and books? Is my dear mother still alive? Is she in Antioch?* Byziana, of course, was married.

We rode along the Black Sea toward home. We had left Dacia in the far north and must need pass through Constantinople.

Justin insisted on visiting his sister there. "I must see for myself how her marriage with the man fares. According to King Olufr, Belisarius is like no other."

"Like no other" was an understatement. He had become all Gaius Justus had envisioned for him.

The top general of Emperor Justinian, Belisarius was a brilliant strategist. Last season, at Dara, he had routed the Persian army. Certainly accolades and triumphant showers of gold had fallen on him and his new bride—though after three years, a man could no longer call his bride new.

My honor forbade me to visit her.

The wound on my soul from the assault of Belisarius's men had flitted away during my service under King Olufr. I had become a man, as happens to all. As a man, I now understood man's prime instinct. We have in us this animal rage that good men can tame, and bad men cannot. I had seen this worked out. Had chosen friends according to this principle. Some men care about proving themselves men, some men care about proving themselves human.

What was it my mother once said? *Never forget the importance of humanity.* She had charged me thus upon our flight from Antioch, our flight from responsibility. Her words had worked their magic, and somehow, as I began to live in the way of the Scrolls, my hatred of Belisarius and anger at those men had dissolved.

They were broken parts of a broken world—brokenness that declared both judgment and hope to anyone who listened closely. I may have dismissed the crime, but I held no respect for the man and had no desire to see her happiness or sorrow with him. Many things disallowed it.

When we arrived in the city, I refused to join Justin.

"I could never stay back and wait for news," he responded. "I shall know what to believe about the marriage when I see it with my own eyes."

We used the gold Olufr gave us to rent lodging, then parted ways: Justin to find Belisarius and I to grieve at being so close to the one I had loved.

Our lodgings were above the street market which added a minimal distraction to my grief. I purchased a pack of apples and ate next to our window, watching the people for awhile. But the distraction did not satisfy. My thoughts were well-trained to dwell on her. I endured the pain and injury of slavery only by savoring each memory I had of my life with Byziana. Like the song of Odysseus by a bard, our song, of the days from the earthquake until my capture, rang over and over in my ruthless mind.

We continually prepared for war—soldier-slaves in the king's private army. Freedom, all we lacked. Food was plentiful. Laughter and friends ever-present. Sword-work, cavalry training, archery all stimulating challenges. And there were women. Mari grew up before my eyes, always looking at me, always with those quickly-blushing cheeks. But my heart knew only one love.

I tallied off days of enslavement by worry for Byzia: she was waiting for us, that first month perhaps.

Today she was selling a Scroll.

Today she was hiring a guide—was he reliable?

Today she was arriving in Constantinople
and finding her father.

Today, the nuptial arrangements.

Today, the nervous bride.

Today, the wedding—a political event
with crowds to hail the general and his new wife.

Today, the honeymoon.

As the first years passed, her story grew more predictable. A son born. A daughter. Parties. Wars. I did not allow her children to look like him. I gave her mosaics and tapestries and scarlet robes. I gave her a large house. I saw the Trunk in her Great Room. I willed her to open the Trunk, to take out the Scrolls. But then I would see that man walk into the room, she would run into his embrace, and the Scroll would fall to the ground and be stepped on.

If you have never been a captive, you cannot understand the tricks the mind plays to maintain a measure of sanity. I spoke not a word of this to Justin, all I did was beg for God's mercy.

Then at one point, when I truly learned to pray, King Olufr summoned me to his throne room tent. And then everything changed. And the consideration needed to manage a real-life miracle took me from my obsession with dreams.

We wonder why things happen. It is human nature to expect meaning, to expect purpose for our lives. For the opposite thought could pummel a man into a chasm of futile insignificance. But it is all for a purpose. The king called me to his yurt. He asked me to tell him of my Scrolls. And the miraculous power of the Scrolls took him, and then his tribe, into the throne room of God.

Yet here in Constantinople, so close to her and her house and that husband, a knot gripped my gut. My thoughts began to dwell on the adulterous memory of her in my arms those many years ago. The soft of her neck where her scent was so strong.

"Do something, Marcellus!" I told myself aloud. "Get busy and you will forget. You must not think of loving a married woman."

As I scanned the neighborhood from the window, I noticed a chapel on a hilly place. *I'll go pray.* Though I prayed like the first disciples, not bound to any one place, sacred chapels still comforted me. King Olufr's village, at first, bore not a single chapel I could pray in. It would have added insult to injury to worship in the tent of Dellingr, their god. Though later on they built Christian chapels, those were tents, nothing to our holy Byzantine brick and mortar chapels.

I strolled through the food stalls and walked along the crowded walkway. Women and children testing fruit, old men selling their wares, young men hoisting boxes of vegetables. Noise, crowd. I closed my eyes and listened to my language and breathed in the smell—I was home! But I was no longer Me. I was part Goth. Suspicious glances of passing people reminded me of this.

The chapel was small, frescoes painted on the wall exactly the way frescoes should be, except for the cobwebs. I lit a candle on the table and crossed myself, then brushed off the dust to kneel at the altar. I spent perhaps an hour in prayer dwelling on Christ.

As I stood from my prayers, and crossed myself again, the ease of worship startled me. *No one asks questions. Why do you cross yourself? Why do you hold your three fingers together to cross yourself? Why do you not offer food to your god? Why do you kneel? Why this? Why that?*

But the ease of worship here also frustrated me. *Why is no one here to ask questions?*

The sound of a man clearing his throat made me turn. A priest watched me solemnly from the narthex. He wore the long black robe, the high black hat, and the short black beard of a young priest. I nodded and picking up my cloak went to him.

His words were strange, slow, simple, in Latin. He spoke using exaggerated hand movement, as if I would not understand, "Greetings, friend. Are you? A visitor? To Constantinople?"

I answered in Greek, "Yes, father. I hail from Antioch, but am here on business."

"Excuse me. I took from your dress," he gestured to my furred robe, cap and boots, "you were from the Gothic netherlands. A horrid people those. I am glad you are not one of them. I expected you were praying to one of your pagan gods at this sacred altar, and I was beside myself in concern."

Did he not see me cross myself?

"I lived amongst them, Father. And I must object to your slander, for many of them are brothers in Christ. How then can we judge them with anything but love?"

His eyebrows shot up. "Indeed? Brothers in the Lord?"

I dismissed his ignorance to lack of experience. "Father, I wonder if you have any portion of Scripture I may read?"

"Portion of Scripture?" He pulled back. "No sir, they've collected those into the monasteries. The patriarch himself has logged them all."

His head tilted and eyebrows rose. "You've read Scripture yourself then?"

I longed for the Trunk of Scrolls we once possessed. For the blank parchment I never found to copy those works of Lady Sophia's. For those two years the Trunk sat in the corner under bundles. I did not regret parting with my Scrolls, except for the Galatians scroll. They were where they needed to be. *'No word would come back void,'* Scripture itself promised. But I so desired those words to minister now to my aching soul. I would placate my desire with memorized Writ.

"Yes. A long time ago in Antioch." No need to explain my whole story to him.

I bade him good day. He crossed and blessed me then I left. After such a peaceful prayer time, the interchange perturbed me. I did not belong here anymore. I, strangely, desired to be back with my barbarian brethren. *With them, things are fresh and new and innocent. Here it's easy to be Christian and not Christian at the same time.*

I found my way back through the street market. I had come back to my people, but they did not want me as one of them. Determined to overcome the prejudice against my dress, I carried groceries for nervous old ladies, shared jokes with nervous shopkeepers, and played knucklebones with a welcoming group of children. This project diverted me enough to get home. And then my mind returned to Justin and his meeting Byziana. *Can she be happy in the arms of such a man?*

The sun set, the market stalls emptied. Rotten fruit and vegetable cuttings lay scattered on the street where tables had been. Poor men and women and their children scurried around like mice, collecting the edible remains. Like me, scraping up leftovers of a dead future, the garbage scrapers shoveled the streets until all hint of sun disappeared from the sky. And still Justin was not home.

I stayed at the window, watching the moon, keeping my eye out for him in case he was lost. When he finally arrived I was furious. "Anything could've happened. Why'd you return so late?"

My frustration with his sister's situation and my displeasure at being home overflowed in a long chastening. He sat down and poured himself a glass of wine, unflinching, watching my tirade as a silent observer.

I finally surrendered to his silence, so he said simply, "She's not here."

"Not here? What do you mean? Have they moved?"

"No. I searched and searched. Looked for any sign of her or my father. Gaius Justus is slightly known, I found one man who saw him 'months or years ago' in his words." He snuffed. "Odd turn of events."

My shock was as strong as my earlier frustration "But what of Byziana? What of Belisarius?"

"No one has even heard of my sister. Everyone knows Belisarius though. I asked about Belisarius's consorts, and they sent me to a brothel!"

I froze.

"A brothel?"

The words hardly escaped my mouth. *Has she been so destitute to have come to this?* I leapt to my feet and pulled on my cloak, fighting back tears. I would find her and take her from that life. *My darling Byziana! What's happened to you?*

"Don't bother." He filled my glass. "I spoke with the brothel madame—"

"You did what!"

He smirked. "Do not fill your mind with wicked thoughts of me, Brother." His twinkling eyes kept on mine with that same mischievous grin, a bit too long.

"Well?" I insisted on elaboration. His tease tormented my soul, and he knew it.

"I explained our story. Our sojourn in Dacia intrigued her."

"I can only imagine the conversation. And the comments of passers-by. You know she was looking for business from a certain young man." My snide comment brought a frown.

"No, Brother, she wasn't. She was from those regions and knew King Olufr. One of her girls is the favorite of Belisarius. And besides her—what was the name she gave?—there is no other woman in Count Belisarius's life."

Belisarius and a prostitute? The same snake.

"Did you speak with the man himself?"

"No. He was at the Great Palace. I tried to get a meeting, but they turned me away after I waited for hours. The doorman explained, local politics are whirring up the whole bureaucracy."

She never made it. The thought weighed down like a stone, pulling me into the depths. I tipped the glass of wine, drinking to the dregs.

Justin poured me another drink. "Marcellus, your life is much too bound up in this situation. There must be a simple explanation. No doubt Theodora wouldn't welcome her to court and she returned home."

My head spun and heart surged.

He pursed his lips together to keep from smiling, mocking me, egging me on.

Yet I could not keep the torrent inside. "They would reject her!" I roared.

I imagined the lovely young woman thrown out the door, onto the streets like a vagabond. *He that is all that, would reject dear trusting Byziana?* I finished my wine much too fast. The heat in my head calmed me. I knew better than to drink away my sorrows, but now I had more questions than answers.

"The madame suggests we return home. To Antioch."

"She does, does she? What would she know about it?" I snapped.

"Antonina!" Justin said.

"Excuse me?"

"Antonina. His consort's name. I remember now."

"Who cares? Where is Byziana? Where is Gaius Justus?"

"The proverbial quest, dear Marcellus," he snuffed. "Step back. Take a breath. I am fatigued and thus excuse myself from your distress."

I ran my fingers roughly through my long wild hair. *What should I do? Where's Byziana? Had she been murdered in the village? Been taken captive herself? Is she destitute? What of the other girls? Poor Natalia! Poor Katerina! Doesn't Justin care?*

I did not want to sleep, my nightmares awaited. I watched the darkness outside the window long into the night, until Justin's deep rhythmic breathing calmed my own, and my eyes shut on this world.

JOURNEY TO TYANA

A week's time found us halfway home, on that long road to Antioch. We had neither located Gaius Justus nor gained an audience with the elusive Belisarius.

As we approached Tyana, the town where Byziana would have waited, memories flooded over us. After many inquiries we met an innkeeper's wife who remembered the girls.

"Yes, dearies. They were here. A big girl, brown hair, comely and smart. A tall, lanky one and a short, darling, tender one. Natalia. I remember her name. She was such a help."

She knew our women!

Justin and I exchanged looks of relief. "How long did they stay?" I asked.

"They lived here for months, maybe. Paid me with worthless parchment . . . . I could not refuse them, three girls all alone. Something about barbarians." She opened a small door under her sales counter and produced three scrolls. "I can't read these letters. Though I know my Latin. It must be Greek."

Never had my eyes beheld such surprise. From the far depths of the dingy cabinet came the Word of God. *The woman unwittingly saved Scripture!*

"I never got around to selling them. Quite forgot about 'em, to be honest. But I thought there were four." She looked again under the counter, producing nothing and shrugging her shoulders. "They were such darling, worried things, those girls. But that giant white dog of theirs was fearsome."

Kyrie Eleison. Sarabi, and Captain! In all these years I never considered the dogs would protect them. God had kept them safe!

Justin took those Scrolls one by one into his hands. He held up a Scroll and wiggled his eyebrows at me—a red string fastened it! Colossians! We have it again!

I reached into my pouch and pulled out three gold coins. "Bless you, dear woman. This is for your trouble if we can have the scrolls." She took the coins giving a happy chuckle.

As I pulled the Scrolls to my chest, torrents of grief threatened to overwhelm me.

Justin pushed her for more information, "Where did the girls go? Did they continue to Constantinople? When did they leave?"

"Sakes alive, sonny," her toothless grin facing him, "I cannot remember when. That was so long ago. In the end they joined a large party of merchants and their families moving to—was it Antioch?"

Her words were like a thunderclap in a drought. "Antioch! They returned to Antioch?"

"To Antioch they went, to Antioch we go. Let us not waste a moment, Brother," Justin said, thanking the woman with a quick kiss, rushing toward the door.

For all his skepticism and joking, he was indeed concerned to find his family.

I needed to make one stop. I found the stable where I had purchased the horse those many years ago, but no one remembered me. No one knew of the Galatians parchment.

I took a deep breath and said farewell to it, wherever it was. At least I had these three.

We traded our horses for another pair of fast runners and purchased food for our journey. Not too far out of town, we pulled the horses up at the fated campsite.

"When they took me, I was sure I'd be dead by nightfall," Justin said. "Yet life turned out differently than I expected."

Alcaeus was right there, by that fire-pit. I relived those brief minutes in my mind's eye. The fighting, the Trunk. The embrace. Questions swirled in my thoughts.

"Never imagined I'd be here again." Justin added.

"Me neither."

He asked for a Scroll so I gave him the Epistle to the Colossians from my pouch. He read aloud, "'*For in him all things hold together.*'"

"Things seem to be holding together in spite of everything, eh Marcellus?"

"Yeah. *'He is before all things.'* My mother repeated many times what the prophet said, *'He knows the end from the beginning.'*
"

"Well, we'll soon know the end as well as the beginning. And oh, I can't wait!" he laughed. We secured the Scrolls and began our gallop home. The road passed below us in a whir. Heedless to the whisking trees, our hearts pulsed to the swift Pegasus hoofbeats.

We pulled up after the Horns of the Taurus Mountains, to stay with Widow Arité. Her grandson Olorix opened the door of her cottage. We had briefly met him that winter. He was now married, and father to a young son. He welcomed us in and, after seating us and offering us a drink, conveyed the sorry news. The widow was gone. "Let me show you where we laid her to rest," he said.

Olorix walked to the gravesite, his little boy in hand. Together we put wildflowers on her gravesite and commiserated. The young boy did not know Arité, yet he toddled to and fro collecting colorful rocks and grass to honor the grave. Neither she nor her faith would be forgotten. I stood up and thanked the man. The memories in this village overwhelmed me. Until I saw my cousins safe, with my own eyes, I would have no peace.

"Let us try to reach Mopsos before dark," I suggested after we said our farewells. Justin, always willing to ride like the wind, hooted and urged his horse into a gallop as an answer.

During the reign of Darius the Persian, his trained couriers could do Susa to Sardis in nine days, along this same road. Our journey to Antioch went as fast, for we hastened it by trading horse to horse. We spared no expense, for both home and hope pulled our hearts toward Antioch.

REUNITED!

I felt as if I were the prodigal son in Christ's parable, riding up to our home on my horse—the repairs in the city, on the hill, lost to me—my only focus the gate. With the slam of a door, out burst Mater running toward me. My eyes poured forth manumit tears. I was home!

I held my mater, encompassed her as if letting go would break my thundering heart. Captain jumped against me, his paws on my hip, his tail swinging from side to side. Next to us, Sarabi's eager guffaw echoed toward the mountain and along the road.

I had thought Justin still behind me, but screams of joy from inside his house heralded the noisy exit of my cousin with three women I had never seen before.

Upon a second look, they were familiar. The third look identified them without question.

Three years does much to a girl. It changes height, shapeliness, hair, posture. Natalia, no longer the eight-year-old I had known, was now a comely young woman with the same endearing smile. And Katerina had become a beautiful woman of—was it thirteen or fourteen? I imagined a line of men awaiting her favor. Three years does much to a girl, and it does more to fervent love.

I suppose it is possible in three years for someone to lose all interest in a passing infatuation.

I suppose in three years one might forget lighthearted promises made in youth. But if three years can take away love, it is not love.

I saw Byziana before me, a woman of almost eighteen, and my legs felt weak. I braced my hand on my mother's shoulder and my tear-filled eyes fixed themselves on the woman I loved.

They say of Helen of Troy one smile caused a thousand ships to launch. I understood in that moment. I could not hear the silence of everyone around me, I could not see their focus or their expressions, I could only see her.

Her face glowed like an angel's. *It's her.* The smell of her, wheat and berries and a spring breeze. All I wanted was a quiet moment in the dark with a torchlight and her. Let there be wolves all around, just give me that moment.

And she touched my arm. "Marcellus," she said, as if from a dream.

Did I answer? Did we speak?

And then I knew I would wake up again from another dream of her. I would again be on my cot in Gothland.

But then, things happened which rarely happen in dreams. She was whisked away for meal preparations, and I was swept by Justin to the city baths.

"My sisters told me to make ourselves presentable, old friend. I can see from your Goth-like appearance I also need to tend to my hygiene."

Antioch is famous for its baths. Antiochenes have always loved bathing. My time in Gothland, with their strange views of water, had not taken away my own love for the old Roman Bath. We had a choice of many, but chose our favorite: the Baths of Trajan.

I walked through the rebuilt city, down the Colonnaded Street, past the fateful spot. The memory's power had faded into the patchwork of my past. Six years since our first earthquake, and the city appeared as a shadow of its former glory. Ephraim had re-built, true. But Antioch lacked its awe-inspiring power of yester-year. The stark changes truly took my mind from Byziana.

"Its old magnificence is gone forever." Justin sighed. "It looks like broken stones re-stacked. Like a decrepit old man."

"Centuries of architecture cannot be replaced in a few years," I replied. Yet I could not grieve. Not today.

We passed by the Big Church, still split. Haphazard clap-boards circled its collapsed dome, making the inside water-tight but pilfering its once-a-time beauty. Reformed paving stones covered the streets. We passed functioning markets, fountains, pools, everything you could want in a city. But having known its glory-days, I saw only a broken-backed city, no longer the region's glorious capital.

Yet the baths stood in perfect restoration. In Antiochene style.

We paid the guard to mind our clothes and braced ourselves for the *frigidarium*. Shivering, we dove into the cold water pool.

A million ideas swirled in my mind as I swam underwater, but nothing settled. The water blocked out all sounds but my thoughts which today soared in joy. *She is not married, and she was happy to see me! Does she still wear the ring? I didn't notice.*

"Hey, let's get warmer!" Justin grabbed my arm, pulling me from the pool just as I was feeling comfortable. Late fall was not the best time to stay in cold water. We passed through a hallway into a steamy room, hot compared to the pool. We sat on the marble and filled our bowls with hot water.

"Is it not wonderful to be home?" Justin watched for my response, eyebrows twitching. "The girls are so grown up."

Remembering her loveliness pressed my heart. But Justin's intent observation put me on guard.

"You always talk on two levels and it makes everyone uncomfortable."

"Why is that?"

"Because you laugh at us, no matter what we answer or do not answer. You find our answers amusing. Like you have your own secret joke about us."

"I do. I have a joke. A secret about you."

"Oh, no. I'm not following you down your rabbit trail. You have no such thing and are goading me."

He chuckled at my answer as if he expected it. "Suit yourself." *Suit yourself? What does that mean? Maybe he's not jesting.*

We poured hot water over ourselves, but in a few minutes our bodies recognized this water as only tepid. After some time our bodies were ready for sweating in the *caldarium*. As we moved to the bath's next section, along the slick blue- and white-tiled hallway, I had to ask, "Do you have a joke about me?"

Distracted by my question, he bumped into a patron leaving the room.

"Excuse me, sir," he said. Then his head pulled back in surprise. "Kasiais! Is that you?"

His old friend and neighbor demanded immediate explanation for Justin's appearance. They bantered updates of their lives, giving me time to lie back onto the smooth marble slab, look up at the blue painted ceiling, and count the gold painted stars through the steamy air while I thought of Byziana.

I knew it would get me into trouble. I knew it then, and I know it now. *She is probably still betrothed. Thinking of her will only dug you deeper into a trap you hardly knew your way out of.* But the pleasure of thinking of her won over the argument. *Her eyes had smiled at me. What did it mean?*

It means nothing, you fanciful fool, I tried to tell myself. But I would not listen. *Why had she looked at me that way? Her eyes crinkled, her face lit up.*

I chided myself again. *Yes, she was glad you were home. But she is a betrothed woman.*

Back and forth the thoughts assailed me, as fists of a fighter left and right, pleasant and painful.

A basinful of cold water splashed over my face and I shot up to my feet. My towel slipped to the wet floor. "What!" I yanked my towel from the floor and tied it around me again.

"Stop thinking about my sister," Justin said.

Why does he think that? I had no time to ask, for he dragged me through the *tepidarium* again to the *frigidarium* for another cold swim and circuit through the baths.

"So what happened to the girls?" I asked as we sat in the *caldarium*, sweating again in the hottest room, scraping our skin of dirt. "Did they ever go to the Capital?"

"I was right," Justin frowned and shook his head. "Justinian turned them away."

"What!" I could not believe my ears. The emperor? How? Why would he reject Byziana?

Justin sat sober-faced for a few tortuous seconds while I fumed inside and burned outside.

"If your face gets any redder you will faint, and I shall have to carry your sorry body out of here, which I am not wanting to do."

I cuffed his arm with my knuckles. Hard.

"Truthfully, from what I got in bits and pieces, the Tyana

innkeeper woman spoke true. They waited for us, sold all the Scrolls, hastened home to Antioch."

"They never went to Constantinople." I was in shock. "They sold every Scroll."

"We need to get back. I'm sure they have killed the fatted calf for us." We rinsed off and headed to the robing room.

As we dressed, I asked forcing my eyebrows high, "Why did you assume my thoughts were on your sister back there?"

He gazed at me in such surprise, then his face opened up into a terrific guffaw.

"No, seriously," I said, still not getting an answer.

He reached his hand across to my opposite shoulder. "Do you really not know?"

"No."

He rolled his eyes at me. Then, flipping a coin to the attendant, we exited the bath.

I stopped him. "Tell me."

"Everyone thinks about my sister, Marcellus," was his not-so-very-satisfying answer. And the thought of everyone dwelling on her made me sick to my stomach.

"Like who?" I asked.

"Don't worry yourself about it. What do I know? I only just got to Antioch today." I followed him up the street.

"Did your friend mention her? Is that who you mean? Kasiais?"

He put his arm around my shoulder and pointed out a new fountain installed on the crossroads. A shepherd carrying a sheep had an engraving labeling it "Ephraim's Fount."

"He must be an amazing man, this Bishop."

I could hardly notice. *How many men in this city have their eye on Byziana?*

"A biblical scene. Instead of his own image. First I have ever seen."

He pulled me into the barber shop and I bade farewell to my Gothic locks and beard. He cut my hair in a typical high circle. *Like everyone else's.* I took a deep breath. *How am I different now? No one will know what we've been through. Now it's like we've never been gone. We're just like everyone else.*

I watched the barber sweep up our hair from the floor. "I'm shedding the whole memory of our time in Gothland. It sits dear in my heart."

"It's just hair."

I lifted my fist to punch him for discounting my words, when he added, "What we lived through will remain with us, Brother. Shears cannot cut it away. It has become as much a part of us as our blood."

We had many years between us, but having shared all we had in captivity, he could understand my deepest thoughts. That was what I loved about Justin.

BOUND TO THE SCROLLS

Before I knew it, we were home.

Home to a house decked out with green boughs and late summer flowers. Home to a house filled with beloved family. Home to a full heart.

My cousins entered the room like prismatic butterflies, whispering and giggling. Everyone in exquisite dress, their braided hair pulled up in swirls, their jewelry shining. They honored us, but I had nothing to give in return. I picked a flower from a vase, and put it behind Byziana's ear, brushing my fingers against her blooming cheek.

They had pulled the two tables into a full circle. "No one wants to miss a nugget of information you men will share," my mother explained.

Byziana sat next to me, and the others were finding places and waiting, it seemed, for the servants to bring in the meal.

"Look at you, Marcellus," she whispered, touching my arm with a finger. "You're all muscles now." One finger, one touch, two honeyed eyes straight into my heart.

I did not know how to answer her. Here I was, master of my own house, and speechless and drunk.

My mother motioned for me to bless the gathering.

Happy for the diversion, I stood and crossed myself, the others also crossed themselves.

Then taking a deep breath, I lifted my hands and prayed, "God of our Fathers, God Almighty, Three-in-one, I thank thee for thy manifold blessings upon us and upon our house this day. After many years apart we are once more together, and for this we give thanks. We beg your mercy upon us . . ." at which everyone replied, "*Kyrie Eleison.*"

"Bless our family, and bless Gaius Justus who cannot be with us. We are truly grateful, God our Father. Guide us, O Lord. Amen."

"Nicely put," Byziana said as I sat down. "You have a cute accent."

"I do?" *What accent?*

"Goth-y."

"Oh." Had my Greek changed in three years? "Uh. Thank you. You look really pretty tonight." She found a loose piece of hair and twirled it around her finger, looking at her plate. And then I saw it.

Belisarius's ring.

It churned my stomach.

That was what Justin meant, the one thinking of Byziana. Belisarius. Belisarius who consorted with prostitutes.

Katerina stood next to me carrying a platter of food. Katerina and Natalia serving food? I looked at my mother in surprise, but a flick of her finger said we could talk of it later.

Katerina dished fava bean *koukia* onto my plate. Oh, my favorite! Natalia served bread and olive oil. I dipped my bread into the fava pureé and took a few blissful bites.

Three years is a long time to catch up on.

I studied Byziana again. She looked nice, her hair all braided and twisted up like a lady's. She smelled like flowers and having her next to me felt right.

I closed my eyelids, trying to memorize this pleasureful moment. The others were talking and laughing with Justin over a battle story he loved to tell. Byziana was quiet. I opened my eyes and caught her regarding me.

"So what happened to you?" we both asked in duet, then laughed.

"You first," I insisted, after a nervous moment.

"Okay. Well, you left in such a hurry. And I need to tell you right now that I never apologized. I never could tell you how sorry I am I slapped you. I've worried over it for years."

"You apologized," I corrected her.

"I did?"

Katerina's eyebrows furrowed as she sat now next to her sister, listening.

"I knew you were sorry before I left. Don't worry about it," I said. "I forgave you a long time ago."

She sighed in relief as if free of a great burden.

"What about you? What did you do?" I asked before filling my mouth with the second dish, hot buttered meat-filled pastries.

"We waited for weeks, sold some Scrolls so we could stay. At the end, Katerina insisted we go home to Aunt Aemilia. I think the desire for the familiar was stronger than the desire for . . . for Constantinople. It happened pretty fast. We met a party of merchants and their wives moving to Antioch, so we joined them."

"Not Kartir from Susa, I hope."

"No. I would not come within twenty feet of that horrid man. They were Romans from Thrace. A nice group of ladies, all bound to make a new life in Antioch. We figured if they could start over, we could start over." She took a few bites of her meal.

"So we never went to Constantinople. I refused to go until we had found you and Justin. The road, like the city we left behind, was too unpredictable. I felt it would open its mouth and swallow me."

"As it had swallowed us."

"Exactly. Well, when we got to Antioch, I sent a letter to Pater. I told him about the betrayal of Gallus. I told him Justin was kidnapped, and you'd disappeared. I wrote we weren't coming, but we'd be at Aunt Aemilia's. He did not answer for a long time. We wondered what happened to him. He's never come back. Because Mater's gone, I guess." She did not speak for a moment, looking at the table.

What could I say? I wished to give her hope, but instead just put my hand on hers. "I miss her, too."

My hand felt the ring, and it burned like acid. I lifted my hand away from the pain.

She seemed to not notice, but kept her eyes on the table. I saw the others were listening as she continued. "Every so often Pater sent money. No message, only money. Not as much as before, but at least we knew he was alive. Infrequent, but always enough, always when we needed it."

"You recovered your property, then?"

She shook her head, "No, our fields fare well, but Gallus bled us dry." I looked at Mater, who nodded to my silent question. This was why there were so few servants.

"We strive to recompense those robbed by Gallus."

"Your difficulty grieves me."

"Oh, please, let us not speak of such sorrow. I still want you to tell me about your time in Gothland," she said, "Justin told the others a bit."

"Certainly."

"You are home." She raised her voice and her glass and looked at me. "It is a happy feast day. The homecoming of our prodigals!" She hoorah-ed, and the others raised their glasses and hoorah-ed.

We told her about the Goths, and our capture, and the military training we went through. She laughed so much she cried, and the smile in her eyes never left. She had changed, somehow. Her attentiveness was delightful. If not for the ring which kept flashing by me as she spoke, I might have thought . . . well, what I might have thought was forbidden, so I kept my mind from going down that path.

The dishes kept arriving, the girls taking turns in serving. They obviously had not dismissed the cook. Roast chicken and leeks arrived next on our plates.

"We read the Scrolls all the time," Byziana said, watching my response. "Every evening. Just as we did in Widow Arité's home, we sit by the fire or on the terrace and read through Scripture portions."

"So you still have some Scrolls? In the Trunk?" My voice echoed with elation.

"A few. I sold four in the village, and three more . . ." with this she cringed, "for our passage home."

I glanced at Justin, who tapped a finger to his lips. I nodded agreement.

"At least you have a few of them left."

"Not as many as we used to. I feel like I have failed our ancestors. They so hoped we would keep those safe. And pass them on. It is a shame. I've failed them."

"Byziana, there's something you should know. It may help you."

She looked up at me, soft eyebrows raised, like a child hoping for good news. At that moment, her eyelids called for me to kiss them. The love in me propelled me to connect with her, to start our fire-circle. *What was I saying?* She waited for me to speak. *Oh right!*

"The Epistle to Timothy says the word of God is '*living and active.*' Another verse says Scripture is '*powerful and effective.*'"

"That's in Hebrews!"

"You're right. But wherever you left those Scriptures, they will bring about a holy effect. They are God's message to this world. It is just as right for the Scrolls to be in the world, not locked in a trunk here."

"Yes, but . . ." she struggled for words. "But while we had them I did not value them."

"But you still have some."

"Yes."

"And you read them."

"Yes. All the time."

"What great news. Surely you are better for it. Gaia Sophia would have been pleased." A slight cloud flittered over Byzia's countenance.

Katerina drew my attention. "We've considered copying the remaining Scrolls, but are not trained in the art. We're afraid to ask the Bishop for help because we heard they're collecting all the Scriptures. And we don't wanna lose the few left in our family trust."

"I heard the same," I said, and recounted the Constantinople priest's comment. A servant helped Natalia bring in stewed leeks with baked fish. I hardly had room for all this food, but the taste of home urged me to keep eating.

"Marcellus, if you go to study—oh, you have heard about Athens, have you not?" Katerina put her pinky nail in her mouth.

"What about Athens?" Everyone watched me with concern.

"Justinian has closed the school of Athens," Mater answered.

The news shocked me. Though I had put aside all hopes of Athens, hearing this distressed me. "Why? Why would he do that?"

"He says it fosters paganism. He has not closed the monasterial schools. The law school of Berytus is open. As is Alexandria. And Constantinople has a new school. But Athens is closed," Katerina said.

"Do you still hope to study, Son?" my mother asked, biting her bottom lip.

I glanced from face to face. The women seemed to think my answer would determine the future of the world. How could I answer?

"I have not given it much thought. I just got home." My chuckle met their sober, worried smiles.

Natalia entered with dessert, a large platter of kopton cakes. The flaky pastries layered with sesame walnut paste and honey distracted Justin and me for a long while. Goths were not known for their desserts. In fact, at this moment, I could not remember a single dessert in the Gothic cuisine.

After we had enjoyed the sweets, we fielded teasing comments on our undistracted focus on those cakes.

Katerina resumed the conversation. I watched her face as she spoke—the complaining child of yesterday had improved greatly!

"If you do go to school, I was going to say, you can learn to transcribe and then we will have copies to give our friends."

"The papyri have completely flaked away." Natalia looked at me as if I could undo the damage.

"They are falling apart?" Justin leaned back in his seat now and folded his hands over his swollen stomach.

"I am afraid so," Mater said. "We are careful, the writing is fine. But the parchments have worn well."

"Taking the Trunk with us was probably not a good idea." Katerina rubbed her arms as if remembering the cold. "They seemed to all breathe in the damp. I cannot believe I suggested we leave those in the Taurus Mountains!"

"They were an added burden, and ours was a hard journey. Yet if we had not taken those Scrolls, we would have died," Byziana chided.

"True. The Scrolls changed our life with the Goths. If Marcellus had not known how to read, if we had not those Scrolls, I dare say we would not be here today. Do you agree, Brother?"

"Yes. At first the king had confiscated our Scrolls. But then once we learned to speak their language, he insisted I translate them. His 'spoils of war' as he called them. I read from the Gospel of John. And our Lord Christ changed his life. He had heard some of Christianity, but had not been interested until he heard the words of God himself. So I know it is fine for Scripture to be in the hands of other people."

"If they read it," Justin added.

"Exactly. If they read it."

A memory burst reminded me of something. "I wonder whatever happened to the Galatians scroll."

"What do you mean?"

"I sold it to a stable owner for a horse. When we went back there, no one remembered it."

"Do you mean in Tyana?" Mater asked.

"Yes."

"Oh, that's interesting. Very interesting."

"What?"

"You lost the Epistle to the Galatians in Galatia! What could be more appropriate!"

"Besides," said Natalia. "If a man sold a horse for it, he must have seen value in it. Horses do not come cheap."

I nodded. "I wonder if we will ever know."

"It is in the hands of God," my mother reminded us. "It's His Word. He'll bring it where He wants it."

"Can we do anything about the decaying Scrolls?" I asked at length.

"Fine parchment, they call it vellum, is the best. People say it will last till Christ returns," Mater suggested. She took an apple Natalia was serving from a wooden bowl.

"But it takes months to make one vellum scroll. And we would need dozens of those." Katerina shrugged her shoulders.

"We could write small," Natalia suggested. "I would help if I could read Greek."

"Which is another complication," Mater said. "I am afraid these days Latin is the common language. It is the emperor's mother tongue, and people have forgotten Greek."

"How about re-using Pater's library?" I suggested. The room became silent as everyone stopped moving to look at me, then my mother.

She did not answer, but thought, finger at her lips. The library represented all Pater had been. His sum of knowledge still lived there on those caudices and scrolls and parchments. Our library was a shrine to my father. I did not ask lightly, and she knew this.

"Would you clean off those parchments?" Justin asked. "They are quite valuable . . . ."

"Not all of them. We can use the less important works," I said.

"It is not too difficult, I hear," Katerina informed us. "Milk and bran will wash the words right off. *Palimsestoi* are not ideal writing surfaces, since the other writing may still be visible, but they are an option."

Mater was indecisive, so I chose to not press her.

"It is a thought we can think of another time. Meanwhile we have our 'family trust' as Katerina said. At least we can hear the sacred words."

Mater adjourned us to the Fireside Room and we leaned back and lifted our feet as Byziana excused herself to get a Scroll from the Trunk.

"Before you go there, I have a gift for you," I said.

"A gift?" Natalia jumped up and skipped to my side. "What about for me?"

"And for me," Katerina chimed in.

"Yes. I have three. One for each of you. Close your eyes." I motioned to Justin.

He ran to his baggage and retrieved the lost Scrolls. "Open your hands." One by one the girls felt the Scroll and squealed.

Byziana threw her arms around her brother. In her hands was the Scroll with the red string. "We have not lost it! We have not lost it!" Tears trickled down her face. "Oh, Mater! I have your Scroll!"

"The lady at the inn kept them in a cabinet all these years."

"Unbelievable." Katerina turned to her sister. "But did we not give the inn four?"

"Only three were still there," Justin answered.

"Oh no," said my mother.

"I wonder which one we lost." Byziana held her mother's favorite Scroll to her chest. "Never mind, three returned is better than seven still lost."

"Well we have the Colossians Epistle. I could not remember which ones were there, which ones I gave. I was so distraught . . . . But I knew we lost this one. Let us read it tonight!"

"We left all four of our Scrolls with the Goths."

"May it do them some good," Mater said.

"I dare say it did! King Olufr never liked the Arian ideas other Goths had brought his way. Particularly that the Son of God was created by God the Father. He claimed Christianity was a tool of kings to gain Rome and to cause war."

"That is too bad." My mother clicked her tongue.

"He longed for peace. Which is what drew him. He was a tried and true pagan until he heard John's Gospel, and the Corinthians Epistle about love."

"You lost that Scroll, too?" Natalia groaned. "I loved that one."

"Not lost. Gave. He said that he had long thought mankind should consider others more than oneself, but he could never persuade his people of it until they heard the wisdom from Saint Paul and Saint John. They loved the reasonableness of love." My family nodded with agreement.

"The people were amazed by Christ, His life, His death, His words. The whole tribe changed. Oh, it was pleasant to speak of Christ to a people so eager to hear. Peace with God and peace with others."

Justin laughed. "It changed their warfare, I dare say."

"How so?" asked Natalia.

"Love-your-enemy and raid-and-plunder do not mix well."

"What did they do?"

"Marcellus taught them about business."

"You did what!" Mater asked, looking at me with a half-raised eyebrow.

"I know. You're asking what I know about business. All I did was suggest they sell their handicrafts, their boots and furs. The king took to action like a horse running."

They threw more questions about the business efforts.

Then Natalia asked, "Do we still have the Gospel of Matthew? Those were the only two Gospel-accounts in our trunk."

"Are we going to read? Or simply talk about how great the Scrolls are without opening them?" Byziana giggled. "I shall check our trunk tonight, and we will compile a list of what we still have. Meanwhile let us read Mater's favorite Scroll."

Joyful firewood crackled, grateful hearts stared into the fire, hungry ears opened to the Word, and I read the Scroll.

When I finished, Katerina sighed. "I wish I could always remember every word of this Scroll. It is filled with such beauty and wisdom. I know why Mater loved it so."

"Is there any way we can visit King Olufr, so we can hear John again?" Natalia asked.

"I hope to. Someday," I said.

Byziana's eyebrows raised in surprise, "You would return?"

"Aha," said Justin, winking at me. "He wants to see his Gothic princess again!"

Justin, if I were closer I'd punch you in the nose for such a comment. I glared at him. *You should not have mentioned Mari.* He understood my look and laughed at me.

"Gothic princess?" Byziana paled.

My frustration with Justin turned into a nervous smile when I saw all the ladies looking at me, gape-mouthed. I licked my lips and smirked, shrugging my shoulders.

If I hadn't left the day I had, I would be married to Mari. That is a fact. I refused to meet Byziana's eyes.

My mother shifted in her seat and straightened her robe. Katerina stared at me, face aghast.

It would have remained a funny unspoken joke if Byziana had not started twisting her ring. Twisting, twisting.

"What were we talking about?" I asked.

"A princess," said Natalia, with awe.

"Oh yes, the Gospel of John," I recalled.

"Right, the gospels. Do you think they have a copy of the other two in Alexandria?" Natalia looked up into my face.

"Which other two?" Katerina asked.

"The other Canon Gospels? Which are those? Philip and . . ."

"Not Philip. It is Mark and Luke," I said. "The Gospels are Matthew, Mark, Luke and John. You seem pretty caught up in gathering the Scrolls."

"Imagine if all the Scriptures were in the same place." Natalia propped her chin on folded hands. "Imagine if you could go to one place, like . . . like Jerusalem . . . and read the Hebrew Scriptures and the Gospel Scriptures and the Epistles, and not have to go to a different monastery to find each one. I would like to live there. If there were a place like that. I mean if I could read."

"It would be a lot of work to track down a full set of all the Canon works," I said, shaking my head at the task. "What we have. . . or had. . . was probably one of the largest collections."

"I have heard," said Mater slowly, "that way back when, Constantine commissioned fifty complete Scripture Canon sets to be copied and bound in caudex and sent throughout the Empire."

Everyone was silent. *Fifty copies!*

What a grand thought. To have it all. All in one caudex, one book. I imagined finding one of Constantine's caudices someday. *I swear, Marcellus, I will find you one.*

"It must have taken a lot of time to copy," Byziana said.

"I wonder what happened to those books?" Natalia asked. "Why do we only have one copy of our own Scrolls? After all these years . . . ? It's been passed on, and we have sold them and lost them, but we still have only one copy of each."

"We are not a monastery, for goodness sake, Nati." Justin yawned, stretched his arms and reached up to stretch his back.

"If I learn the craft of transcribing—I give you my word—I'll make you your own copy of our Scrolls," I said. "That will be a start for your collection. And I will teach you to read. It is not a bad idea, little one."

"I'm not little. I am twelve years old."

"No you are not." Justin's face twisted with the petty disagreement. "You're—"

"Well, almost. I am almost twelve."

"You know, I was betrothed . . . when I was . . . when I . . . ," Byziana's voice tapered off.

My throat tightened. *Again Belisarius and his hold on her ruins our beautiful family time!*

"Well, well," Mater tried to rally our spirits. "It is late, and our travelers are no doubt tired and ready for bed. We always have tomorrow to talk, children. Come now."

She stood up and swept the girls toward the door. I walked with Justin and we waited for the girls to go into their house, and for Mater to walk toward her bedchamber.

"Welcome home, Brother," he said, holding out his hand, the other hand on my shoulder.

"Welcome home." I took his hand. My eyes were still on the

doorway where Byziana had disappeared.

"Do I not please you?"

"What?"

"I am here." He drew my attention, waving his hand in front of me. "Your long face can wait until you are alone in your room. Will you not wish me good night?"

You speak nonsense. How much could you know of my troubles? "Good night, Justin."

"You have a bad case of the sickness, Brother."

Sickness? What sickness? "I'm not sick. Perhaps, as Mater said, I am tired." I looked again at their door and sighed. "I shall retire, then."

"Good idea."

"Good night."

"Good night," he chuckled as he walked across the path to his house.

GLASS BOTTLE DAYS

A glassblower once came to Antioch when I was a child. Using his thin glass bars and fire, he showed us his skill. As we stood near his elbow, he lit the glass on his shaping stick, using the fire to make a molten ball of glass. The glass glowed red as fire. And then he blew into his shaping stick, gently sending breath into the glass ball, opening the body of his fragile bottle. The art form was beautiful. Fire and glass. Breath and a new bottle.

My time in Antioch those next two weeks resembled that glassblower's bottle. I had gone through fire, my life now at the glassblower's table. Hopes were enlarging my life, showing me the shape it should be. I saw my home in Antioch. Our time in Arité's cottage had been a foretaste of this complete dream I had. Byziana, me, our family, Antioch. And now it was mine. Ours.

I was home again. We sat together, read together, ate together, walked together. The dream was lovely those few days.

Byziana and I reclined on Mount Silpius one day, near the spot we watched the earthquake happen almost six years ago. She was no longer that carefree girl, arms outstretched to the sky.

"Remember what happened here, Marcellus? Remember the rocks rolling down this hill?" She traced the path those boulders had taken.

"What a big change for our lives," I answered.

"I was so angry at God. But do you know what was worse? For me? You and Justin being gone. Disappeared. I'd much prefer an earthquake to losing you both."

"It ended up well, though," I said. "We're back."

"You might not have come back, and I . . . I don't know how I could've lived the rest of my life."

"You would've gone on with your life. Like Grandmater Emmilia, after Naucratius."

"We turned to the Scrolls. Aunt started us reading them. She was inconsolable. We read every night. One evening, through the Epistle to the Hebrews, our dear Saint Paul reminded us to '*endure hardship as discipline.*' '*The Lord disciplines those He loves,*' and though unpleasant, this will bring holiness."

Byziana spoke as her mother had of Scripture, with love for the Word of God. She adjusted the hairties on the back of her head.

"Remember reading that? In Mopsos, the night we lost everything? I always hoped I could be like you. You are so strong. So trusting of God."

I chuckled and shook my head in disagreement. *If she only knew who I really am.*

"How do you do it? How do you stay so faithful, Marcellus?" She untied her hair and shook it out behind her, flowing wavy hair. Her intoxicating scent swirled around me.

"Before Gothland I was not who you claim I was. I wanted to trust God, but didn't. Not yet. Something happened that redirected my thinking."

"What happened?"

I took a deep breath and exhaled, reliving the memory. "When we got there, King Olufr informed us he'd execute us if we tried to escape. What a great burden. I was responsible not only for my own welfare, but for Justin too. Then one day I was sitting by a river, feeling sorry for myself. Regretting all the difficulties I had lived through."

"I had many of those days."

"I can believe it. But this one time I was thinking about . . . a particular painful misfortune that made no sense. Something from when I was a boy."

She looked to ask more. I am glad she did not.

"I was with the other soldiers resting on the riverbank after our noontime meal, looking out at the trees on the edge of shore. Tall trees with their roots pressed down into the soil. It reminded me of those kittens, the day of our earthquake. Do you recall how eagerly they pressed their mother for milk?"

Byziana nodded.

"I always thought it'd be nice to have that kind of trust. In God. But then the earthquake happened, and sorrow upon sorrow."

My eyes found the spot on the street way below, and I spoke to the Street of Colonnades.

"Then I noticed one crooked tree on the river. It leaned over the river as if there was a time it was going to fall in." I tilted my hand at an angle. "But the tree's top half was as straight as the others in the woods." Curving my hand I matched the strange angle of the tree trunk.

"Fascinating." She ran her fingers through her hair, straightening where the wind had blown it.

"Yes. It refused to fall. I like to think it sent its roots down deeper to drink of earth, it lifted its face to heaven in prayer to God, and it righted itself, refusing to give in. Finding its balance again."

Byziana stared out at Antioch below us, humming in thought.

"So I decided to live that way as well. To survive. To stand strong, to look to God and live on. No matter what tried to knock me down."

She turned back. "Did you? Were you able to?"

"I moved on with my life, did what I was told, learned the language. That's how I righted myself. The tree didn't choose where to grow, either, I figured. Soon after, the king called me to his yurt to ask about the Scrolls."

She pointed to the city. "Remember we used to ask, 'What does God want from us?' Maybe that's what He wants from us."

"I think that tree knew, in some strange way," I said.

"When hardship came, the earthquakes and everything, our cries in the night, we shook our fists at God. Blamed Him. But if we hadn't been outside Tyana that night, if those exact Goths hadn't taken you, you wouldn't have told King Olufr about our Lord Christ."

I followed her profile. Smile-lines smoothed her face. Her hair fluttered with the wind, tempting me to touch it. "I understood now. It's not about us. It is about God. It is about His holiness, and our becoming holy. And about His desires, which are far wiser than ours. Your story confirms this."

She spoke of God in a bright eager fast way—this was a new

Byziana. *She must have found peace with God, with her mother.*

"Do you know when I knew all this?" she continued.

"No. When?"

Her eyes were on the city, then returned to me. "The moment I saw your bearded, Goth-y face!" She touched my cheek where the beard had been. Without thinking, I took her hand and kissed it. I could not pull my eyes from her. She turned away again, blushing, but kept her hand in mine.

Deep in my gut, I knew this was dishonest. *She is betrothed. Another man's.* But my heart defied Belisarius. *Stop me if you can.* Her hand in mine felt wrong and delicious and right at the same time. I felt the challenge call out across the miles from my deeply beating heart.

Where are you? Where have you been? Have you wiped her tears all these years? What kind of man are you to not protect people? The wind carried my challenge along the Pilgrim Way.

The wind whipped her hair around her neck and she straightened it. Her hair look so soft. Thankfully, her mind was still on God, and her next words stopped me from much.

"I still have many unanswered questions since then. You know my biggest one."

I hesitated. "Chalcedon?"

"Yes. Still my mind doesn't understand it, or why it matters so."

Why it matters. My distraction dissolved away as a flood of memories from Tyana came to mind. The answer to her big question. A peace to the Debate.

"I know how it's true. I was going to tell you years ago, but never did." I looked into her eyes and formed the words. "Only a man could bear man's sin. But no mere man could have borne its weight."

She said nothing, only looking at me as if I would say more. Her reaction confused me. I shook my head and frowned.

"What's wrong?"

"I know it's an important idea. But my words can't put the color and texture and depth into the importance." I tried again. "I mean, our Lord Christ had to be God to survive the caliber of sin. He had to be man to take our place."

She shook her head, still not understanding. I looked at her hand in mine, feeling dejected again. Words could not suffice.

She brushed back a strand of hair. "I hear what you are saying. But how can it be true? And why does it matter, Marcellus?"

Why were my words inept?

"Lady Sophia said it mattered more than anything," I said, shaking my head again. I still had no answer. "I do know that Christ being man matters because He had to be our high priest." That was related. Why didn't it make sense to Byziana?

She waited for me to continue. My answer had fallen flat and old questions began resurfacing. Two natures in one person still seemed contradictory. And if so, Reason would not demand it?

"But why?" Byziana continued. "Hebrews said He makes intercession as high priest. But that could be God the Son interceding. What is significant about Christ's humanity? Why is it essential?"

"I cannot explain why Christ needed to be man, metaphysically. I know it says so in the Scriptures. And what I told you makes sense to me. Maybe we're missing some information about the world."

"Hmm," she leaned back onto the grass with a sad frown.

"I will find out for you, though. One day, when I study."

With all the horrors that await us in life, our tears seemed to require an ethereal answer just out of our grasp. She traced my fingers. "Thanks. I look forward to finding out." I watched her touch each of my fingers, and the fire-circle raged. My eyes found her lips.

It was quiet for a while. Then she asked, "So do you truly have a princess, in Gothland? Waiting for you?"

"I do not know if she's waiting."

"Is she your princess?" Her eyebrows pinched.

I took a deep breath. "Many desire her to be mine. She desires it. The king desires it."

Her face lost its color and she sat up. "And so you will return? To Gothland?"

"I am not sure," I said, standing and pulling her hand to help her up. "Should we go home?"

She did not stand, nor did she pull her hand from mine. "Don't you wish to speak?"

"Not of Gothland."

She continued as if she had not heard me. "Does she mean anything to you? Your princess."

I could not answer. Mari had become a good friend.

"Will you marry her if . . . when . . . you return?"

What can I tell her? That I left Gothland because I wouldn't have Mari? Because I loved someone who I thought had married another? What can I say?

"She must be pretty, your barbarian princess."

"She is. Inside and out. She was my nurse. Fed me. Kept me from dying. And she taught me to speak her language."

"So you have her accent. And you spent a lot of time with her?"

"Well, yes. But I was also busy fighting wars."

"And you won her heart."

I shrugged my shoulders. I put my other hand over hers.

"But you left her. Why did you leave her?"

Should I tell Byziana the truth? Should I tell of my pleading with the king to not give Mari to me? To let me go home? Should I tell of Mari's tears when I told her I would leave? Should I tell this to Byziana?

She twisted the ring, which twisted a sword in my heart. The irony of it all took my breath away. *I could've been a prince among the Goths. But declined so I could come home to Byziana, who will yet marry Belisarius.*

"Marcellus, come. Sit with me." Her eyes rested on our hands. "Let us not think of it, then."

I sat down again, our fingers intertwined.

And after that she spoke neither of Gothland, nor of Mari. Those few days were perfect. Gothland was forgotten. Belisarius was forgotten.

Those days brought me true and perfect happiness.

Sometimes life feels complete, like two opposite realms of your life have come together as one. Then one morning it all changed.

The early morning hoofbeats pattered up our road pummeling the ground like a hailstorm. After the courier left, I heard Byziana come to our door and ask to see my mother. They sat in our Fireside Room reading and talking. I hovered at the door, but Mater chased me away.

Byziana called me in a few minutes later. She stood, letter-in-hand.

"What is it? Good news, I hope. Is it from Gaius Justus?"

"Yes, it's from Pater. In Constantinople."

"He's in Constantinople? We looked for him when we were there, and couldn't find him."

They're acting as if they received bad news.

"Is all well?"

She handed me the letter, half-size and on washed parchment. "See, even your father reuses his parchment," I quipped.

They acted as if someone had died.

I read:

"Gaius Justus of Antioch, Constantinople, Front Street, to Byziana of Antioch, Mount Silpius

Greetings daughter. Count Belisarius, has been amazingly successful of late. He would like to marry soon. Please come with haste to Constantinople. Do not delay. Received word Justin was in the Royal City. If he is in Antioch, please bring him.

With apologies, Gaius Justus"

It was a messy letter. Awkward. Different from his others. The word choice atypical, I could not put my finger on it. *Why's he apologizing?*

"You look worried," I said, hoping they would identify the problem. The ring twisted, round and round.

"What should I do?" Byziana asked me. Mater watched me as if I were to decide for Byziana.

"Why do you ask me?" We knew this moment would come. I was not the one to ask. "The pater says to come." I spit out the words.

"That is the point, is it not, Byzia?" Mater said. "Marcellus points you right. The pater makes the decisions, and we trust the Pater. Gaius Justus must not be crossed."

My passions raged, hearing those words. "Why is there a question?" I barked. They had some gall asking me. Mater held her finger up to quiet me. I whipped my robe around and left the room, furious at being crossed, furious at being quieted. My precious glass dream bottle shattered across the floor, and nobody cared.

A CONSECRATED LIFE

After a while I returned to the Fireside Room where everyone had congregated.

"Did you hear the news? Father has called us to Constantinople again." Justin tried to read my feelings.

"Well, then my mother will be alone again. Since I plan to go to University. And upon return I'll join a monastery."

Byziana's face blanched. "Marcellus, are you? Truly? You will take vows?"

Katerina ran up to me, "No. You can't. You mustn't."

"Maybe I can copy those Scripture scrolls for you, finally, Nati," I said with an empty chuckle that sounded like the bark of a dog. But not even Natalia looked pleased.

Mater's expression was enigmatic.

"Is it not a noble calling, dear Mater?" I asked her, wishing my words would injure those who hurt me.

How could they so easily leave behind this special, precious time together? Two weeks was not long enough. *I waited three years. This is not long enough!*

After an extended pause Mater answered, looking from face to face. Her words were not full of enthusiasm as I would have expected. "Your father always wished you to go to study. Finances are not an issue, at least for us anymore." She looked again at Byziana.

"But if you wish to be a monk above all else, My Son, then it is your calling, I suppose."

The "I suppose" irked me more than any other words. *Is it not she, who taught me from the cradle to love God? Is it not she, who impressed upon me the need to live a righteous life?*

"Will you be up on a pillar, too, dear Brother?" Justin snorted. "Just the kind of impact you would like on this world."

A pillar? I fumed inside. *A pillar? Me?* "I do not know," I said aloud, feeling like I was falling down a well and not asking a soul for help. "I suppose if it comes to it, yes."

I shot an angry look at everyone. *How can you not understand? How can you not see? She shouldn't marry Belisarius. It shouldn't be his hand she holds!*

Natalia touched my arm with featherlight fingers, "Will you take Byziana to Constantinople?"

I threw down dear Natalia's hand. "Don't involve me!" I yelled and left the room again in a rage.

My mother came into my sleeping quarters a couple hours later. She sat next to me on my bed and combed my hair with her fingers. The calming touch from my childhood soothed me some today. "Is this what you truly wish? Do you desire to consecrate your life to God, Marcellus?"

How could I explain to her? How could I explain what I had seen? What I felt now?

"Of course I want my life consecrated to God," I wept, the tears bursting through the dam. I was young again, being knocked down again by the laughing soldiers, being hurt repeatedly again by things out of my control. And I could do nothing to stop them.

"Then you should consecrate yourself to God. Your pater's great wish was for you to be a scholar. You have an inherent proficiency for study and thought."

She pulled me to herself. My mother's arms were once a great retreat, a great refuge, a loving haven. But the tenderness I felt in her arms no longer met my needs.

She must have sensed my tension. Pulling away, she put her hand on my cheek.

"You've changed, Marcellus . . . ," and nodded in her sympathetic way. "Good for you."

"But Mater, why is it either one or the other? Why can I not consecrate my life as a man and not as a monk?"

Mothers have a way of understanding their sons as no other woman does. It is a fact of nature, perhaps. Is it not mothers who pick up their weeping infant to placate their hunger? Is it not mothers who wipe away the blood on the skinned knee? Is it not mothers who watch their awkward sons become men? *Why is it that now, when it matters more than all these, she doesn't understand my problem?*

"In our world, only monks can live consecrated lives. Saint Paul showed how worries of life pull married men away from serving God. If you must consecrate yourself in this way, with vows of poverty and chastity, you must do it now, before you make a tie you may regret."

She did not know it was too late. I could never consecrate myself to God. I would always be a ghost in my heart, searching for Byziana's hand that could not be found.

Return to Gothland. The idea started as a seed in my mind.

"If this is what you are determined to do, at least do your duty to Byziana and her family, and take her to Belisarius. Let her family be established again. Then go to study."

Established? With Belisarius? He frequented prostitutes! Even my mother had turned her back on me. I groaned and rolled onto my side, away from her. My pillow was soon wet with tears. I did not hear her leave.

I thought again of Gothland. The quick growth of my idea seemed to bring salve to my aching heart. *I shall collect other Scriptures to take to them. I can be a scholar under King Olufr. Read everything I find.* My mind swam in the thought of those scrolls and parchments around me on the tables and chairs.

But then he will make me marry his daughter. I groaned again. *How can anyone live a life of right decisions when he is bound to the foolish desires of others? Why had Gaius Justus made such a promise of his firstborn?* A word came to my mind.

Constantinople. What had Katerina said? A new university in Constantinople.

I can study there.

PATER'S PROMISE

I returned to the family for dinner. The servant clanked the dishes against each other, the wine was sour, the food bland. My soul was raw, and whenever Byziana tried to catch my eye, I looked beyond her, as if I did not notice.

She would marry Belisarius, after all this time, and he such a man. The storm clouds hovered over my sky, and I did not speak.

Justin sat next to me, refilling my wine glass, laughing in his way, slapping my back to emphasize a joke. Natalia came over with a bowl of fruit. How many years had it been since Byziana had likewise danced her way between guests with a fruit bowl? Had her father been here, would he marry Natalia off as well to the first scoundrel he met? Byziana sat at the other end of the half-moon-shaped table. Silent and straight-backed she pushed around the food on her plate.

Katerina started crying. "Oh, how I wish Mater were here! Everything's ruined now. I don't wanna live in Constantinople!" She jumped up from the table and ran from the room. Natalia followed her out.

My mother was not eating, but observed the interactions with a gentle frown. She nodded to herself, and then asked Byziana, "Is it settled then, dear? Will you go to your father?"

'Will you go to Belisarius?' was what she meant. At her words, Byziana's eyes flew to mine with a concerned question. I straightened my back and studied a bird flying in the sky behind her. She would ask me to escort her. But I refused. *Not this time.*

"Yes, Aunt Aemelia. I believe I must. My father wishes me to come. And as he said in the letter, time has passed too swiftly."

Her braided hair in perfect curls surrounded her face like an angel's halo. What had happened to us? How could one letter wreak such havoc on our lives?

And that was when Mater betrayed me and all I stood for. "Then I shall send Marcellus with you again. You must take the horses and speed your way."

"Speedy horses? Count me in, too," said Justin.

Byziana's eyes were on me but I grit my teeth to not reveal my thoughts. *I can go against my mother's wishes, but she knows I won't. She will make me the hangman of my darling.*

Mater's finger was on her lips, further planning her design. "I am afraid I must ask a favor from you, dear Niece. Would you leave Natalia for me? I need a friend, a nurse to stay with me, and she is so perfectly created for that—aren't you dear?"—for as she spoke, Natalia came up to her side.

Katerina, listening from the hallway, called out, "I refuse to go that bandit road again! If Natalia will stay, please Sister, may I stay? Please, Aunt?"

So with these manipulative words, and arrangements that followed, my mother forced me to escort Byziana and her brother yet again to Constantinople.

And then I broke my vow of silence, "Mater, if that is your desire, I shall arrange for my studies afterwards. From Constantinople I shall continue on to Alexandria or Berytus or Rome. And perhaps be gone for several years," I said. It was a lie. I would not move on.

Byziana did not seem to care what I said. She kept folding and unfolding her hands in her lap, looking at her plate in thought, most likely distressed over being separated from her sisters, I figured. She stood, chin-up like an empress, and asked quiet leave of her aunt.

After she left, I informed my mother, "I go to discuss our affairs with Steward Dynamius. But I believe you will continue to be cared for in my absence."

Mater assented, but also seemed worried by the preparations, or some other concern privy to women.

EYES WIDE OPEN

I packed up much as a man in a daze. Experience lent me ideas for the necessary and the unnecessary. Speed being of the essence, we would travel light. She could send for her possessions and the Trunk later if needed. After all, the clothes and belongings of a mistress in Antioch would seem backward in Theodora's court.

I pushed aside all of my personal interest and approached my work as I had under my enslavement to the barbarians.

Early on departure day before the sun rose, I was fastening the final bundles onto the pack horse when I saw Byziana scrutinizing her seating pillion behind Justin's saddle. The horse, used to heavy riders, would not be hindered by the weight of two.

"I prefer to travel behind you, Marcellus. Justin takes too many risks."

I nodded and without a word secured the pillion behind my saddle. I had no energy to argue with this woman.

She did not like my silence. "You mustn't behave this way, Cousin. If you do not want to take me to Constantinople, you should refuse. I can hire a guide to travel with Justin and myself."

Cousin? Her words flared my indignation. *Hire a guide?* This was our exact argument of three years ago.

But her hand on my arm put out the offense and started another fire. I reached down to the horse's leg, flicking myself free myself from her touch. When I stood, her eyes met mine, questioning. My heart was not used to such heights and depths, and tears welled.

She turned away, "If it's such a burden, you shouldn't have agreed."

Why do women misunderstand men? Why do they believe their own inventions about your thoughts and punish you accordingly?

She began to walk away, and I grabbed her arm. *Since the beginning when Adam told Eve not to take the fruit, women have been going against wisdom, acting on their whims, and ruining lives. She won't listen, but I'll say it, anyway.*

"Do not marry him."

She blinked twice, shaking her head in uncertainty. "Then whom shall I marry?" As she asked me this, I heard her answer from many years ago. *The Pater makes the decisions. We trust the Pater. The whole system will collapse.*

I saw in her the pain of obedience, and an innocent submission. Gaius Justus would not be crossed. We both knew him. It was the same argument all over.

"Whom should I marry, Marcellus?" her earnest pleading carried something else—was it grief?

"Do you know I waited for you? When you were gone. I refused to go to Constantinople, wondering if I had caused your death. I waited for news of you. I would have blamed Belisarius, Pater, everyone, if you had never come back."

She put her fingers to her tears. "And after all that waiting . . . after all that, you punish me by this condemnation."

No one understood my disapproval. *Why is this world filled with people whose lives pivot around money? No marriage guarantees security. How can they not see?*

I took her hand into mine. I longed to lift it to my mouth.

Cold, small, fragile, I knew this hand. I put my other hand on top, wishing to never let it go.

Why will they sacrifice her life for an unsure future with such a man? Certainly Scripture is against this.

I thought of Ruth and Boaz. *No hope there. Ruth married out of economic necessity. Rachel and Isaac. Money again. Even for holy women of the past, money made the sun cross the sky.*

Without thinking, I drew her to myself and held her against my chest, the lava in me raging and burning into our fire-circle. "What do you want from me? What should I say?" I whispered in her ear. My hand felt that warm curve of her neck.

She did not answer right away, but rested against me. I imagined this was the pain Patriarch Epiphrates felt in the vat of pitch. Fire. Torture. Unable to resist.

"I need you to not be angry with me," she said at last.

"I'm not angry with you, Byzia," I said. Not with her. I breathed in the floral scent of her hair. *Oh God, please help me.*

"I told you before. All I have is this ring. All our hope rides on that promise, I suppose."

The words cooled me like a tonic. *That cursed ring.* I dropped my arms and began re-strapping a securely strapped bundle. Gaius Justus was forward-looking, true. I could give her no valid reason to defy his will. No answer sufficed. The storm-cloud glowered over my head again.

All her hopes? Her father had sealed her fate. Either submit—and gain Belisarius and all he stood for, or object—and lose her good name in Antioch and all that stood for. *The Pater's will must be done.*

"I pray for your happiness," I promised, with a bite of sarcasm, re-strapping the baggage yet again.

She replied in the firm voice of a martyr, "Happiness is not my intention."

I sighed and turned around. "Happiness can be no one's purpose. Life assures us that happiness is fleeting. Joy, peace, purposeful living, family, godliness, these alone should be our intention." It may have been true, but the platitude sounded cold and calloused even to my bitter ears.

"Cousin . . . Marcellus . . . please understand something. We face destitution. You think that my being in Constantinople means my being unfaithful to God. That if I live there I'm going against everything our forefathers believed in. That old quarrel again. You are wrong. I wish you saw it like I do. I must do all in my power to help my family regain its position. Belisarius has proven he is destined for greatness. Since our engagement he has become great in this Empire. This is the only way I know."

Greatness? I crossed my arms and looked at her pinching my lips shut.

She bit the inside of her cheek. "It may be a world-based greatness. Oh, I know it is. But his home cannot fall. Our family depends on me."

Did she really believe that? I could not tell.

"Don't do it." Did I say it aloud, or just think it so strongly that I thought I had spoken?

Why can I speak candid words to a Gothic princess, but to Byziana only stumble over honesty? I knew I should have fallen to my knees and confessed everything. But I refused to beg. I refused to force her against her will, against her father, against all she lived for.

By her response she had not heard me. "Do I have any other option, Marcellus? Do I?"

I straightened my shoulders and stuck out my chin. My teeth clenched. *You'll never consider marriage to me as a valid option, in light of your father's wishes. You told me as much. To offer is absurd. If you attempt to break the engagement for me, my own honor will be in question.*

She watched me for some time, her eyes asking again for something, I knew not what. *How can I counter what your pater sealed with Belisarius, in front of the whole of Antioch? I will be chased out of town.*

Then she sighed. "So I go to my destiny. Waiting these years has taught me much. Sitting at your mother's feet. Listening to the Scrolls. Do you remember that Saint Paul said, *'The things that have happened to me have actually turned out for the furtherance of the gospel'*? Saint Paul understood nighttime weeping. Sufferings worse than mine, I'm sure. . . . As have you, in Gothland. What if our Lord desires me to make a difference in the Emperor's Palace, as you did in captivity?"

I could not counter this reasoning. She spoke true. And yet if she were with that man, I doubted those hopes could ever come true. She had lived over five years in the prospect of marriage to Belisarius. None of her time in the Scriptures had swerved her from that goal. I could not change her. Her next words were a sword in my heart.

"In light of all this, I go in with my eyes wide open. Wide open."

If she will go, I will go, and never leave Constantinople. I will shadow her in that city—and God forgive me—swear I'll kill Belisarius if he betrays her, if he once makes her cry.

ON THE PILLION

*E**yes wide open**,* she had said. There was no debating our return to Constantinople. We said farewell and left at first light. She rode behind me, her warm arms around my waist. As a general taking his queen to marry the enemy king who would slaughter her on the wedding night, I rode on in solemn and morose duty.

Justin gave up trying to speak with me and rode ahead as fast as his horse could carry him. I refused to warn him that tiring the horse extended our journey. Let him learn that himself.

Byziana rested her head on my back and was silent. Day in, day out. Often sleeping, always leaning against me, arms around me. *Oh, bitter warmth!*

It took four days to Mopsos. We crossed the Cilician Gate in a day, thank God. The village inns were a day's ride from each other. *Why had we ever walked those many years ago?*

One night, as I carried my sleeping charge into an inn I made a decision. Justin opened the door for me and I took her to the bed. Her peaceful face—eyes which had closed in trust on my watch. Her limp arms—hands which had locked around my waist to keep her safe. I lay her down and knew I needed to tell her.

Sitting on the edge of her bed, I traced her face, her neck with my eyes. How many peaceful days did she have left? Belisarius, and the life he would give, would strip her of every decent thing. *I must speak. Tomorrow. On the road tomorrow I'll tell her everything.* Looking at her I framed the words.

Byziana, may I tell you something? . . . No, too weak.

You must not marry that man . . . also weak. And I had already said that.

Do you remember the night of your betrothal? . . . Yes, a good beginning. *After we left your mother's bedside, after the party, I saw the troops outside. I followed them down the hill. Curious . . .* I liked my phrasing so far and hoped it strong.

By the time I was at the base of Silpius Hill, they were already propositioning the night ladies. Following the example of Belisarius . . . .

No.

I threw out my plan.

I can't bad-talk her betrothed. The union is set. It will do no good. And she might cut me off from her life forever.

Justin peeked his head in, "Everything okay?"

I stood up and pulled the blanket over Byziana's chest. She rolled to her side mumbling something, then brought the blanket up to her chin.

"I'm coming," I said to Justin, disappointed at my weakness. I stepped out the door, but the self-loathing was too strong. I went back in, shut the door firmly and sat on the floor next to her bed. *I know myself. I'll find some excuse tomorrow and keep my secret.*

"I know you're asleep, Byzia. But I can't. . . or I won't tell you while I'm awake. It's too horrible to tell anyone. But I need to tell you."

I watched her eyelids. "You're not awake, are you?" There was no sign, so I took a deep breath.

"I need to warn you about Belisarius. He's not who you think he is." I sighed. *Am I really going through with this?* I made sure she was still asleep, tried to steady myself, then pressed on. I could feel my pulse increase.

"The night of your engagement, after your banquet, he went out to the streets. To the prostitutes. I was. . . propelled. . . to follow the soldiers down to the city. And they saw me watching them. Belisarius was busy with the prostitutes. And his men. . . they hurt me really bad. In a way no one should ever be hurt. And it broke my heart."

My breathing increased as I remembered in vivid detail every injury, every sword flick, every fist, every jibe, every guffaw. "I didn't know men could be so mean. So evil. And I called to Belisarius."

Predator-eyes narrowed. Beastly smile stretched over hidden fangs. "He saw what was happening, but he laughed at me and returned to that woman. Byziana, they did not kill me, though I wished they had."

His troops, the ugly Indulf, leaving me face-in-dirt, now propositioning the women of the brothel. Imitating their captain.

Byziana gasped. *Did she hear me?* I watched her breathe deeply. *No. She's still asleep.* I let out my breath and continued.

"I don't hate them. Not anymore. They have no Christ, just the name. No honor, just the robe. And yet here you are. Sleeping. On your way to him." I took her hand in mine.

"I haven't had the. . . the courage . . . to speak of it. And so I wait till you are asleep. Because I was not strong enough to stop them. Because I am not strong enough to tell you. And because he is your betrothed."

My head shook at the dilemma. "So this man you must marry will do you wrong. And I am too proud to confess what he is." *The Pater makes the decisions. Trust the Pater.* The words chided me, though I claimed them dutifully. "So forgive me for being weak. Forgive me."

I had done it. I had told her, in a way. I tried to evoke relief, but to no avail. Instead a vision rushed at me.

In my mind's eye the scene changed. No longer was I on the ground surrounded by soldiers.

Wolves had Byziana on the ground by her throat . . . teeth about to pierce her white skin.

She called to me for help, reaching out to me . . . like Thomas grasping the dirt, like the buried men asking for deliverance.

But I laughed at her . . . and I turned from her . . . to the woman at the wall . . . for I was busy kissing the lovely lips . . . of Megalopsychos.

The vision terrified me. I was more horrified than that night when it had all happened. My heart cramped as if in a vice. *It's me. I am her greatest enemy. I am taking her to her death. I am culpable in this. My silence is party to her fate.*

A soft knock drew my panicked eyes away from her and to the door. Justin entered. "I thought you were coming down."

I gulped and stood. I could not control my breathing.

"Your face is white as a sheet. Are you sick? What were you doing here?"

This was supposed to relieve my conscience. But I stand condemned. Her blood is on my hands. I shrugged and forced a smile. But distress flowed in my veins.

He looked back at his sister, still sleeping. "Is she awake? Were you talking?"

"No. We can go down." I deflected, running my fingers through my hair.

We sat at the inn's fireplace. Justin spoke of our days in Olufr's army, trying to get me to laugh. If I slept that night, I know it not for I awoke with the same weariness I had brought to my bed.

Silence made me a traitor. Condemnation's sword stabbed my heart, *strike-step-guard-strike-backhand.*

And yet I continued my hypocrisy. At each inn, each night of that three-week-long journey, I faithfully carried her to her room, place a slow Judas kiss on her cheek, and watch her for a moment before closing the door.

Her innocent face at peace, unaware of what awaited her. Because I loved my honor more.

She will share her husband with the army, her marriage bed with the brothel. He will not be good to her, yet she will reestablish the family fortune. Eyes wide open, going to her death. And I am serving her on a platter to the wolves. I am no different than him.

I prayed day and night. *God, is there no other way? God in heaven, can you not rescue her from this deadly embrace?* Silence from heaven, no Scripture in reply, became my retribution.

By the time we had reached Ancyra, I could no longer sleep. I did not speak. My jaws ached from clenched teeth. And then we met John.

THE TOME OF LEO

One day a young monk caught up with us. Justin, eager for some daytime conversation, invited him to lunch when we stopped. Old pines surrounded the wooded area under which we sat. From the base of one, an artesian spring burst forth from the dirt, its bubbling water trickling past the fire-pit in the center of the trees. Only early morning sun could reach into this darkened solace, making it a perfect, natural refuge for weary travelers. I gathered wood and lit a fire as Byziana and the monk conversed.

His name was John, hailing from Ephesus. Empress Theodora had summoned him from Zuqnin Monastery to discuss religion.

"Oh, then you must be a Monophysite," Byziana exclaimed.

"Absolutely. All intelligent people are," he answered.

Her eyebrows raised, and she looked at me in surprise. The monk looked at Byziana, his eyes strolling down her body. In a moment, Justin's gaze met mine. In a coordinated move, he stepped into the monk's line of vision and I urged Byziana to be seated at the fire across from the man, blocking his gawking look.

As he spoke, the arms of this long-winded John of Ephesus undulated up and down. I gave him a wide berth, watching the interchange from across the campfire to avoid his flailing appendages. The topics he introduced changed almost as soon as they began.

Justin took his arrows and came back within minutes, carrying several wild pheasants. He feathered them, then skewered them over the fire to roast.

"Barbarians fill this empire. Do you know they sacrifice to every stone and tree they see?" The monk's nasal elocution vibrated through very large teeth, producing a sound not long tolerable. "Look beyond, see you the tree at the top of yonder hill? Those strings and cloths tied to those trees are pagan symbols of worship. They believe the tree will grant them their wish."

Byziana mentioned she had seen these trees starting at the outskirts of Caesearea after the Cilician Gate.

"My lady, these divine trees litter our landscape. They are a sign the empire is filled with pagans."

"They haven't heard the gospel of Christ?"

"Madame, they heard the gospel and rejected it!"

I asked him his sources for this information.

"Everyone knows this, my good sir. Since Constantine made our great empire a Christian nation, every inhabitant and every citizen is to be a Christian. One state, one law, one church. This paganism must be countered. The gospel truth must reach into every home."

Byziana agreed, to which he replied,

"Our Divine Augusta Theodora also agrees. She has called me to discuss a way to spread the truth to these heathens. My dear friend and brother Anthimus of Trebizond plans to join me. Together we will help these poor inhabitants. Our illustrious emperor has stated, if our society is to have one religious belief, we must eliminate the paganism practiced throughout the empire."

The mention of Theodora, and her role in this plan, made me uncomfortable. Why would the empress need be consulted in the work of evangelism?

Byziana responded to this before I. "How, sir, can the matter be solved? If they refuse to believe, the model from Scripture is to try elsewhere. Is it not the Gospel of Matthew?"

"My little lady, do not fluster yourself with such ideas. Model from Scripture, indeed. History has shown how to subject a people to Reason." He winked, wiggled his eyebrows then, SMACK! struck his fist into his hand.

Byziana drew back in surprise. I diverted the conversation so she could regain composure.

"Is it not true Theodora and Justinian have differing views on Chalcedon? Have they joined opinion?"

Then, ignoring Byziana's presence altogether, he began a long tirade into the deception of Chalcedon, their rejection of the Ephesus Council, the maneuvering of emperors in the affairs of religion.

Byziana looked at me and asked, "Marcellus, do you believe emperors should have no say in affairs of faith?"

She saw the contradictions in the monk's claims and was suggesting I challenge him.

"Wise King Theodoric said, 'We cannot order a religion, because no one is forced to believe against his will,'" I said.

"Aha. The 'wisdom' of a Gothic barbarian. Do you quote an Arian to me? One who allowed Jews free rein in his empire?"

"Good sir, please let me hear your views. What has race to do with Reason? Is it only the Roman who has a foothold on wisdom?"

"Yes. You summarize my views."

"And what of King Solomon? Was he not a Jew?" asked Byziana.

"No, not a Jew. He was a Hebrew. He was the Son of David and an ancestor of Christ. Jews are the ones who killed Christ."

"So does race then predispose people to either foolishness or to wisdom?" I asked.

"I would say, yes."

"The wise race being Roman?" I glanced at Byziana. She was nodding, understanding my train of thought.

"Yes."

"Justinian is a foreigner, hailing from Thrace. Is his race foolish?"

"He himself is wise." He grimaced and scratched his neck, for he understood his contradiction. "After all, Justinian has proven himself a Roman."

"I think you see your reasoning falls apart," I said. "I purport both the rich and the poor can be wise. Barbarian, Jew, and Christian can all know Truth and Reason. There is a standard far superior to race. Truth, dear friend, does not depend on a leader's claims of Truth. Truth holds itself irrelative to man. Scriptures point us to Truth, man's whims do not."

John of Ephesus disagreed. "If the leaders do not reclaim the people's faith, they will return to paganism in a generation's time."

Justin laughed, patting John on his back. "But a moment ago you criticized an emperor, sir, for negating the Council of Ephesus. Surely you speak from two sides of your mouth."

"Justin!" Byziana scolded. "You insult our guest."

The monk was speechless.

She tried to rally his spirits. "Sir, please tell us of your monastery. What Scriptures do you possess?"

"We have the entire Canon."

We all faced him dumbfounded. At that moment, all thoughts of Constantinople faded away. *Zuqnin. They have the whole Canon.* I imagined myself sitting, scrolls and parchments surrounding me, absorbing the sacred Word of God. *The entire Canon! Then I could make copies for myself. Rome cannot be so blessed.*

Byziana glanced at me. "Perhaps Marcellus, here, will come to your monastery. He plans to be a monk."

The reminder of my foolish words were like another slap in the face. I jumped up and left to check on the horses.

"We also house copies of other famous works," he was saying. "In fact, I carry a copy of Pope Leo's Tome, for the emperor himself has asked for it."

A motion from Byziana and Justin asked, "May we see the Tome?"

"By all means," John said, running to his saddlebag. He handed a bound book to Justin saying, "The man twists Scripture to make it say what he wishes. Read the blasphemy if you wish."

"My sister has in the past inclined toward your position, Brother John. Byzia, why not read this yourself and let the blasphemy persuade you fully against Chalcedon?"

She secured the book with a curtsy and hastened over toward me.

"I would like to ask you, Brother John," Justin interjected, drawing John's lingering eyes from her. "What is it about Chalcedon you Monophysites do not accept? Besides the rejection of the Ephesus Council."

"Young man, I see you ask a deep question. I wonder if you have the knowledge to understand my answer. I shall answer briefly. It is illogical for God to also be man. It is impossible by definition. If he is man, he is by definition not God. If He is God He cannot be, by definition, limited by manhood . . ."

While he turned the pheasants over the fire, Justin listened to the monk give his brief answer at great length. I admired Justin's patience.

Byziana sat on her pillion against a tree and read the book with an ever peaceful, ever confident, ever brightening look on her face.

A while later, Justin called Byziana and me back to the fire. "The fowl are cooked, my friends!"

I gave her my hand to help her stand.

"What does it say? Byzia, your whole face is glowing."

She touched her cheek. "Is it really?" Then she closed the thick book's binding, sighing. "I wish I had a copy of this text. I wish you could've read it. Pope Leo speaks as you do, as one who knows and loves the faith of our fathers, the faith of Emmilia. He speaks the words of Scripture with love and power."

Her eyes opened wide. "Do you think he had one of Constantine's Fifty?" My heart seemed to skip a beat at the notion.

"Justinian would be a dead horse to not be influenced against the Monophysites view. If you know Scripture, this rings as true as a bell," she whispered, putting her hand on mine. "I understand you now. And I understand Mater. Why it matters. It matters because the Bible is clear about it, even if we cannot reason through its metaphysics."

Approaching the fire, she handed the book back to the monk. "Thank you, sir. I found the words quite, quite inspirational."

"You agree with me, then? Leo twists Scripture to fit his own agenda?"

Byziana licked her lips and scratched her cheek. "He does use Scripture to back up his points. Have you read the complete Canon, Brother John?"

"Perhaps I have," was his non-committal answer. "But I know all about Scripture, having been a monk all these years."

How long could those years have been? He's not much older than me.

"I see," said Byziana. She helped serve the meal and then sat down next to me.

John's large teeth tore the meat. He smacked his lips and spoke with food in his mouth, talking about the superior Monophysite philosophy and faith, swinging his food around to empha-size his points.

Justin and Byziana both listened with pulled smiles on their lips. At a break in his verbiage, Byziana asked in her sweet voice, "Brother John, how then can Christ empathize with our sinfulness and frailty? The Epistle to the Philippians claims He was in very nature God and took on the form of a man, being made in our likeness."

I stared at her. She debated Scripture—as a scholar with ready ammunition. I wondered about this Tome.

"And Leo says, "To pay off the debt of our state, invulnerable nature was united to a nature that could suff—"

"Dear lady, do not trouble yourself in things beyond your understanding," John interrupted, waving of his meat-filled hand.

She blanched and looked at me, shocked.

I stepped over to the fire and poured dirt over the flames. We had spent too long here, and my tolerance of his voice had expired. "You should be amazed by this lady, John of Ephesus. She has read as many Scriptures as most of us."

"I know not of that. But you must recognize. We at Zuqnin possess the complete Canon. Your incomplete knowledge of Holy Scripture disqualifies you to challenge me, for our sources are much superior."

Byziana was biting the inside of her mouth, but stood up and bowed her head in respect. "You have been welcome at our table, Brother John. May God bless you in all ways—"

Justin added, "We will surely hinder your speed, sir. You may continue on without waiting for us."

From his hesitation it was clear he planned to travel with us. He soon overcame this surprise as Justin ushered him to his horse.

We wished him well as he hastened on toward Theodora and the frightening plan of his.

"I so wished to warn him of his error," Byziana started. "He can't have read Scripture. He can't have truly read Leo's Tome himself. No one can read it and not feel . . . empowered in his spirit."

Justin put his arm around his sister and kissed her cheek. "Not everyone is as kind-hearted as you, dearest. You would better speak to this pine tree for all the good it does. That monk's mind is satisfied with error, and no amount of persuasion could pull him from it."

"Marcellus, you've been saying the same all these years. But until I read the treatise of Pope Leo, I didn't see it all in one place. I understand now. I understand what you meant. My heart is still ringing the true tone his letter struck."

"What did it say, Sister?"

"Justin you must read it for yourself . . ." she squinted down the road, toward the distanced monk and sighed. "Alas, you cannot."

"Well?" I asked. "Share with us his message to the council. You're our only link to it, Byziana."

"Pope Leo wrote regarding a heresy that Christ was not man. He wrote in particular against a priest named Eutyches who taught this but was himself ignorant of Scripture. Leo spoke of being *'pupils of the truth.'* That it is essential to study Scripture to know Truth. But more so, he asserted our creeds teach all one needs to avoid heresy. His words sounded like the creed you recited those many years ago in Widow Arité's house."

"You remember that?"

"I wish I remembered it better. But when I read the words of Pope Leo, I heard familiar phrases." She touched her chin to remember.

"He stated if you are not pupils of Truth you are masters of error. And I remember something else, absolutely persuasive. I shall never call myself Monophysite again. Never. Why anyone cannot know Christ is man is beyond me. What a fool I was. He quoted from the Apostle Paul who quoted from The Beginnings when God says to Abraham: *'in your seed shall all nations be blessed.'* That was it for me."

"You were persuaded that easily?"

"And there is a verse in the Prophet Isaiah, *'Behold a virgin shall conceive and bear a son and shall call His name Immanuel which means God with us.'* He was born, from the seed of Abraham. He was not only an apparent man, He was an actual man. He had ancestors. Do you understand what this means?"

She had never been so animated. I shook my head, so she gave her answer. "It means I understand!" Her joyful spark —the one I had sorely missed, the one despair had all but smothered— that smile was back.

She took a deep breath and let it out with a loud sigh. "I feel so free! I used to think logic defended only the Monophysite view.

My father had taught me that intelligent people lean on Reason, and that Reason can shape our faith."

"But that is true. Reason is essential," I said.

"Yes, but Pater insisted on more. Reason points to the impossibility of a man having attributes of God, he said. If God became man, and God is one, who was looking after all of creation during that time? Therefore, God must have only 'appeared' as a man, but remained purely God—His divinity swallowed up any humanity. I don't agree with him anymore. Because reasoning this way demands we disregard much of Scripture. As Leo showed, Scripture logically presents Christ's essential humanity. Not just Scripture, but Reason."

"What did you say? How does Reason require it?"

"Leo wrote, '*It does not belong to the same nature to weep out of deep-felt pity for a dead friend, and to call him back to life again at the word of command.*'"

"Good point," said Justin, nodding his head. "Two natures functioning together in one person."

That was it!

She pulled her arms around herself in an embrace. "It matters. Regardless of my being able to explain the dynamics of how God could be man, His actions showed That Jesus was God and Jesus was man, though we never are told How. And That he was both is enough. The reasonableness hits my heart. Do you remember, Marcellus, what I said a long time ago? About believing and understanding?"

"You said you couldn't believe what you didn't understand," I said.

"Right. But His humanity-divinity is more reasonable than trying to explain why Christ's death mattered if He was solely God—Widow Arité said as much. Or why Mary was necessary. It matters!"

"Praise Christ," I answered. The change in her was God's doing, a miracle wrought through the melding of four years of Scripture reading with a passionate eighty-year-old letter. Thank God for His servant, Pope Leo!

Her eye caught on the glimmer of her ring, and her radiant face paled. "Oh no! What am I going to do in Theodora's court now?"

My condemnation rushed to its place in my heart, sobering the mood. Was this how Judas felt as he plotted for Christ's death? I watched her in horror. Her joy reprimanded me for I conspired for her demise.

Justin finished loading the horses. "I can only hope Justinian is as affected by the Tome as you were, Byzia."

"I fear that monk will do these people wrong."

She scanned the hills surrounding us. "Would John actually injure people to spread his beliefs? He suggested Theodora was complicit in this plan with him."

"I don't know." Shrugging, I hoped against it, but was sure of his character.

I helped her onto her pillion. She did not let go of my hand. "Will I be any help at the court of such people?" Belisarius's ring cut into my palm as the words sliced into my heart.

Pulling my hand away, I mounted the steed. I did not wish to answer such a question.

"We must continue if we will reach Malagina before dark." Our monkish diversion and Byziana's renewal had darkened my storm. And yet, when Byziana put her arms around me, I found my possessive hand over hers. Cold winter threatened to approach, and she pulled close, cheek onto my back. Like a sponge I absorbed the glowing fire of our touch. So few days were left to us. Thus we rode until sunset when we arrived at the village of Malagina.

CHALCEDON VIRGIN

After Ancyra and Malagina, we crossed a mountain ridge then through Nicaea and Nicomedia. Having been unconscious and tied to the back of a horse, I did not see these cities my first time through. Likewise, on our return I gave no notice to the sights, my only attention on the blurred road passing on either side of me.

This time, my final time with Byziana, was different. Riding behind me, chattering about everything she saw and heard in this countryside, she brought a lightheartedness I had not felt in weeks.

When we arrived at the Bosporos Strait, my hand was over her two hands, keeping them warm. Coming over the crest we beheld the glorious city of Constantinople northwest across the strait. I helped her off the horse as she gasped. "The city is enormous. What a striking picture of civilization."

I stretched my legs, sore because we had ridden long to make it by noon. "It is our capital, it has to be impressive." Our hometown had been large, too. And more grand. *I wonder if she's also thinking about Antioch.*

Below us ships and barges and ferries tatted to and fro across the busy strait. Fisherman shanties, the wharf, wagons along the seafront all spoke to the industry and significance of this bustling seaport.

Chalcedon, the famous city, reflected the midday sun on its marble and brass palaces.

I looked southwards down the coast. *Somewhere is Rufinianae Monastery one of Belisarius's mansions.* I did not wish to think further on his eminence.

"Thank you. For bringing me here," Byziana said. "I know I put you into all sorts of trials. Me being the hardest one."

She put her hand on mine, and her fingers between mine. "You sacrificed a lot for me. Your time. Your accounts. Your studies."

If only you knew the extent of my loss. And the cost you pay for my honor. I pulled my hand out from hers.

"But you made it possible for me to get here. You were the perfect companion on my biggest life journey...." She stopped herself and looked out over my shoulder, eyebrows furrowed.

Her face brightened at the sight of her brother. Justin came riding up the hill. "I found the ferry crossing. Follow me."

We made our way down to the Bosporos. The coast was alive with peddlers and pedestrians. Justin and I left Byziana to watch the horses and went to pay the ferryman for passage. When I returned, she had disappeared.

I searched up and down the street, but then heard her calling me from between the storefronts. She was on a side street by a chapel where I joined her.

"I apologize for leaving. The horses pulled me here. Isn't it a sweet little place?"

The beauty and intricacy of the stone-carved geometric designs on walls reflected the building's age. We tied the horses and knocked at the gate. A black-hatted priest opened it wide.

"Welcome to the Cathedral of Saint Euphemia."

From the outside, the church was small, so the expansive insides surprised us. Innumerable candles and a superabundance of gold-gilded saint icons bolstered awe and a poignant feeling of our own insignificance.

We lit our own candles in the narthex and set them with the others, saying a prayer. At the priest's call, we walked deeper into the chapel's gold-flickering shadowy recesses.

Our attention darted from icon to icon on the walls, coming to rest on Saint Euphemia's candle-embraced reliquary. *I wonder who has Saint Emmilia's or Saint Basil's bones.* Then I recalled the Trunk of Scrolls, a more powerful reliquary. *We don't remember our ancestors by their remains. We have their godly heritage and—some of—their Scrolls. More powerful than bones.*

"Have you heard of Saint Euphemia the martyr?" the priest asked, rolling onto the balls of his feet. We had not, so he told how, though a young woman, she had refused to bow to the gods of Rome. The pagans threw her to the animals at the circus, and a bear mauled her to death, "Right here in Chalcedon!" he said with eyebrows raised.

"But that is not the end. Her sacred body performed a miracle at the Council of Chalcedon . . ." The rest of his anecdote was lost on me, my eyes locked on Byziana's.

The Council? It happened here!

She smiled amazement.

"This is the site!" she whispered, when the priest had finished his story, and started tending to priestly duties.

"What site?" Justin asked, coming up.

"This is Chalcedon. Where the council was."

A gentle, dusty breeze blew through the chapel.

"Can you imagine six hundred bishops and priests and scholars sitting here debating?"

"I doubt they sat. Look at how you riled like fighting cats whenever anyone brought up Chalcedon." Justin studied me and his sister. "Are you two through fighting yet?"

"Yes we are. Don't bring it up again." Byziana jostled her brother.

"You know what's interesting?" I said. "They say, after reading Leo's Tome there was no more debate. Just like your experience. They unanimously affirmed that Leo stated their common belief about Christ."

"I wish you could have read the Tome, too."

Clearing his throat, Justin shook us out of our reverie. "I hope you both are comfortable wading in winter waters. I spent my last denarii on passage. So if we don't embark on this ferry in five minutes, we'll have to swim our way across. I just heard the bell."

"Our last denarii? Good thing Pater is across the strait!" Byziana laughed.

"I have a bit left." I shook my pouch. "But let's still not miss the boat." We hastened out and barely had enough time to put up our horses at the ferry stables and board the vessel.

HARKEN TO
THE GOLDEN HORN

Thus we crossed the river from Chalcedon in Bithynia to Constantinople to give away our lady to the emperor's court, into the hands of God—though to such a man. She believed in Chalcedon. I had fulfilled my promise to Lady Sophia, I tried to reason away my worries. But my heart would not let go.

The sun glittered on the water, the ferry crashed over waves, a spray of sea misted over us, and seagulls glided overhead in restful ease.

It would have been all peace, except that she went to him. And we would part. My torrid love fought my reasoning mind, and the clash brought a tremble to the deepest part of my soul.

Byzia stood next to me at the railing, eyes closed, the sun warming her, the spray of waves misting her face, nothing like a woman going to her death. In a flash, my nightmares returned— the same worries and sorrows I had imagined in King Olufr's land.

If I can no longer protect her, will Byziana become a living martyr? Will the court of Theodora spoil her? I had heard of inner-room conspiracies, of assassination plots and plans for power. *What will happen to her there?*

Justin put his arm around my back and patted my shoulder. "How are you doing?"

He led me to the seating area. "I do not wish to talk about my thoughts, Brother. They are foreboding and dark."

"About my sister?" he asked. His eyebrows twitched in

mock solemnity.

Two children ran in front of us, one of them had a small sack of bread pieces.

"Throw it! Throw it!" a boy said, giving a chunk of bread to his younger sister. The little girl tossed the bread toward the sea birds. It landed on the water, and dozens of seagulls dove for the bread, tearing it to pieces. That poor bread.

"Do again. Do again," the little girl laughed, holding her hand out for more bread. Her laughter drew Byziana's attention.

The boy gave his sister another piece and she threw it. An alert gull caught it in midair and flew off with it. Several birds perched on the railing, cocking their heads at the children.

Innocence lost was not a new thing. Esther from the Hebrew Scriptures had lived through the same.

What would lovely Byziana be like in one year, five years, ten years of life at court? *No matter what she becomes, I'll always remember her as she is now. Standing at the rail, eyes closed, the light and wind on her soft, beautiful face.*

I will pray for her, will hope she, like Esther, would make a difference for goodness and truth in the dark world of politics.

Justin asked again, "Do you have fears for my sister?"

I turned away from him. *You wouldn't understand.* My soul pulsed with sorrow. With worry. With frustration. *And I have no patience for your humor, Justin.*

"Marcellus, do you remember? The first time you went off to war with Olufr's troops, I begged you. I said you should not go. You were leaving me alone, that I needed you. I even went to the king himself, trying to get you recalled."

I did remember.

"You told me something that went deep into my heart. 'If it's God's will for me to return, I will return. If it's His decree for me to die, even staying here cannot save my life. Man's decrees can be changed and broken. They are impotent. But God's will remains potent for all time. Trust in God, Cousin. You can't die unless it is your time.'"

Justin turned me by the shoulder to face him. "That meant much to me. Those words have kept me through difficulties. So I remind you, Brother, in the same way. Do not worry about tomorrow. It is in God's hands." He winked at me, as if he understood the conflict within me, which I knew he could not.

Byziana watched the children. When the boy noticed her he lifted a piece of bread to her.

"You wanna throw one?"

"Sure," she answered.

"Try to throw it in the air, and see if a gull can catch it," the boy suggested.

The little girl giggled with joy when a quick bird caught the bread Byziana threw. Byziana bent down next to her. "What is your name?"

"Anna," she answered.

"Oh, it's like mine. I'm Byziana."

"I like your name." Anna put her finger in her mouth and twisted her shoulders side to side.

"I like yours," Byziana said, kissing the girl on the cheek. Anna lifted her arms and Byziana picked her up, hugging her with delight.

Byziana seemed at peace, accepting of her future, eager almost. *I wonder if the virgin martyr Euphemia had that same peace on her face when she faced the bear.*

A seagull swooped almost hitting them, then soared along the ferry's side, up into the sky.

She looked our way, and seeing us watching her, put the girl down and came over.

"Hey."

"Pretty hungry birds," Justin said.

"Oh yes," she laughed. "You know, those birds just live for the moment. Whatever food comes, comes. Not so me. I was thinking of tomorrow."

She could not know how her words dug coals into my heart. *Tomorrow she will be with him.*

But what she expressed next showed her thoughts were not on the man. "I feel content. With my lot. I believe the reason the Leo's Tome affected me so much is that he spoke Scripture. Almost like Mater talking."

She sat down next to me.

"Mater knew this. When she died, she made me promise something that seemed unreasonable. Those promises made me furious. I know I took a lot of that anger out on you. I apologize."

She looked at me as if she knew she was already forgiven.

I smiled to let her know she was right.

"I hope she can see me now. She would be pleased."

"She would."

"What about you? May I ask? What did Mater say to you the morning she died? Did she talk about the Debate?"

"Yes. The debate was close to her heart. Obviously her greatest concern. She wanted me to help your family to stay in the faith."

"I am glad. I realize God is clear about what He wants us to know and believe and do. It's in His Word. Mater knew it. Tried to tell me."

Take my family to Chalcedon, Lady Sophia had charged me. Here we were together, both in the city and in the faith of Chalcedon. *I've fulfilled my promise to Lady Sophia. Perhaps if Byziana's faith is intact, she can face the lions of court, in spite of who that man was.*

"Remember what Euphrasius preached once? From Job's trials. *'Though He slay me, still I will trust him.'* When I first heard it, I laughed at the idea. But now I know the idea exemplifies wisdom. It is about troubles in life, big or small. Trusting, no matter what happens. You know, I had wanted other things for my life . . ." She sighed and scanned the sea again.

"What things?" I asked.

"It is of no import." She shrugged her shoulders. "My life is before me, and my future is in God's hands. My fortune is with Belisarius which is part of God's plan for me. As of tomorrow, our family troubles are over, and I will have honored my father and lifted the family out of shame and ruin."

She brushed her robe straight and lifted her chin, then looked toward the water.

What a great burden to bear.

She stood up and went to the rail again, and I joined her. Our eyes followed the seagulls soaring alongside the ferry.

"Still, a feeling haunts me, chiding me I should have brought my Scrolls."

She cocked her head at me, adding, "And do not roll your eyes, Marcellus."

"I'm not rolling my eyes."

"I know we were packing light. But I wish we had the Scrolls. We must read them, but with our souls. Think of all those nights Gallus just stood at the door as we read. But did he really hear? I doubt it."

She put her hand on mine. "Tell me the truth, don't you think our journey would have been less . . . less morose," she glanced at me to test the word, "if we had read Scripture together? Be honest."

"I am sure it would have helped me with my concerns," I said, pulling my hand out from under hers.

"What are you worried about?"

My eyes met hers, but I turned away. I did not want her privy to my deepest thoughts. I mumbled something, trying to divert the conversation.

Justin, on the other side of his sister, came to the rescue. "Our cousin is going to Berytus, you know."

That was a secondary worry. As I watched seagulls diving for bread, questions about my future assaulted me. *Shall I study law in Berytus, and gain the knowledge Mater desired and Pater had willed for me? Or shall I return to Antioch and run our home? I can never be a monk, and I will never marry.*

The birds fought over the bread. One seagull was king. The others feared him and left him if he ever approached the bread. *Like with men. The strongest ones always get the bread and the weaker ones had to scramble for the leftovers. Like me.* I fought the thoughts of Byziana by thinking of the Scrolls again.

I might copy, perhaps even translate our Scrolls. A man of learning, a man of wealth, can in his leisure do what he wished. As I copy them I'll learn them by heart. But I could not teach. Teaching was left to the bishops. Except in Gothland. *I should go to Gothland.*

The warmth of Byziana next to me rebuked me. *No. I should not go to Gothland.*

I sighed. *Why is a consecrated life left to the monks, and the everyman left to strive?* Then she did it again, she set her feather-light hand on my forearm. I looked down at her.

"Are you worried about me?"

I watched her face, the porcelain features I had memorized spoke of deep concern. And I nodded.

"Thank you, dear Marcellus." She leaned toward me, her hands on my forearms, tipping up on her toes to kiss my cheek.

My arms slipped around her as if drawn to a lodestone. The

warmth of spirit radiating from within the most precious of souls, the warmth of trust which had fallen asleep against my back this past three weeks, her sun-warmth resided now on my chest.

That fire-circle raged in me and I held on. I clenched her to myself. I smelled the fragrance of her hair—like what the wind carries in summer: lilacs and wheat and oregano. I locked her to myself. *You cannot leave me.* Until my brain screamed at me to release her.

Stolen! It shrieked. *This warmth is stolen! It belongs to another!*

"I apologize," I said, opening my arms wide.

Justin covered a snigger and turned away, whispering, " I apologize."

She did not move away though I had released her. I felt her gaze on my face. She stood, as if held still, close. Her heat pulsated against my chest. I did not trust myself to look at her.

If I look away . . . from watching the seagulls sailing by the railing . . . if I look down into her eyes again—warm, affectionate hazel eyes stayed on me . . . I will lose my resolve.

Why I did not keep her, hold her to myself, profess my love for her, beg her to not marry Belisarius, I do not know. To be true to her, I conceded. *Here our road divides. I, my road to Berytus or Gothland or wherever the devil I was going. She, her road to the courts of Constantine.* The divided road tested all I knew of faith.

She stepped away, breathing out a weary sigh, and joined Justin, who put his arm around her back and stroked her shoulder.

The ship bells rang, the sailors hustled to prepare ropes and planks for mooring.

"When do you leave for University?" she asked me as we watched the sailors.

"I am not sure. There is no set arrival date for me."

"Then if you have no time constraints, you can be here for the wedding! I am so glad. I was worried you might be gone before—" She stopped speaking when she saw me shaking my head.

"I will not be here for your wedding."

"What?" Her face paled, and she stumbled back as if I had pushed her. "What do you mean? I don't accept this."

"You must accept this." I crossed to the rail on the other side of the ferry. "I cannot be there." She followed me.

"Please, Marcellus. Please be there. I want you there. After all we have been through, I need you there."

This was where I drew the line. I was indignant. *How dare you ask that of me? How dare you ask me to be at your wedding?* I kept my back to her.

She came next to me and stood looking out at the golden city's bustling port. "I wanted you there," she said with an acquiescent sigh.

"I will stay with you until you see Belisarius again. That's all I promise."

Justin slid his arm around his sister as we walked toward the exit plank and disembarked.

St. Euphemia
Chalcedon
Waterside
St. Sophia
Basilica
Cistern
Hippodrome
Priorium
Palace
CONSTANTINOPLE
500 m

CONSTANTINOPLE THE MAJESTIC

Face to Face

JANUARY 13, AD 532

S uffice it to say, the next morning we left our inn after breakfasting and arrived at the gates of Priorium, the city residence of Belisarius. Simple to find, known to all, the future dwelling of my beloved and that man.

"Priorium, not Aesmior?" the innkeeper asked—Aesimor being his estate in the southwest countryside of Constantinople.

"Priorium, not Rufinianae in Chalcedon?" the stableman inquired—informing us that Justinian gave Rufinianae to his Magister Militum Belisarius after the battle of Dara two years ago.

"No, the Constantinople home of Belisarius, Priorium," I demanded, growing more and more irate. And so after being assured of the height and length and width and depth of his prestige, they directed us to Priorium, the renowned general's modest semi-palace on the pinnacle of the Great Hill overlooking the wide city of Constantinople.

On the outer door, a heavy bronze knocker sported the face of Oceanus. This brazen statement pronounced to the world that the owner considered himself superior to the sea itself, for the sea itself summoned him. I lifted Oceanus and knocked five times.

A young woman, clad in the linen tunic of a servant, opened the door.

"Justin, son of Gaius Justus. Byziana, daughter of Gaius Justus of Antioch here to see Count Belisarius," I said. "Tell your master we have come a great distance."

The maid nodded, giving a subservient nod of her head. "Yes, sir." She curtsied, then closed the door.

I turned toward Byziana. This was the moment she had been waiting for all these years. She was no longer the lovely young daughter of a nobleman. Six years had straightened her shoulders, grown her figure, lustered her hair, grown her character.

"Why do you clench your teeth, Marcellus?" she asked me. "If I could read myself in the mirror of your face, my looks will repel him. Do I look as bad as that?" She smoothed the folds of her dress and cloak and brushed back stray hairs of her curled locks. I had no answer for her.

"How do I look?" she asked again. "Will he still want me?" She wore an unnecessary self-consciousness. The muscles on my cheeks softened.

Who was I to answer that question? My heart surged at the injustice of life. Oh yes, he will want her. Instead of an answer, I tucked a final loose lock of hair behind her ear, brushing my fingers along her cheek, my thumb caressing for the last time the beloved of my soul. He could not but want her.

The latches opened in front of us, and the maid ushered us in. Removing our winter cloaks and handing them to the doorman, we followed the maid through the passageways.

Her eyes darted from wall tapestry to onyx vase to floor mosaic. The decor of this small city home rivaled any Antiochene manor.

Along the floor, the symmetrical borders of a black and white mosaic marble directed us toward the Great Room. Grand pillars and green trees filled every corner with a sense of easy-come luxury. His home was the house of Byziana's dreams.

As we passed the Great Room, a large tapestry caught my eye. Christian virtues Love, Faith and Hope stood side by side to the Greek Graces: Aglaia, Euphrosyne and Thalia. Goddesses of Splendor, Mirth and Good Cheer. Pagan gods and Christian virtues living side by side caused my gut to tighten. Was this his version of *megalopsychia*?

Cushioned couches overloaded with pillows . . . side-tables of bowls crammed with fruit . . . golden bowls, silver pitchers, rubbed vases . . . broadcast the wealth he had no scruples flaunting.

She will be more than well cared for. Yet the gods and virtues side by side haunted my soul. *Belisarius and Byziana, side by side.* My stoic mind tried to accept my fate. *The time I've had with her, as her protector, as her friend, finishes at this end. I made my choice to be silent and she will receive her fate. God be with her. A home and a husband and*—the thought fought its way to life—*a family await.* My naïve heart defied her fate, for he was such a man. *What have I done?*

The sun reflected through the glass beads on golden threaded swags hanging along the hallway. Glimmers of color fell over the walls and floors and our garments. Toward the sun we walked, toward the balcony hovering the city, toward the couches presenting the sea at your feet, toward the raging fire-pit in the terrace center.

Count Belisarius, his esteemed Magister Militum, stood up upon our entrance. Behind him another well-dressed man, much older, remained seated facing the fire.

The general's presence struck me as regal and dignified and mature. The perfect new Roman. He bore a nobleman's haircut, not a soldier's—rounded and short. His short beard declared him diplomat, his Herculean body declared him seasoned warrior.

As the renowned general walked toward us, his tapestry robe swished and swaggered side to side. The jewel-trimmed fabric, woven in reds and purples and blues and blacks, presented a cacophony of birds: crows, hawks, eagles, vultures. If the garment displayed songbirds or peacocks, I would not know. I saw only the clawed avian.

The count's arm stretched out toward Byziana. "My dear! After so many years, to see you again delights my eyes!" She took his hand and looked to the floor, breathless and speechless. She thought still of her appearance, and his words pleased her. She smoothed her robe again, peeking into his face like she had that banquet night six years ago.

Is she considering him as a husband? Is she wondering if he would be loyal and faithful and loving? Does she know that he . . . I commanded the thought to cease.

Her look pleased the man who smiled with the swollen air of a cock. He lifted her hand, resting it on his arm, turning toward Justin. "You are Justin, the brother, so grown as well—almost rivaling your sister in improvements. It has been too long."

My cousin bowed, "Greetings, Count Belisarius." The count did not respond, but glanced at me, perplexed.

I expected some kind of displeasure, that he would read my secret, know my disgust and envy. Perhaps he disapproved of a strange man accompanying his betrothed. Surely he could not remember me.

And no such memory came to mind. Instead, "You, sir, are welcome as well. May I ask your name?"

"Marcellus Pontus of Antioch, son of Gaius Dorotheus, at your service," I bowed my head. He gazed at me for a long moment as if to drudge up from his past my place in his betrothed's world. But instead of any verbalized thought, his indifferent stare turned into a drawn smile. He spun toward Byziana, whipping my leg with his robe.

His words to her I did not hear. With the sweep of his garment, I lost all fear of the man. With the flick of his robe I knew I was his equal, or more. His behavior showed his true colors even if I alone saw it. He did not wish to be of my acquaintance, he had no use of me, and so he gave me no honor. What a relief, for now I had no need of his acquaintance, either.

He might be a count, chief military commander, confidante to the emperor of Byzantium—yet he lacked breeding, he lacked the genteel grace required of those born to this class.

The general introduced Byziana at his arm to the man on the couch. I never wanted to be that man's friend. *Now my Byzia is his. I am outside her life. Sliced off like a cancer.*

"Let me introduce you to Senator Hypatius," he said to Justin and Byziana.

I waited until they were seated, then dropped myself on a cushioned bench near the entryway. A servant offered a bowl of fruit. I had no appetite, but took an apple. When a maggot wiggled out of a rotted hole, I set the fruit on the table.

The silver fruit bowl in the servant's hands. I studied it. The twisted grapevine relief. *It can't be. Is it?* Was this the one Gallus stole? It was, I was sure of it.

I studied the group at the balcony. *Had Gallus given this to Belisarius?* My head began to ache. *Would Byziana recognize it?* If she recognized the bowl, she would know the truth. Whatever that truth was. That intricate knot of details. I tried to catch her attention, but she was enthralled with the conversation.

"Senator Hypatius is the leading Green senator. Nephew of our illustrious former Emperor Anastasius—may he rest in peace."

"May he rest in peace," replied the others.

"You do well to acknowledge this man," Belisarius continued. "He is esteemed by both the masses and the emperor, even though the emperor is Blue. Of course if the emperor were Green or a Green the emperor, what a different city we would be. Do you not agree, Senator?"

"I do agree, Count." The senator's pleasant, deep laugh resounded through the house, but he offered no more on the subject. *Are they tiptoeing around treason?*

The comment troubled me. *Is he courting Hypatius to become the next emperor? Impossible. Why open that topic among practical strangers?*

"We will be at the races tonight. Have you been to the Hippodrome, Justin of Antioch?"

"Not yet. Perhaps we might visit tod—"

"And which color do you support, Justin?" Belisarius's eyebrows rose in mock interest.

My cousin began, "We do not kn—."

Again he disregarded Justin's answer and offered a new topic for discussion.

"Senator, these are the children of your illustrious Gaius Justus."

Byziana's proud smile warmed me. Justin's shoulders became straighter, until he saw the senator's amusement. He looked at his sister whose eyes met his then moved to mine.

"Indeed?" the senator replied, his face pursed-up. He looked away from my friends and began to rise from his bench. "I should leave you to your business."

"Stay, Hypatius. Stay. You should be here. Shall we call the man?" Belisarius laughed. "Yes, we shall."

I found myself on my feet. He ran to the passageway, pushing past me. "Indulf! Indulf!" Again we passed each other questioning gazes.

A moment later, the man I had seen so many years ago stood before me, the man I had called ugly, the man my heart had insulted, the one who had taken the pouch from Gallus, who had met me at the Colonnades. Indulf.

Yet now, where I thought there would be hate, bitterness, anger, there was something else. Could it be? Joy? Oh, how my heart was drawn to him. His beard, his mannerisms, his dress. Oh, how I missed my dear Ostrogoth friends. He was brother Goth.

My hand reached out. *But for a word with him in his native tongue. To ask of his family. Perhaps I know them. Has he heard King Olufr's new faith?*

"Indulf, bring Gaius Justus at once. He will be at his home on Front Street."

"Pater!" Byziana's whisper drew my attention. Her hands clasped together at her chin, eager eyes sparkling. It had been years since she had seen her father!

"Yes, your honor," Indulf said—that delightful Gothic accent flavored his Latin words. He bowed, and was about to leave, when he caught sight of my furred Gothic boots and my outstretched arm. An intrigued look met mine for a fraction of a second. Then he vanished.

While waiting for my uncle, the two men chatted a few moments over the games and a recent execution of troublemaking rioters.

The senator alerted my attention when I overheard him say, "Our emperor has too heavy a hand on our people. He is trying to prove his power to the Persians, but at our expense. Do we want an emperor like this?"

"Bold words, Senator," Belisarius said holding back a chuckle. Amused at another man's words of treason?

"Count Belisarius, I know you are a man who holds the emperor's ear. And you are one who understands the times. Justinian has sacrificed his own people, in war and in peace, is it not so? Increased taxes burden us since the Cappadocian came. Has he no thought for the common man?"

The general glanced at us before saying, "Senator, you are wise. But I dare not answer you. The emperor was not pleased by my failure at Callinicum last fall."

"Failure? Nonsense," the senator replied. "Merely a stalemate. Do not trouble yourself over that."

I turned to Byziana. Did she not feel unsettled at these words? Her gentle attention followed the parley, back and forth— her hands folded in her lap, her ankles crossed below, her thoughts hidden within.

These bodacious criticisms of our emperor had no place in my world. Had they no fear of us carrying tales of their treason? I shifted in my seat, catching Justin's attention. He raised his eyebrows and flicked a shoulder.

The sun shone on the floor below my feet, highlighting more mosaics and criss-cross patterns. My attention darted around—at the shelves of Egyptian vases, at the black- and red-figured Greek urns, at the frescos on the wall—all goddesses and gods raised to positions of honor in the room. I clenched my teeth again. His wealth made him imprudent.

Byziana's furrowed eyebrows matched a worried frown. A hint of Hypatius glancing in her direction erased the expression. She stretched her mouth into a smile and nodded in polite agreement when Belisarius answered the senator.

"If you say the people feel abused, then the emperor needs to address this."

"I believe he shall, Belisarius," Hypatius said with a cryptic wink. "I believe the emperor will address these abuses."

They exchanged such strange, knowing smiles with each other— *what do these unspoken looks mean?*

Treason. Derision. Discourtesy. I looked toward the entrance, finding my cloak, having a mind to leave this awkward gathering.

Ratt! Ratt! Ratt! The door knocker drew everyone's attention. I watched Indulf slip into the hall's darkness without another look. Then the servant announced Gaius Justus.

PATER'S FATE

When Byziana's father had entered my home six years ago, when he appeared in form and countenance of a ghost, the shock we felt was nothing—nothing to the horror we felt upon seeing him here and now. That ghost of a man was now a crooked pallid creature.

I mean no dishonor to call him creature. When I lived in the Gothic wilderness, one day a village boy brought me a small sickly wolf pup.

A hunter had trapped a she-wolf the night before—its thick winter pelt stretched across the tanning ream in the village center. Seeing the pelt, I knew that the pup's mother was gone, and the pup would soon also be no more. But the boy, Alrick, had cried for me to help the pup.

"It will not survive," I had said. "Its destiny is death."

"But it is a wolf." Alrick's answer carried an idealistic confidence. "Wolves must live."

The wolf pup, smaller than my hand, licked my finger. Its stomach empty, its fur matted, its body trembling and shivering and sneezing. It would die. Seeing Gaius Justus stripped of his glory by some unknown fate brought that pup to mind. Death had its grip on him. Not just Death. Gaius Justus, regent of Antioch, stood before us altogether destitute.

Abandoned by God.

Could this be the man who wrote that letter two months ago?

He limped in pain, using a cane. Wearing no hat or scarf on

his head, his robe tattered as a beggar's, his feet bare as a dead warrior's, his nose and eyes red, draining, dim, crusty.

I could not breathe.

He flinched as the general approached him. *That cringe—had that beast struck my uncle?* Belisarius put his hand on my uncle's shoulder. The squeeze made him wince.

"Pater." Byziana rushed to her father's side. "Oh, Pater!" I ran to our robes at the entryway and brought them to swathe his thinned tunic and moth-eaten cloak. Then I covered his bare feet with my furred boots.

Justin thrust his shoulders back and his chin out. "How dare you? How could you? With all this"—he waved his arm at the surrounding decadence—"let my father become this?"

Belisarius glanced at Gaius Justus and rolled his eyes, shaking his head and tutting. "Please, sit." He slid his hand toward the chairs near them. But Byziana and Justin remained standing on either side of their father.

Hypatius took a loud sip of wine from his silver goblet. He choked on a suppressed laugh and started coughing.

The general dropped on the couch next to the senator and patted his back. He flicked his finger for the servant to fill the glass again. Then he examined the scene before him. We still waited for an answer.

Crossing his leg over his knee, he said, hands pointed to heaven, "What business is it of mine? He is your father. Why did you never seek him out?"

Justin stared at Byziana who stared at me and then back at Belisarius.

"Or do you expect me to tend to every beggar in the city?"

Byziana took her ring off at her brother's request. He held it between two fingers as if plagued. "Did this mean nothing to you? My faithful sister has worn it all these years, yet you treat us thus?"

"Oh, that . . . ?" His voice trailed off as he looked at my uncle. "Do you not find it amusing, Justus? Have you led your family on since then?" His lack of courtesy toward my uncle shocked us. My uncle gave Belisarius his start, his introduction, his status. What could have happened?

The Pater's belated and insincere chuckle turned to an influenzic cough.

"That was in the heat of the moment, my dear young Justin," the count continued without waiting. "I meant nothing by it. Surely, Byziana, you did not take it seriously?" He lifted his eyebrows and a farce of concern contorted his face in calloused innocence. "Surely Justus has not misled you. He has known for years how I regarded it."

For years?

He waited for her to respond, to which she said, "No. Certainly . . . uh, I did not take it. . . uh . . . very . . . seriously."

My breathing quickened and my fists clenched.

Setting her shoulders square, Byziana stretched her face into a big smile to cover her wounded heart. She found my eyes, and for some reason a calm expression smoothed over her face. "I mean, I did know."

Had she heard my confession that night at the inn?

She nodded at me this time. "I knew."

Justin mouthed the word, *What?*

Oblivious to what was happening within her, the general spoke again. I know not why.

Sometimes wisdom is limited by dull wits. With these words he severed himself from our family and from the Old Antiochene Order, as would a swift executioner's blade: "Can you imagine, Senator, if I were married to this beauty"—he gestured to Byziana—"I'd have this beauty"—he gestured now to Gaius Justus—"as a father!" Belisarius roared laughter, chin up to the sky, teeth open to the world.

Antioch's *patrikios* grinned with his broken and missing teeth, he cried with his tearless and crusted eyes, eyes he refused to lift from the floor. I felt like a tethered lion. My soul tore forward and ripped the scurrilous traitor limb from limb.

"Well, General, you've proven your colors," Justin snapped. "You may have the emperor's ear, but I have the ear of the King of Kings. I shall pray for you. But God forgive me, I have no hope for you." He tossed the ring in the fire and turned to escort his sister from the room.

The senator chortled, "Sounds like a Blue."

"Justin, watch your words," Byziana begged as her brother spun back around. "Please, he is right. The engagement was a youthful jest."

My young cousin's lips clamped together but his glare shot flames.

"Brave words for one so young. I could use a fire-pot like you. Have you considered a career in the military?"

"Come now. We must leave," I said.

His arm around her, Justin hurried his sister toward the exit. I embraced the old man's shoulder and tried to usher him out but he resisted my help.

Justin came back into the room.

"Come, Pater."

Gaius Justus kept his face to the floor, clenched his teeth, and stayed in place.

Byziana returned, and bent to catch her father's eyes. "Why do you stay?"

"Only wise one among them," Belisarius said. His leg still crossed over his knee, he lifted a goblet of wine to his lips, watching us as if at theatre.

We stood dumbfounded. A heavy log slipped and thudded in the fire and sparks crackled into the air between us.

"Justus does not wish to tell you. It is clear," the senator said.

"Pater?" She tried to lift the chin of her once proud father. "What do you fear to say?" A tear streaked her face.

"Enough melodrama." The senator clapped his hands in applause. "Enough. It kills me. I will tell you and be done with it."

We turned to the men.

Behind us seagulls cawed and soared in the vast expanse of sky over the city and over the harbor. On the balcony wall, a hunting fresco framed the two men in front of us—men who held casual goblets to their lips, who held our breath with their silence.

"I own your father," Hypatius said at last. "I bought him out of debt." My uncle lifted his head in objection, but a flicker of the senator's frown, and a flash of his hand, and the leader of Antioch lowered it again in submission.

"Yes, yes. We need not be particular about details, but in fact I bought him in lieu of debt he owed me."

Byziana, standing next to me shoulder to shoulder, grabbed my arm in terror.

"It will be fine," I whispered. "We will take care of it. Just listen."

"Debt? What debt?" Justin waited for his father to answer. Gaius Justus took a long breath and blew out slowly.

"It is neither here nor there. He can clear that with you later," Hypatius said. "But the fact remains. I own him and I allow him to live in his own home out of my own good will. He is my slave."

Their father cleared his throat and licked his lips but added not a word.

"He sent for Byziana at my request, truth be known," Belisarius added. "I thought that perhaps we could come to—shall I say?—an agreement regarding the debt."

"What kind of agreement?" asked Justin.

I closed my other hand on top of Byziana's.

When I looked back, I saw the general's gaze on our entwined arms. He raised his eyebrows, a contemptuous smile stretching onto his lips.

"It looks as though her chastity is in question." He flicked his hand toward me. "Perhaps she is not worth what you said, Justus. And here I thought I was being so generous to your family . . ."

I could feel a vibration of rage shaking within me. I stared at him through narrowed lids. She held tighter to me, and my eyes found my sword hilt.

"What agreement?"

He looked back at Justin. "Your sister for your father. Fair trade. I will have your sister. Not as wife, I'll have you know. As my—shall I say—as my personal slave."

He raised his glass in salute. "And I will pay off your father's debt to Hypatius."

The words echoed in my veins. His slave. His personal slave! His mistress for life!

"Not as wife?" Justin's roar had the echo of Gothland in it. Byziana's fingernails gripped my arm.

"What is this about, Pater?" He forced his father to look at him. "Is it true?"

His father bit his lip and lifted panicked eyes to his son. But he still said not a word.

"It is good she arrived now. After all, I am to be married to Lady Antonina in the spring." His off-handed comment to Hypatius tore further at our pain. "And we are no doubt off to war."

As if she were his property already! I wanted to defend her. To say something to make this untrue. The man in front of me was Cyclops in Odysseus's story, who grabbed and ate and grabbed and ate the men while Odysseus stood paralyzed and watched. *It can't be true. I refuse to allow it to happen.* I remembered the battles I fought for King Olufr. Side by side to the king. *I can defend her.* I scanned the room. Belisarius did not have a sword nearby. Justin still wore his.

We can defend her. I grabbed the hilt of my sword, "You cannot have her," I said.

"Aha. The lover finds his voice."

Did my face turn red? I do not know. But red fire burned in my gut. I felt my torso tighten, my teeth grit, my eyes narrow again. I stepped in front of Byziana, hand on my undrawn sword.

The soldier's attention was on my sword, but he remained seated. "The law is behind us, young lover." He drank the dregs of his goblet. Then out of nowhere a sword appeared in his hand and he rushed at me.

Byziana screamed. I shoved her away from the fight.

My sword out, I blocked his attack.

Strike-Step-Guard! Strike-Backhand-Spin-Strike!

He scurried to the center of the room.

Justin stood in front of his sister and father, knees bent, sword raised.

The furor of Gothic battle consumed me. I raised my sword, a fierce raging battle cry coming from the depths of my soul, and I charged.

Belisarius raised his free hand and sword and shushed us, backing away. "Shh. Shh. Stop, stop. Let us talk law."

I restrained my greatest desire. My blade just wanted to touch the man.

Indulf appeared at the doorway, lowered sword but curious eyes stayed on me. Other guards appeared from the woodwork. Their general motioned for them to stand down.

He kept his distance, but walked as he spoke. My cousin stood next to me, sword raised, Byziana behind him.

"If you can pay the debt, it's no use talking any further. Or fighting. You are welcome to make your own agreement with the honorable Hypatius. I only offered to help offset the debt of Justus."

"Gaius Justus," I said.

"Gaius Justus then. No use killing a rascal like you, who has known fierce battle."

Justin shot out, "What is the debt? We will settle."

The old man sighed and his shoulders sunk more than before.

"Do you see, Justus? You only needed the right pressure and your debt would be paid."

To Justin, he added, "Once you hear, you may reconsider. Six pounds of gold, or four hundred fifty solidi, more or less, if I am not mistaken. Is that not right, Senator?" Hypatius tilted his head in acquiescence.

An unnatural silence followed, the seagulls quiet, the waters quiet. The only sounds were the echoing beat of my heart at my throat and the fire's crackle in the middle of the balcony.

Impossible. A king's ransom.

As I calculated it, more than ten years of full harvest income would still not pay this off.

Justin's glare shot fire, unyielding. "We will settle. You may not have my sister."

"Thank you," Hypatius said, shifting in his seat, eyes flitting from us to Belisarius to the guards surrounding the room.

Justin took his father's arm and led him to the door.

Hypatius called after us, "I expect the payment tomorrow, per our agreement, Justus. You children, do not think of leaving this city. I know you will not."

I walked with Byziana on my arm again. If they watched us exit, I did not care. But as we closed the door, I heard the men burst out in laughter.

Things That Have Happened

Byziana gasped outside the front door—she had been holding her breath.

"Pater?" She dropped my arm and rushed toward her father. "What happened? How could you amass such debt?"

"Aaagh!" Justin grabbed his knife and stabbed it into the wooden door. "Why'd I promise to pray for the man?"

I could not chastise him because I was calculating my value in gold.

Byziana surrounded her father's back with her arm, whispering, pulling our cloaks tighter around him and stroking his cheek. Soon her comforting words eased away his shame. "Come now, to Front Street." Byziana took her father's arm in hers, strolling along the street as though there were no bounty on her life.

Would the army take me? Would that earn me much gold? What was the worth of our estates in Antioch? We could sell both. No. Surrendering the property was no solution. For where would our family live? *Selling myself is the only feasible option. But who'll pay a king's ransom for my life?* I found my thumbnail in my mouth again.

Justin walked on the other side of Gaius Justus now, so Byziana let go of her father and took hold of me.

"I like it here." She squeezed my arm. "Holding onto you."

"I like you here, too."

We moved down the hill. Though still early afternoon the overcast sky shed a twilight glow on the road to the water.

"You raised your sword to Belisarius. You could've been hurt."

"Oh no. He would've been hurt."

It was a fact. No one fought like the Goths, not even Belisarius. Which is why he needed Indulf.

"Was he right? About you?"

"That I was a warrior? Yes." I nodded. "He was right."

"No. The other thing." She stopped me and looked into my eyes, waiting for my answer.

A lover, she was asking. I refused to allow another minute go by without making myself clear. I had been silent too long. And who knows what the future holds?

"He was right." I felt a warmth pour from my heart into my cheeks, but kept my gaze on her. *I love you, Byziana. I've loved you all these years. I've loved you since the day of the first earthquake, maybe even before. Yes, I am your lover*, I wanted to say.

Aloud, I said, "I will not let you be taken to Belisarius."

She looked away, but I saw her cheeks smiling. She inhaled and sighed, her smile glowing. "I know you won't, Marcellus. You are my protector, and my friend."

"And your friend," I repeated.

My thumb caressed her hand as we continued along the road. The cursed ring was gone.

"Marcellus, if you hadn't been with me I could not have lived through the pain of this morning. You were with me every step of the way."

I nodded. *I wouldn't have been anywhere else.*

She gasped and stopped in the middle of the street. Her mouth gape-open, she shook her head, wide-eyed.

"What?"

"That's it!" she said.

"What's it?"

"You were with me every step of the way. It is why it matters more than anything!"

"What matters?" I tried to pull her onward. "Keep walking. We'll freeze if we stop."

"Wait a moment. It's important. I know why. It's not just that He was man, it's why He was man. Christ—I know why He had to be really, truly man. He had to walk through the mucky battlefield with us."

I did not understand and shook my head. Lifting my bare feet one by one helped stave off the stone road's chill. "I think you're in shock, Byzia."

"No. You said it once, we deserve none of it. The broken world declares a punishment to come. Yet we have hope in Christ's tears!"

Christ's tears?

"He knows our pain because He walked through them. *'Jesus wept'* He wept!" Tears filled her eyes, but they were tears of joy!

"He lived this sad, sorry, beautiful life. He knows our pain. *'The ungraspable willed to be grasped,'* Pope Leo said. Which is why Christ needed to come in the real live flesh."

She giggled and embraced me, "Isn't it wonderful?"

"You mean about Him being our High Priest? Relating with us in our weakness? Bearing our sin?"

"Relating with us in our tears. Our tears. *'Jesus wept.'* He understands this pain."

She gripped her chest, a brokenhearted expression turning into a sudden, radiant smile and her hands opened. "But He is God! He is holy. He could have just kept us in constant punishment. Yet in His mercy He holds back that suffering. We suffer so little for how selfish we are, for how hurtful we are to others."

A flock of pigeons took wing and Byziana followed their flight from the street to the rooftops and into the sky. Then she continued, "But instead of doling out the punishment we deserve, He came and grieved with us. We do not face them alone."

I put my arm around her. That message she had not understood came to mind again. "The sin of man could not be borne by a holy God, neither could the wrath of God be borne by a mere man. Reason demands a God-man."

She cocked her head and then nodded, "Exactly. He took it on himself. He showed us the way to be free from this broken world even while we live in it."

Bless you, Lady Sophia. This is what you meant. He had to be here with us. "Like a shepherd walking the dark valley, or in the rain, with his sheep," I said. "Suffering the miseries of this life. A man of sorrows."

"Right. In the rain. I know why God is waiting—it's for people to see Jesus's tears! Oh the shining cross. Oh joyous day!"

My mind gyrated with the memories of the past hour. The gods and virtues. The creature, my uncle. The Gothic roar. Their laughter at the closed door. Six pounds of gold. My cold feet. *And she called it a joyous day!* But Jesus had wept, and that made sense of all things.

"Do you remember when you told me I hated God?"

I nodded.

"You were right, I did hate Him. Because I didn't know His true nature."

"I shouldn't have said it like I did. It was mean and spiteful." I stroked her cheek, and she pressed my hand there.

"It hurt. But it made me think. How could He punish people for disagreeing on such an important topic? No. The split church demanded to be repaired. But Reason repairs it—it proves the reality of both Christ's humanity and His divinity. That is the God who was championed at Chalcedon."

She lifted her arms to the sun making its way to its zenith. "I look to heaven, to the golden sun high in the air, and I send up a prayer to God, You who know my pain, How can we be freed of our debt? Our eyes are on you. God of Chalcedon. God of the Earthquake. Word become flesh. You are the God I look to now."

Some women looked down from their windows at the young woman whose arms were lifted to the sun. Children stopped playing in the street, cocking their heads with curiosity. She did not notice. Tears brimmed again.

"Is this what it is like? Is this what faith is like?"

"How do you feel?"

"I pray these things. But I know things will work out. I've no worries, though my whole future, all my honor, depends on something impossible. And I need it by tomorrow." She laughed. "Six pounds of gold by tomorrow."

"Yes, then. That's faith."

I tried to recall a particular verse in Scripture, but it eluded me. All that came to mind was her words the day we left Antioch, *"The things that have happened to me have actually turned out for the furtherance of the gospel,"* I said, realizing for the first time that it all pivoted on the word 'actually.'

"Sometimes when we realize only God can solve a problem, all we can do is throw it into His arms. Byziana, He's the One who turns possibly into actually."

"Well then, God," she threw her hands up, as if tossing a great bundle into the sky, as if letting a caged bird free and watching it fly away, "Here is my problem. I call on the God of the Earthquake to help me. Only that kind of power can save me from this horrid future." She laughed again. "Six pounds of gold! Or slavery!"

I wish I could say thunder resounded in the sky. It did not. Not in the sky. But in my heart there was thunder, a raging thunderous storm. *I will do all in my power to save her.* And I hoped God would, too.

She slipped her arm back through mine, and leaned her face against my shoulder, and we walked again. For all my life I will remember that mind-spinning moment, and the feeling of joyful trust as we strolled together toward the home of Gaius Justus on Front Street.

The squalor Gaius Justus called home had half a front door. The moment we stepped into the room we felt crowded. On the windowsill, even a potted shrub could not muster the will to live in this damp, dark place. Her pater lifted a chair, tipped on its side, and placed it in front of the three-and-a-half-legged table propped against a mildewy wall.

He shook off a frayed cloth and rodents scurried out from under it and around a corner. Looking at the would-be tablecloth, and at the table, and at his children, he lost his last ounce of courage. His knees gave out beneath him. Sinking to the sleeping mat against the wall, he curled up into a ball and wept.

What a change from the man who had stood to announce the betrothal of his daughter to the young promising Captain Belisarius—the man lifting his glass amidst the bounteous table.

Byziana sat next to her father. Justin whispered something to her, then picked up our robes, and we left.

"Here we are at the beginning of winter, and his place is already ice cold!" Justin said outside.

"I wonder what happened." I remembered my mother's words that his money had been infrequent, and she had covered the loss, giving from our own larders. But she had failed to express his neglect. He was not forgetful of his family. Destitution had kept him from it—to such a point he would even agree to sell his daughter into slavery!

"If only I'd been here. If only we weren't taken to the Goths! I could've helped Pater. I'd never let him—or our family name— sink so far."

"In Antioch, your father's name still stands. No harm that cannot be amended."

He considered my point. "How will I ever save my sister?" He looked back down the street toward his father's hovel. "What do we have left? Gallus's work was thorough!"

I stretched my arm over his shoulders. "Your mother told me once, 'When life knocks you down you've only got two choices.'"

He cocked his head. "Two choices?" Then its meaning lit on his face. "Oh. I see. But how do we stand again now?"

"Did you ever think, when we were tied up in Gothland, that we'd stand free in Constantinople one day?"

"No. I never foresaw it."

"The things Gallus did are known to God. Leave it to God's vengeance. Meanwhile, hope dies at death. Until then, there's always a way. The point is to not stay down."

"Is there no life worse than death?"

I considered his words. "But at the end, there awaits for us a life better than life. With a God of such love and kindness. We've nothing to lose." I made a fist and hit my chest with it. "They can make my life hell, but they cannot take heaven from my heart."

Justin stopped, eyes closed, jaw clenched. I waited for him to speak.

He nodded in resignation, "You're right, Marcellus. I can't let it keep me down. But...." His teary eyes spoke what words could not.

"I will not let it happen. Not to your sister."

"You say that with as much faith as you talk of heaven. There's nothing we can do."

"I am not a planner, Justin. I've no idea but one. Yet my idea will solve it all."

We arrived at the bakery and bought two loaves of fresh bread. Then I stopped at the cobbler and bought a cheap pair of shoes, and a wool blanket for my uncle from a neighboring shop.

In my half-filled money-pouch I had enough for their return trip, and for several days in the city before that. A few storefronts down from the cobbler was a stand of fresh fruits and vegetables. I bought a small parcel of these, and we turned toward home.

"Marcellus," Justin said at length. "What's your idea?"

"I shall not speak of it." If he knew my plan, he might hinder me.

I'm a warrior, I can sell myself to a military man. But who would pay my debt up front? Would Hypatius trade my services for the debt? He did not seem to lack finances, but would he like a Gothic warrior like Belisarius had? *Maybe he had use for a bodyguard. I'll speak to him.*

Had Justin read my mind? Or was it written on my face? He decried the idea. "Shall we then lose you? You can't take it on yourself. It's our family's shame, not yours! What of your mother?"

"My mother can take care of herself and the property. Think of her competence during our capture." I grabbed his arm. "And you are my family. It is my business."

"Whatever you plan to do, I refuse to accept." He grabbed me by both shoulders, looking into my face. "It cannot be. It is our debt, we must bear it. You are free, stay free."

"It is my life to give, not yours to save. We can save your sister from shame. I freely give it."

He dropped his arms. "What is it your plan?"

"Hypatius intended to go to the races," I added. "I will speak with him there."

"At the Hippodrome? Wait for me. I am coming, too," he said, demanding my agreement. "Tarry for me at Holy Wisdom Church." He ran back to the waterfront to take the food and blanket to his family.

HOLY WISDOM

As I walked up the steep hill, women shook and hung their laundry on lines above the street, shopkeepers swept their porches, children chased friends, young men marched arm in arm toward the Hippodrome. Life continued.

The sunlight streamed at a sharp winter afternoon angle. In spite of the bite in the air, the early afternoon had enough promise that windows were open to share life with neighbors.

In a short time I entered the Church of Holy Wisdom, the Hagia Sophia church. I had expected a larger church, for it housed the emperor's seat. Yet Hagia Sophia took only half the space that Antioch's Domus Aurea took.

In the central court of the church Justinian's throne was roped off-limits to the general crowd.

I lit a candle, set it in the sand tray, then walked around to see the saints. Saint Andrew's portrait drew my attention. Andrew of the Cross. Our first bishop, here in Constantinople.

Andrew, who had known Christ, had walked with Christ, had brought the loaves and fish to Jesus. He had been here. Had walked these streets, perhaps on the very cobblestone outside.

Looking at his portrait on the fresco warmed me strangely. *We are connected, he and I.* He had crossed through Antioch to Constantinople, he had been at this church or near-abouts. And he had crossed the Donarus—or Danubius as we call it—into the land of the Goths. There had been no Goths in his day. It was Scythia back then.

He had risked everything, taking the gospel to those up the Borysthenes River. *And I brought the gospel there in my day.*

Andrew of the Cross. Blessed Andrew, tied to a cross in Peloponnese because he brought them good news. Darkness has always hated the light. Some of his bones were here in the Capital, at the Holy Apostle church. If things had been different, I might have thought to visit them, to see witness the relics of Saint Andrew.

But if Hypatius accepts my offer, I won't be my own man tomorrow. Why is this world so full of loss? I knelt at the bench and prayed like I had never prayed before. More than I had prayed in Gothland. I called upon the God of the Earthquake, as Byziana had—the God who can be both man and God at the same time, who does amazing things, to rescue the family of Gaius Justus, for rescue was outside of my power.

I left Hagia Sophia with a lighter heart, and strolled through the nearby colonnaded hall, Stoa Basilica, until I saw Justin coming up the road.

"How were they?" I asked Justin.

"He apologized. Can you believe it? He apologized."

"For what?"

"For going into debt."

"Unheard of. How did it happen? Did you find out?"

"Tragic, really. He said that to maintain his position, and to not lose Belisarius, he would host parties for the upper class. And take gifts to their parties. After the treachery of Gallus, he was too ashamed to stop. He said he should have listened to you. What did he mean?"

It saddens me it has come to this. No need to drudge up the past. We all make decisions we regret. I shrugged my shoulders. "What else did he say?"

"He had to keep up appearances, he said, for our sake. So he borrowed from Hypatius."

How many parties would cause such a debt? I could not even fathom. Then a freedom dawned on me. *I had not been silent about Gallus.*

"If it had only been the debt itself, Pater could have paid it off. The problem was Hypatius committed usury in response to the unpaid debt. Thirty percent interest."

"Usury? From a senator?" I blew through my lips. *Why hadn't our laws protected him?*

"Gaius Justus should have come home to Antioch. He was needed there, and could have relieved himself the pressure to fit in."

"He said the same, but that his vanity kept him in Constantinople." He chuckled. "While we were suffering, his pleasure-seeking was killing us all."

"I don't think I'd ever agree to sell my daughter into slavery."

"It is always the final step before destitution, Marcellus. You know that. Either one of us, or all of us."

Gaius Justus's pride had brought that debt upon the family, but who was I to speak? My pride had made her face the man. *I hope my plan solves everything.*

"What are we doing tonight?" How would I spend my last evening in freedom?

"I told them we would be back after the races. Byziana said she would have dinner for us." I took a deep pensive breath as I considered his words.

Dinner for me. What a short-lived dream—a home with Byzia. She knows how I feel now, and I will prove the extent of it.

A trembling tried to take hold of me, but I resisted it. *No self-pity,* I swore to myself. *If I don't do this, she'll become Belisarius's slave. There are no other options.*

"I hope the games are loud," I said, "I need to dull my thoughts."

More and more fans passed by us, calling their team's victory song.

The Blues chanted,

"As the water is Blue

. . . as the Sky is Blue

. . . the world is Blue

. . . so the one to win is Blue!

Nika for the Blue!"

Against that, Greens across the street marched and sang, with newly arriving fans joining up from side streets and alleys,

"Green as a tree Oh-lay,

emerald green Oh-lay,

our team Oh-lay,

our team Oh-lay."

Faithful Reds and Blacks sang their soft songs, yet drew little notice. Apparently, "Do no offense," was the byword.

"Let's on to the Hippodrome." Justin pulled me toward the long oval structure bordering the Royal Residence.

The songs seemed to be friendly banter as I had seen many years ago in Antioch. Little did we hear the winds of change.

After a ten-minute walk, past the baths and past the minor palaces of the rich, famous and heartless, we arrived at the Hippodrome. Our garments supported neither team—we still wore the tapestry-accented robes from our ill-fated interview this morning.

The Blues, wanting more representation in their section, enticed us with complimentary banners and whistles, so we took the bribes to support their team, and walked up the stairs leading to those seats. I looked at my whistle and cringed. *Why am I here? Everyone is singing and laughing. Why am I here?*

"Justin, what are we doing? We must speak to Hypatius. Let's not stay for the races."

He rolled his eyes. "Taking your mind off of your problems is not a sin, Marcellus. We might discover new solutions! Besides, I've always wanted to watch the races at this Hippodrome."

"You what!"

His sister is the one whose life was at stake. Time is against us. And he wants to watch a horserace!

"This Hippodrome will be exactly like ours, I'm sure," I tried to reason. But as we walked through the entrance arch, I took back my words. This race arena was three times as large as Antioch's.

My eyes could not gaze on the living horses until they took their fill of four gigantic golden horses frozen in a trot over the starting gate. Huge specimens of majestic excellence! Justin whistled as he pointed at them, to make sure I saw them over the Gate of Death.

The eight sets of eager horses drew our notice, tugging at tight reins—two chariots from each team, four horses on each chariot. Thirty-two cream-of-the-crop horses pulled at bit to get started.

"Look at those grays!" I nudged Justin as we moved across to some empty seats. The light grays wore Red team markings. Disapproving murmurs of nearby fans reminded me to keep my mouth from accolades of the Red team, in spite of their superior appearance.

"I'm going to get myself a horse like that." Justin pointed one out to me. "A fast and strong horse."

"Your horse is the fastest you've ever owned. Why do you need another?"

"Because I am sure these fly like the wind. If I could, I would harness the wind itself, and go Whoosh!" He slipped his hands across each other in a smooth and fast movement. His face dropped as he remembered. "Poor Byziana." He too could not be distracted long from our family's dire situation. Clouds covered the sun, and we both pulled our robes tighter around ourselves.

"If this race doesn't start soon, we'll turn to ice." I put my arm across his back and patted his shoulder, pulling his attention back to the horses, and certain clothes of the charioteers. I could see my breath, so crossed my arms and bounced on my heels.

We stood high enough to see, over the top of the stadium, dolphins tumbling in the Propontis. Ships sailed to and fro carrying their cargo to all the ends of Byzantium and beyond. Seagulls soared above us. Clouds gathered.

To our right, the *Kathisma*, the Grand Box of the Emperor, hovered above the common seating. A direct passageway connected Justinian's box to his palace. I pointed it out to Justin.

"There's the emperor," Justin said. "At least we know he's alive today. Usually he rules unseen."

His eyes scanned the stadium and then his demeanor dropped. He pointed across from us, beyond the *Kathisma*. "Look. Hypatius."

My heart dropped. The wounds of this morning's interview surged in my heart. The senator sat in a roped-off section of the Greens. A dozen men fawned over my future master. I studied the men. *Soon I will be one of those flatterers.* The thought gripped my stomach.

While the Blues, as favorite to the Crown, sat in the honored section next to the emperor's box, the Greens sat in the Sphendone, with neither a good view of the emperor, nor a good view of the racing corners. Today that made the difference.

Pouches of Gold

What kind of man is this Hypatius? I observed the interaction for a while, more and more disliking my prospects. The extortionist took advantage of a fellow citizen and brought dishonor upon a patrician of Antioch. He might be the nephew of a dead emperor, but his overall demeanor at Belisarus's house bordered on ignominious. Such is my fate, to fawn at the foot of such a man.

But he was my polar star. Without him, my plan was empty. "I'll be right back," I said to Justin. I'd burn in hell before leaving Byziana's fate to Belisarius.

He held my arm, "I'll come with you. Wait'll after the races. He may be in a better mood. We may be in a better mood. Step back. Take a breath."

A feeling of dread came over me—as if waiting would not be wise. I tried again to pass Justin, but he stopped me, pulling me into the conversation with his neighbor.

"They say the Blue's charioteer, Captain Zenobius, has his own drinking house."

How could he ignore our predicament?

"A drinking house?" Justin asked. "Is he that wealthy?" His hand held me tightly.

"Yes. He more than doubles his income by selling beer and wine to Blue fans."

"Does he not make that much racing?"

I tried to pull away again, but Justin insisted. He lifted a finger. "Please. Wait."

Waiting is not efficient. I only have today. Yet I've never gone wrong trusting my cousin.

I nodded in agreement. *I'll give him an hour or so.* He let go of my arm.

"Can anyone ever make enough?" the stranger next to us laughed. "I heard of a charioteer. His name escapes me. But after ten years of racing, he done gets—through his wins—a hundred years of laborer salary! Moved away somewhere. I'd be gone, too, if I was him."

A nearby fan contributed his thoughts to our conversation. "Did you say you did not know our Zenobius? The Captain is one of the richest plebeians in the city. His Blue City Drinking House has wine far surpassing any other you'd find anywhere but Rome itself."

Another fan sunk his fist into the first man's shoulder, "Rome has nothing to our wine, you numbskull! Why'dya think the Ostrogoths want control of our Imperial Court? First, they make a Goth a Pope. Next thing you know, they want our throne."

"Keep yer hands to yer own brainless body," the first man responded. "It's John the Cappadocian who wants control of us. He's robbing us poor with his taxes. How can Justinian not see this?"

"Sit down and shut your complaining yappers!" A man behind us shouted. "It's starting!"

The spectators to a one forgot everything but the races. Money. Politics. Games. All forgotten.

I looked across at Hypatius again. Next to him was Belisarius! *I thought he was a Blue!*

I nudged Justin to point out the man across from us, but his eyes were on the start of the race.

What's Belisarius doing over there? Their eyes never left the conversation, even as the Commencement ceremony began. The horses started off, trotting around the stadium in an introductory circuit, the top two favorites of each team, if the Blacks and Reds could be said to have favorites. My eyes went back to the senator across the Hippodrome.

Even at my distance I could see Belisarius was unhappy. Hypatius would lean in to speak into Belisarius's ear, and in reply Belisarius would speak into his.

As he spoke, Belisarius surveyed the emperor's box next to us. With reluctance Hypatius consented. Belisarius patted the senator on the shoulder, then left with the smile of a cat that caught its prey. My eyes followed him as he walked up the stadium, and out the tunneled archway behind the Green seating.

As he left, fans roared their approval of horses, chariots, drivers, life. They had no idea, nor did I, of the critical interview which had just taken place. They had no idea, nor did I, of how life would soon be changed forever. They only watched the horses as did I now.

The horses and chariots trotted around the track, drawing my eyes to the rows of tall *spinae* lining the center of the track. Near the center stood a towering, proud Egyptian hieroglyphic stele, and nearby the mouths of a strange bronze triple-headed serpent poured water into a font.

Other statues were indistinguishable. They could be Roman gods for all I knew. I sighed. *What strange creatures we worship.* The fascinating columns hosting our grand and infamous history made up the narrow center barrier which the chariots would circle. Sky-touching pillars on either end signaled the *meta*, or the circuit's turning point.

Of a dozen additional commemorative statues, six honored the same notorious character: Porphyrius the Charioteer, hated by Antioch for the massacre he led against the Jews in our neighboring town of Daphne. Remembering Daphne reminded me of my hometown, the earthquake, and all we had been through. Then Byziana.

I found Hypatius again, curious how my future owner viewed the race. Though the circus brewed with anticipation, he still regarded not the chariots. Now, he held a man by his tunic, had pulled him to speak into the ear. In any other circumstance, it might have been a wage being placed. But the man's scraggly black mane, his mode of dress, and his sneer told me he was a ruffian. Then Hypatius shoved him away.

As I watched, the ruffian walked up the steps, but not toward the exit. As he got to the walkway, he pulled a pouch of money from the top of his tunic, weighed it, and strolled off under the *Kathisma*, tossing the money-pouch in his hand.

My eyes were back on Hypatius. But his eyes were on the race now, so my attention likewise returned to the action.

The first set lined up, a team of each color. Each charioteer wore colorful tapestry garments woven with their team color. The chariots and charioteer helmets bore the color. Fans as well wore the same colored garments. Horses panted and pulled. Tightly muscled charioteers resisted. Crowds raged. Intoxicated hopes surged.

Then the white flag dropped, the gate opened, the first race began.

A slow team at the gate caused the Black team to lunge, then horses trampled horses in a tangled mess of equine limbs. The charioteers urged their horses back and forth to get untangled, and in a moment they gained speed attempting to catch the forward teams. Meanwhile, a near-collision at the front, between the Blue and Green team, caught our breath, drawing our attention to the quick moves of the charioteers. Nothing was off-limits, anything permissible if only to win.

If you have ever been in a crowd during a competition, you can understand how we get pulled-in to forget, for a moment, the troubles we have.

I cheered for the Blues aloud, but inside kept my eye on the beautiful pale horses of the Reds, amazing specimens of agility and strength. The first goal of each team was to vie for position, which could decide the end from the beginning. Chariots moved and maneuvered in front of each other, each attempting to cause their opponents to "shipwreck" as they called it. Horses ran fresh and alert, the drivers ready for opposition.

"Look at the Green and Red drivers!" Justin said, "They are both whipping the Black!"

"Barbarian!" a man behind me yelled. For they now had ganged up on the Blue.

I cringed at the word, offended at the unknown affront against a people dear to my heart. That epithet brought me back to today and our problem.

We had been to races before, but none so cut-throat. Vicious charioteers whipped their horses, whipped the other teams' horses, whipped the other charioteers, in the same way Hypatius had whipped Antioch's *patrikios*. My attention again moved to the senator.

Across the Hippodrome, Hypatius had another man's ear. This man did not seem a ruffian. But when he walked off and took a pouch from his tunic as well, I suspected as much.

My eyes had been on Hypatius for a long time when he caught me. And then he stared back, his glare frightening.

He was threatened. Who am I to be watching his doings? He must assume I'm spying. If so, he'll never accept my proposal? I've got to clear this misunderstanding. I've got to explain.

I stood up, explaining to Justin that nature called, and walked to the Blue Gate. But the exit was filled with spectators. I couldn't get out, so instead of exiting the Hippodrome I walked around the inner walkway .

Halfway to the starting gate, a crowd blocked me. I stood back as they passed and studied the spinae statues part of the stadium. Athena beckoned toward the emperor's box. Pan, Hercules, the Muses, a Boar raised in honor. A statue of a man and donkey boasted importance, dead center of the stadium. A donkey, of all things, represented victory. *Where is victory in a Christian world saturated with Greek gods, screaming race fanatics, usurious leaders and prostitute-mongers? Where is Christianity in this city?*

A murmur through the crowd drew my attention back to the race. Finishing the first lap, the leading team caused the first ball to be dropped. Then taking a bend too fast, the Blue chariot almost overturned.

Our whole section gasped. But the driver threw his weight at the last moment and the wheel jarred itself onto the ground, the horses pulling the vehicle on. His axle had withstood the shock, but would it endure the rest of the race?

At a turn, each charioteer had to slow down to make the sharp curve around the gilded pillar on each end of the track, doing so while keeping his own horses safe but hindering the other teams in any way possible.

I had not realized the competition had drawn me in again until Justin put his arm around my back.

"Almost lost you for a moment," he said. "I thought you'd wait for me."

"He saw me looking at him."

"It is of no matter. Let us be wise. I am in no hurry to throw your life to the lions."

He turned me around and pushed me back to our seats.

"And Byziana? Inaction brings her closer to her lions."

"That is more my responsibility than yours."

"It would already be mine if I had spoken to your father of my intentions."

"Then I thank God you did not. Trust God we will find another way." He directed me back to our seats, but a huddled group of men blocked our path.

"Make way!" Justin pressed through the gathering.

". . . But you must not be near each other," I overheard a man say.

I turned to see the speaker, and to my shock it was Hypatius's first ruffian!

"You'll be paid half now, half at the end. Torches . . ." His voice trailed off.

What wicked plans were these? I tried to slow Justin down.

Peeking back at the other faces, I heard the faint jingle of coins. But my cousin yanked me along. I stopped him after a while and tried to explain.

"You're imagining things. I'm sure they were betting on the race."

I explained what I had seen with Belisarius.

"If that is the case, Brother, we must stay away from Hypatius until this conspiracy is over," he reasoned. "Let us keep our eyes open and hope for the best."

He steered me back to our well-situated seats, which other fans had grabbed. So we stood in the aisle. After this I feared looking at Hypatius.

One by one the races came and went. And the more races that passed, the more I began to doubt what I had seen. We should return to Front Street. This was my last day of freedom and the sun was going down.

We found new seats but were blocked from the races by fans standing before us. I glanced up at the emperor in his *Kathisma*, then scanned the crowd behind us.

Spectators gawk at horses. Meaningless voices scream. Anything goes. No rules. Dog eat dog. Only the strong survive.

Somehow my mind returned to Thomas reaching out to me from under the stones. "Help me!" he had said. Us against the stones, and the stones had won.

I tapped my cousin on his back. "Shall we go home?"

A scream from the track shot us to our feet. The Green chariot drug a body below it. The Black driver had fallen. The Green charioteer steered his horses straight along the track, and with a final thump over the body, maneuvered his horses toward the front running Blue team.

He did not even look back.

A team of horses ran, riderless, panicked. After the chariots passed, a couple medics approached the broken rider. Meanwhile, the riderless chariot hopped and bumped from the missing weight, and soon a wheel broke loose. The horses continued on, the chariot axle digging into the soil, a long trench dug in the track, until the axle wedged into the track, stopping the horses.

The crowd went wild. Around the bend, the Blue team headed toward the unseen chariot.

A groom ran into the track, racing against time to release the team from the chariot.

On the other side, the doctors took the charioteer off the field. With loud relief, the Blue team cheered for the winner.

I stopped paying attention to the race. Justin slouched in his seat next to me. The frenzy was not worth the cost.

"Have you ever heard of Iuvenalis?" I leaned to speak above the ruckus into his ear.

He shook his head, "No."

"Decimus Iunius Iuvenalis. A Roman poet. He said, '*Bread and circuses. That's all the people want.*' How can we take pleasure watching others get hurt?"

He nodded. "The tension, the peril pulls us in."

"An insatiable appetite for death and pain."

"Maybe we're glad it's not happening to us."

"But why should we be entertained by it?"

He shrugged. We had been absorbed into the same frenzied fanaticism of our compatriots sitting around us, pulled in to lose our conscience.

A rush of people around us hurdled over each other toward the emperor's box. Hundreds of gold coins rained down into our section from the *Kathisma*, the emperor rewarding the Blues for their wins. The Greens threw bitter glares at the patronage.

And then another race, and another win for the Greens.

"Another point for the Monophysites, may they be damned to hell," a Blue nearby said when the Greens won.

Those words froze me in place.

"Did you hear that?" I shouted again in Justin's ear.

"What?"

I looked back, wondering if I heard right.

The crowd gasped again. Another chariot crash. Another life lost. And on went the race.

"Green!" the team shouted in unison. "Oh-lay! *Nika* for Green! Victory!"

"Blue will win! Blue!"

"Mercy!" the words came from the crowd.

Mercy? I searched for the cry's caller. Soon the cry echoed throughout the stadium. "Mercy. Have mercy upon our men!"

Justin elbowed me. "What's it about?" he yelled.

I did not know.

"Have mercy! Mercy Great Emperor!"

"Release our friends from prison!"

Words drew attention to the *Kathisma*. Spectators eyed spectator. The crowd eyed Justinian. Waiting. For something.

"What does this have to do with the games?" I asked a neighbor.

"Soldiers arrested Green and Blue activists. They escaped and we want their pardon."

Another man near me added, "It's our only recourse for mercy—when the emperor is pleased and at the races."

"Long Live the Merciful Augustus! Have mercy, Augustus!" The words echoed, a whirlwind of noise and discontent.

The emperor did not respond, his face like flint watched the racing chariots. Blue was due to win.

Strange murmurs ran around the Hippodrome like wildfire, fueled by coins spread by Hypatius.

We had seen twenty-two seven-lap races before this change.

No longer waged Blue against Green. No longer waged horse against horse. Now waged the contest between state and citizen, emperor and man. Man called for mercy. Man called for justice. Man called for substance beyond bread and circuses. Beyond this immaterial horserace.

Raging Torches

Emperor Justinian's apathy to the cries for pardon caused a different chorus.

"Long live the merciful Blues and Greens! Long live the merciful Blues and Greens!" the new chant rang.

I turned in my seat to find, not to my surprise, the chant had originated with the ruffian's crew.

Belisarius and Hypatius. It had all begun with that. Both men were cutthroat. And considering their treacherous dialogue this morning, I could only imagine where this would end!

Eyes left the race, focusing on the many pockets of complaint across the stadium. Everyone stomped in rhythm, looking at the emperor.

A scurry in the *Kathisma,* and Justinian and Theodora were gone, ushered by their *excubiti* down secret corridors into their safe royal residence.

I felt an urgent need to leave. Grabbing Justin by the arm, "Come now!" I said and pulled him to the Blue gate.

Behind us we heard the chariots spinning yet another circuit, but attention was on the gathering fans demanding justice.

A strange sound came from the stadium depths, a demonic echoing shout, "Get 'em! Down with the emperor! *Nika! Nika!* Victory for the people!"

Haunting the stadium, the same words and stomping reverberated over and over across the Hippodrome. The mob's dark shadow blocked dim lamplights around us and the exit archway was too far away. *We won't make it out!*

Shoving Justin to the wall, I pressed into the corner. *God keep us safe.* This decision saved our lives.

Like the demoniac's legion, raging men raced as one twisting screeching horde down the stairs, brushing past us, knocking each other to the ground, trampling any who stumbled on the steep steps.

Justin turned his head to see the crowd. Something hit his cheek, and he yelled, pulling back into our safe spot.

When the possessed throng dissipated into the streets, we pushed away from the stairway corner. "Do not let go of my hand," I said, hastening to the light. "We cannot be separated in this furor!"

At the stairway base several old men lay trampled, several young men lay slit-throat.

In front of us, the city was in an uproar. We ducked into a dark alley and watched the mayhem.

"What in the name of all that is holy has happened?" Justin whispered.

"I have no idea. We will know soon enough. Meanwhile we must get to Front Street. To your father and sister. This cannot end well."

Across Mese Way, along the double- and triple-storied residential dwellings of the senators, young hooligans with lit torches chased people and lit aflame whatever they could touch. In a matter of moments even the mansions were blazing.

"*Nika*! Victory! *Nika*!" the shouts rang out.

"This can't be about the games," Justin said.

"All I can think of is what I saw between Belisarius and Hypatius."

"It is almost like the kindling was ready for the fire."

I nodded. Who would know the heart of the people more than those two men?

"Can you get to Front street?" I asked him.

He pointed to a street on fire.

The people on the streets, who risked a pause to see the fire, wept at the loss.

Children wandered in their sleeping clothes, crying for Mater.

Babies whimpered on the ground next to their slain mothers.

Fires. Frenzy. Feverish inferno.

Pockets of silence were impossible to find. Children needed

help. But the moment we reached them, hooligans on horses would race by and trample them. Trample the children! And this in a Christian country.

I could barely stand. The sounds and screams melted together like a furious hurricane too big for a ship. Surrounded by death, a crowd of us spun in place witnessing horror, horses surging, houses burning, ashes flittering down from the sky like snow.

Justin slapped my face, shaking me to the present. "Pater! And Byziana!" The words drew me from shock and delirium.

My young cousin pulled me by the hand. We ran northwards, down the Mese, with all our strength, turning at the quietest downhill side street. Running like the devil himself was after us. For he was. Humanity unleashed was wicked without its Savior.

Clattering hoofbeats warned us of the approaching rioter. We ducked in a dark corner holding our breath until he passed by. Again we took to flight. Down, down the hill. Toward the port district. The city was aflame.

Most residences, built of wood, did not withstand this inferno. A gargantuan blaze promised that the whole city would be homeless by morning. But what of our family? What of Byzia? Gaius Justus? Would they be among the living? Or the dead?

We raced on. A man plowed into us, dashing in from a side alley.

"A-ha-ha-haaa!" He laughed at the collision, and standing up, picked up his torch and lit Justin on fire! Then, as if nothing had happened, he kept running along the street with that maniacal laugh.

"Heeelp!" Justin screamed and started to run.

I threw him to the ground, tearing off my robe to suffocate the flames. Another panicked scream burst in my ear. I pinned him with my chest and patted the fire out.

"Calm down. You will be fine. Shh."

When his breathing steadied, I unwrapped him. The fire was quenched. He was safe, but our clothes scorched. We wrapped our blackened robes around us again and hastened downhill.

The fire soon widened the close streets of the wooden residential district, approaching the large brick commercial warehouses. But the fire, no respecter of persons, showed no mercy. Cemeteries, ecclesiastical complexes, parks, fields . . . all succumbing to the power of flame. The Church of the Apostles was on fire, along with Saint Andrew's bones. Not even relics could stop this blaze.

The glowing sky ahead of us pulsated. The shouts of those fighting that fire reverberated in the bedlam. Granaries and warehouses on fire. Most of the homes below us, raging red. The poor districts inland, aflame. The damage on this city irreparable. Constantinople burning down!

MERCILESS INFERNO

I remember as a child the moment I had first faced fire. I was, I think, five years of age. In the fields behind our house our servants were burning brush and wood.

The golden red glow drew me like, I am sure, the ancients had been drawn to the first fire. I watched the flickers of that molten red, pulled into its magical entrancement. I knew fire was hot. Up to this point of my childhood, I had heeded my father's restriction on approaching fire. But I saw the big boys poking sticks in the fire. So in my innocence, I took a stick, caught it aflame, and held it aloft, swinging it around, drawing pictures in the sky.

"Do not play with fire, Son," my father had warned me again.

He had threatened me, but I still insisted, "I am a big boy. I won't get hurt." And I spun the stick in the air above me.

With my eyes up, I did not see my feet, and I fell face-first into the fire.

I rolled and rolled and could not get free of the fire. My clothes burned, my skin blistered. I screamed. Pater came, lifted me, pulled the clothes off me, bathed me, comforted me. Never did he scold me. The fire's voice was firm enough.

Now, surrounded with that same beautiful, consuming, all-powerful orange flickering glow, I was entranced, I was petrified. Smoke was everywhere. Adults and children were running, stumbling, grasping, gasping, calling for children, calling for mothers.

A grandmother leaned out a window screaming. "My stairway is on fire. Please help! Help me."

"Jump!" I shouted up to her, lifting my arms.

"You will drop me. I cannot." She searched for help, around her and behind her again. "I am too weak."

Flickers of orange pulsed behind her, the heat fluttering a curtain.

"Throw your curtain down! We'll catch you on it. Hurry!"

She dropped it down to us.

"I am too afraid!" she cried.

The flames behind her told her she could jump so she climbed up next to the window.

Justin and I held the fabric between us, but it would not take her fall. A man stepped up next to us. "Let me help." He took the last corner. Between the three of us, we held the cloth taut. The woman clambered onto her windowsill and teetered on the ledge. Flames consumed the room behind her.

"Jump, Grandmater. Jump!" Justin called. "We will catch you. You will be safe! Jump!"

She screamed and jumped toward us. We positioned ourselves under her. And the next thing we knew, she lay on the curtain on the ground, breathless.

We hovered over her. Had she died?

Her eyes flickered. Pushing herself up into a sitting position, she threw her arms around our necks with a joyful groan.

A sound from her home pulled our eyes to the burning wreck. The roof caved into the flames. Kindling waiting to burn.

"Get away!" Justin shouted.

We helped the feeble woman out of danger, then I felt something at my side.

A little tear-stained four-year-old boy took my hand. "Where is Pater?" I scanned the once-neighborhood. *How can I find one minuscule boy's father in the midst of this monumental chaos?* A pack of Greens rushed past us with torches raised, almost trampling the boy. I lifted him to myself, swinging away just in time.

"Where do you live?"

"I don't know." He looked at the smoldering burnt shells of homes around him. "I don't know."

"Help me!" A feeble voice called from nearby. I looked to the left, right, up and down. I found no one.

"Hello! Where are you?" We waited for the voice. It never spoke again.

If I stayed in one place, ghostly need would assault me from every side. We needed a plan!

"Can you find your house from Hagia Sophia?" I asked. He nodded. I hesitated to return as the Agora seemed to be the heart of the rage.

"How about Front street?" Justin was next to me again. "Can you find your way from there?" The boy put his fingers in his mouth shaking his head "No."

"You've never been to the water-side?"

"Water-side? Yes. I know Waterside." A hopeful nod of his sooty face met my eyes.

"We must find my father and sister," Justin said. "They are out there somewhere, too."

The smoke and noise and heat and fire and cries had so filled my mind I had forgotten about myself or my friends.

We hurried along the smoky street, boy and grandmother in tow, coming now to the heat of a still-burning part of the city. Bodies lay strewn, burnt, slain, trampled.

The city was dying. More dead people than alive lined the streets, yet the riot burned on. Men and anger and torches. We continued to the hill base, yet we were not at the sea. "Which way to Front Street?" we asked. No one could answer.

Smoke blocked our path, filling our lungs with coughing black, until we noticed its movement, pulling us toward the water. We followed the smoke, finding ourselves at Front Street. The grandmother ran to a huddled crowd.

"Arturus!" a woman's scream startled us. The boy pulled his hand from mine and ran to the lady. Two sooty people clung to each other. I approached. "Is Arturus your son?"

"My nephew," she answered, tears in her eyes. "Thank you for bringing him here. How can I ever repay you? Oh, Arturus!"

I observed a large group of children, all mustering against several priests. The holy men held the crying, frantic children, consoling them, making promises they hoped to keep.

"We will find Mater. Don't you worry."

"They will come here and you will be safe."

"Just stay close to us, darlings."

"Do not let's cry, little one."

Babies in their arms, toddlers clinging to their legs, frantic boys and girls demanding comfort.

"I do not envy them their job." Justin shook his head back and forth.

And yet the look of hope, of faith in their young eyes at those promises surged in my heart. I thought of all the wandering children, the lost parents we had passed. A sudden desire to return up the hill and help them overwhelmed me.

"We've got our own father to locate," Justin said, holding me back. "And sister. You can be a monk later."

"I'll never be a monk," I answered.

Justin snuffed in reply. "I am glad to hear you come to your senses."

The wharf swarmed with people, cats, dogs, beasts.

"Where is your father's house?" I shook off a rat climbing my leg. "Where's he live?"

He was not sure. No one had their bearings so no one could direct us to safety. All anyone knew was the water was safe.

Hooligans jumped off a barge. A moment later the barge caught flame. "Nika! Victory! Nika!"

"Will they never stop?" I asked the air.

"What kind of victory is this?"

A voice spun me on my heels. "Marcellus!" Her cadence burst my heart with joy and hope and love and pain. I turned to find her, my friend Byziana, in my arms.

I would never give myself to Hypatius. I could never serve him after what he had done to his city. I would never let Byziana go to him, either.

"Is Gaius Justus safe?"

"He's with the monks. He is safe." She pointed to him sitting by the group of lost children, some of them on his lap. She squeezed her arms around my chest.

The sound of crying drew our attention. A little girl sat on the ground in wet nightclothes shivering and weeping. Byziana ran to her. "Darling! Do not cry!"

Without a thought she pulled off her robe. I noticed it as if a great light shone on the event. Yet, for her, she acted as if she had done nothing significant. She threw the robe over the frightened child, saying, "We'll help you. Let me take you to where the other children are. My own Pater is there. He'll keep you safe until Mater and Pater come for you. Don't worry, darling."

In a moment we were with the monks and other children, joining their work.

Gaius Justus pulled the girl into his arms, warming her arms and wiping her tears. He recognized the noblewoman's robe on her, and his eyes shot up to find Byziana.

But she was out in the crowd in a mere linen tunic, looking for others needing help. He raised his eyebrows in astonishment, then gave his attention back to the child.

It would be nice if I could say the fire went down, the parents were found, and the city went back to normal the next day.

In fact, this was only the beginning. It was like a nightmare where you are drowning in the sea and cannot breathe. All you want is a breath but you cannot breathe. And you swim for hours and days under the water until you finally come up for air. Those were our days under the dark, sad smoke of Constantinople's burning.

GOD OF HIDDEN WATERS

Our strength was all but sapped. We were hungry, and tired, and breathless as we sat. For three days we scrounged and fished for food for all the homeless at the wharf. For three days we aided and comforted lost children. Now, a friar named Dominicus told us worse news.

"Many young ones can no longer stand. They need water or they may die. Several infants passed on last night."

"Oh, no!" Byziana covered her mouth in horror.

Then, she remembered, "The Hippodrome must have water. Justin, you told me there was a snake fountain in the center under all the statuary."

Justin disagreed. "The Delphi statue, but we can't go there. You know that's the riot headquarters."

The friar looked back at his charges. "If we go, as monks, they may let us get some for the children."

That was also dangerous. "No," I said. "If anything happens to you, the little ones will be the ones to suffer."

"Could you loan your robes to three men?" Byziana asked. "They could go, dressed as monks, and could request the water in your place."

"It would be dishonest," Dominicus said. "Taking-up the cloth is a holy action, and it represents a commitment to a consecrated life."

"Yes, it would be deceptive," said Justin.

"But the children need to drink. We need to be shrewd in our actions. Did not Christ leave his divine appearance and come in human form? If he had not come as man, he would not have been able to relate with us. He also cloaked himself in mystery."

Dominicus put a finger to his lip, considering her words.

"If our men cloak themselves in mystery, they can bring life to these children."

"Byziana," I said. "We must not twist what Christ has done for our own benefit."

I studied the monk. "What does taking-up the cloth represent?"

"It represents all the good deeds and good intentions of the life I have sworn to live for Christ, for the world's betterment," he replied. "I chose myself to take-up orders and wearing the cloth is the sign I am set apart."

"May I ask you something, Father? If I have committed myself to a life sworn to Christ, for the world's betterment, for the honor of our Lord—which I have—do I not have the right to wear the sign of this commitment for the brief time it takes to retrieve two or three bucketfuls of water?"

"Well, you have a persuasive case. Yes, then."

Justin followed with his own statement of commitment.

He crossed my forehead, and Justin's forehead, and had three of his fellow monks take off their robes. Underneath they wore short tunics—we gave our dirty, burnt robes to the men.

"Who is the third?"

I scanned the crowd for another capable man who might risk going into the lions mouth with us.

"I am," said Byziana.

We frowned at her with a stern, "No. Absolutely not. Never!"

But after similar persuasion Byziana donned a habit. We pulled the brown hoods deep over our foreheads to keep our faces in the shade. Then we tramped up the smoldering street toward the Hippodrome.

She walked next to me, shoulder touching shoulder. Had it been so long ago that we had spoken outside Belisarius's house?

"You should have stayed behind. I don't like you to be in harm's way."

"I know." She kept her face down, as did I, but I could hear a smile in her voice. "Marcellus, we must help. What makes me any different than any of them? They come from rich or poor—who can tell when we all have soot all over ourselves?"

I laughed. "Soot doesn't differentiate, does it?"

We continued up the hill. The houses in this area were shells, roofless. Anything flammable had disappeared in the inferno that had raged. People poking through the ashes with sticks lifted their eyes to us briefly.

I felt the knife at my belt, ready to protect if they attacked. But they preferred their looting. After assessing our harmlessness they returned to their poking in the ash.

Byziana said, "I realize, since we are destitute, that—"

"You are not destitute. Not as long as I have a breath in my body."

"Mater said that. She said, 'God has not forsaken us. Not as we have life in our bones.' That is what I realized. That's what matters. Life. If we have life—not money, not pleasure—life, God is still faithful. No matter what comes."

"That may be, Byziana. But I still don't want you facing danger. The danger and harm a woman can receive is much heavier than any a man receives."

She did not answer, but walked a little closer. After we turned a corner and approached the Stoa Basilica Hall, across from the Hagia Sophia, the extent of damage stopped us short. The Hall's portico had fallen down, almost every pillar knocked from its place when the foundation corner had sunk into the moist earth below it.

Across the road, men carried torches across the Hagia Sophia's roof. *How can people vandalize their city?*

"Marcellus," she said after a while. "How will we pay Hypatius?"

We had not discussed the debt since our walk away from Belisarius's house, though it weighed on my mind.

Hypatius had staged this riot. He had directed those first hoodlums. He must have known payment would have been impossible. 'Do not think of leaving this city. I know you will not,' he had said. Now the strange words made sense.

There seemed to be no way out. "I have an idea," I still said.

"I can guess your plan, and I hate it. We have no way to pay, that's plain. But a little hope burning in my heart tells me God is guiding my steps to clear it."

"I feel it too. Let's get water for the children, and then we can design a plan that will persuade Hypatius to forgive our debt."

"Our debt?"

"Yes, our debt."

Leaving their posts at the Hippodrome's vast Gate of Death, men with torches and swords moved toward us like guard dogs in attack. I motioned for Byziana to stop speaking. Justin turned to us.

"There's soot on your feet, Byziana" Justin said, "and the soot on your face and hands should hide your gender. As long as you say nothing, and you keep your eyes down."

"I'll do my best."

"Let Marcellus and me say what's necessary."

"With all due respect, Father, you gotta leave," a burly man said, blocking our path. "We been instructed here to not let nobody in." Several guards approached from the gate.

I gulped. These men were huge. But the children needed water. *Please God let our disguises work.*

"Dear son, we come from Front Street, where there are orphan children dying of thirst." Justin kept his head down. "We beg permission of whomever is in charge to grant us water from the fountain at the *spinae*."

"It is not for me to decide, Father. It is for Hypatius to decide. He is in charge of the city now."

It took all the strength in me to keep my eyes lowered, to not look at Justin and Byziana, to not cry out my surprise at such news. *In charge of the city? Are they calling him emperor? How can things have turned so sour?*

"Please, then, my son," Justin's voice had a nasal whine, as if trying to imitate the voice of John of Ephesus, "lead us to this great Hypatius that we may beg his pardon for the sake of our charges."

If the stakes had not been so high, his impersonation would have been humorous. But a greater danger gripped my heart. *We can't let Hypatius see our faces, or nothing will save us from this newfound power. He already hates us.*

We walked through the starting gates and into the Hippodrome. No longer did spectators stand in great excitement watching their horse wagers win or lose. Instead, thousands of people, Greens and Blues and Blacks and Reds, sat talking in groups, waiting for something. In the Blues section, several senators conversed together.

The guards walked us up to the emperor's box, and with a quick glance I could see that Hypatius sat in Justinian's place in the Kathisma. He spoke with two men in Red tunics. They left him, then he lifted his hand for our request.

"Go ahead." The gatekeeper signaled Justin. "Ask the senator what youse all need."

Justin kept his head lowered, "My son, if you could request in our stead, it would be a great service. The smoke has damaged my voice—" he coughed for effect, and in fact he had a surprising congestion.

Byziana moved closer as we waited. Someone called down for us to speak or leave the Hippodrome.

"Senator Hypatius, sir," the man said with an unnatural civility, "these fathers are asking for water for some homeless waifs down at that there port district."

Hypatius waved his hand in a permissive, dismissive motion. *That easy? I never would have expected.*

We approached the water source, the three twisted bronze snakes from Delphi, and first filled our hands to quench our own thirst. Then we dipped our buckets in the pool and turned toward the exit gate.

We got halfway to the exit when a burst of wind blew on our cloaks. I yanked my cloak at the chest which kept my hood on, but Byziana did not catch hers in time, and her hood flew back.

No Purple Shrouds

Byziana pulled her hood in place within a split second, but the revelatory damage was done. Every bored one of them had watched our appeal, so every bored one of them had glimpsed those lovely twisted plaits upon her head. Everyone knew no monk, priest or hermit would have hair pinned up like that.

"It's a lady!" someone shouted. The brawny men ran to block us, others ran from the stands to stop us.

"Get them!" Hypatius shouted, propelling others toward us. Had he recognized her?

Justin knocked three men down, opening a gap for his sister. She threw her bucket toward another group coming from the side. Without watching what came of her attempt, she lifted her robe and ran like the wind toward the exit.

The front man stepped on the rolling bucket. He slipped onto the ground. Three men behind him tripped and fell as they attempted to avoid stepping on him.

I floored several men. Then picking up my still-full bucket ran after Justin to the gate.

My cousins had turned left away from the starting gate. They ran along the Hippodrome's western side. My water splashed a trail behind us so I stashed my bucket under a stairwell and continued after them.

Byziana ran with almost supernatural speed into early evening shadows. She dashed to the back of the Hippodrome, and if Justin had not been close on her tail, I would have lost her.

They turned a corner. I turned there, entered a park and froze. They had disappeared. Staccato footsteps approached from behind.

An arm grabbed me and yanked me through a narrow doorway. A firm hand clamped my mouth.

The pursuers ran past the door, footsteps fading at the park's far end. Justin let go of his restraint.

"What do you think this place is?" Byziana whispered, looking up the small stairway behind us.

I shrugged my shoulders. The musty smell of old wood and thick air pressed over us.

"How did you even find this place?" Justin asked. "I saw you run up to a wall and open a panel in it."

"A light shone on it. I cannot explain, but I ran to it and knew it was a door."

"*Kyrie Eleison*," Justin said. "We could not have continued at that pace."

"*Kyrie Eleison*," we echoed in a soft whisper.

The door seemed to be an afterthought to the construction, and the steep stairway built after the rest of the building.

Sometimes life is like that. You move in the way you are pulled. Byziana started to climb the winding and tight stairs and we followed, ending on a narrow, dark catwalk. Above us the roof's support beams criss-crossed the cramped walkway. Looking over the ledge, I saw gold-spangled pillars and lush greenery of the Royal Courtyard.

"We're in the Imperial Palace!" I whispered. *If they catch us, we'll be hung.* Justin pointed for us to back away, but Byziana ignored her brother and pressed forward, drawn on by curiosity, or something stronger.

This waist-high parapet alone separated us from a long drop into the royal courtyard. Lines of light shone up and across at odd angles into this dark walkway. Talking!

We froze. Justin shoved us behind a short wall under the low roof to our right, just in time to avoid being caught by a party of three.

"Please, my darling. Let us leave at this moment," a deep voice said. "The exit is right ahead of us. You know this riot will not end until I am dead."

"I will not leave, Husband."

"You must. There is a way of escape. A boat awaits to take us across to Chalcedon. We can be free of this disaster and survive with our lives!"

"What is my life? What am I? I am Augusta. Empress."

Byziana grabbed my hand and squeezed it. The emperor and empress. I could not breathe, knowing what would happen if they found us.

"If I leave what am I? A fugitive queen. A refugee. I will not have it."

"Then the rioters shall kill us."

"They will have to enter our fortress first."

"Perhaps they're already here." I stopped breathing altogether. My life flashed before my eyes—which is not an idiom, it really happens. Mater waving goodbye, the letter about Gallus, the boulder rolling down Mount Silpius, riding the rounds in front of Pater. I saw it all and said farewell.

"Impossible," Justinian said.

"You are the emperor. Does that mean nothing to you?"

"My Lord, we must depart," the third person, a bodyguard I assumed, spoke.

"Please, Theodora. Wife. Do not stay behind. Come with me."

"Do not go, My Lord. Do not go. You are Emperor, Augustus of the New Rome. Your place is here."

"They will kill me."

"I wear purple. If I leave, I must leave it behind. I wear purple. It makes a good death shroud."

The only sound was the beating of my heart at my throat. Justinian sighed. "Yes, Wife. Your words are wise. We cannot live a hunted life. Ulric, we will not be going. Go inform the boat captain." The third man passed by our hiding spot and continued the way we had just come. We heard him descend the secret stairs.

Then I heard whispered words that froze my blood, "*Gabei-dan her.*" The bodyguard had spoken in the Gothic tongue! And not to the emperor. Wait here, he had said. But to whom?

"If you had not spoken, Augusta Theodora, I'd have laid aside my crown for my life. But if I die, I shall die with my crown, not as a coward." They had turned around. Their voices got fainter as they walked back down the parapet.

A rustle of cloth and Ulric was back with the same Red men who had been huddled with Hypatius. Ulric led them to my emperor! The moment they passed us, as a unit, Justin and I hurled ourselves down the narrow walkway, landing on the men.

Theodora screamed.

"Treason, My Lord!" I shouted, as I reached for my knife and sought to disarm the assassin.

"What is this!" Justinian roared, approaching the scuffle.

My opponent pushed my face with one hand, hacking his knife at my throat with his other. I turned and twisted to keep my head intact.

Out of the corner of my eye I saw Ulric pull out a knife and run for the emperor.

"No!" I shouted. I hit the man under me as hard as I could on the chin and leapt up, my momentum just enough to land on Ulric's feet, pulling them toward myself, out from under him. He landed on the floor chin-first, his full bodyweight snapping his head back.

The emperor's steps approached. I rolled the bodyguard over. He was already dead.

I jumped to aid Justin, but he was standing, brushing off his monk's robe self-consciously. "Are you all right?" I asked. He pointed behind me with his chin and kept his eyes to the floor.

Turning around I froze. The emperor approached! I then realized what a terrible situation we were in. We had broken into the Imperial Court. My knees threatened to buckle beneath me.

I can explain, Your Honor, I wanted to say. And yet I could not speak to the emperor without his permission.

"Do not be afraid. Everything is clear, young man," he said with a nervous laugh. "You have kept these assassins from me this day. For that I thank you." Tears welled in my eyes.

He reached out his hand, and I touched his ring to my lips. Then he gave his hand to Justin.

"Pray, what is your name?"

"Marcellus of Antioch, Sir. Son of Gaius Dorotheus of Antioch."

He cocked his head and raised his eyebrows with pleasure. "And you?"

"Justin, son of Gaius Justus of Antioch, sir." We lowered our gaze.

"And how do you warrior monks come to be in this most fortuitous of places tonight?"

I explained how we found the door. Byziana, coming out from our hiding place, drew the emperor's attention. She brushed off her robe as she approached and curtseyed.

"This is my sister Byziana, Your Grace."

"Aha. And a girl monk." He nodded in her direction.

Theodora approached. "Three non-monkish monks," she said, eyes askance. "You must have a story."

Byziana curtseyed to the empress. "Madame, we come from the ports. Many children are dying of thirst, so we volunteered to disguise ourselves and bring them water from the Hippodrome."

"They were found out and as they ran away, they stumbled upon the secret door. No doubt Ulric had unlocked it for the assassins to enter. If they had not found the door first, we would be dead in that purple shroud you mentioned, Wife," Justinian said. "Thanks be to God for your entering first."

"Amen," Justin and I chorused. Satisfied, Theodora turned around and departed into the dark passage.

"If I survive the night. If I survive this riot, I hope to meet you again, dear sirs, and dear miss."

The emperor followed us down the stairs, "Gaius Justus of Antioch, you say? I know him. And I sympathize with his troubles."

"Yes, Your Honor."

"I give you my thanks, again." As soon as we left, we heard a heavy bolt slide in the door behind us.

"We should have told him what you saw in the stadium before the riots," Justin said. "It would have helped him find those to blame."

"If only we had the water for the children," Byziana said.

I pulled off the brown priestly habit, in case the same men awaited us, and ran in tunic to the stairwell. My bucket still had water within it. I took it back to Justin and Byziana, who had taken off their robes.

"At least we have this water." Byziana pointed to my bucket. And yet one bucket won't suffice for everyone at the port.

The raging riots had ascended into ruthless vandalism and manslaughter. *We have to avoid those lawbreakers at all cost.*

In the manner of the Gothic warrior, we followed silence.

We haunted the dark shadows around the Stoa Basilica's edge which lay between the Hippodrome and the Port Road.

"Aaah!" Byziana cried out and grabbed my arm. "Wait. My leg is stuck."

A muddy crevasse along the portico's edge held tight to her leg. We helped her pull it out, and Justin leaned down to peer into the hole.

Shouting and running and the smell of smoke came from the other side of the basilica. I crept to the corner and found, to my dismay, across from us, the Hagia Sophia—that the delightful chapel which had reminded me of Andrew's great work, that triumphal creation of Theodosius—was now aflame.

Shame on them!

"I think we may have found something here." He drew me back and pointed at the gap between the foundation and the earth. It was a damp cave under the portico. Then we heard the dripping of water.

"It might be an ancient cistern! There must be a water source feeding into this spot."

Next to the cornerstone of Stoa Basilica, a tree had reached its roots deep into the earth, deep into the source of water.

Is it not strange how nature replies to man's destructive hatred by peacefully pushing onward toward life? This tree's roots had over time lifted the foundation as to make a man-sized hole, its roots providing a strong support for us to lower ourselves into the cavern, its sooty branches hiding the hole from any but those whom God willed to show the passageway.

Byziana stood guard as Justin and I slid down the hole.

Justin whistled. "Wow. What a place." His voice echoed over the muddy cavern into the darkness. "This has been here since before Constantine, I'm certain."

Vast pillars held the roof from collapsing, old Greek and Roman stones now supported vaults all about this underground cistern. I broke off a stick of root and sounded the depth.

"I can't even touch the bottom."

"That hole's been hidden all these years by brush and weeds. No one knew."

The deep cistern was tranquil, away from the storms of rage and fire. Placid water, earthy mud and strong pillars. Musty and cool and at peace. A secret gift waiting.

Byziana called, "Hidden waters! Is there enough for the children?"

"This cistern has enough to drink for everyone left in the city! I hear trickling water. It must be fed by an underground stream."

Byziana helped us out of the cistern and took me by the shoulders. "Marcellus, God brought us to this water."

"True. But if we make this known far and wide, the marauders will block us from it."

"But it's is a miracle!"

"Anything good is a miracle, Byziana," I answered. We put our robes back on to cover our muddied tunics.

When we arrived at Front Street, we surrendered our robes to grateful monks, then found trustworthy men to make regular cistern runs until the riot was over. The sea provided fish, and the hidden cistern provided water. Now we only need wait for God's wind to bring about peace for the people.

And those winds soon came.

MY PRINCESS

A week since the torches set the city aflame, there was now nothing left to burn except the whims of man. This was the final ember Belisarius took up and doused.

Petrus, the lad on water duty, ran back to Front Street with the news, "It's over! It's over!"

Blacken-clothed homeless hoards gathered around, waiting for the fate of Byzantium.

"What happened?" Justin asked. "Quiet everyone! Let him talk."

Mothers wiped joyful tears across sooty cheeks and pressed in eagerly. Fathers lifted their sons to hear history's story, which way the winds had pushed their nation.

"Over? Who has won?"

"Is the emperor dead?"

"What of Hypatius?"

"Do we have peace?"

"It just happened. I never seen such slaughter."

All chatter stopped when the boy said these words.

"Hypatius was standing in the Kathisma. A line of senators was marching toward him with a crown. To name Hypatius our emperor. When Eunuch Narses comes in, all weak and hunched over.

"They always let me in the Hippodrome cause I know people there. So I am sitting swirling a stick in the fountain, when Narses comes in. Everyone gets all quiet and watches him.

"And I run along the *spinae* toward the *meta*. So I can see what is going to happen. And then Narses goes right to the Blue senators and says, 'A message from your emperor.'

"And the stadium men all yell real loud. They say 'Hypatius will be emperor!' But Narses continues talking soft, so they stop talking.

"He says, 'Justinian sent me to remind you he has always favored Blues. The Blues have always been the best political faction. And the best racing team. He has sent gold to remind you of your great value.' Then Narses throws pouches of money to the Blue senators.

"No one else noticed, but I see Belisarius and Mundus making their way along the stadium edge. And I get worried.

"Narses says, 'Justinian says you can have whoever you want as emperor. But he wanted me to remind you, you are choosing a Green to be your leader.'

"Belisarius and Mundus approach the *Kathisma*. And I know it's not going to go good. So Narses turns away. He walks through the Gate of Death. And after a short talk, the Blue senators holding the crown follow him out, and the sitting Blues walk through the arena out the gate.

"Just then Belisarius breaks open the Kathisma and seizes Hypatius. I run off as fast as my feet can go. And they let me out. Thank God. And after the Blues get out the gate, soldiers close off the Death Gate." Petrus ran his fingers through his thick hair. "And they slaughter all the Greens, and any Blues that stayed, and everyone left in the Hippodrome."

He grabbed the back of his neck. "God have mercy. I'll never forget those screams."

I could not believe my ears.

Justin thanked the young man for the news, and Byziana handed him a cup of water and pat his back to comfort him. Several others huddled around him for more information.

"Belisarius betrayed Hypatius?" I was still in shock. "Why would he do that? Hadn't they planned this together?"

"Welcome to the world of politics," Justin snuffed, as we walked toward the fire.

We sat by Gaius Justus. "Did you hear, Pater?" Byziana said. "The emperor has taken back the city."

"Yes, I heard."

"Uncle, you knew these men. Why would Belisarius arrange a coup and then turn on his choice of new emperor?"

"Because the emperor lives," was his reply. "Belisarius will do what is good for Belisarius. If he can usurp Justinian, he will try. If it fails, he will betray Hypatius. Belisarius is for Belisarius."

Byziana held her hand to her heart, horrified. She touched the place her ring used to be and twisted the emptiness.

"*Kyrie Eleison*. So we can finally go home." She glanced at Justin and then at me.

When she said "home" it carried the weight of my hopes for a life with her. We looked at each other, thinking the unspoken question. Searching for our daily needs and meeting needs of those around us had taken our minds off of the larger problem.

"Is a debt valid if the bond bearer is dead?" Justin spoke the words.

"I am afraid his family will carry the debt forward. It is the law." Byziana sat next to me with a heavy sigh.

"We must appear before the courts as soon as our city has restarted," her father said.

"But he swindled you out of the money, Pater," Byziana said.

"It must be invalid," Justin added.

But their father did not reply. If we could not find six pounds of gold, Byziana would still be a slave. I could think of no recourse to help them out of destitution. With no Hypatius to appeal to, my own plan faltered.

We went to our makeshift tents that night bearing heavier burdens, though the riot was over. The next morning no one spoke of the debt. We ate fish, again, and drank water, again. Today the city would right itself. Today people would remake their fragile lives. Men of power threw it around, while the everyman was left to pick up the pieces and stabilize the scale. We knew all about that, about rebuilding cities and burying the dead. Though we longed for our own home a king's ransom bound us to this charred city.

After we ate, Byziana took my hand and walked me over to the water. We sat down on the tall rocks, our feet hanging over the Bosporos. Justin waved to us from a barge where he was net-fishing.

I studied the skyline. The city would unbreak itself today. The darkened structures across the Golden Horn and along the waterfront would soon have light. For the city there was hope, for the family of Gaius Justus, none.

The words were ready on my tongue. "I won't let you become a slave."

"Yes. I know." She squeezed my hand.

"Do you remember the day outside of Belisarius's house? Do you remember your laughter?"

"I do."

"You called to the God of the Earthquake."

"He's the God of Hidden Waters, too!" she chuckled. "What names we have for God!"

"He takes care of us and brought me back from Gothland."

"Yes, back from Gothland."

"You will go back to Antioch. I promise. As long as there's life in my bones."

"But what will we do?"

"If God could figure out how to make a seed turn into a tree, I'm sure he can figure out how to help us. We just have to keep doing the right thing. Hang on to that joy we had. It's what makes us different from pagans. They fear their gods. We know our God."

She crossed her arms in front of her and held her chin, looking out onto the water. "You're right. I do still have that joy."

"The Who of God is what we need to grasp. He can fix this. And even if it doesn't go the way we expect, still trust Him. Don't let it steal your joy. Whatever the situation. When you trust God, you can face whatever comes against you. Just do the right thing."

"It's not always easy, but it reminds me of that bent tree you saw. You'll think it strange, but the thought just came to mind that even this adversity is a part of my joy."

"How is that?"

"Like the dark clouds around that cross in the sky the day Mater died. We couldn't see the cross if not for the darkness. Light is clearest when darkness is around. I have hope, in spite of the dark night my future promises."

I took her hand in mine again. I preferred the light. "Did I tell you my plan? It might work."

"I fear it." She lifted my hand to her lips.

"I can wield a sword. Gothic style. They pay good money for that these days. If I find the right master, he can pay upfront." It would be harder without Hypatius. Who else had money in a broken city?

"Don't do this, Marcellus." She stroked my fingers one by one. "You should become a scholar. Go to study."

Her nails were all torn, her hands black from the ashes. But they no longer wore a ring. And they were in my hands. *She'll be no man's slave.*

"I cannot."

"Or go to Gothland. And marry your princess."

Her words sliced the moment like a knife. *What? My princess?*

"Do not get tangled in our prison." A cloud covered her face again. "My dark future should not be yours."

Burning anger gripped my chest. "My princess? Why do you bring her up?"

"I just—"

My princess?

"Why do you push me away?"

"I want—"

"I'll stay by your side."

"But Marcellus—"

Did she still think I had a princess in Gothland?

"If it kills me, I'll protect you. You won't be anyone's slave."

Did she still not understand?

She was the only one I wanted.

I put my hand on her cheek and stroked the line of her jaw. "Byzia, what do I have to say to persuade you she meant nothing to me?"

She shrugged her shoulders and looked out at the water.

"You must know how I feel about you."

She pulled my hand to her mouth and kissed my palm.

The future was in God's hands. Like the ever-changing clouds, he moved in ways we would never understand. But we had to do the right thing. That's all we could do. Only one thing could prove this to her.

"Will you marry me?" I asked. "Right now. The priests can sanctify it. Marry me."

"But we will be parted!" she cried. "What good is that?"

"I will never be severed from you." I pulled her to her feet and toward the fire.

We walked to Gaius Justus, her hand still in mine. I tucked the furs over his shoulders and then sat next to him by the fire.

"Uncle, I wish to marry Byziana," I said. "Will you grant me her hand in marriage?"

He did not lift his eyes from the fire, but his face softened. After a while he took a deep breath and studied me. "You were right, about Gallus. You tried to keep us on track. But he tricked me to leave Antioch when I should have stayed."

I studied the man. Had he recognized the silver bowl at Priorium? It did not matter. "Gallus, Belisarius, they deceived us all. How else do we learn but by mistakes. And we're still alive." *What can be done now?* I shook my head, *Belisarius is for Belisarius.*

My uncle's look was like a street dog kicked too many times, weary and broken, like that wolf pup trying to survive. "Yes, perhaps. But consequently we have nothing to offer you, son . . . "

"I need nothing. I have everything to give."

" . . . and we are slaves."

"I'll buy you out of slavery if it takes my very life. Will you give me your daughter's hand?"

His eyes rested on Byziana. Justin came over with a net full of fish and sat down.

"Why is everyone so serious?" He looked at each of us.

I ignored him and waited for Gaius Justus to answer. But he was silent again.

"What is happening, Byziana?" Justin said, looking from his father to me.

"Hush. Marcellus just asked for my hand." She watched her father, eyebrows knit.

"Well it is about time! About time. Finally became a man, eh? Congratulations!" Justin patted me on the back.

I kept my eyes on my uncle.

Justin eyed me and Byziana, then his father once again. "What? Pater, have you given no answer?"

"Justin, hold your tongue," Byziana said.

"Haha. Oh this is fine. Pater, this is one fine joke." He bent to catch his father's eye, bringing a slight smile to his father's mouth.

"See. Pater has given his approval, have you not, Pater?"

Byziana kneeled at her father's side. He was still so weak and tired and cold, but to us he was that man who had held up the goblet with all the pomp of the patriate.

"Pater?" Byziana asked.

Gaius Justus took her hand and patted it. "Does it make you happy, Daughter? Shall I say 'Yes'?"

Her face glowed excitement and beams of joy.

"Your mater saw this, from the beginning. She said this should be, but I refused to accept it. My lovely Sophia would be happy. If she had been here."

He looked up at me next to him, and taking his daughter's hand from his, he put it into my hand.

I jumped up and spun Byziana around, hooting a Gothic song. Her head back, her face to the sky, restful, free and joyful, we spun round and round. Gaius Justus started to laugh, but his joy turned into a hacking cough. We all stopped our spinning and brought him water and a warmer cloak.

And so Friar Dominicus married us. We stood next to each other in front of that fire and vowed our love to each other, and as simply as that we were married.

GOD OVER ALL KINGS

As we were receiving congratulatory handshakes from the other homeless citizens, soldiers arrived at our makeshift camp.

"Gaius Justus of Antioch?" we heard them ask.

We brought the troops to my uncle.

Though he had lost everything, he sat straight as he welcomed their message, chin up in dignity. "The emperor summons you and Justin of Antioch and Marcellus of Antioch into his presence," they said.

The soldiers waited as we brushed off our sooty, dirty garments and washed our faces, then they marched before and behind us, past the Agora and to the Mese.

Byziana, my wife, walked next to me.

We took a circuitous route, passing the house of Hypatius. The house, untouched by fire amidst charred neighboring homes, stood out like a bold soldier at a battle's end. The emperor's men were at the door, voiding the house of its inhabitants.

"Where will I go?" the wife of Hypatius cried.

Women surrounded her, wiped her tears, held her to their chests, stroked her face, "We will help you, Mary. You tried to stop him. You will not go hungry. We will care for you."

Gaius Justus gazed on the scene. I eyed Justin, and he shrugged his shoulders. We knew the desperate family would demand repayment.

I heard a squeal of joy. A girl wearing Byziana's robe waved at my wife, letting go of her mother's cloak and running up. Byziana pulled the girl to her chest. I kept marching as they fell behind, watching over my shoulder. Byziana met and embraced the girl's young mother. At that moment—as I strode under armed escort to the court of Justinian—the robe changed. Almost miraculously, almost physically glowing, it was no longer Byziana's robe. The girl wore Christ's robe. And in that moment I understood the Incarnation.

God in a man robe, God and Man.

Our Lord Christ had come to earth. He took off His robe, rolled up His sleeves and went to work—His work as a carpenter, His work as a teacher and prophet, His work as a Savior in a broken world. Reason demanded that a man bear man's sin, and only God could bear that caliber of sin and survive.

Like Pope Leo wrote, *It does not belong to the same nature.* But because Christ had borne the wrath of God for me, I was free. Christ paid our debt to holiness by having a robe. He had wept, so we could rejoice. Whatever the circumstances. His death conquered this broken world and made peace between man and God. Because only man could die.

We could all be curvy trees by the waters, our roots digging and branches lifting in trust. We could even be heedless, nursing kittens because our mother would not fail to save. Because He had a robe, He could put that robe on us, to cover us in our cold, homeless, sooty-faced desperation.

He who willed to touch became touchable.

He who willed to embrace became embraceable.

The ungraspable willed to be grasped.

And that was what God required of us. To be graspable. And to grasp.

Byziana caught up and took my arm again, happily marching forward to our fate.

Scripture portions rushed to mind,

'The religion that God finds faultless is to look after the orphans and widows in their distress, and to not become defiled by the world.'

'A body you have prepared for me.'

'Who for the joy set before Him endured the cross, scorning its shame.'

'Christ . . . though He was in the form of God, did not count equality with God something to be grasped.'

God's forbearance said it all. He was waiting for Christ to bring peace to the world, through us. Because Christ was my peace,

I could love others. He condescended because He loved us, and out of that same divine love we must condescend. God required our mercy to be no respecter of person—rich or poor, male or female, young or old.

We had been doing what God required all along! Valuing humanity. Helping. Standing faithful. Serving. Telling others the gospel. Reading the Scrolls. Rolling up our sleeves. Giving our cloaks away. Refusing to fall. I trembled inside at this revelation.

Whatever awaited us at the Court of Justinian, whatever waited—slavery or servitude or poverty—whatever waited, I knew I could please God.

We entered the Hippodrome through the Gate of Death. The Hagia Sophia in ruins, Justinian held court here. Dirt had been thrown over pools of black on the seating, and the racing sands had been raked of any other signs of blood. Yet violent death hung heavy over the sorry racetrack.

The bronze serpent from Delphi trickled its water from unknown depths, its sound reminding me of hidden waters. *No matter what happens to us, no matter where they send me, no matter how they force from us the six pounds of gold, our God will meet our needs. He always has.*

The guards stopped before the emperor. *Come prison, or exile, or confiscation. His waters will continue. They can take it all, but heaven remains in my heart.* I held my wife's hand firmly. *And we are together.*

Justinian sat in regal splendor, soldiers-at-arms surrounding the box, Empress Theodora in her purple robe sat by him, and another woman by her.

He rose from his seat and commanded in a loud voice. "Bring forth the prisoner!"

I thought he meant us, and I grit my teeth in apprehension. But instead, from within the Black Gate, Belisarius brought Hypatius down the stands to stand before the *Kathisma*.

"Hypatius, Son of Royalty, you are hereby charged with treason, with moving to steal my throne, with inciting a riot, with being the direct cause to my golden city's destruction. How do you plead?"

Hypatius, the man who owned my uncle, fell to his knees. "I apologize, My Liege. Forgive me."

"You apologize!" Justinian roared. "You think an apology is all I want, when you've caused the death of my citizens, the death of innocent children in my city? Tens of thousands are dead, you snake. Guilty. Or Not Guilty?"

"I am Guilty, My Lord," he said. He looked up at Belisarius. I knew he desired to speak of that man's part. But a flash from Belisarius's eyes turned him back to the emperor. "Mercy, Augustus. Mercy." He opened his hands before him and dropped his head.

"Second charge against Hypatius, Son of Royalty."

Hypatius lifted his chin to the emperor. "Second charge?"

"Gaius Justus of Antioch. Step forward."

My uncle stepped toward the *Kathisma* and lowered his eyes to the ground.

"Gaius Justus of Antioch. I opened a case in your name against this former Senator Hypatius. I understand he committed usury against your debt to him. Is this true or not true?"

"True, My Lord," my uncle's voice was weak, but clear.

"How much debt do you owe this man?" Justinian asked.

"Sir, I owe four hundred fifty solidi."

Belisarius shifted his gaze from my uncle to Byziana on my arm. His eyes caressed her foot to head then he licked his lips. I pulled her to my other side to block his view. He shifted his grin back on the *Kathisma*.

"In how much time did you accrue this debt, Gaius Justus?"

"Over three years, Your Grace."

The woman next to the empress—this was Lady Antonina, I learned later—lifted her finger, ever so slightly, to Belisarius. At this signal his face sobered, he cowered his head and shifted his back to us, careful to not ogle her again.

"What percentage usury did he charge?"

"Thirty percent gross, monthly."

The emperor frowned and took a deep breath. "Hypatius, Son of Royalty. In my empire we are in pursuit of one state, one law, one church. I place great weight on law. And we have a law forbidding usury."

"Yes, Your Honor," Hypatius said.

"Specifically, a nobleman can be charged no more than four percent per annum on loans."

"Yes, Your Honor."

Justinian paused and observed Hypatius. "Although I cannot see your heart, I find your deeds reflect malicious intent."

"Yes, Your Grace," he whispered.

"Take a look at this man." He eyed Gaius Justus in a sooty robe, a weakened frame leaning on a cane. He returned fearful-eyes to the emperor.

"This great man, a retired officer of my *limitanei*, defended our frontiers for years. More so, he is a patrician of Antioch. One of four. But now he is broken. Broken. Because of your greed."

Justinian's firm voice echoed across the Hippodrome. "Hypatius, I need my *patrikioi*. They bring order and stability to my Realm. When you break them, you are breaking my Empire. Do you understand this?"

"Yes, Your Honor," Hypatius said.

"Do you plead Guilty or Not Guilty to breaking my patrician?"

He sighed and glared up at Belisarius next to him. Belisarius kept his eyes on the *Kathisma*.

"Guilty, Your Grace."

"Marcellus son of Gaius Dorotheus of Antioch, step forward."

Gaius Justus stepped into place next to Justin, and I stepped in front of our small group.

"Marcellus of Antioch, I did not know your father personally. But he was reputed to be a great and wise scholar. Although you are not from this city, during the riots, you cared for the children of my city. You risked your life to provide them water and food. And while you were busy with that great service, you rescued my dear empress and myself from certain assassination."

Tears welled up in my eyes. I had only done my duty.

"You have protected my realm, protected my children. You are to be commended, Young Patrician. Your father trained you well."

Patrician? Am I a patrician? I looked up at him. He stepped back, and the empress spoke to him. After a moment he approached the window again. "We have learned you were taken against your will to live with the Gothic raiders, and by obeying Christ's command to love your enemies, you brought the King—King Olufr—to our Faith. I commend you for this. I find it . . . intriguing. In fact, Marcellus, I would consider you for ambassadorship . . . if you would so desire."

I glanced at Byziana. Her smile was radiant.

"Thank you, Your Grace," I answered.

"You are welcome, Marcellus of Antioch. We can discuss this at a later time. Justin son of Gaius Justus, and Byziana daughter, please step forward."

Byziana stood by her brother now.

"You two as well were active in protecting my realm. With the children, and in saving our lives. Thank you. I commend you to your father. He must be proud of you."

Gaius Justus nodded his head.

"Now, Hypatius, turn and look upon these four fine citizens."

He turned and faced us, a man stripped of honor. How different he was from that man who laughed at our "melodramatics."

"Hypatius, look upon what you should have been. These have been commended for living according to the ideals of our Empire. Let me see your face again."

He turned back, his eyes resting at length on Belisarius. When he lifted his attention to the emperor, the verdict began:

"For crimes against the society and physical property of Constantinople, you will surrender your homes, and your possessions, and your monetary worth forthwith to the Crown. For crimes against the Crown and the Empire, you will forfeit your life, and the freedom of your wife and your daughters."

A weeping came from the top of the Hippodrome. His seated wife leaned onto the laps of her friends nearby, in heartbroken anguish. Hypatius turned and watched his wife with hopeless eyes.

Justinian continued, "For crimes against my Patrician Gaius Justus, you are required to forgive... to negate... any standing debt he or any other debtor has accumulated to your name. Neither your family nor posterity have any claim whatsoever to that debt. Negate these debts now."

"I negate all debts," Hypatius said, a deep sigh following the words.

"Hypatius, Son of Royalty, you began this life with the Empire at your feet, you end this life with your head under the Empire's foot. You have used your life foolishly and have received just compensation for your criminal behavior."

He leaned back again to hear a word from the empress.

Then he added, "I understand your wife is a wise and prudent woman. You would have done well to listen to her. She now will suffer for your crimes."

"Gaius Justus," he turned his attention to my uncle, "before I send this criminal to his execution,"—with that word a shriek came from Hypatius's wife—"I wish to tell you, in front of your malefactor, the reward I shall bestow on you and your family, for your praiseworthy, honorable actions. The homes of Hypatius, his possessions and his monetary worth are forthwith legal property—to be divided equally—of the house of Gaius Justus, and the house of Gaius Marcellus."

Gaius Marcellus? Byziana squeezed my hand.

"In addition, the family of Hypatius is now forthwith your legal slave property—to be shared or sold—at your discretion. May God bless your homes and give back to you for the honor you have brought the Empire."

"Thank you, Your Grace," Gaius Justus said, standing a bit taller.

When the emperor signaled for Hypatius to be taken to his execution, he fell to his knees. "Mercy, My Lord. I was not alone. May all suffer who brought this upon me!"

Theodora pulled Justinian's attention, and after a short conference he approached the *Kathisma* window again.

"You may charge those complicit in the crime."

"Your Grace, I have nothing to lose, I've lost everything. But I can die with a clean conscience, not leaving the Empire in disgrace."

Belisarius peeked at the former senator. I saw him smirk, ever so slightly, and I remember thinking Belisarius was immune.

The accused pointed at the general. "Belisarius. He put me up to it."

Justinian stared at his top general standing next to Hypatius. Belisarius stood straight-backed that oily arrogance on his face.

"You are saying my faithful Belisarius caused this riot?"

"Yes, sir."

"Do you have any evidence?"

"Yes, I do."

Belisarius gazed at him, amused, licking his lips again.

"We planned it for weeks. I went to his house. We arranged looters and torches and the, and the . . ."

"Evidence. Proof."

"My word. It is all I have."

"General Belisarius, forgive me. For this to be legal and valid, I must ask you if you are Guilty or Not Guilty."

"Not Guilty," was his confident reply.

"Hypatius, I see right through your accusation. Do you seek to injure me back? You have no reasonable proof. Yet, I have proof to the contrary. General Belisarius is the most faithful commander I've ever had. He has never, ever given me cause to lose that trust in him. Shall I list his merit and deeds? Furthermore, it makes no sense that he'd want you to be emperor over me. He has too much to gain from my leadership and friendship. So unless you can offer proof, I consider this a frivolous vengeful accusation.

Do I have proof? What did I see? Only Belisarius speaking with Hypatius before the races. What had I heard? Only Belisarius responding to Hypatius's treasonous talk. I have no proof, only suspicions. Perhaps I'm wrong about Belisarius's part in the coup. The emperor is right. I have no evidence and it does not make sense.

I kept my peace. Yet I have always wondered if I should have said the little I knew. What I would say was all conjecture. I myself had no concrete evidence against anyone. This is how I think Belisarius got away with treason. For better or for worse.

TWO BANQUETS

They took us to the palace, where they purged us of our filthy clothes and lavished us with fine garments worthy of royalty. We partook of a luxurious meal with the emperor, the empress, Belisarius and Antonina. Thankfully we sat far from Belisarius at the large gathering, the remaking of court.

Peacock, dolphin, pork, unknown sea creatures, unimaginably delicious vegetables, all presented with parades of grandeur and flourish. Buttery, savory herbs my mouth had never known blended in heavenly ways. Yet we lacked one thing. Salt. This palace was not our home. My uncle's—that is my new father's—health required we make a short night of it, so we did not stay late. We left the loyal nobles to remake court on their own terms, and we hastened to the solace of our own company in the upper-level palace room Theodora provided.

The next day Justinian transferred the city home of Hypatius to our name. They brought his wife and daughters to us as slaves. Byziana sat on a couch next to the wife, Mary, for a long time. Then she came to see me. I was in the library, looking through the vast collection of scrolls the man had collected.

"How do you feel, Marcellus?"

I took her in my arms and kissed the soft of her neck. "Having you as my darling wife? Never better."

"I mean about living in Hypatius's house."

"Do you remember the story of Esther? Do you remember how Haman's property became Mordecai's?"

She nodded.

"It is not unheard of to receive transferred property."

"I see," she said. She lowered herself to a chair and straightened her robe.

"How do you feel about living in Hypatius's house?" I asked.

"Guilty," the ready word filled the room.

"We were given this home legally."

"And a widow is our slave. Orphans, our slaves."

"Legally."

"Yes. Hmm. Have you spoken to Mary at all?"

I had not.

"You should. She reminds me," Byziana smiled, "of my mater."

I looked at her in surprise. "Lady Sophia?"

"Yes. She's like us!" Her face glowed. "I have a suggestion, and I hope you will accept."

"Then I hope I will accept it, too. What is it?"

"What if we take Mary and her girls to Antioch with us. And free them there, so we don't offend Constantinople or the emperor. We can buy her a house. And she'll no longer be a slave."

I took a deep breath and scratched my chin.

"I do not object," I said.

"When can we go home?" she asked, with a smile, her rested, at-peace smile, her all-is-well-with-the-world smile.

"On the morrow," I said. "What do you say we take a ship this time?"

And so we returned home to Antioch.

What shall I say of our reunion in early spring, of the joyful cheers from Natalia and Katerina, of my mother's surprise at my being a married man?—just that it took hours to relate how it all happened.

What shall I say of the poor widow Mary, and her orphan daughters?—just that she received a home, and became a beloved friend to both my mother and my wife, and her daughters to my younger cousins.

What shall I say of the warm home and hearth I wanted?— just that my wife, Byziana, was all I needed.

We were home, and we had a banquet. Just my mother, my wife, my new father, my sisters, my brother and me. I held up a goblet and praised God, and we sat around the fire and talked and took and read the blessed Scrolls.

What can I say?—except *Kyrie Eleison*! God had mercy on us. The God of the Earthquake, the God of the Scrolls, the God of the Hidden Water, the God over all Kings—He willed to be grasped, and by His touchable blood enabled us to grasp onto humanity.

THE FACTS OF THE MATTER
FOR MORE INFORMATION

Study Guide
https://darlenenbocek.com/trunkofscrolls_studyguide

Internet *Facts of the Matter* for Trunk of Scrolls
Anatolian Saints http://darlenenbocek.com/facts/
anatoliansaints/
Ancient Antioch http://darlenenbocek.com/facts/
ancientantioch/
Barbarians and Goths http://darlenenbocek.com/
facts/barbariansandgoths/
Belisarius http://darlenenbocek.com/facts/belisarius
Byzantine Life http://darlenenbocek.com/facts/
byzantinelife
Character of God http://darlenenbocek.com/facts/
characterofgod
The Creeds http://darlenenbocek.com/facts/thecreeds/
John of Ephesus http://darlenenbocek.com/facts/
johnofephesus
Justinian http://darlenenbocek.com/facts/justinian/
Monasticism http://darlenenbocek.com/facts/
monasticism/
Monophysite Controversy http://darlenenbocek.com/
facts/monophysitecontroversy/
Relics and the Spirit of God http://darlenenbocek.com/
facts/relics/
Sarabi Dogs of Alexander http://darlenenbocek.com/
facts/sarabidogsofalexander/
Story of Scripture http://darlenenbocek.com/
facts/storyofscripture/

Trunk of Scrolls Timeline of Early Church and Byzantine History

*If you want to understand
the intricate problems of the Church today,
you must study the Byzantine times.*

When St. John the Beloved, the last of the apostles, died in Ephesus in AD 90, the Church of Christ continued to be led by godly men who earnestly sought to follow Scripture. Amidst a pagan world set on ridding itself of the non-conforming Christians, Church bishops like Clement of Rome, Ignatius of Antioch and Polycarp of Smyrna showed the early Church by sermon and lifestyle, how to bravely live and die for Christ.

With the spread of the Church came the influx of false teaching. After the legalization of Christianity in AD 312, whenever doctrinal tension in the Church threatened the empire's stability, emporers such as Constantine, Theodosius, Marcian, and Justinian would call for the convening of bishops for a council.

Duly-ordained Church bishops of all large cities and towns, would gather together and compare the conflicting ideas with Scripture. These Church councils identified in concise creed and confession the standard, orthodox teaching of Scripture. Always back to Scripture.

The more you study the early Church councils, the more you will recognize the same heresies today, in the 21st century. It does matter what you believe. As Lady Sophia said, "It matters more than anything.... Your belief on Chalcedon identifies the very God you worship."

-

FACTUAL   DATE AD   FICTIONAL

FACTUAL	DATE AD	FICTIONAL
St. John the Beloved, in Ephesus	10-90	
Polycarp, Bishop of Smyrna	69-155	
Widespread persecutions and martyrdoms of Christians	33-312+	
Macrina the Elder	270-c340	
Euphemia martyred	303	
Edict of Milan Constantine the Great legalizes Christianity	312	
Basil and Emmilia of Caesarea	315-375	
First Council of Nicaea	325	
Nicene creed (relationship between God the father and God the son). The Council met to combat the heresy of Arianism which denied the divinity of Christ.		
Macrina, Basil, Gregory, Naucratius, Peter	**c330-July 19, 379**	Isodorus born, brother to Basil & Gregory
Codex Vaticanus & Codex Sinaiticus written (Alexandria/Rome) *The Pope had a full copy of Scripture. Alexandria had a full copy of Scripture*	c325-360	
Three Cappadocians: St Basil, St Gregory of Nazianzus & St Gregory of Nyssa lived /worked	329-394	Basil and Gregory collect Scrolls in Trunk.
		Personal copies of parchments & scrolls selected, added to Trunk as monks under St. Gregory's watch copied the Scrolls. He said, "Scripture belongs to the people, for the 'Word of God took human form.'"
Constantine Commissions 50 Bibles	331	
Asked for Eusebius to make 50 copies "of the sacred scriptures which you know to be especially necessary for the restoration and use in the instruction of the church."		
John "Gold-tongue" Chrysostom	347-407	
	360	Arite's Grandmother born
First Council of Constantinople	381	
This council formed a creed that expresses the truth of Scripture regarding the doctrine of the Trinity. Various errors with respect to the Trinity occasioned the meeting of this council. The confession of Nicea was enlarged to also include the Holy Spirit.		
	382	Marcus born (father Isodorus)
Synod of Hippo *identification of formal Canonical books*	393	Trunk passed from St. Gregory to Isodorus
	400	Arite's Mother born

FACTUAL	DATE AD	FICTIONAL
	418	Twins Mary and Elizabeth are born (father Marcus)
	425	Trunk passed from Isodorus to Marcus
Council of Ephesus	431	
The Council of Ephesus condemned two heresies: Nestorianism, which taught that God merely lived in Christ, and Pelagianism, which taught that the sin of Adam was not passed on to the human race.		
	432	Trunk passed from Marcus to Elizabeth
	438	Ioseph born (mother Elizabeth)
	439	Arité Born
Council of Chalcedon	451	
The Council of Chalcedon established confessionally the truths of the unity of God and the distinction of both the human and divine natures of Christ. It condemned three heresies: Monophysitism, which denied the dual nature of Christ, Apollinarianism, which denied the completeness of the nature of Christ, and Nestorianism, which denied the unity of the divine nature of Christ.		
	472	Helena born (mother Mary)
	479	Gaius Justus born
	485	Gaius Dorotheus born
	493	Aemelia born (mother Helena)
	495	Sophia born (father Ioseph)
	497	Ioseph & wife die. Helena adopts Sophia
	500	Trunk passed from Elizabeth to Sophia
Hypatius Lived	c460-532	
Flavius Belisarius lived	505-565	
John of Ephesus lived	c507-c588	
Antioch Pogrom of Jews in Daphne by Porphyrius the Charioteer	507	
	Nov 18, 510	Marcellus born
	Mar 3, 514	Byziana born
	Dec 13, 516	Justin born
Reign of Justin I	518-527	
	June 20, 519	Katerina born
Epiphanius serves as Antioch Patriarch	520-535	
Simeon the Stylite lived	521- May 24 597	

FACTUAL   DATE AD   FICTIONAL

FACTUAL	DATE AD	FICTIONAL
	July 1, 522	Natalia born
Great Fire of Antioch	525	
Antioch Earthquake	May 20, 526	
Glowing cross observed in sky	May 23, 526	Trunk passed from Sophia to Byziana
Theodoric's death	526	
Simeon, at 5 years of age, *goes onto pillar at Monastery of the Admirable Mountains in Antioch*	526	
Reign of Justinian I	Aug 527-565	
Second earthquake in Antioch	Nov 28, 528	
	Nov 29, 528	The Family departs Antioch
	Mar 529	Justin and Marcellus kidnapped
Justinian closes School of Athens *for teaching pagan thought*	June 529	
Battle of Dara *Belisarius victorious against Persians*	April 530	
Battle of Callinicum *Belisarius defeated against Persians*	April 531	
	Oct 531	Justin and Marcellus released
John of Ephesus begins work *to destroy by force the "wicked heathenish error" in Anatolia*	529-535	
Nika Revolt	Jan 532	
Death of Hypatius	Jan 532	
	--	Return to Antioch

About the Author

Darlene N. Böcek lives in the land of old Byzantium, in Izmir, Turkey. She and her husband Fikret Böcek, graduate of Westminster Seminary in California, have planted Izmir Protestan Kilisesi (The Protestant Church of Smyrna), and are working on the *Turkish Standard Version Bible* translation and other book projects. A former public school teacher she homeschools her teen and pre-teen children and writes on history and homeschooling at darlenenbocek.com.

Acknowledgments

A special thank you goes to my children, Anya, Ela, Selen, and Han who learned how to cook, serve tables, and run the estate during the final stages of this novel, when mom would disappear into nowhere. Gratefulness to my mother and father Ruth and Paul Pirolo, who, like Emmilia and Basil, first taught me to love the Lord and then let me go, at great cost to their hearts. Thank you to Val Marsh and her kids who were my first fans and greatest critics. And finally, much gratitude to the men and women of Izmir Protestan Kilisesi who have been a great encouragement and the true motivation for my writing this novel.

Lost Trunk Bookmarks

A special trunk image appears at three places in this novel. *Trunk of Scrolls* is a novel about the 6th century, but it is also about our lives in *the 21st century. The Lost Trunk: a serial novel*, is a modern-day connection to *Trunk of Scrolls*, taking place in Escondido, California. If you are willing to break the 4th wall in your reading, when you see this bookmark click over to http://darlenenbocek.com/thelosttrunk for a free download of the episodes: *Prologue, Mesologue* or *Epilogue.*

www.ingramcontent.com/pod-product-compliance
Lightning Source LLC
Chambersburg PA
CBHW032208180726
48284CB00001B/243